Turn the page for more acclaim . . .

"I recommend this book to anyone wanting to be left with a good feeling after turning the last page." —*Old Book Barn Gazette*

"Alexis Harrington has written an enchanting novel in ALLIE'S MOON. Filled with down-to-earth characters and a tight, well-conceived plot, ALLIE'S MOON is an exceptional read . . . I eagerly await her next novel." —*BookNook Romance Reviews*

"Ms. Harrington has another winner with ALLIE'S MOON . . . A beautiful love story. Ms. Harrington's masterful weaving of the relationship between Allie and Jeff is very tender, moving and believable. The characters are strongly defined with amazing strengths and real human weaknesses. This one is a keeper." —*Reader to Reader Reviews*

HARPER'S BRIDE

"A tender story of the healing power of love."
—*Affaire de Coeur*

DESPERATE HEARTS

"Highly recommended!" —*Manderley*

A TASTE OF HEAVEN

"Charming, warm-hearted." —*Romantic Times*

"A TASTE OF HEAVEN is everything its name has promised."
—*Affaire de Coeur*

A LIGHT FOR MY LOVE

"A very special love story between two unforgettable characters."
—*Affaire de Coeur*

MONTANA
BORN *And* BRED

Alexis Harrington

St. Martin's Paperbacks

MONTANA BORN AND BRED

Copyright © 2000 by Alexis Harrington.

All rights reserved. No part of this book may be used or reproduced in any manner whatsoever without written permission except in the case of brief quotations embodied in critical articles or reviews. For information address St. Martin's Press, 175 Fifth Avenue, New York, N.Y. 10010.

ISBN: 0-312-97587-2

Printed in the United States of America

St. Martin's Paperbacks edition / December 2000

St. Martin's Paperbacks are published by St. Martin's Press, 175 Fifth Avenue, New York, N.Y. 10010.

10 9 8 7 6 5 4 3 2 1

When the going gets tough, these people always pitch in to help. I am eternally grateful for their support and consider myself lucky to have such wonderful friends—Catherine Anderson, Maggie Grover, Nikki Harrington, Lisa Jackson, and Margaret Vajdos.

To RLS and DBB, you made Zach and Sarah come to life.

MONTANA
BORN *And* BRED

Chapter One

Sarah Kincade lied about Danny Kincade. She lied about him to everyone she met.

Well, now, who's this little buckaroo?

My nephew, Danny.

Or . . .

Oh, isn't he just a sugar bun! What did you name him?

He's my late sister's boy, Danny.

Worst of all . . .

You didn't tell us you had a young'un, Miss Kincade— it's Miss, right? Schoolmarms aren't s'posed to have babies.

I'm his aunt, his only living relative.

But Danny wasn't her nephew, and she'd never had a sister.

He was her baby and she could admit it to no one.

In her arms, four-month-old Danny wailed at the top of his lungs, just as he'd done most of last night. His shrieks accentuated the headache pounding in her ears. She paced the plank floor in the dark, musty schoolroom where she would spend the next nine months teaching the children of Lame Horse.

"Froggy went a'courtin' and he did go—" she sang brokenly, and stroked his silky hair.

As she paced, she paused at the filmy window and glanced down the street that cut through the center of town, checking for strangers. The small, plain schoolroom sat at the end of the street and gave her a good view of the sparse traffic that ambled along through the dusty summer morning.

Though she'd tried to break the habit, every day she peered into the face of each person she encountered on the street, each person who passed her, spoke to her, exchanged looks with her. She sought not the faces of people she'd come to know during her time in Lame Horse. Rather, she looked for the unfamiliar, the stranger, because Danny's father was the kind of man who would stop at nothing to get his son back.

She knew that she was only making herself crazy with this fear she carried in her heart. After all, Lame Horse was just a flyspeck of a town on the Yellowstone River in eastern Montana, with a higher population of jackrabbits than people. If Ethan Pembroke sent someone to track her down, this rough little place would be the last they'd check. That had been one of her reasons for coming here. But the fear persisted, and she kept searching faces.

She'd also traveled here because she'd needed a teaching job immediately, far from Helena and Bozeman, and the one in Lame Horse had been the first she'd found.

Danny wailed on and she paced a little faster, growing more frazzled with each passing minute. She cupped the back of his head in her hand and kissed his sweat-dotted forehead. "Sweetheart, please! Please stop."

She turned and crossed the floor again, trying to settle him down. She rocked him in her arms and crooned to him, but his face remained pinched, his open, toothless little mouth taking up most of his expression. His fists were clenched on either side of his head. As she walked, she considered all the work still ahead of her. It would be a monumental task to prepare the schoolhouse for the first day of classes next week, to try and make something out of this—this *nothing*. In Helena, she'd taught in a new two-story brick building that featured every modern convenience. But she suspected that the term *modern convenience* was all but unheard of in Lame Horse.

Here—she sighed just looking at it—the school was a squat, ugly cabin, unpainted and weathered outside to a silver-gray. Inside, the walls were lined with old newspaper pages, floor to rafters. It smelled closed up and unused, with a lingering smoky odor from all the winter fires burned in the fireplace. If she could call it a fireplace. It was nothing more than a heap of rocks, sticks, and mud with a chimney.

As for her lesson plans, they'd flown out the window the day she'd met with the town council. In addition to *McGuffey's Eclectic Readers*, she'd hoped to introduce the works of Charles Dickens, Herman Melville, and the Brontë sisters. But her suggestions had been met with chair-fidgeting and throat-clearing. The young folks just needed their three R's, nothing more, ma'am, and nothing fancy. *McGuffey's* would do just fine.

So *McGuffey's* it would have to be.

Danny purpled with his screaming, and Sarah felt if she couldn't quiet him, she might join him. "Hush, little Danny, hush. Everything is going to be all right."

Passing the dirty window again, she paused when she saw Clarice Flanders at the far end of the street, striding purposefully in this direction with a dog in tow at the end of a rope. Oh, God, she hoped Clarice wasn't coming here.

Sarah had spent most of the night sitting up in the chair next to her bed, worrying about the baby's health and trying to comfort him. The idea of dealing with Mrs. Flanders now was more than she could bear.

Sarah's teacher's pay consisted of two dollars per student per month, and board and room with Clarice and her family. Clarice was a narrow-minded prig, married to a man who sat on the town council. She was determined to see that Sarah earned every penny of her salary and was less than generous with the room and board.

Life in the crowded Flanders household was far from ideal. Her five noisy children, out of school for the summer, were always in one scrape or another. Voices were raised from dawn till after dark, not necessarily in anger, but as if the family didn't know how to communicate any other way. Taciturn Bob Flanders was the conspicuous exception in his home. He was the town's undertaker, and in Sarah's opinion, he fit the role perfectly with his pale silence. Even worse, at the dinner table, Bob considered Sarah with furtive, sidelong looks that were both curious and downright lascivious.

Her loss of privacy, the never-ending sense of being an unwelcome guest, the unruly Flanders children—it was all horrible. But unpleasant though it might be, she would endure anything to protect Danny. He made it all worthwhile.

Holding him, she inhaled the delicious baby scent of him. His piercing shriek was deafening, his little face nearly plum-colored with the effort, but Sarah could rise above it. She had to. Her attachment to him had been immediate and more intense than she had ever dreamed. From the moment of his birth she had fallen completely and hopelessly in love with him.

He kept on howling, as he had most nights for the past two weeks. Mrs. Flanders had said it was colic, and the local doctor had confirmed her diagnosis. She'd tried all the remedies suggested—warm compresses, peppermint tea, even a drop of brandy in water. They all helped a bit, but the colic came back.

"It's all right, little Danny," she crooned again, feeling anxious, jogging him in her arms. His dark hair against her cheek was as soft as a duckling's down. "Everything will be all right. You'll feel better soon. And no one will find us here, I promise."

Suddenly the door swung open, making Sarah jump. She whirled to find herself staring at Mrs. Flanders. "Miss Kincade, I have to talk to you!" God, she dreaded facing the woman after the night she'd put in.

Clarice Flanders stood before her, a plump, brown wren of a female in a faded Mother Hubbard. Her fine hair was pulled into a tiny, hard knot on the top of her round head. A frown completed her appearance. It seemed to Sarah that she was always frowning at her, despite her own unfailing courtesy that bordered on servility.

"Miss Kincade, you know mighty well that even though I didn't hold with the town council's decision to hire you, what with this—*nephew* of yours"—again, she looked Sarah up and down with a narrow-eyed gaze—"I agreed to let you live in my home. I've boarded the town's teachers for as long as I can remember. And I've tried hard to be understanding of your circumstances."

"Oh, yes, Mrs. Flanders, and I appreciate it so—"

The woman lifted her voice dramatically to be heard over Danny's wails. "But you've been under my roof for three months and this just isn't working out. The baby is keeping the family awake at night with his crying. Your goat is just as noisy." She yanked on the rope and a clatter of hooves sounded on the floor. From behind Mrs. Flanders Sarah heard her goat's loud *eh-eh-eh-eh*. It had been Isabel following her down the street, not a dog. Clarice continued. "I've got chores of my own to do, and I need my rest. Doc Bentley said you ought to give the boy laudanum for his colic, and I agree."

Sarah might not know much about infants, but she'd seen what laudanum could do to adults. "We've discussed this already, Mrs. Flanders. I wouldn't dream of giving a baby such a strong drug!"

Mrs. Flanders's dark brows formed a sharp vee above her small, close-set eyes. "Well, you can dream whatever you like. But I'm putting my foot down."

Sarah flinched, almost feeling the woman's big foot between her shoulder blades. She clutched the baby more closely, half expecting this crone to fix him with the evil eye. "What do you mean?"

She huffed impatiently, and her nose rose just a notch. "The truth is—Well, I have to speak my piece. I knew this would be trouble from the beginning, but the town council wouldn't listen to me. They offered to take you on because we needed a teacher, bad, since the last one left in March. Even so, they had no business hiring a—a loose woman to oversee our children and give them immoral ideas."

Hot blood flushed through Sarah's face. "What are you implying, Mrs. Flanders?"

"I'm a charitable Christian and I was willing to look the other way." The woman lowered her voice and snapped, "This isn't your dead sister's boy, like you told everyone. I know he's yours, just as sure as I know my own kids, and you're only trying to cover it up, *Miss* Kincade. Why, he looks like you! He's got your dark brown hair and will probably get those green eyes of yours, too."

Sarah set her back teeth in the face of this accusation. "It isn't true! Danny is my nephew, and my poor sister gave him to me with her last breath the morning he was born." Sarah almost choked on the lie—it broke her heart to deny that he was her own.

Mrs. Flanders stared her down. "I don't believe it." She drew herself up to her full five feet, putting the top of her head at Sarah's brow. "And now you're setting your sights on my husband. Oh, don't think for a minute that I haven't noticed you making eyes at him, and right in front of me, too, at my own dinner table. I saw it again last night, and I can tell you, I've had enough. Women like you are all the same, on the prowl for any man, attached or not!"

Sarah sputtered, groping for words to defend herself against this outrageous accusation. "You could not be more wrong—" Attracting a man, *any man,* was the least of her desires. And creepy, monosyllabic Bob Flanders, with his nasty, slinking glances, made her skin crawl anytime she was in the same room with him.

"There's still another week before school starts," Mrs. Flanders continued. "That should give you time to find somewhere else to live, because you won't be staying with us anymore."

Sarah gaped at her, dry-throated, with a taste of dust in her mouth. "Somewhere . . . else?" All of her tenuous, carefully made plans were suddenly tumbling down around her.

"I know I said I'd watch the baby for you while you worked, but I never should have made the offer. His diapers take up half my clothesline, and anyway, I won't have a tart in my house. I hate to lose the money the town paid me, but there are some things that money won't solve. Since the council hired you, let them pay someone else to board you. Of course, I don't know that they'll look too kindly on a woman with a bastard baby who lied to them—"

Sarah felt as if her heart had stopped in her chest. "You wouldn't tell them such a horrible thing!"

"Why shouldn't I? I don't want you giving my innocent girls the wrong—"

The sound of bare feet running on sun-dried earth added to the din of raised voices, the crying baby, and the bleating goat. One of the Flanders girls trotted up to the open door and complained, "Ma, you gotta come on back home! Cody took my favorite hair ribbon, the one that Gramma gave me!"

Isabel increased the volume of her own contribution to the chaos. *"Eh-eh-eh-eh!"*

Clarice Flanders turned her head and barked, "Well, make Cody give it back, Jess!"

"He used it on his kite and now he says it's stuck in a cottonwood down at the creek!"

Turning back, she said to Sarah, "I don't have time to worry about this problem. You have to go. By tonight. Get a room at the hotel until you find something else."

The hotel consisted of two tiny, airless rooms over the general store. Sarah had stayed there when she first arrived in Lame Horse.

"Ma!"

"Land sakes, Jessica!" Mrs. Flanders turned and charged out, leaving Sarah adrift in the doorway, her sharp retort caught in her throat.

Finally it surfaced and she hurled it at the woman's back. "I'd rather sleep in a—a cow pasture than spend another night under your roof!"

Danny stopped crying.

To Zach Garrett, Blaine Hodges looked like the sheriffs in every other piss-ant town like Lame Horse—slow-moving and unaccustomed to any trouble beyond a drunken cowboy now and then. A little thick around the midsection, a little thin across the hairline. The sheriff leaned back in his chair on the other side of his desk.

It was plain to Zach that the trouble he was presenting now was something Hodges did not want to deal with.

He endured the inquisitive gaze of the lawman, who considered him from under the bony ridge of his brow. Zach resisted the urge to shift restively, and merely returned the look.

He wanted to be done with this whole business, to get Sarah Kincade and her baby back to Helena. When he did that, and Ethan Pembroke paid him, he'd finally be able to start his life over. God knew he'd spent enough time on the road, nearly a month, tracking down the woman and the kid. Before that he'd spent *more* than enough time doing work that other men had turned down, just for the chance to start over. Now that chance was so close he could almost smell it. He only had to do this one last job.

The lawman returned his attention to the official documents in front of him. They were heavy with ornate script and bore seals with ribbons.

"Who did you say you were?"

"Zachary Garrett, from Helena."

"And you're a bounty hunter?"

Zach suppressed an impatient sigh. His identity and his reason for being in Lame Horse had been established ten minutes earlier. "Nope, I'm just doing a job for the pay. The baby's father hired me to bring the woman and kid back to Helena."

Hodges arched a brow at him. "And you're saying this baby was kidnapped by some stranger?"

"I didn't say that at all." Zach pointed at the papers. "Look, Hodges, I have a court order here, signed by a judge in Helena. And here's the contract the woman signed, agreeing to give up her baby to the Pembrokes. It's all pretty clear. And it's all legal."

Sheriff Hodges rubbed the back of his neck, a reluctant expression on his long face. "I don't know. She told everyone that the boy is her nephew, given to her to raise when her sister died birthing him."

"She's lying."

Hodges shook his head and peered at the contract. "Maybe some folks around here thought it was kind of unusual, an unmarried teacher with a baby, but if he's really her own child—I just don't like the sound of all this. You say she made up the story, but I'm inclined to believe her." He straightened in his chair. "After all, she's a *schoolmarm*."

As if that explained everything. Zach leaned both hands on the desk. "Yeah, and Doc Holliday was a dentist with a fancy gentleman's education. It didn't stop him from whoring and gambling and getting into gunfights. Now you've seen all the proof you need that this woman has done wrong. I don't have a personal grudge against her. I'm just doing what I was hired to do. And nobody wants to arrest her—they only want her to bring the baby back to Helena. If you know where she is, I'd be much obliged if you'd tell me." He picked up the documents from the sheriff's desk, refolded them, and tucked them inside his shirt. "If you won't, I'll knock on every door around here until I find her."

Sheriff Hodges pushed himself back from the desk and stood up. "No, no, I can't have you doing that. Folks wouldn't appreciate that at all. I'll take you to her." He reached for his hat and eyed Zach again. "I'll tell you this much, though—I wouldn't have the stomach for the kind of thing you're going to do to her. It wouldn't matter how much someone was paying me. I wouldn't be able to sleep nights."

Zach turned a flat gaze on him. "Then I guess it's a good thing Pembroke hired me and not you."

Humiliated and desperate, Sarah needed less than an hour to jam their belongings into her bag and leave the Flanders' house. She didn't own much and neither did Danny. She'd had to abandon most of her clothes in Bozeman the morning she escaped on the stagecoach that had brought her to Lame

Horse. What she had left were a couple of dresses she'd had to alter once to accommodate her pregnancy, and then again to fit her current shape.

Before Sarah knew it, she had Danny nestled in her arm and was walking away from the house, clutching her valise, with Isabel tied to the handle. The goat's bell clanked behind her with a dull sound. She wanted to cry, she felt so lost, so alone in the world, but she choked back the tears and forced herself to keep her chin high. She sensed six pairs of eyes watching her from the windows, and it occurred to her that she knew how conspicuous Hawthorne's Hester Prynne must have felt with a scarlet *A* sewn to her bodice.

She headed toward the general store, dragging her forest-green skirts over the dry weeds that grew along the edge of the road. It promised to be another hot day, one that would turn the sky to silver-blue by afternoon. As the sun pounded down upon her bare head, a dozen worries and questions swam through her mind. The most frightening concerned the future. Clarice Flanders was bound to tell the other members of the town council what she suspected about Danny, that he was really Sarah's own and not a nephew. It was such shameful, delicious gossip, an unmarried woman passing off her illegitimate child as a nephew, Clarice would be unable to resist. Though there was no real proof, they'd be far more likely to believe the woman's suspicion than anything Sarah might tell them.

If she lost this teaching job, she didn't know how they'd survive. She had so very little money and no security at all. She couldn't even nurse Danny to feed him. She'd had to wean him as soon as possible to goat's milk, and one of the neighboring farms had donated Isabel. After all, an aunt couldn't very well breast-feed a baby, and anyway, when school started she wouldn't be able to leave class to feed him. He'd need milk and clean clothes and safety. Icy coldness radiated from her stomach to her limbs when she thought of their uncertainty.

Sarah shifted the valise handle cutting into her palm. Imagine that pumpkin-headed Clarice Flanders implying Sarah was a loose woman, that she had designs on her husband, that she couldn't be trusted to educate children. Sarah Kincade, who had once held a position of respect and esteem.

She glanced down at her baby, who waved sleepy fists as she bundled him along, and recognized an inescapable truth: just a little more than a year ago, her own view of an unmarried mother wouldn't have been much different.

A teacher, she had learned in normal school, was charged with the vital task of molding children's minds and souls, and therefore had to be more decorous than most people. In Helena, Sarah had been so careful of her conduct, no one had thought to question it. Seen as a paragon of moral virtue and right-mindedness, she had been very proud of the dignified example she set.

Still . . . though her life had been full, it had not been truly fulfilling. Telling herself that she had her dignity and the town's regard hadn't filled the emptiness she sometimes felt. It hadn't tamed the yearning, bittersweet and piercing, for more than dignity and a different kind of regard. Ethan Pembroke had identified that yearning as clearly as if she'd worn a sign, and singled her out as surely as a mountain lion targeted a doe.

How could she have been so foolish and naïve? she wondered bitterly. *This* was true loneliness, with despair and an uncertain future thrown in for good measure.

Passing the plate-glass display window at Miller's General Store, Sarah caught sight of herself, the baby in her arms and the bag in her hand. She wasn't sorry she had Danny—she adored him. He was her reason for living. But a child deserved a better life than this, and they were off to a terrible start. Just a little more than a year ago, and a world away . . .

She continued to Miller's entrance, a fancy double-door setup of which Winslow Miller was very proud. The only one in these parts, he claimed. He was a member of the triumvirate that made up the town council.

Leaving the goat tied to her valise on the sidewalk, she walked into the cool gloom of the store and inhaled the scents of coffee and leather, bacon and talcum powder, fruit and vinegar. The walls behind the counter were lined with big glass jars that held rice, hard candy, beans, dried peas, lentils, and spices. Sarah had fed Danny his bottle, but she hadn't eaten since dinner the night before. If her circumstances were not so dire, her mouth would have been watering. Instead, it still felt as dry as paper.

"Miss Kincade, how do," Win Miller hailed. He stood behind the counter heaped with new merchandise, excelsior trailing from it like Spanish moss. With a pencil poised in one hand, he was comparing the order to its shipping list, the high plane of his forehead furrowed with the effort. "Out shopping with young Daniel before the heat of the day sets in, eh? Good idea. What can I do for you today?" He squinted at an item on the list, then checked it off with the pencil that he touched first to his tongue.

Sarah swallowed and approached the counter. "Well, Mr. Miller, it seems I am in need of a hotel room."

The shopkeeper looked up from his accounting. "Eh? What's that you say?"

"I'm afraid Mrs. Flanders has decided that she doesn't want to open her home to me and Danny, after all."

He shoved a crate of tinned peaches down the counter.

"Why not? I admit it's a little out of the ordinary, a teacher with an orphaned baby, but Clarice has that wild tribe of her own. I don't know what difference one more would make. She and Bob have always boarded our teachers, since, well, since I can't remember."

In seconds Sarah considered and discarded several reasons to give Winslow Miller, but before she'd decided, her reply popped out of her mouth. "She seems to think that Danny is my son and not my nephew." Had she actually said that? Perhaps it was best, though. Get the jump on the woman and her tale-bearing. Even if it did Sarah no good, she would deprive Clarice Flanders of the perverse joy in being the first to relay her nasty little piece of gossip. She put on what she hoped was an expression of injured dignity and hated herself for once again denying her own baby. *Danny, Danny, I'm sorry*—He squirmed in her arms, and the smell of wet diaper reached her nose. "Since I am unmarried, I'm sure you realize all that is implied."

Miller stared at her for a moment, his pencil still poised in midair, then his face turned a vivid shade of crimson. He glanced at Danny again. "*Your* son? Uh, yes, yes, I see." He pawed at the papers on his counter and looked as if he wished he were anywhere in the world except here.

Sarah had just one advantage and, slim though it was, she intended to play it for all it was worth. "I'm worried that in her zeal to do what she feels is the right thing, Mrs. Flanders will want to persuade the town council to look for another teacher. But it's so late now, I don't know who they would find. Lame Horse's children might go without schooling for the whole year."

Miller's brows shot up. "Yes, yes, I see we have a problem here. Maybe Clarice is looking for trouble where there isn't any." He fidgeted with a jar of candy sticks on the counter. "But even so—a schoolmarm is supposed to—Well, we got to have some standards, Miss Kincade. Right and wrong is a mighty important part of a youngster's education, even more important than book learning. If there's a question about . . ." He nodded at the baby. "Well, the town council will have to have another meeting about this. But you try not to worry, ma'am. We'll get it all sorted out."

They stared at each other across the counter for an endless moment, and then Danny let out a short squawk, causing a break in the eye contact. Sarah felt her shoulders droop, as if the weight of her troubles and the world's were pressing down on them. She was tired and scared, and though no experience in her life had prepared her for this, something told her she must keep a confident—and innocent—appearance. To do anything else might jeopardize her already precarious position.

To do anything else would mean that Ethan Pembroke had won.

She straightened. "In the meantime, Mr. Miller, would you be kind enough to rent a room to me? I don't have a lot of money but I need to tend my nephew, and we both need a place to sleep."

Miller tugged at his high collar, as if it were too tight. "Now, now, we promised you room and board, and until we can get this business figured out—" He pulled out a strongbox from beneath the shiny counter and plucked a key from its depths. "You take number two again, just up the stairs outside. You can tie up your goat out back, and I'll talk to Mrs. Miller about fixing your meals."

Sarah took the key he offered and tipped her head in assent, not trusting her voice to answer. Her throat felt as if a clenched fist were lodged in it. Boosting Danny a bit higher on her shoulder, she crossed the floor to Miller's fancy double-door entrance. On the plank sidewalk, she looked up the tall flight of stairs that climbed the outside wall of the building and led to the two rooms on the second floor. She wanted nothing as much as a place to lie down and the time to do it.

"Miss Kincade—ma'am, wait."

Sarah turned to see Sheriff Blaine Hodges hailing her from the hitching post in front of his office. She paused and he trotted across the dusty street, kicking up little plumes of dry Montana soil with every step. Another man followed him, someone she didn't recognize. He was handsome, perhaps the most handsome man Sarah had seen in a long time, but she saw a shadow of callousness in his eyes. He carried himself with a deliberate gait, and he stared at her in a way that conveyed an odd dislike. A chill shivered through her.

"I never thought I'd have any trouble finding a body in this town," the sheriff said, "but I've been all over Lame Horse looking for you. Clarice said you'd be here, though."

Oh, Sarah would just bet Clarice had told him that, and a thing or two more. A cold hand stole around her heart, but she did her best to put on a brave, unconcerned face. It was an exhausting task. "Really? What can I do for you, Sheriff?"

Sheriff Hodges jammed his hands in his back pockets and actually scuffed his boots in the dust. Sarah had seen this self-conscious behavior often enough in her students to know it probably didn't bring good news.

"Well, ma'am, um, this man here is Zachary Garrett, from Helena, and he says he has some business with you. About the boy."

Sarah backed up a step and pressed Danny closer. *No, no! Dear God, no.* She didn't know this man, but without being told, she knew what his "business" was. At night, her dreams had been haunted with images of a dark, faceless stalker who would steal Danny from her arms. She'd wake, shivering with cold perspiration and her pulse hammering through her body with the singular terror of the pursued. She felt like that now. Her nightmare had come true—somehow this stranger had tracked her down. She wanted to run but, just like in her dream, her feet were as heavy as lead and wouldn't budge. And this horrible man—how had he found them, how?

Zachary Garrett stepped forward to close the gap. "You're this boy's mother? Sarah Jane Kincade?"

Staring up into his cold hazel eyes, she felt like a rabbit trapped by a fox. Her pulse throbbed in her temple but she could not respond.

He laid his shotgun in the crook of his arm, then reached into his shirt and produced two documents, both creased many times. He shook them out to unfold them. "I have a court order here, signed by Judge Wallace Driscoll, authorizing me to take you and the baby back to Helena."

Sarah looked at it but she couldn't focus on anything written there. Court order. *Court order.* From the corner of her eye, she saw Win Miller edge close to his door under the pretense of rearranging an umbrella stand filled with walking sticks. She found her voice, although her words were only whispered. "Do you mean to tell me that I'm under arrest?"

Garrett sighed and took no trouble to lower his voice. "You aren't under arrest. Look—" He shoved the other document into her face. "This is the contract you made with Ethan and Priscilla Pembroke, agreeing to let them adopt your baby in exchange for their charity. Isn't that your signature at the bottom, next to theirs?"

It was. What had she been thinking of to sign her child away? Snared by a web of lies and outrageous deception, she'd been backed into an impossible corner, and the pen literally put into her shaking hand. If only she had it to do again—

"Ma'am? Isn't that your signature?" Garrett repeated.

"Yes."

Now Miller boldly stepped outside to join the meeting, adjusting his sleeve garters the way a lawman might hoist his gun belt. "Well, by God, we can't have a woman like this teaching our young folks, a woman with a bastard baby!"

"Aw, Jesus, Win, pipe down," Hodges said, plainly embarrassed. "Now isn't the time to talk about that."

Sarah turned a frantic gaze on Blaine Hodges. "Sheriff, surely you can do something about this!"

Hodges shrugged apologetically. "I'd like to, ma'am, I really would. But the court order is all nice and legal, and there's this contract. I've read it. I'm afraid the Pembrokes are within their rights, and they've hired Mr. Garrett, here, to bring you back." In a more cheerful tone, he added, " 'Course you can probably get a smart lawyer once you get to Helena and fight this if you want."

Get a lawyer! With what? She didn't have enough money to even buy a stagecoach ticket out of this town that was supposed to have been her refuge. All of her fretful planning to safeguard her son had done no good. God save them from this man, Sarah's mind screamed. Yes, he was handsome, even more so than Ethan, with a lean jawline, a straight nose and smooth brow. But his heart was probably as black as Ethan's. Didn't they say the devil could assume a pleasing form? Meeting Ethan had certainly taught her that. This man had come to take Danny from her and he had the authority to do it. Well, he wasn't going to. She wouldn't let him.

Zach Garrett pressed his point. "One way or another, you and the boy have to go back to Helena. You signed a contract. I was hired to see that you make good on your promise."

Sarah cast frantic, pleading looks at the sheriff, at Win Miller. But they looked at the sidewalk, down the street, everywhere except at her.

"You can't have my baby!"

Panic and a mother's instinct racing through her veins like sheet lightning, she backed up again and whirled toward the stairs. With the room key clutched in her icy fingers, she dropped the valise with Isabel still tied to it and hiked her skirts to gallop up the steps. The long flight seemed to tower into the sky, but she ran as though the very devil were after her. Indeed, he was, bent on stealing her child from her. Danny bounced against her shoulder and began howling again, but if she could just reach that room up there, if she could reach that room she would lock herself and the baby inside, and barricade the door if she had to.

"Hold on, Miss Kincade!"

She spared one glance over her shoulder and saw Zachary Garrett right behind her. Dear God! She took the stairs two at a time but she couldn't outpace him and his long-legged stride. His gloved hand shot out and closed around a fold of her skirt. Abruptly he checked her momentum, and with a cry she fell to her knees on the next step, her shins crashing against its sharp edge. She wrapped both arms around her wailing child and twisted to one side to keep from crushing him beneath her. The muscles in her back wrenched, complaining with white-hot pain that was almost paralyzing, and she landed hard, wedged against the banister with Danny on her lap.

Sarah heard a cowardly, murmured protest from one of the men at the bottom of the steps, but she knew it was hopeless. She couldn't keep running—she had no job, no money, and no means of transportation. Danny would starve.

She could no longer keep the tears from welling up in her eyes.

When she lifted her head, she saw Zach Garrett looming over her, offering her a hand up. She looked into his eyes and found no compassion. No pity. Only her own fear, reflecting back at her.

Chapter Two

Sarah sat on the hard spindle-back chair in her hotel room above Miller's General Store. She watched Danny, finally asleep in a dresser drawer that served as his bed. Even though the day had turned hot, she huddled in her shawl, chilled to her heart and bones.

Zachary Garrett had taken the room next to her, the one closest to the stairs. She'd heard him come and go three or four times, and each time he peeked into her window as if making sure she was still there. The last time, she yanked the blind down, cutting off his view.

So this was to be the end of the folly she had begun nearly two years earlier, a horror that she had never once imagined in her romantic flights of fancy. Sarah leaned her head in her hands, reliving a heartache that, even now, was still sharp and brutal.

She had loved Ethan Pembroke. All the more hurtful, she'd believed he loved her. For a while, anyway.

Sarah had met Ethan at a church ice-cream social. He was handsome and educated, and interested in polite female company. She had her teaching job, and she enjoyed it, but she hoped for more from life. Something for herself—a real home, family. Ethan had made that seem possible.

With a taste for fine things and the ability to pay for them, he'd shown Sarah a side of life she'd never pictured for herself—champagne, elegant, intimate dinners, Sunday picnics during which he'd read poetry to her and fed her orange sections. He'd also been very careful of her reputation; he knew how the town would view a schoolteacher who was being courted, so he kept their meetings discreet.

Sarah fell hopelessly in love with Ethan, and assumed that a marriage proposal was in their immediate future. But he kept telling her they had all the time in the world. And as a financier with several wealthy clients, he told her that he could take the tidy nest egg she had in the bank and invest it for her so that she could begin their marriage with money of her own. Accustomed to independence, the idea appealed to her. Together, he promised, they would build a fine house on fashionable Madison Avenue, and she could almost see the imposing dwelling he described. The future he painted with words sounded like a dream come true for a lonely schoolmarm who had so hoped for a husband and family.

Without hesitating, she added Ethan's name to her savings account—and shyly invited him to her lonely bed.

But over the next few months, Sarah found herself beginning to wonder if Ethan was truly the man for her. She felt the relationship had changed subtly. She'd made herself vulnerable to him, not just emotionally, but financially too. He controlled all of her money. And though he never took a dime, never did any of the investing he'd said he would, she felt bound to him. His double-edged comments and tiny criticisms spawned horrible doubts in her heart about a future with him.

But then she realized she was pregnant. Her terror consumed her—an unmarried teacher expecting a baby. Even now Sarah cringed, thinking about the scandal that would have caused. She sent a note to his office, telling him that she needed to discuss an urgent matter with him. Delicacy prevented her from putting the details on paper, but she worded her message in a way that left no question about her predicament.

The memory of what happened next sent new chills through her until she trembled like a windblown leaf. How could she have been so stupid, so gullible? She was worse than any of Brontë's heroines she had so loved.

When Ethan finally came to see her, he brought a woman with him—*Mrs.* Ethan Pembroke. Not only was he already married, but his wife had known all about Sarah's relationship with her husband. But Priscilla Pembroke didn't seem upset. In fact, she looked rather pleased.

So eager were the Pembrokes for a child, and apparently unable to have their own, they had selected Sarah to bear one for them, trapping her as neatly as a spider tied up a fly. Knowing full well the position they'd put her in, they offered her the chance to escape from Helena and the inevitable scandal that would follow if news of her pregnancy became public knowledge. As long as she surrendered her baby to them, they would finance her months of seclusion in Bozeman. Then after he was born, she could return, telling people she'd gone on sabbatical, and no one would be the wiser.

Stunned but still capable of making a decision, Sarah refused. She would go away, yes, but she would leave permanently. She'd start over someplace where no one knew her. But when she went to the bank, she learned that Ethan had emptied her account just that morning. Without money, she couldn't run. Yet, how could she stay? The townspeople who'd put so much faith in her would shun her and her baby. He would be treated like an outcast, less than human. She couldn't do that to an innocent soul. To her child.

Sarah had agonized over the decision for two long, sleepless days and nights. Finally, her heart breaking, she signed the Pembrokes' contract, letting herself believe they could give the child a better life than she could. But on the hot, endless night that Danny was born and he was put into her arms, the rush of love was so fierce, she knew she couldn't go through with the plan.

Three days later, she'd bundled him up, grabbed what clothes she could, and sneaked away from her boarding-house to the train leaving Bozeman. She hadn't cared where it was going. She'd gotten off a stop or two later, just a few miles east, but she'd bought herself enough time and breathing room to plan her next move. And that had brought her to Lame Horse.

Sarah rested her head on the edge of the drawer where Danny slept. Now there was nowhere else to run to.

Zach Garrett stopped at the top of the stairs, in front of the door that bore a tarnished brass numeral one. He'd rented the room for himself. Sarah Kincade and her child were in the other room at the end of the landing, with the blinds drawn. If she decided to run again, she'd have to pass right by his windows and creep down the flight of stairs that squeaked like a pair of new shoes. He could be on her in a second, the way a bobcat pounced on a gopher. Now that he'd found her, he didn't intend to let her slip out of his grasp. She was worth a pretty penny to him.

He leaned over the railing and looked at the stairway below. Unwillingly, he remembered her fall on the steps a couple of hours earlier. She'd been haggard-looking and her dark hair tumbled around her shoulders. The baby lay screaming on her lap.

He'd offered her a hand, but she pointedly ignored it and struggled to her feet, clutching the baby to her. Zach had felt the disapproving stares of the men below him bor-ing into his back. He'd meant only to check her flight, not to push her down. What had happened troubled him, more than he wanted to admit even to himself, but now he did his best to dismiss the thought.

He leaned his elbows on the railing and stared at the open prairie beyond Lame Horse, where a pheasant bolted out of the brush. Over the past couple of years, Zach had made an occupation of doing his best to dismiss troubling thoughts, to blunt his conscience and temper his nerve. He'd had to in order to pursue his goal. After all, if a man gave it too much thought, would he take a job delivering a mining company's payroll when it had been routinely held up and its drivers killed by one outlaw or another? If he didn't abandon his sense of decency, at least temporarily, would he work as a bouncer in a whorehouse? The one where Zach had worked for six months entertained all manner of men, including a prominent Helena minister. With a wife and three children at home, the man enjoyed his flock's admiration and respect. But, the girls whispered, he demanded services so profane that Lady Rose, the madame, charged the good reverend double. Hell, if Zach hadn't seen him with his own eyes leaving the place at dawn, he wouldn't have believed it. He wouldn't have been so disillusioned, either.

Zach had seen and done a lot in his life that might haunt his sleep for the rest of his years. All he could do was keep his sight on his goal and the money it required. But although it had been an accident, driving Sarah Kincade to her knees on the steps had very nearly scaled the wall he'd built around his sleeping conscience. He wouldn't let that happen again. Damn it, if she hadn't given her word and then broken it, she wouldn't be in this spot to begin with. Blasted women were always running out or running away. His early years on the New York streets had taught him that. He'd tried hard to forget that part of his life, but it lurked in the corners of his memory. Random images, shadowy and dark, pushed forward now and then the way an old bone break ached in damp weather. Nights spent in alleys . . . running from the police . . . stealing just to eat . . .

Zach slammed the door on the ghosts and forced himself

to think about his goal. He wasn't looking forward to dragging the schoolmarm and her kid across the territory. But
Ethan Pembroke's offer had been too tempting to pass up.
He and his wife wanted that boy back. They'd extended
the hand of charity to Sarah Kincade, and now they were
willing to do everything they could to make sure she held
up her end of the deal. So determined were they that to
obtain his help, they'd offered Zach the very prize he'd
been working toward all this time—the promissory note
Pembroke held on his land.

To get that, with the words *Paid in Full* written on it,
Zach would deliver the devil himself to the man's fancy,
book-lined study in that new house he'd built in Helena.
But all he was asking for was a woman and a baby. A baby
that, by contract, belonged to the Pembrokes. Zach didn't
know Sarah Kincade's sad life story, and he didn't want to
hear it—hell, *everybody* had a sad story. He didn't know
or care why she had agreed to give her son away for adoption and then changed her mind.

This, thank God, would be his last job. It might even be
the worst one yet, but it would be his last. After this, Zach
would be able to rebuild the ranch house from its ashes.
He'd sit on his front porch in the evenings and gaze at the
good, blooded breeding stock he'd bought, while they
grazed on acres of fine Montana grassland. All paid for in
cash. He'd be able to hold up his head in Helena again,
and forget the things he'd done, work that other men had
brushed off as too unsavory or risky.

Straightening from the railing, he walked to Sarah's door
and knocked sharply. No answer. He knocked again, louder
this time. God, she couldn't have gotten away already—

"Miss Kincade!"

At last he heard stirring from within and the door opened
a crack. Sarah Kincade glared up at him with a pair of the

greenest eyes he'd ever seen. He was struck by the fact that she didn't look like the kind of woman Pembroke had described. She looked—well, respectable, like a schoolmarm.

"Forgive me for not moving faster. I was tending some bruises on my lower limbs."

Zach rubbed the back of his neck and cursed the flush he felt rising past his chin. He'd be damned if he'd give her the apology she was fishing for. She shouldn't have run. Then the accident wouldn't have happened.

"What do you want, Mr. Garrett? Checking to make sure that I'm still here?"

By God, but she was a sassy woman. "No, ma'am, but I don't intend to lose track of you, just in case you have any ideas about running. I came by to let you know that we'll be leaving at first light tomorrow, so you and the boy be packed up and ready to go. I want to get back to Helena as soon as possible."

Sarah opened the door a bit wider. She had tidied her dark-chocolate hair, pinning it high on her head to show off a slender, pale neck. She was a small woman, with faintly rounded shoulders, full breasts, and a slender waist. "The stagecoach comes to Lame Horse every two weeks. It won't be here again till next Friday."

"I'm not buying stage tickets. I bought a horse for you to ride, a mare. She's at the livery."

Sarah blinked. "A horse . . . We're going to cross the territory on horseback?"

"You know how to ride, don't you?" He couldn't imagine that she didn't. Not if she was from Montana.

"Yes, but I haven't been on a horse in years. Traveling in a stagecoach would be a lot easier."

Zach stared back at her. This woman obviously didn't know the value of a dollar. Pembroke had given him expense money, but every penny Zach saved was one more

penny he could keep, and he intended to do just that. "Jesus, the passage would cost a fortune. At least I can sell
the horse in Helena and I won't be out the money."

Sarah's jaw tightened slightly. "And what about my
baby? Will I carry him on my back like a Cheyenne wife?"

Well, hell. He hadn't thought about that, and Pembroke
hadn't mentioned it. He'd just said to bring the pair to Helena. How Zach accomplished that was his responsibility.
Although Zach was in charge of this expedition, the way
she was looking at him made him feel that he was the one
at a disadvantage, and he didn't like it one damned bit. "I'll
rig up something. Maybe a sling you can wear over your
shoulder."

She opened the door wider still, giving him a view of a
narrow iron bed. The bedding was rumpled, and he figured
she must have been lying down before he knocked. Her
sleeves, rolled up to the elbows, revealed willowy forearms.
"And what will Danny eat?"

Unable to resist the dig, Zach let his gaze drop and linger
on her bosom for a moment. "That's your problem, Miss
Kincade."

A flush stained her white cheeks, suggesting a complex-
ion of rose petals and cream on a better day, and her
dagger-filled stare fell away. It wasn't the kind of prim
reaction he'd expect from a woman who'd allowed herself
to get in trouble. Oh, he could see how a man could get
tangled up with her. Sure, she was pretty, and some women
sent out signals that invited a lot more than a kiss on the
hand. But now that he got a better look at her, he realized
she wasn't what he'd pictured at all.

"Danny is weaned to goat's milk and that's what he'll
need. Isabel—my goat—won't be very happy if she's
dragged along behind a horse."

"Isabel." He'd seen the animal earlier, but in the chaos

on the stairs, he hadn't paid it much attention.

"She's tied up downstairs behind the building."

Zach crossed his arms over his chest, losing patience with this snippy female. "Where would a *goat* have sat on a stagecoach? Was I supposed to buy a ticket for her, too?"

Sarah responded with a frown that creased her forehead, and briefly she pressed a hand to her throat. She had a small, slender hand, Zach noticed. "I probably would be able to get goat's milk at the stage stops. But if we take horses, the goat can't graze and drink all the water she needs to give enough milk." The daggers were back in the gaze that she leveled on him. "That simply won't do, Mr. Garrett."

No, he could see that it wouldn't. And didn't she enjoy pointing that out. "I'm not buying stage tickets, so you can forget about that."

Sarah's voice dropped to a whisper. "Isn't it enough that I'm being forced to give up my child? Can't the trip be arranged so that I can properly care for him until he passes from my arms?"

Hate radiated from Sarah Kincade. Not in what she said, or even how she said it. It was just there, pulsating between them. A man could fry an egg on that hate. That was just too damned bad—he didn't care what she thought of him. But almost without realizing it, he took a step back.

"Yeah, well, I'll see what I can do. You just be ready at daybreak." He turned and walked back to his room, opened the door, and closed it. Hard.

That horrible man.

That horrible bully of a man.

Sarah shut her door and locked it, then lifted her skirts and bent slightly to look at her identically bruised shins. The sharp edge of the step had left angry purple and blue

contusions as big as the oatmeal cookies her mother used
to bake. Zach Garrett had done this to her. He was nearly
a foot taller than she was and probably outweighed her by
eighty or ninety pounds. All lean and long muscled, he was
very much different from Danny's father, the only man outside of her own family that Sarah had ever known on a
level more personal than conferring with a student's father.
She found Zach's very maleness intimidating—he plainly
bore the look of a man who'd spent most of his life in the
weather instead of behind a desk. Did it make him feel
important to tower over her and order her around?

Dropping her hem, she picked up Danny, still fast
asleep, and glanced around the plain-walled room. It was
more than two hundred miles to Helena. God, to cross
Montana Territory on horseback, with a baby? To be out
in the wilderness with gruff, cold-eyed Garrett, the man
who'd made her fall on the stairs, with no regard for the
child in her arms? She looked down at her sleeping baby,
the very heart and soul of sweet innocence. No, she
couldn't do it.

Once more escape crossed her mind. As she paced over
the pine flooring, frantic ideas swooped around in her head
like wild birds. Her own fear made her squeeze Danny so
hard he let out a startled cry.

"Sweetie, I'm sorry!" Swiftly she kissed his forehead,
but her steps only quickened.

She didn't have much money, certainly not enough for
a stage ticket, but she could sneak away from here and hide
with a family on one of the surrounding ranches . . . No,
no, that wouldn't work. Her throat grew dry and her hands
were still icy. She passed the window, with its wilted ging-
ham curtains, and glanced at the schoolhouse at the end of
the street.

Maybe she could appeal to the town council again. Not

for a job, because surely that was out of the question now. But perhaps she could beg for a secret place to stay and the loan of enough money to find her way out of Lame Horse. Yes, that was good. She'd repay the loan when she found work in another town. It would have to be any kind of work—trying to find another teaching position would be nearly impossible at this point. She could appeal to the council's decency and plead her case of basic maternal possession. Maybe Danny was born without the benefit of a married mother, but that didn't give anyone to the right to steal him from her arms. She paced faster. Danny cried in earnest. What decent person would stand by and watch that demon Garrett carry her off on horseback across the hinterland for the purpose of taking her child and only God knew what else? Who could do that?

A lot of people could.

The realization stopped her cold.

Sarah sank down on the stale-smelling bed, making the springs underneath screech. There was no point in fooling herself—no one was going to help her. This morning, the men watching Zach Garrett chase her up the stairs had just stood there, shuffling their feet and looking away.

If she had just herself to worry about, it would be different. She could take her chances. But Danny would only suffer from a life of running and hiding, and she had to put his welfare first.

"Oh, Danny," she mourned and pressed her cheek to his forehead. He was such a miracle to her. She drew back to study his face—the fine, almost invisible silky brows, the long lashes, and big blue eyes. His howls stopped and he stared back at her. As she dabbed at his tears with her sleeve, she recognized herself in her son's face, just as Clarice Flanders had. Odd, but he bore little resemblance to Ethan Pembroke. That was just as well. Not that Ethan had been bad-looking. In fact, he'd been quite handsome, but his cold heart and cruelty were in his face too. If only she'd seen them sooner—But then, she wouldn't have Danny.

She'd had such hope for their future in this town where no one knew them or their circumstances. She glanced down at her scuffed valise standing next to the bed and reached down to open its stiff brass fasteners. Inside, between one of her two chemises and Danny's diapers, was a well-worn volume of Dickens's *Oliver Twist,* and her copy of *McGuffey's Eclectic Fourth Reader. McGuffey's* was a mainstay of schoolteachers everywhere. In Helena, Sarah had owned the whole set of seven readers, but she'd left them behind, not expecting to need them. After all, she'd planned to have her baby, surrender him to the Pembrokes in secret, and return to her teaching job with no one the wiser. It had been an insane idea.

Sarah kissed the little hand Danny stretched out to touch her nose. "Do you know how much I love you?" He grinned and squawked, showing off toothless gums, and waved his fists. Her heart throbbed in her chest, as if it were truly breaking, and she swallowed hard.

She knew then that her only real option was to return to Helena with Zach Garrett, that devil's henchman with the expressionless eyes. When she got there, she'd do her best to appeal to whatever shred of honor Ethan and Priscilla Pembroke might still possess and plead for her son. If she failed—well, she couldn't think about that now. If she did, she'd go crazy with grief, and that wouldn't help at all. She had to keep her wits about her.

Sarah looked over Danny's head to gaze out the window again, at the endless miles of open prairie. Tomorrow, she and her son would be forced to venture out into that empty expanse, led by a man who had been paid to fetch them back like criminals.

"May Ethan Pembroke roast in hell," she intoned bitterly, "and take Zach Garrett with him."

The sun was a brilliant ruby on the eastern horizon when Zach pulled a wagon around to the side of Miller's General Store the next morning. His horse, tied to the back of the tailgate, followed behind, its hooves clopping along with the mules'. Dew glistened on the dry weeds sprouting from the edge of the wooden sidewalk, and for that moment their desiccated plainness was transformed into gold and diamonds. Even Lame Horse, not much more than a smudge on the landscape with its weather-beaten buildings, looked clean and new in the kindly light of sunrise.

Zach loved the beginnings and ends of days, sunrise and sunset. On one side was the chance to start over, when life seemed less punishing and possibilities abounded. At the other end was satisfaction or relief, sometimes regret. The hours in between was where the struggle lay.

This morning, though, just one thought occupied his mind: the journey to Helena. He'd lain awake most of the night, some of the time listening for the sound of soft footfalls on the landing outside his room, and the rest wondering how much trouble Sarah was going to give him. For a woman in her circumstances, she wasn't nearly as cowed and meek as he'd imagined she would be. She'd already gotten her way over this wagon and they hadn't even taken the first step out of town yet.

The whole outfit—covered wagon, mules, and a small pen—had cost far more than he'd expected to spend. But after his encounter with her yesterday, he'd realized there was nothing else to do. The owner of the livery had taken back the mare and sold him everything but the goat pen. The old man had brought the wagon out from Missouri years earlier, but luckily, he'd kept it in reasonable repair and under a tarpaulin in his barn, just in case a golden opportunity to sell it came along. Its canvas wasn't in the best shape, though, so Zach hoped the weather would co-operate.

The goat pen had come from Win Miller himself, along with the rest of the provisions Zach had bought for the trip. With a guilty expression, Miller had thrown in two glass baby bottles for the kid, free of charge.

"She might need them. Miss Kincade, that is. Tell her we're all—well, I'm mighty sorry things didn't work out for her."

Sorry. Despite what he stood to gain, at that instant Zach had been disgusted with Miller and the rest of Lame Horse. They'd willingly served up Sarah and her baby to him and an uncertain future, because suddenly she didn't measure up to their ideal of morality. Well, Zach wasn't judging her, although he supposed he couldn't say she'd done the right thing. But she was still the same person she'd been when she came to town to be the schoolmarm. What the town had learned about her didn't affect her ability to teach their children or change the knowledge she had in her head. They could have helped her if they'd wanted to. Instead they'd turned their backs.

Aw, damn it, it didn't mean anything to him. There he went again, taking his eyes and mind off his goal. He couldn't afford to do that yet. Not until he had that prom-issory note in his hand. Determined to get this trip started, he set the wagon brake and jumped down from the high seat while the mules waited in the traces. At least Sarah's gear already stood on the bottom step, so she must have taken his order seriously and he wouldn't have to go back upstairs to roust her out. When he glanced up, though, he halted in his own tracks.

Sarah descended the stairs carrying the baby. She wore

her shawl draped over her head, with its tails crossed and tucked into the waistband of her skirt. The same sunrise light, kind to the landscape and life's possibilities, fell upon her with a gentle touch. Again he was struck by how small she was—if he didn't know better, he might mistake her for a girl. But she carried herself with a cool, quiet dignity that exceeded whatever her true age might be. Pembroke had said she was twenty-six or so. Looking at her, with her back straight and head up, a vague uncomfortable feeling shimmied through Zach, not a lot different from the one he'd had yesterday. He shrugged at the sensation, then pulled on the cuff of his leather glove.

"Miss Kincade."

"Mr. Garrett," she replied as she reached the plank side-walk. She glanced at him and then turned her attention to the conveyance stopped alongside the building. "A covered wagon?" There was that edge in her voice again that seemed to say much more, and the look in her eyes that could slice a man at twenty yards.

"Yeah, and I bought enough food and supplies for three weeks." He crossed his arms over his chest. "Will this be good enough?"

"Yes, it will do, Mr. Garrett. I'm just surprised." Her lacerating gaze softened the tiniest bit. "I didn't expect— well, I expected something less."

"Sorry to disappoint you. Get on up there. I want to put fifteen or eighteen miles behind us today. I stopped by the telegraph office last night and wired the Pembrokes to tell them we're on our way." He stepped forward to take the baby so that she could step up to the wagon seat, but she pulled away. He lifted his brows and fixed her with a look of his own. "It's pretty hard to climb into a wagon with both of your hands full."

Still she stood back, plainly not trusting him to lay one

finger on her boy. "I can manage." Shifting the child to one arm, she put her foot on a wheel spoke and, with a big push, lunged for the edge of the wagon box. He didn't know how she got up there, but she settled on the seat and adjusted her skirts. Then she craned her neck and looked around. "Isabel—where's my goat? We can't leave without her."

Zach half hoped she'd forgotten about the damned nanny. "I know, I'm getting her. There's a pen in the wagon for her." He headed to the back of the building to fetch the goat.

Watching as Zach walked away, Sarah caught herself staring at the flex of his shoulders, with his dark hair brushing them. She tilted her head, considering the way he moved. He had long legs and carried himself with a certain grace, she supposed, one that seemed natural to him. But graceful or not, he was still the one taking her back to Helena so that the Pembrokes could steal her child, and he was hired by them to do it. That made him just as much her enemy as they were.

She turned to look inside the canvas enclosure behind her and sighed. This was to be their home for the next few weeks. Well, as she'd told Zach, it was more than she'd expected. The morning sun brightened the gray interior and the arches stood out like dark ribs. She saw a few barrels and boxes neatly stowed in a corner of the wagon box, and down at the end, a small, sturdy pen waited for Isabel. Its floor was lined with clean straw.

There was a clatter as Zach dropped the tailgate and struggled to get the goat into her coop. Isabel's bell clanked wildly, and she complained with enough vigor to wake the entire town. Zach added his own fervent, low-voiced swearing, bringing a hot flush to Sarah's cheeks. What else could she expect of such a man?

"Don't hurt her!" she called, trying to see what was happening.

"I'm *not* hurting her," Zach ground out between gritted teeth.

The tailgate slammed shut again, the pins were slid into place, and he tied his own horse to the back. Sarah heard his determined heel strikes on the hard-packed earth as he came around to the front of the wagon and climbed to the seat beside her. Vertical streaks of dirt, undoubtedly from Isabel's hooves, marked the front of his tan shirt, and a flap of fabric that had once been the pocket hung by its bottom seam.

"What happened?"

"Damned animal—that goat is as bad-tempered as a wolverine." He unwrapped the reins from the brake handle with angry, impatient movements.

"No she isn't. She's very affectionate and friendly."

He flicked his torn pocket at her. "Oh, yeah? Well, it wasn't a kiss that ripped my shirt. That goat bit me!"

Good for Isabel, she thought, and turned her face so Zach wouldn't see her satisfied expression.

"Shirts don't grow on trees—they cost money."

Everything about this man seemed to circle back to the subject of money. "Maybe Mr. Pembroke will reimburse you when you explain what happened." She looked into his hazel eyes, her brow arched. "You can blame the goat."

Zach frowned but didn't reply. Slapping the reins on the mules' backs, he barked, "Heyup, there," and the wagon lurched forward.

There he was, right next to her, his thigh almost touching hers, and there he would be for the better part of more than two hundred miles. The seat was narrow but she scooted away and pulled her skirts closer.

They reached the end of the only street in Lame Horse. The vast, empty grasslands of Montana lay before them for as far as the eye could see.

Chapter Three

The day proceeded uneventfully, with Zach stopping now and then so that Sarah could milk Isabel and change Danny's diaper.

She knew that Danny was a sweet baby most of the time, except, of course, when his colic acted up. And, while the general rocking of the wagon soothed him, if one of the wheels hit a gopher hole or a rut and woke him, he complained. Then, as babies were inclined, he turned fussy, and he screamed vigorously when he was wet or hungry.

Sarah sensed Zach's impatience with each stop but there was nothing she could do to make Isabel give her milk any faster, and Sarah diapered as fast as she could. At least she could feed the baby while they were moving, although the ride was much bumpier than a stagecoach would have been and he tended to spit up a lot more. Somehow the thin towel she carried was always in the wrong place when this occurred, and by afternoon her shoulder and bodice were stiff with sour, dried goat's milk, adding one more foul odor to the panoply of smells she already wore.

Dear God, what a place to try to care for a baby, she fretted, feeling his wet diaper against her midriff. She wished for nothing more than to be in a clean, safe place with the humble conveniences of a stove to heat water and a roof over her head. Yet Sarah was torn. She had no desire to spend one minute longer with Zach Garrett than she had to, or be stuck out here in this wilderness. Hurrying as he wanted, though, only brought her closer to that horrible moment when she would have to relinquish Danny to the Pembrokes, and her heart would be broken for all time.

Zach sat on his side of the wagon seat in a fine grump. He didn't know much about kids, but in his opinion this baby peed more and hollered louder than a new calf, and his nerves were beginning to fray. Between the squalling boy and the Sour Pickle Queen of Montana sitting next to him, stiff and indignant, his patience had thinned to the breaking point.

"Mr. Garrett, I need to change the baby's diaper again. Please stop the wagon."

Zach bit down hard on his back teeth and rewound the reins around his hands. At the rate they were going, stopping every hour or so, they'd be out here until kingdom come and gone. Maybe that was the point, he realized, and glanced at Sarah again. She'd made it no secret that going back to Helena was the last thing she wanted. Well, he'd be damned if he'd let her stand in the way of his plans. Not now, when he was so close to achieving his goal.

"I'll slow down, but you'll have to take care of this while we're moving, Sarah. Hell, the wagon trains on the Oregon Trail didn't come to a halt every time some baby needed his pants changed. I plan to get home while I'm still young, and if I have to stop whenever that kid wets his drawers, we won't make it back before winter sets in. Days mean dollars and time lost out here. You'll just have to manage."

She glared at him—those sharp daggers she threw at him with her eyes that almost made him squirm. It wasn't hard for him imagine her staring down a kid who'd brought a frog into her classroom or had been caught throwing spit wads. With her jaw set, she said nothing and climbed into the back of the wagon, dragging her heavy skirts and petticoats over the seat. He could see that balancing the baby in her arms and climbing into the wagon box was tricky, but she did it. He almost admired her for it—almost.

The baby continued to howl behind him and Zach hunched his shoulders to block it out. It didn't work. At that moment, he'd have given almost anything to see the hazy outline of Helena's buildings on the horizon ahead.

"Hush now, Danny, sweetie, hushabye." Sarah's murmuring came to Zach over the sound of wheels crushing the grass beneath them. "You'll be dry in a minute."

Just then the wagon bounced over a sharp-edged rut and Sarah let out a squeak of pain.

Zach turned to look inside, but Sarah's back was to him. "What's the matter?"

She didn't respond.

"Is everything all right back there?"

He heard the sound of ripping fabric and moments later she returned to the front with Danny, grabbing for the back of the seat with one hand while negotiating the tricky climb in the rocking conveyance. He took her arm to steady her, but she pulled away and settled beside him with a flounce of skirts. Her right index finger was bandaged with a length of white cloth, and a bright spot of blood seeped through the layers.

"What happened to your hand?"

"I jabbed myself with a diaper pin when you hit that bump."

"Jesus, it was deep enough to bleed that much?"

She kept her gaze fixed on the horizon ahead. "Yes. But I did as you commanded, Mr. Garrett. I *managed*."

Shame, a really unwelcome feeling, stuttered through Zach. Oh, damn it . . . He couldn't afford to feel guilt, or remorse, or regret. Not now. Not yet. Guilt had never troubled him when he'd stolen food or clothes or money when he was a kid. He'd had no other choice, and snitching a loaf of bread or a sack of potatoes had meant the difference between surviving and, well, not.

*   *   *

When the wagon was rolling they drove for hours, it seemed, without a word passing between them. The only sounds were the mules' hooves, the rattle of the harness, and the wagon, which seemed to creak in every joint of its construction. The landscape was vast and rugged. Endless green and yellow hills rose and fell as gently as the curves of a beautiful sculpture, contrasting with rough outcroppings that fostered Ponderosa pine and low scrub. The wind carried the scent of trees and grass, clean and wild.

At first Sarah sat with her back rigid and her nose up, determined to let this man know through her haughty silence just what she thought of him and his mission. But distance and time stretched into endlessness, and she wasn't sure how long she could maintain her pose. Her muscles were beginning to quiver with the effort, and Danny, though he weighed hardly anything, grew heavier in her arms with each passing mile. She hoped they'd stop for the day pretty soon but wasn't about to suggest it.

Zach sat hunched forward, his boots planted firmly on the footboard, the lines wrapped around his gloved fists. When she chanced a peek now and then, he looked to be lost in deep thought. So, late in the afternoon, when the sunlight grew golden and mellow, he took her by complete surprise when he spoke.

"What school did you teach at? In Helena, I mean."

Sarah started and cleared her throat. "I had an elementary class in the First Ward building, up on Warren and Pine Streets. Do you know it?"

He shrugged and kept his eyes on the mules' ears ahead. "Nope. I don't get into that neighborhood."

She risked another glimpse and noticed his forearms, hard with muscle and dusted with dark hair, flexing with the effort of driving the team. "Are you from Helena?"

"No, not originally." He nodded at Danny. "Wasn't that baby born in Bozeman?"

Instantly, Sarah was carried back to the dreadful night Danny came. She'd seen the sun set, rise, and set again during her labor, certain she'd die before she had him. Dr. Pickert's nurse had been a scrawny, sour woman who'd hung over the bed like a ghoul and told Sarah to keep quiet and suffer with more dignity. If the old battleaxe had had her way, Sarah would never have laid eyes on Danny, much less been able to hold him. "Yes, he was," she murmured.

"How old is he?"

"Just over four months." Suddenly wary, she shifted Danny closer again, though her arms felt like lead. "Why?" Why would he want to know something like that? Maybe it was just fatigue that made her so skittish. What with holding Danny, her own emotional turmoil, and the awkward tension humming between herself and her escort, Sarah was worn out.

"No reason." Zach knew she was tired—she was even more jumpy and suspicious than before. Hell, he was tired himself. He'd been driving the bumpy wagon since dawn with Sarah, rigid and angry beside him, and that damned goat bleating without a break in the back. With all that, plus the baby howling intermittently, it was about as much as one man could take for the day.

He didn't even know why he'd bothered to try conversation with her. For the most part he'd made a mighty effort to pretend she wasn't sitting there next to him, her leg brushing his when the wagon hit a rut or a bump, but it hadn't worked. He wanted to ask her a hundred questions— she spoke with the voice of a no-nonsense, educated woman. How had the baby's father broken through her thorny defenses to get her into his bed? Did the man even know he had a son? Did she have family somewhere? Not that any of this mattered to Zach, he reminded himself. His job was clear-cut and uncomplicated, his reward priceless, and remembering that would be his best bet.

"We'll camp over there, under the brow of that hill. I hope you know how to cook."

She glared at him, her resentment turned on full force again. "Not only are you abducting me and my child, but you expect me to cook for you as well?"

He turned the wagon toward a flat, grassy spot against a hill. A clear creek burbled nearby. "And yourself too. Lady, trust me—you won't like it if I do the cooking. All you'll get is sourdough biscuits and coffee. Besides, I'm not *abducting* you."

"We see things quite differently, then." She surveyed their campsite. "I'm to cook while you do what? Whittle by the fire? Your wife has spoiled you, Mr. Garrett."

Sarah was used to being in charge, there was no doubt about that. But Zach wasn't accustomed to taking orders from any woman, and he sure as blazes wasn't a naughty ten-year-old in her classroom. He'd already lost one battle to her today, that disagreement they'd had over diapering the baby in the moving wagon. He'd stopped every time she'd asked after that, although grudgingly, part of him wondering if she'd jabbed herself with the pin on purpose just to make him feel guilty.

He knew if he lost this round with her, she'd gain the upper hand and he'd have a hell of a time getting it back. That wasn't going to happen. After he set the brake, he grabbed his shotgun from under the seat, jumped down, and looked up at her. "For one thing, I have to tend the team and my horse." He slapped one of the mules' rumps. "For another, I'm not married. You're going to cook, Miss Kincade, or go hungry."

Sarah remained on the seat, stiff as a fence post, coral

lips pursed, and fixed him with a withering gaze. She might look like a girl from the distance, he thought, but up close there was no mistaking her for anything less than a full-grown woman. And no matter how hard she tried to imitate a sour pickle, she was a fine-looking woman, at that. But she was as stubborn as the whole team of mules. He returned her stare, unflinching, unblinking.

Finally, she inclined her head in assent, and the low sun caught black-cherry glints in her hair. "Very well. But only if you'll also see to Isabel."

That damned goat again. He looked down at his flapping pocket, annoyed. "I'll take her out and tie her to a wheel, but if she puts up a big fuss again, we might be having *her* for dinner."

Zach took Sarah's silence for concurrence. He'd won. This time. As he moved to the mules, he wasn't fool enough to congratulate himself too heartily. With his luck, she'd deliberately catch her skirt on fire to make him feel bad, and the first thing he knew, he'd be whipping up a skillet of biscuits. Dealing with this kind of woman was a whole new experience for him. He understood men a lot better, even the ones who'd cheat him out of his last dollar. At least he knew where he stood with them.

She climbed over the seat into the back of the wagon. He saw her line an empty crate with a blanket and lay Danny in it. Then he heard her rummage through the boxes that contained the provisions he'd bought—a keg of salted beef, coffee, sugar, cans of beans, sourdough starter, a sack of flour, a Dutch oven and a frying pan, a coffeepot—

"Your biscuits and coffee will be a start. We'll need water for both, so if you could go down to that creek over there—"

"*My* biscuits—"

She poked her head out the oval opening in the canvas.

"Yes. You have the team to take care of, and I have the goat to milk, Danny to feed, and washing to do. We all have our jobs, it would seem, so you can help with meals. I'll start the fire for you, and I guess I can put together some kind of supper with what you've brought along here."

She made it sound as if she were doing him a big, damned favor. He almost told her she could go whistle "Dixie" in a cloudburst, but decided against it. If she decided to sabotage dinner, at least he'd be assured of having one edible thing to put in his stomach.

He drew a deep breath and then grabbed a pair of empty buckets that hung from the side of the wagon. As he strode off toward the creek, he glanced back over his shoulder at the form of the woman-child, and reconsidered his victory over her.

Maybe he hadn't won after all.

Sarah gave Danny his bottle as she stared at Zach across the fire. She'd put together a rather unimaginative meal of boiled potatoes and boiled beef. She wasn't a bad cook but she hadn't had a lot to work with. The food didn't have much flavor but at least it was filling, and after the grueling day she'd put in she was ravenous. Zach had grudgingly contributed biscuits and coffee, and they tasted wonderful, but she was unwilling to compliment him.

He sat there, ankles crossed, his tin plate of potatoes and beef resting on one knee. Sarah tried to keep the tartness out of her voice—she was no peerless example of virtue and had no place to find fault. It seemed to her, though, that his was the worse sin. Maybe all transgressors felt that way, that the world was a place filled with more wickedness than they themselves committed. Some may take that view to ease their conscience, but Sarah believed she was right in this case. Still, just because he was an unprincipled scoundrel taking her on the worst journey of her life didn't mean she had to abandon her manners. She'd try to keep the sting out of her words.

She asked, "Tell me, Mr. Garrett, do you have another line of work?"

He looked up at her with bottomless, inscrutable eyes and sank his teeth into the biscuit he held. Chewing thoughtfully, he took a moment to answer. "Yes, ma'am. Lots of them."

"Such as?" Sarah couldn't help herself. She wanted to know what kind of man would do this deed, and one way to find out was by how he earned his living.

His smile didn't reach his eyes. "I've worked in a whorehouse and I've dealt cards in a saloon. I drove nitro-glycerine for a mine in Butte and I dug graves. I take whatever job pays the best and I take jobs no one else wants."

Sarah sniffed. "Your mother must be very proud." She couldn't resist the tart comment.

Zach gave her another even stare. "I never knew my mother. Or my father." He took a last swallow of coffee before he tossed the rest of the cup into the fire. The liquid hit the coals with a sharp hiss and released a cloud of steam.

Sarah felt the blood climb to her cheeks. "Oh, I—I'm sorry. I apolo—I'm sorry." She tripped over her tongue like an idiot, embarrassment flooding her. This was where rudeness got her. "I didn't mean to—"

He arched a dark brow. "Yeah, you did."

It seemed impossible, but Sarah's hot face grew hotter still. Of course, he was right. She'd been snippy and sarcastic, and it had backfired on her. She tipped her head down and made a big show of straightening the baby's clothes and wiping his face.

"If you want to know something about me, ask a civil

question. Naturally, I might not answer if it's none of your business."

Sarah said nothing, and the only sounds to be heard were the faint snap of the fire and the call of birds winging their way across the pale evening sky.

"Look, I don't expect you to like me, Sarah—"

She shifted the baby to her shoulder and patted his back. "I'm sure you can understand why I don't."

Zach unfolded his long body and stood over her, his plate in his hand. "I don't expect you to like me, but we're going to be together for three weeks or more. This trip will go a little easier if you keep a rein on that razor tongue of yours."

"How do you expect me to behave, Mr. Garrett?" she demanded, looking up at him. "As if I'm off on a grand adventure with a happy ending waiting for me in Helena?"

He turned and tossed the empty plate into a bucket of water, splashing it on his boots. Then he reached down and gripped her chin between thumb and forefinger. "Nope. But I'm not going to take the blame for things you did before I met you yesterday. You set this whole damned business in motion, not me."

Sarah cringed at the reminder and at his touch. She jerked her jaw out of his grasp. "Why are you doing this? Why?" she begged to know, her voice hoarse with emotion. "Ethan Pembroke is a horrible man, and his wife is no better. You could let me go in some town and tell them anything—that I ran away again, that I died—"

"No I can't. Even though you think I have a personal grudge against you, I don't. You're just a means to an end. Ethan Pembroke holds the promissory note on my ranch and he'll give it to me when I give you and the baby to him. So, see, you're a way for me to get my ranch back from Pembroke. That's all. I'd do just about anything to get that land, right or wrong, fair or not, so the sooner I get back to Helena the better." He shifted his weight to one hip and folded his arms over his chest. "Now, you entered into an agreement with the Pembrokes that I don't know anything about and had nothing to do with. Whether it was an honorable deal or a good deal is none of my business. All I know is that they say you didn't hold up your end and they made me an offer I couldn't turn down. I've been working for two years solid to pay off the money I owe them, and this job will take care of the last of it. The only thing that will stop me from seeing it through is if you kill me, Sarah. If you try that, you'll have a hell of a lot more trouble on your hands than you do now. That's a promise."

He picked up his shotgun and slung it across his shoulders. Sarah watched him walk away, long legged and resolute. She knew he meant what he said.

The sun was still hovering on the horizon as Zach sat on a rock, adding a column of numbers on a piece of paper with a stub of dull pencil. He'd tended the mules and hobbled them, and Sarah was down at the creek, washing clothes. The sound of splashing water came to him as a pleasant background noise but his attention was fixed on the figures. He knew to the penny how much money he had on deposit at the First National Bank in Helena. He carried all of his deposit receipts and the bankbook they'd given him when he opened the account. But it had become his habit to double-check the numbers from time to time. He knew there was no error in the figures—he'd been over them often enough to be certain of that. Instead, he was looking for a sense of security. He couldn't hold the dollars in his hands, so he had to content himself with scribbles in a book.

Just opening that account had been a decision Zach

struggled with. He'd wanted access to his money, in cash, whenever he chose to look at it, touch it, count it. Banks failed, banks were robbed—he didn't trust them much. But practicality had finally won out. He knew he couldn't carry money bags on himself at all times—silver and gold were heavy. Besides, his work took him to places where a man might be beaten and held up for the gold in his back teeth, never mind the gold in his pockets.

He squinted against the sunset at the dates entered in his passbook, recalling the source of each deposit. April 7, 1889—thirty-five dollars. That had been pay for driving the nitroglycerine. May 15—fourteen dollars and sixty-five cents. He'd helped with a spring roundup. July 3—six dollars. A Butte undertaker had paid him to transport a shot-up miner back to his wife in Marysville. Six dollars was a lot of money for the trip, but then the man had been lying in a ditch under a summer sun for about four weeks by the time he was found, and he'd turned pretty gamy. Even though he was nailed into a coffin, Zach could smell him. But he'd tied a bandanna over his nose and mouth, and made the journey.

All the dates and amounts added up to one fact—Zach would be rid of Ethan Pembroke in the near future. Sarah may not know it, but he didn't like being under the man's thumb any more than she did. Her position was more precarious, though. Traditionally, women were far more vulnerable to exploitation and criticism. He glanced up and saw her kneeling by the edge of the creek as she wrung out her wash. Her movements were deliberate but slow, as though weariness dragged at her. The baby was beside her in a basket, presumably sleeping since Zach couldn't hear him wailing right now.

Sarah straightened for a moment and pressed her wet hands to the small of her back, leaving two damp spots on her skirt. Then she reached up to secure strands of her dark-chocolate hair that had come loose from their pins. With her arms raised that way she struck a classic, very feminine pose that pushed her breasts forward and lengthened her torso. Zach stared. By God, he'd bet a man could almost span that small waist with his hands—to look at her, he'd never have guessed that she'd given birth four months ago. In his heart he knew that she'd be warm and tender to the touch—she'd have a special bit of lush softness that made her womanly in a way that nature bestowed only through motherhood. The peaceful tableau of a woman kneeling on a carpet of emerald grass beside a sparkling creek, enhanced by the bronze sunset with a baby by her side, was as perfect and beautiful as a painting. Zach sat just as still, the bankbook under his elbow and the list of figures on his knee all but forgotten.

At thirty, Zach had never formed any serious attachment to a woman, but he'd had more than his share of encounters with females. Lust he knew very well. It was easy to satisfy it and then move on. Love, on the other hand, was a mysterious emotion that could interfere with a man's judgment, make him act like an idiot, and ask too much of him. Zach had no experience with it himself, but he'd seen its effects often enough to want to avoid it.

Someday he might have sons, he supposed, but whenever that day came it would be far into the future. And anyway, nothing in his early life had taught him about being a good father. It was just as well that his immediate plans did not include anything domestic.

What would Sarah do after she gave up that baby? he wondered. Would the whole thing be kept quiet enough so that she could return to her teaching job at the school in the First Ward building? Or would she find herself cast adrift again, with this stain on her reputation dogging her

for the rest of her life? Ethan Pembroke could arrange that
if he had a mind to.

Sarah could rail against Pembroke and his wife, Priscilla,
but Zach knew what she apparently did not—the man always got what he wanted, and he thought nothing of grinding people under his heel if they got in his way. Zach
despised the merciless bastard. He was powerful and had
contacts among several influential people. He also had a
judge in his back pocket, Priscilla's own uncle. Judge Driscoll had signed the court order to bring Sarah back that
Zach carried inside his shirt.

But out here, in this sea of rolling grass that eddied and
flattened in the wind, he could almost forget all that. With
nothing else to look at but the vastness of the land and a
woman sitting by a stream, everything else seemed to recede.

The realization brought Zach up short, jerking him upright on the boulder. Damn it, that was exactly what he
didn't want to happen. Nothing mattered as much as getting
his ranch, and nothing would stand in the way of that. He
went back to studying his figures, concentrating on them
nearly as hard as he tried to avoid looking at Sarah.

It didn't work. He saw the numbers, but they were just
a blur to him while his mind stubbornly wandered over the
curve of her hip and the sunlight caught in her hair. So
involved in these cross-purposes was he that he actually
jumped when her shadow fell across his passbook.

"Where will Danny and I be sleeping, Mr. Garrett?"

She looked as worn out as an old dollar bill, and he
supposed he couldn't blame her. She'd washed the dinner
dishes, she'd done the baby's diapers, and now he saw
she'd draped them over a line she'd strung inside the
wagon. A lot of farm and ranch women worked harder than
that every day, but Zach was pretty certain she wasn't used

to it. At least she wasn't as snappish as she'd been earlier. Probably too tired to fight, he thought dryly.

"You and the boy take the wagon. I'll bed down out here." He glanced up at the pale sky. "It looks to be a nice night."

She nodded, not bothering to follow his gaze. "I will say good night, then. I assume you'll want to get an early start again."

"Yes, ma'am. The earlier the better."

Sarah turned without another word and walked to the back of the musty old wagon. She washed herself and Danny with water she'd carried back from the creek with leaden arms. The wet laundry made the air damp and heavy inside the enclosure, accentuating the smell of old barn that permeated the canvas.

The sooner the better.

The earlier the better.

You're just a means to an end.

In the past year, Sarah had known a full range of emotions from love, to hate and anger, to betrayal, to fear. But not until tonight, as she wiggled into her nightgown with her back and arms aching from the rigors of the day, had she felt so completely discouraged.

She made a bed of the blankets on the wagon floor and took Danny in with her. The glow of the fire outside gave dim light to the inside of the wagon. Propping herself up on one elbow, she stared down into his sweet, smiling face, and her heart gave a hard wrench. "I know I promised you we'd be safe, sweetie," she murmured to him with a shaking voice. "That everything would be all right and that I'd take care of you no matter what." Tears coursed down her face, making her low voice shake. She pressed kisses to his cheeks and hands, fighting the hard knot in her throat. "But I don't have any more promises for you. I don't know what's going to happen and all I know for sure is that I'm just scared. For both of us."

Outside, the slimmest crescent of moon rose in the eastern sky. Zach Garrett leaned against a wagon wheel beside the dying fire, tossing bits of dry twig into the coals with short, angry motions, wishing he hadn't overheard Sarah.

He'd felt guilty a time or two in his life. But never more so than he did right now.

"Read the telegram to me again, Ethan."

Looking up from a stack of papers on his carved teak desk, Ethan Pembroke regarded his wife with carefully concealed impatience. She stood in the doorway of his study, dressed in expensive moiré taffeta the color of Madeira port grapes. She advanced no further because it was understood between them that this room was his sanctuary, a place of business and mental concentration. The leather furniture, dark paneling, the floor-to-ceiling bookshelves, even Bell's new invention called the telephone that sat on the corner of Ethan's desk—they all bespoke a man's room where a man's work was done, and basically was not accessible to her unless a dire emergency arose. Or unless he invited her in, something he seldom did.

The low angle of the evening sun cutting through the leaded-glass windows wasn't kind to her face, which showed every line of its thirty-nine years. But her smooth, upswept hair retained its rich wheat color, and in the warm glow of candles on a well-appointed dining room table, she was a satisfactory-looking woman, enough so to catch admiring glances from one or two of their male guests. *Satisfactory*. It was a fairly accurate description of his wife overall. "Now, Priscilla, I've already read it three times since it came yesterday."

She folded her hands in front of her. "I know. You're

so patient with me and I'm such a ninny, but after nearly losing our dear baby, I just want to hear the words again. I don't believe I'll be able to sleep until that horrible woman has returned him and he's under this roof where he belongs."

Ethan had been a penniless but enterprising and ambitious clerk working for Anaconda Copper Mining Company when he'd caught the notice of Priscilla's father. Armistead Driscoll had been an associate of copper baron Marcus Daly, the company's founder. Driscoll had recognized Ethan as a willing protégé and a sharp-eyed opportunist. Over the course of time, he'd also come to view him as a fitting suitor for his daughter, Priscilla, despite the fact that Ethan was seven years her junior. Her family's wealth had made her an attractive object of attention from men that Driscoll found eminently unsuitable, each for different reasons. But he liked Ethan. And more importantly, the plain, somewhat awkward Priscilla liked him too.

A skillful negotiator, Armistead offered his daughter in marriage to Ethan under two conditions—he must make Priscilla happy, no matter the cost, and he would use his natural talent for business to increase the Driscolls' already considerable holdings. It didn't matter one whit to Ethan that under any other circumstances, he would not have given Priscilla a second glance. Recognizing a prime opportunity when he saw one, and eager to align himself with the wealthy and powerful Driscoll family, he leaped at the chance. Love was certainly not an issue, not on his part, and he didn't believe on hers either. But to the best of Ethan's ability, he had kept both bargains—Armistead and Ethan had made a considerable fortune thanks to his canny transactions in land, minerals, and cattle, and he put forth a great deal of effort to please Priscilla. He sent her on European tours and excursions to New York and Sarasota.

She wore only the finest modiste-made clothing to be had, and he gave her jewels of every color in the rainbow. Most recently, after living four years in Butte, he had moved her to the more sophisticated Helena and built her a grand home not far from the financial wizard Samuel Hauser's twenty-nine-room mansion on Madison Avenue. Of course, they'd lived on the town's outskirts while the house was being constructed. This had kept Priscilla out of town so that he was able to masquerade as the smitten bachelor to Sarah Kincade.

Priscilla had shown herself to be a respectable wife and hostess, with the ability to manage large dinner parties and other social gatherings so vital to Ethan's business interests.

But satisfactory or not, wealthy or not, in their seven years of marriage Priscilla had also proven to be as barren as a rock, and in Ethan's bed, just as cold and inert. No pregnancy—not even a miscarriage—had ever resulted from their infrequent joinings.

Two years ago, they had adopted a foundling child, an infant girl left with the Sisters of the House of the Good Shepherd. She had turned out to be sickly, nearly dying several times before she finally succumbed in her cradle before reaching her first birthday. Almost immediately following her funeral, they'd adopted a healthy toddler, another girl, also from the sisters. She had died as well, and under practically identical circumstances. Priscilla had been inconsolable, taking to her bed and requiring round-the-clock nursing for weeks afterward. Ethan had been mildly suspicious of the children's deaths, in a distracted sort of way. But he'd promised he would do whatever it took to find another child for her.

And so he had.

"All right, of course. I'll read the wire again." Ethan put down his pen and reached into the inside breast pocket of his coat. Withdrawing the telegram that had been delivered yesterday afternoon, he unfolded it and read the terse message. " 'Located Sarah Kincade and baby in Lame Horse. Will start for Helena tomorrow. Should arrive with pair in four weeks latest. Signed Zachary Garrett.' "

"Four weeks." Priscilla closed her eyes and pressed a lace-edged handkerchief to her mouth. Her smile was beatific. "Four more weeks—I don't know how I shall stand it. Do you really think we have Sarah this time? We've waited before, while she was in Bozeman, only to have our hopes dashed when she ran away."

Ethan sat back in his leather chair. "Garrett is the perfect man for this job. When I offered him that promissory note, I know he wanted to leap across the desk to grab it. I saw it in his eyes. Nothing is more important to him than having that land back. He'll get here with Sarah and the baby, come hell or high water."

"Oh, I do hope so. After Caroline and Eleanor—well, I just don't think I could go through that again."

"Try not to worry, Priscilla. You have four weeks to ready the baby's room—a boy this time. A son." Ethan reached for his gold watch chain and withdrew the timepiece attached. "For the time being, though, we have dinner guests arriving in an hour. You'll want to make sure that everything is in order."

She nodded. "Yes, of course, Ethan." She looked as if she would say more, but apparently changed her mind, and turned to walk back down the hall, her taffeta skirts whispering as she went.

He glanced at the telegram again. If Sarah Kincade hadn't yet learned that he always got his way, she would now. Ethan Pembroke was man to be reckoned with.

Chapter Four

Sarah came slowly awake, opening her eyes to find herself looking at freshly washed diapers hanging over her head. In the faint light of dawn they resembled limp, ghostly sails moving ever so slightly in feeble drafts that passed through the wagon. Mostly, though, the air in here was humid and stale, and smelled faintly of goat and barn. Beside her, Danny stirred but was quiet, obviously fascinated by the sight of his diapers suspended above them.

She could hear Isabel outside, her bell clinking and the sound of her strong, ruminant jaws chewing grass. Last night Zach had tied her up to a wagon spoke just on the other side of the canvas. He'd given her a long length of rope so she could graze in a good-sized area. So far the trip hadn't interfered with her milk production, thank God. Sarah didn't know what she'd do if something happened to that goat.

She rolled slowly onto her side. Every muscle ached from sleeping on the hard wagon bed, and she'd developed a tightness in her neck and shoulders that never left her anymore. As she rubbed her gritty eyes, snippets of yesterday flashed through her memory, all painted against a backdrop of endless grass and rolling hills. Where were they now? she wondered. How far from Helena? How soon would she have to give up her child . . . how long did she have with him?

She tucked Danny closer. He was warm and soft and vibrant against her breast, and she desperately regretted that she'd had to wean him so early. She touched kisses to his downy head, not caring that his diaper was wet and soaking through her nightgown, not bothered that he didn't smell as clean and sweet as he did straight from the bath. He was her own flesh and blood, her child, and it was her *right* to give him her mother's milk, if only she still could. It had stopped flowing weeks ago. Well, maybe she hadn't gotten to nurse Danny, she thought grimly, but at least that heartless Priscilla Pembroke would not be able to either.

If she had to relinquish him—and that was so difficult for her to even contemplate—she knew he would have no memory of her at all by the time he reached his first birthday. If he saw her on the street someday, would he have some vague feeling of recognition? No, of course not, she acknowledged sadly. If he was taken from her at four or five months, no matter how closely he snuggled with her now, she would be forgotten.

The realization made her think of something Zach had said yesterday during dinner, that he'd never known his parents. What did that mean? That he was raised by wolves? No matter how unconventional his upbringing or inferior his lineage, even a man who saw a woman and her child as nothing more than a means to an end must have had some sort of parents and been raised by someone. His cleanly sculpted good looks and tall, long-muscled build suggested at least one handsome forebear.

Curious, she rose to her knees and lifted the bottom edge of the canvas an inch or so to peek at him. The light was still thin and gray, and shapes were not immediately distinguishable. She made out the mules and his horse grazing under a couple of trees, and a dark winding ribbon that was the creek. Her gaze moved to the rough circle of rocks that had enclosed their fire and quickly scanned the immediate vicinity. Craning her neck, she tried to take in the whole landscape on that side of the wagon. He wasn't there.

Where on earth—Then she lowered her eyes and saw

him asleep on the dry yellow grass directly beneath her, close enough for her to detect his breathing in the rise and fall of his chest. Dear God! She dropped the canvas and muffled a surprised gasp, automatically closing the neck of her nightgown with one hand. What was he doing *there*? He should be out—well, out farther, where he could get early warning of an approaching animal or some other intruder. Where he wouldn't be as close to her as little more than an arm's reach.

Hesitantly, she raised the canvas just enough to peer down at him again. He lay on his back with his head turned toward the wagon and his ankles crossed. The heavy shadow of his beard, very plain in the coming light, accentuated the line of his lean jaw. His dark hair, thick and longer than city men considered fashionable, spilled over the rolled-up blanket he was using for a pillow. She considered the bow of his mouth, which bore just a hint of fullness and in repose was neither hostile nor cruel. In fact, she thought she detected vulnerability in its curve. He still wore the dirty shirt with the flapping pocket that Isabel had torn, a plain tan thing that looked as though it had been washed so often and worn for so long that its only remaining strength lay in its buttons and seams. Surely he had another one, she hoped. He held his shotgun against his right leg, and even in sleep he kept his hand wrapped around the stock. His other hand rested on his chest.

Daylight continued to creep over the land, throwing the plains into sharp relief and creating shadows in the hollows around Zach's eyes and under his cheekbones. Sarah found herself staring in guilty fascination as he slept on, giving him a head-to-toe inspection. He must have spent most of his life outdoors, probably working horses and cattle, she'd guess. His shoulders were wide and muscled, his hands large and detailed with tendon and sinew, all suited to controlling spirited animals and doing other work that required brute strength.

When her perusal wandered down his trunk to his hips, Sarah's gaze riveted on the bones of his pelvis. A heat, an energy surrounded him, as if he had experience with life and men and women together that Sarah, despite her own circumstances, knew nothing about.

And didn't want to know about, she was positive of that.

In all, Sarah suspected that Zach Garrett was a dangerous man, and one who seemed accustomed to dwelling on the edge of society and life itself. Why or how she knew this she had no idea, but the impression was strong, and certainly in keeping with a man who claimed to have no knowledge of his own parents. Dangerous he might be, but he was sinfully handsome, too, and it irked her. In fact, she wasn't sure which annoyed her more—his attractiveness or her recognition of it.

Sarah continued to study him through her peephole, tracing the line of his long legs with her eyes while her fingers grew numb gripping the side of the wagon. Suddenly, Isabel let out a loud series of *eh-eh-eh*s.

Zach's eyes snapped opened and he found himself staring at the long face of Sarah's stinking nanny goat. When he turned his head and glanced up, he caught the telltale flutter of canvas and a fleeting glimpse of a fine, feminine nose before it withdrew. Well, hell, that schoolmarm had been watching him—it unnerved a man to know that he'd been stared at while he slept.

"Good morning, Sarah."

No response.

"Come on, I know you're awake in there. I caught you peeking."

A long pause and then finally, "Good morning, Mr. Garrett."

"Zach."

"What?"

"Look, if you're going to study me while I sleep you can at least call me by my first name, don't you think?" It seemed strange to have a conversation with someone on the other side of a curtain. It reminded him of talking with the girls at Lady Rose's sporting house. They'd bare all for a customer without a moment's pause, but they always changed clothes behind a dressing screen when Zach was around. One of them had said it was because he knew them better than any of their "regulars," even though he never engaged their services, and it made them shy around him. It still baffled him, but who knew how women's minds worked?

"I wasn't looking at you. I was looking at Isabel. She needs to be milked."

Right—Isabel. He glared at the goat again and suppressed a sigh. "Then I guess you'd better see to it. We need to get cracking. We've got a long day ahead of us."

He sat up and rubbed his face, feeling as creaky and tired as a pair of boots left out in the rain. Sleeping in the open was nothing new to him. He could usually sleep anywhere and in all kinds of weather, so that couldn't have been the problem. But he'd woken up several times with Sarah on his mind, and that had made the night stretch on for an eternity.

He hadn't meant to bed down so close—he'd planned to wrap himself up in his blankets over by the dead fire. But after overhearing her frightened, tear-choked words to the baby the evening before, he'd begun edging nearer. He told himself there was nothing he could do, *nothing,* to change matters. Fate had conspired to put all of them in their own situations, and none of that was Zach's fault. But it didn't help much with the nagging sense of wrong that nudged him now and then. He almost wished he could tell her that, although it shouldn't matter to him what she thought, whether or not she blamed him. At any rate, as long as Sarah and Danny were his responsibility, he intended to do a good job of watching over them, and that required him to stay close by. No one could accuse Zachary Garrett of not earning his pay.

The second day had dawned as bright as the one before, but when he climbed out of his bedroll and looked at the sky, Zach figured that it would be hotter. At least for a while. That wind blowing in from the southwest seemed to carry something with it, maybe a storm.

He went down to the creek to wash and shave, and when he returned he saw Sarah struggling to put a bucket under the cranky Isabel, who bellowed loudly.

"Come on, now, Isabel," she urged, her voice colored with vexation. Her skirt was streaked with the same hoof prints as the shirt he'd just taken off and stowed in his saddle bags, and her dark hair, woven into a long braid, swung like a cow's tail. "Danny needs his breakfast. Anyway, it's way past time for you to be milked." The goat, her udder plainly distended, kicked over the bucket and danced away from Sarah to the end of her tether, giving her a baleful look. "Isabel!" From within the wagon, the baby screamed even louder than the goat.

Damned animals, Zach thought again. He strode through the grass and grasped the rope he'd tied her with, then hauled her in like a fish to snub her to the wagon wheel. Somehow, the goat managed to turn her back to him and deposit a considerable pile of droppings on his boot. Zach swore again and shook most of the dung off his foot.

Sarah's harried expression changed to anxiety, and she laced her fingers together. "Mr. Garrett, be careful with her!"

He looked up. "Sarah, did you grow up in a town or in the country?"

"In town."

He nodded. "I thought so."

"And why is that?" she demanded. She glanced over her shoulder at the wagon, distracted by the baby's caterwauling.

"Because you think this goat is a pet. Farm animals aren't pets like lapdogs. They have jobs to do, and this one's job is to provide milk for that boy of yours. He sounds pretty damned unhappy, so bring me the bucket."

Sarah scowled at him but delivered the bucket anyway. He crouched next to Isabel and gave a firm tug on a conical teat to produce a stream of fresh, warm milk. Isabel, apparently realizing that she'd met her match, offered no further resistance.

Zach felt Sarah standing next to him although she said nothing. All the while the steady *wish-wish-wish* of milk hit the wooden pail. Finally she asked, "I suppose you grew up in the country?"

He shook his head. "Nope. I was born in New York City, as far as I know. At least that's where I started out."

"New York!"

"Surprised, huh?"

"Well, yes. You look like a cowhand, and you said you have land. New York City . . . I'd expect you to be a dandy, more like Ethan Pembroke."

Zach tightened his jaw and kept his eyes on the rich, frothy milk. "You haven't seen much of life, have you?"

"I'm hardly a child. I have traveled—I'm educated."

It couldn't have been the kind of education *he'd* had. "The streets aren't really paved with gold back there, you know."

"I didn't think they were—"

"There were children starving in doorways, covered with rat bites and weak because fleas sucked so much blood from them." Images of his childhood flooded back, flipping across his memory like Mathew Brady's still photographs of battlefields, and every bit as horrific. "Sometimes, just the hope of a stale bread crust could send a dozen kids scrambling over a garbage heap. I don't think too many dandies grew up out of that."

The tight, low-voiced vehemence of Zach's words took Sarah aback. She wasn't naïve, at least she didn't believe she was. But she'd grown up in Stockett, a small, safe community where everyone had looked out for each other. There had been church every Sunday, grange dances, and if someone in town fell on hard times, everyone pitched in to see them through. Her parents still lived there, running the dry-goods store and believing, along with everyone else, that their daughter was off on sabbatical. None of the children she'd taught in Helena had lived with the kind of deprivation and hardship Zach described either. Perhaps some were worse off than others, with poorer clothes and thinner faces, but not starving, for heaven's sake, or rat-bitten. Dickens had raised such images in his works, but they were fiction, weren't they? Sarah had dedicated her life to caring for children's minds and souls, and couldn't imagine that anyone would let youngsters suffer so.

"Did that happen to you? Did you go through garbage heaps looking for bread?" she asked.

He tipped a sideways look at her, and his sudden grin was hard and almost cynical. "Sometimes, but not usually. I was good at stealing food, and then when I finally got caught, the reform school fed me and washed off the lice and fleas."

"Reform school?"

"Yeah, the New York Juvenile Asylum. Sounds nice, but

it was really a reformatory. They taught me to read and write, anyway—something I wouldn't have learned in Mulberry Bend." He pulled the bucket from beneath Isabel and held it out to her. "All right, here's the milk. I'll get the fire going."

Sarah stared at him. Maybe she was wrong—it certainly wouldn't be the first time; she might be far more naïve than she realized. Next he'd be telling her that he spent time in prison, and her hard-won, meager sense of safety wobbled. But when she took the bucket handle from him, her fingers brushed his, and a rush of heat shot up her arm. For the space of a baby's breath their eyes met, and this time she saw more than her own fear and uncertainty reflected back at her. She saw what looked like surprise in his handsome face, and perhaps even a whisper of kindness. His dark hair was slicked back with water from its dousing at the creek and the ends were beginning to curl slightly where the sun had dried them. Before he rose from the crouch, she could see his bare muscled chest where his clean shirt gaped away from his body.

Sarah's attention to the tasks at hand evaporated.

"Fire—"

"For the coffee and bacon," he prompted.

"Oh, yes, of course."

Her emotional equilibrium, already in a precarious state, stuttered within her. She sat down on a boulder near the front end of the wagon and strained the milk through a piece of cheesecloth she'd laid over a funnel, then let it trickle into a clean baby bottle.

As she watched him light bits of dry kindling with a match, she wondered again, What kind of man was Zach Garrett? And where was Mulberry Bend? She'd never heard of the town. It seemed the more he revealed about himself, the less she knew.

After she fed Danny, changed his inevitable dirty diaper, and put him in his makeshift cradle in the back of the wagon, the sun was a bright, yellow-white disk climbing the sky. She hurried to the campfire, expecting to find Zach waiting impatiently for her to cut slices from the slab of bacon to put in the frying pan. But he already had breakfast cooking and the coffee boiling.

Her surprise must have been evident because he gestured self-consciously at the meat sizzling in the cast-iron skillet. "Well, I figured you probably had enough to do." He handed her a tin plate and a steaming cup of coffee, as fragrant in this wilderness as the finest perfume, and in that moment an uneasy truce was born between them.

The wagon rattled along again, hitting ruts, jarring the baby, and crossing the endless plains and slopes of Montana's rugged beauty. The air, hot and increasingly oppressive, was driven by a wind that carried no coolness. It reminded Zach of the feeling he got when he opened the door of a line shack in the winter—inside it was hot from a stove, but the dampness of snow-wet clothes and men made the air almost steamy. As the morning wore on into afternoon, he kept one eye on the thunderheads beginning to build off to the south and west. If it rained, the old wagon canvas probably wouldn't hold up very well.

They bounced along, he and Sarah, with Danny in her arms, and the tension between them eased just a little, he thought. At least her back wasn't quite as stiff as it had been yesterday. But conversation was still stoppered like a new liniment bottle.

He was aware of her. How could he not be, with her leg and shoulder and arm bumping into him constantly? No matter how he wanted to, he couldn't seem to ignore her clean smell of fresh laundry laced with a touch of spice, like carnations. Or the fact that her skirt occasionally lapped over his leg. Although the sturdy denim of his pants lay between his flesh and that skirt, he swore he could feel the fabric drifting over him the way a curtain brushed a windowsill. He could offer himself a lot of excuses for his distraction—he hadn't been with a woman in months, he was a loner unaccustomed to company, and she was a bothersome female (although she rarely uttered a peep).

But the hard-boiled truth of the matter was that she intrigued him. Not only was she a surprise—he'd imagined a slightly coarse woman with a come-hither manner—he was becoming curious about how she'd gotten herself into this fix. She reinforced that curiosity every time he saw her gaze at Danny with a maternal love so strong that even Zach recognized it. Strange that he should. He'd had no such nurturing himself, and had rarely seen it while he was growing up. And his own part in the pending separation of mother and son chafed at him once in a while, like a pebble in his boot or a shirt that was too tight through the shoulders.

He could see she was getting tired holding the boy, mile after mile. She *could* put the baby in his bed in the back of the wagon. "You'll spoil a baby if you pick him up every time he cries or hold him too much. You ought to put him down for a while."

She turned a sharp look on him. "Spoil him? How would you know that, Mr. Garrett?"

He shrugged, now feeling a little awkward, and rubbed his sweat-damp chin against the shoulder of his shirt. "Well, that's what I've heard, anyway."

"I don't believe I've ever met a child who was spoiled by affection and kindness. Cruelty and deprivation, not love, make a child mean." She turned her head and stared at the mules' ears, bouncing along with their gait. "I wish I could know what Danny's future will be."

"The Pembrokes are pretty well set up. They've got a big fancy house and a servant or two." He offered the comment as empty consolation. Pembroke was a son of a bitch as far as Zach was concerned, and his wife, Priscilla, seemed odd and bloodless. "They'll probably give the boy everything he could ask for."

Servants, Sarah grumbled to herself. Who would make cookies for him, as her own mother had? Would a servant take him fishing, and show him the best way to bait a hook, the way her father had shown her brother? Ethan probably wouldn't. He'd be too busy, and he probably didn't know how, anyway. "That doesn't mean he'll get what he needs."

Zach exhaled, an impatient, gusty sigh. "But maybe he'll be better off with them. Look, Sarah, what can you give him? An unmarried schoolteacher with an illegitimate son?"

She lurched on the seat, feeling as if she'd been slapped. There it was between them—not an accusation, not a judgment, but the bald facts of the matter.

"Fair or not," he went on, "people still use the term 'bastard,' and it carries a load of misery for the unlucky kid stuck with it. At least the Pembrokes have money."

Sarah lapsed into humiliated silence, and knew he was right.

Bastard.

Illegitimate.

And that other word again—*money.*

"Not everything is about money, Mr. Garrett," she murmured, fearing he'd hear her voice crack with angry tears if she spoke any louder. One front wheel thumped into a rut, throwing Sarah against him. She struggled to right herself, unwilling to have any more contact than necessary.

"Oh, yeah? Try and get along in the world without it. You saw for yourself that it's just about impossible."

"I did have some savings, but I—I lost it."

"Gambled it away, huh?" he taunted.

She whirled to look at him, stricken. "What do you mean by that?"

He waved it off, plainly exasperated. "Aw, nothing, *nothing*." Silence fell between them and then he cast a side-long glance at her. "Does the baby's father know what's happened to you?" The question took both of them by such surprise, it was as if a third person had asked it.

Sarah gaped at Zach, aghast at his prying. Danny felt like so much a part of her only, carried and born and loved by her only, it was sometimes hard for her to remember that he hadn't been conceived by her alone. She wished that it had been possible. Just thinking about the cold-hearted heel who had fathered her child, with his trickery and lies, filled her with a simmering rage and resentment that did her no good. "That is none of your business, Mr. Garrett."

"It seems like if he was any kind of man, he'd have married you. Short of that, the least he could do is help you and the baby."

"It's none of your business," she repeated coldly. An awkward moment passed, as wide and empty as a canyon, and then she added, "But even if I told you about it, I doubt that you'd believe me."

Chapter Five

A storm was brewing, all right. The thick, humid air seemed to grow heavier with each passing hour, and the sky turned eerie with its gray-pink glow. Thunderheads boiled up ahead in the distance, tall columns billowing out of an ever-darkening base of clouds, all moving this way. Zach scanned the hazy terrain for a sheltered place to stop, but there was no sheer cliff face or even a berm to huddle the wagon against. They were out on a flat plain, several miles away from any swell of land, a bad place to be with lightning on its way. Only the occasional tree dotted the landscape and a tree was worse than no shelter at all. He'd seen more than one split from top to trunk during an electrical storm, killing the dumb cattle that had crowded under the bows.

He glanced at Sarah and noticed the sheen of perspiration that gleamed on her face and throat. Damp, curling tendrils of dark hair stuck to the nape of her neck, as slender and pale as the throat of a calla lily. He was familiar with the flower—a customer had once sent an armload of the things to a girl at Lady Rose's whorehouse. The sight of Sarah's dewy profile distracted him momentarily from the misery of his own shirt glued to his back like a mustard plaster, but he forced his attention back to their predicament. Something was going to happen soon. Even the team was lathered with sweat in their harness.

Late in the day he heard rather than saw the beginnings—the first rumble of thunder sounded. It rolled from one side of the sky to the other, distant and low-voiced. The mules' ears flattened. A lightning bolt zigzagged to the faraway hilltops, and a rain shaft loosed itself above them.

He felt Sarah's uneasy gaze on him. "Do you think that's coming toward us?" she asked.

"Yeah, probably, and it looks like a big storm too."

The wind picked up.

She craned her neck, looking around as far as she could stretch. "Shouldn't we stop and wait it out?"

"Not yet. We'll keep moving as long as we can, and maybe we'll make it to a good place to hunker down. There's no sense in just sitting here like birds on a fence rail, waiting to get shot at."

The wind blew harder, carrying with it a breath of coolness and the smell of rain. Overhead the clouds scudded past, moving faster now. Another fork of lightning split the sky, throwing the landscape into brilliant relief, followed by a louder thunderclap. Danny woke up, frightened by the noise, and started wailing.

They moved forward another mile or so and rain began falling, fat, soaking drops that drummed against the canvas. Danny was still crying, adding to the din, and Sarah would have liked to hold him and comfort him, but she put him in his bed in the wagon to move him out of the rain.

"Maybe you should climb into the back too," Zach suggested, raising his voice over the wind, rain, baby's howling, and the goat's frantic bleating. "You'll get soaked out here."

"N-no, I'll stay." As much as she'd rather be under cover, something about Zach challenged her, and she didn't want him to think she was a helpless, frightened schoolmarm. Why that mattered she couldn't guess, but the fragile remnants of her savaged pride demanded it. On top of that, their circumstances looked dire enough that she didn't want to be stuck in the wagon bed, unable to see what was happening should an emergency arise. Danny was tucked into a safe corner, and it seemed to her that anticipating danger was the only way to help avert it.

So she remained at Zach's side, and the firmament opened over them. Lightning, closer now, snaked across the blackened clouds with long bony fingers, a thousand times brighter than a photographer's flash powder. No words passed between them. The mules shied and reared in their traces, and Zach struggled to control them, the lines wrapped in his gloved fists, his face set and grim. Sarah planted her feet on the footboard and kept a death grip on the narrow wagon seat.

The rain became a heavy gray veil that shortened their sight distance and drenched them to the skin. All the fury of heaven seemed to be pounding down upon the wagon. Fierce winds flattened the tall yellow grass and whipped it back and forth, revealing the silvery undersides of the blades. To Sarah it seemed they were as insignificant as ants, caught out in the open with no place to hide from the uncaring hand of nature that could plummet from the sky and kill every one of them. She lost her bearings and for all she knew they were traveling in circles. Zach's strong profile gave her courage though, and she watched him handle the lines, the muscles in his arms flexing with the effort.

Suddenly a huge gust dove under the wagon canvas and seemed to lift it like a sail before ripping long rents in its rotted creases. Rain poured in through the tears. "Danny!" she screamed, and scrambled over the seat to fling herself on top of the baby in his bed.

Zach glanced back at the collapsing canvas, just in time to see his horse break loose from the tailgate and take off running past the wagon, across the plain. It would be impossible to catch the gelding now. He uttered a curse, and then another as the deluge turned to hail. Chunks of ice the size of musket balls pounded them like rocks, stinging and bruising, and bounced all around them. He'd lost his hat to an earlier wild draft and the pellets pummeled his wet, bare head. Keeping the mules in check required every ounce of strength and determination he could summon because they wanted nothing more than to bolt and follow his horse's lead. If that happened they'd all be hurt or maybe killed when the wagon flipped. Of course, they weren't in good shape as it was.

On he pushed them, the deafening lightning strokes hitting so close he could smell them, while he peered through the gloom. Finally he spotted what looked to be a shallow, rocky overhang jutting out of the earth. It wasn't much but in this waking nightmare of noise and confusion, it was a godsend. He set his jaw and pulled the team hard to the left.

"Haw, there, haw!" he barked, lifting his voice over the raging weather. Drawing the wagon alongside the wall as closely as possible, he was able to squeeze it under the low overhang with scarcely inches to spare. It didn't cover the whole wagon bed but at least the left half was out of direct fire of the hail.

Zach set the brake and jumped down to hobble the mules. Turning, he called to Sarah, "Are you two all right back there?"

When she lifted her head to look at him, he thought his heart would stop. Terror had drained the color from her cheeks, but blood, red and brilliant against her paleness, trickled from her scalp and down her face.

"Jesus, get out of the wagon!" He stepped forward to help her and put his hands on her waist to lift her over the side. Clutching Danny to her, she trembled like a newborn colt under Zach's touch. When her feet were on solid ground, she put a shaky hand to her head and looked dully at the blood on her fingertips.

"You're bleeding but we'll get it stopped."

"Y-you are too," she replied, and gestured at his head and drenched shirt where red, diluted splotches streaked the right side.

He dragged the back of his hand across his forehead and turned his gaze upward. "I guess God hates us today, doesn't He?"

Even in this dire emergency, she could get that sour-pickle look. "God doesn't hate anyone, Mr. Garrett!"

"Yeah, well if the mules stampede with the wagon and strand us in this place, I'll have my answer for sure." He pushed her flat against the wall. "Stay here. The overhang isn't very wide but it's better than nothing. Be sure to keep your skirts away from the wheels just in case the thing starts rolling."

She nodded and crouched between the wall and the wagon, still holding the boy tight to her chest. Zach followed, sitting cross-legged next to her and looked out at the landscape, now as white as if from a snowfall. No sooner had he settled his butt on the ground than they heard a frantic *eh-eh-eh!* The goat was in a dither!

Oh, hell. Zach tensed, because he knew what was coming. Sure enough, Sarah turned to him, anguish in her eyes.

"Now, damn it, Sarah, that goat is just fine."

"Aren't you going to get her?"

He gestured at the mules. "I had to leave the team out in this. At least she's got a little canopy over her head. That's more than they have." A tattered remnant of canvas flapped over the pen, providing a little shelter. She scowled at him, and then without another word she put screaming Danny in his lap and crawled back out into the storm to rescue the goat.

"Sarah!" He started to go after her, but hampered with the baby, who was distinctly unhappy with the change, he didn't dare. A moment later she returned, dragging Isabel by one of her horns. It wasn't hard for him to picture her pulling on a naughty student's ear the same way.

"Hold her," she said, and dragged the goat's head within Zach's reach so he could grab the other horn. Without an instant of hesitation, she lifted the hem of her skirt and tore a strip from the edge of her petticoat, creating a makeshift lead to slip around the goat's neck.

While her skirts were up to her knees, Zach caught a glimpse of her shins, bruised as dark as two stove lids. In the confusion of the moment, he almost asked her how she'd hurt herself. But before he opened his fool mouth, he remembered the scene on the hotel stairs, his hand closed on her skirt, and her tumble with the baby in her arms.

"Why didn't you use the rope?"

"I couldn't find it and I didn't want to stand there looking for it," she snapped.

She tied the other end of the lead to her ankle and sat down again, forcing Isabel to crouch next to her as the hail turned back into rain. From the pocket of her skirt she withdrew a handkerchief and pressed it to the cut on her scalp, while lightning forked down from the sky, nearer and nearer. Just as she took Danny back into her lap, another bolt of lightning, hot and sizzling and closer than ever, demolished a tree less than a quarter mile from their puny shelter. The oak was split down the center in a deafening explosion of fire and sparks that looked as if God Himself had struck the blow. Sarah screamed and hid her face against Zach's shoulder.

"H-have you ever seen a storm this bad?" she asked, her voice muffled by his sleeve.

"Hell, we get thunderstorms in Montana every year."

"Yes, but as bad as this?" she repeated insistently.

"We aren't going to die out here, Sarah," he asserted,

taking no comfort from his own words. They could very well be killed, with lightning falling like spears. The wind lashed them with rain and the team danced in the traces, teetering on the same hysteria he felt coursing through Sarah. "You just hang on, girl."

"I wish I were home," she answered in a plaintive voice, and guilt elbowed Zach again. He didn't know which home she was talking about—her childhood home, Helena, or Lame Horse. But the blame for her being out here in this tempest with her child could be placed squarely on him and no one else.

Shit.

He put his arm around her small form and pulled her close.

The four of them huddled together next to the wall while the world crashed down around them.

The sun finally broke through the clouds in the west, a brilliant band of light that grew wider as twilight began to fall. It seemed to Sarah that an eternity had passed while they'd sat—waiting for the storm to move on, or waiting for it to take them. Now, though it still poured rain, the flashes and rumbling had turned toward the northeast, and they had survived.

"It's over?" She ventured a peek at the sky. Zach's arm was still around her, and Isabel lay with her muzzle hidden against Sarah's hip. Amazingly, Danny slept.

"Looks like. That was a hell of a goose drowner."

"*Goose drowner*. That certainly can't be a New York expression," Sarah said.

"No, it isn't. At least that isn't where I learned it." At that moment she glanced up into his eyes and saw a flicker there that gave her pause. Suddenly Sarah was very conscious of their physical closeness.

With the faintest sense of reluctance she pulled away from the shelter of his arm. She didn't mind the weight of it over her shoulders, or the warmth that radiated through his wet shirt. He had a menacing edge that gave her an ironic sense of security, and the trickle of dried blood on the side of his face reinforced the aura of danger. If she or Danny were threatened she had no doubt that Zach would jump to their defense. But in light of what he was doing to her, he was the last man on earth she'd seek out for protection. Well, next to the last, she amended in her mind.

She opened a noticeable gap between them and leaned against the wall. "Where *did* you learn it?"

Zach considered her as they sat out the last of the rain, as if debating what and how much to tell her.

"I was born in New York, but after the reformatory and before I made my way west, I spent time in Illinois. On a farm." A dark expression swept across his features. "I learned a lot of things there."

"Really? How did you get from the East to the Midwest?"

"Have you ever heard of orphan trains?"

"I've heard the term but I don't really know much about them."

"Hundreds of kids are shipped west from New York every year, usually to be adopted by families waiting at the other end. Most of them are sent out from the Children's Aid Society."

"Oh, yes. I remember reading about that."

"Some of them, like me, come from prisons and reformatories."

Prisons. "Did a family adopt you?"

"No. I was indentured."

"Indentured!" She sat up straight. Isabel dared a peep out from behind Sarah's skirt, then rested her head on her mistress's lap. "Do you mean as a servant?" Her teacher's mind flipped through her knowledge of history, lighting upon the practice of indentured servitude that had been part of early colonial times. Looking for a way to leave Europe but with no means to pay for the transatlantic crossing, people sold themselves into bondage for four to seven years. Often the indenture turned out to be a form of slavery.

Absently he slapped the flat of his palm against his knee and gazed out at the clearing horizon. "Not the way the Juvenile Asylum told it. They said a family was waiting to welcome me. That I'd get food and shelter and 'learn the moral Christian value of honest work.' The man who took me in signed a contract promising all of that, but in the end, yeah, I guess I was just an unpaid laborer."

"How old were you?"

"Eleven." The dark look crossed his face again—abruptly he pulled away from the wall and stood up to survey their surroundings. "It's stopped raining." Plainly, he'd answered all the questions he wanted to, but Sarah's curiosity was aroused now in spite of herself, and she wished she could ask more.

He climbed into the wagon bed to investigate the damage, his boots crunching on the layer of hail. Sarah followed his movements with her eyes, peeking at him between the rents in the canvas. His jeans were wet, molding themselves to his legs and backside, and his shirt clung to him, outlining the muscle and bone in his shoulders.

The hail was melting now, forming puddles of cold standing water. It bowed the canvas and dribbled into the wagon through the tears. Zach stuck his head through one. "We've got a hell of mess to clean up." She heard him move boxes and blankets around, and shove aside the crates. "Everything is soaked. Do you have a needle and thread with you? We might be able to patch this thing." He waved at the cover.

Sarah nodded and once again set about the business of trying to salvage something out of nearly nothing. There was no point in complaining or pouting—that wouldn't get the job done. But she could still dream, and she wished to heaven she and the baby were in that clean, dry room she'd imagined, with its simple conveniences of a roof and a stove on which to boil a kettle of water. Instead, she was stuck out here with Zach Garrett, interesting or not, with a wagon that looked as if its wheels might come off the next time they rolled.

Her first priority was Danny. Zach's was the team. Fortunately, her valise had protected most of the baby's things from the rain, so she had a clean diaper to put on him. She found a dry nook under the wagon seat in which to lay him, and after he was fed, she helped Zach spread out their wet belongings on the tailgate and any other flat or vertical surface.

He gathered enough wood from their campsite to get a fire going. It smoked a little at first but once the surface water burned off, it blazed. There they sat, she on a small crate and he on an overturned skillet, eating a plain meal of beans and coffee. Sarah arranged her heavy, damp skirts before the flames, hoping they'd dry.

Zach studied her for a moment, then shifted his gaze to the wagon, draped with its tattered cover and sodden blankets. He scooped up a forkful of beans and gestured at the two of them, wet and huddling near the fire like pathetic refugees. "God, we look like we came through a war. I lost my horse, our gear is drenched, the wagon took a beating, *we* took a beating—" He carefully touched the tender place on his scalp where hail had left a gash. With obvious reluctance he added, "I guess a stagecoach might have been a better way to go, after all."

Sarah sighed and shoved the beans around her tin plate with her fork, not really hungry. "In the end, it would all come to the same result. You get your reward, I lose my child."

Another awkward moment of silence fell between them. Then he asked, rather casually, "What will you do after we get to Helena? Go back to your teaching job?"

Sarah didn't know the answer. "I suppose I could. My position at the school is still there, as far as I know. I'm away on sabbatical, and I don't think anyone knows the true reason why I've been gone. I'm not sure I'd want to stay though." She looked up and caught his gaze for an instant, unguarded and perhaps even concerned, before it faded into indifference. If only he weren't so handsome, so distracting, with his dark hair, cleanly sculpted features, and lean, rugged frame. If only they were making this trip for some other reason, any other reason. She hurried to explain. "It isn't that I don't want to teach. I love teaching. That's what I wanted to do from the time I was little. I'd line up my dolls, round up our cat and dog, and I'd pretend I was showing them their ABCs. I had a wonderful classroom in Helena, and a good life."

"But?"

"I'm not sure I can stay there. In Helena, I mean. I'll have to go to another town."

"Why? Didn't you say they're holding your job for you?"

"Yes, but it's more complicated than that."

He shrugged and took a cautious sip of scalding coffee from his tin cup. "If no one knows about what happened, you should be able to pick up where you left off."

The monotonous hours and miles had given Sarah a lot

of time to think about this. She'd weighed the problem in her heart and mind, and considered it from every angle. To give voice to it, though, and to Zach of all people, made her throat constrict. "I—I played the organ for my church and I sat on the library committee. I was respected and counted upon to do the right thing, to set a good example. If I went back to Helena, pretending that I've been traveling and studying, I would betray the trust all those parents and citizens have put in me. I'd be lying to them, and I'd be the worst kind of hypocrite. They deserve better than that. I've had my trust betrayed and it's a terrible feeling . . . terrible."

"Hell, what they don't know won't hurt them. You have the right to earn a buck. Why turn your whole life upside down and lose out on a paying job?"

Sarah frowned and couldn't keep the sarcasm out of her response. "It's more than the money. I have my sense of honor, but I suppose I should expect that kind of answer from a man who'll do anything for a dollar. How do you sleep nights, Zach?" She realized she'd called him by his first name, but she was beyond caring about the preservation of formalities.

His already closed expression turned stony. "I know what I want and how to get it. I don't lie awake worrying about it."

"How fortunate for you."

Zach stood and tossed his plate into the dishpan Sarah had taken out of the wagon. Then he walked away through the wet grass, heading toward the mules.

Just when she'd reached the point where she thought she could tolerate Zach, he'd changed her mind again. He appeared to have no conscience, while Sarah's conscience had tormented her all these months. Then again, who was *she* to judge him? She looked up at the clearing sky, growing pale with the sunset, and felt miserably small.

Regardless of the breathless, moonlit promises made to her well over a year ago, she knew she'd done the wrong thing.

Sexual commerce outside of marriage.

At the time, it hadn't seemed to deserve such an ugly, glaring description. Oh, no, she'd been *in love,* and her beloved had been a dashing, gallant man. Or so she'd believed.

Fornication.

Now she could think of it no other terms. She had paid the price for her bad judgment and romantic gullibility in so many ways. Her heart had been broken, and she knew it would be broken yet again. During scores of sleepless nights, she'd seen a parade of people march past in her mind, all of the people she had let down, whether or not they knew. Reverend Davidson in Stockett had written a letter of recommendation to Agnes Middleton Academy, speaking of her character and propriety in glowing terms. Her parents, loyal, encouraging, loving, and so proud of their daughter—they'd pinched and stretched every penny to pay her tuition. Aunt Zoë had helped Sarah sew a new wardrobe to take to her first teaching job in Helena. Michael, her brother, had made her a beautiful inlaid pencil box to put on her desk. The day she left Stockett, most of the town had come down to the train depot to see her safely on her way. She could still see her mother on the platform, alternately waving her handkerchief and using it to dab at her streaming eyes. Even her father had brushed away his tears. But all of them had smiled and cheered and wished her well.

And she'd let them down. All of them. She bowed her head over her damp lap, squeezing her eyes shut to force back the tears.

Finally, she took a deep breath and turned her gaze to the wreck of the wagon. For now, she still had Danny, and she had work to do.

She rose to get her sewing kit from her valise.

A piercing scream shot up from the bowels of the house. It ricocheted off the crystal chandelier in the entry hall, echoed around the high, coved ceilings, and seemed to make the dark velvet drapes shudder on their poles.

Ethan Pembroke jerked bolt upright in his black calfskin desk chair, knocking over his inkwell in the process. A puddle of brown ink streamed its way across a blueprint rolled out on the blotter in front of him. It was a plan for a grand hotel and natatorium, an important pet project that he'd already spent months on.

"Goddamn it!" he muttered and jumped up before a drizzle of ink cascaded over the edge of the desk.

"Mr. Pembroke!" Louisa, their plump maid, cried breathlessly from the doorway, fear in her voice. She was pale and obviously frightened, as if she'd seen her own grave.

"Louisa, what the hell was that?"

"It's Miss Priscilla, sir. I mean—"

"Where is she?"

She pointed behind her. "In the cellar, sir."

Baffled, he repeated, "In the cellar. What's she doing down there?" He dropped the pen he was holding, further splattering the drawing with ink. Rushing past the maid, he hurried through the main hall to the kitchen, and down the back porch stairs to the cellar. Louisa followed in his wake, almost running to keep up.

"It was that mama cat and them kittens down there," she reported, beginning to pant. "Miss Priscilla has been feeding the mama, and I carried a tray down for her a few minutes ago. When we got there, she said the mama cat was hurting one of the babies and she wanted to save him. But somehow—"

Ethan vaguely recalled Priscilla talking about the litter of kittens under the house. She'd seemed to take great pleasure from watching their progress and feeding the mother cat.

They rounded the corner of the house and found the cellar doors thrown open. The cool, damp smell of earth and cordwood wafted from the opening, and Ethan could hear the sound of Priscilla's sobs. Bounding down the stone steps, he waited for his eyes to adjust to the low light provided by the windows in the foundation. At last he spotted her in a corner on her knees, clutching a gray kitten to her breast. The mother cat's hair stood on end, making her look twice her normal size. Her babies, about five weeks old, huddled behind her. She hissed and growled wildly at Priscilla, sounding like a mountain lion. Her mouth was open wide enough to display all of her needlelike teeth, her ears were flat, and a furious frown wrinkled her brow and nose. Tensed and ready to lunge, she could do a lot of damage with her sharp claws and fangs. His wife was about to be mauled.

"Priscilla, for God's sake, what happened?"

"She was trying to hurt this kitten. I wanted to save him—he's the one I was hoping to keep for myself when he was old enough. B-but when I tried to pull him away from her—" She held out one hand that bore long, bloody scratches. "It was too late!" The kitten's head flopped lifelessly against Priscilla's arm when she moved.

Ethan eyed the mother cat warily and then his wife. He wasn't sure how any of this had come about. Something seemed out of kilter. But he had to get her out of there. Spying a broom propped against the brick wall, he grabbed it and shoved the bristle end toward the cat, giving her a new target. "Priscilla, come away from there right now!"

The feline caterwauled and Priscilla wailed on, still cradling the dead kitten. "The poor little thing," she sobbed. "Poor, poor baby."

"Priscilla!" When she didn't move, he motioned Louisa toward her with an emphatic nod.

The maid stepped forward and took Priscilla by the shoulders. "Come on, now, miss. We'll bury the kitten."

Priscilla stumbled to her feet. Her cream taffeta skirt was smudged with dirt and her hair was coming loose from its smooth upsweep. "He was just a little baby. I tried to save him. I really tried so hard."

"Of course you did, miss."

Something about this seemed so very familiar to Ethan.

The two women crossed the hard-packed dirt floor and climbed the stairs while he held the angry mother at bay with the broom. Then he followed and slammed closed the cellar doors.

"It's all right, miss, it's all right," Louisa soothed as they walked the path to the back door. "I'll find a nice little box to put the poor mite in, and after I'll bring you a pot of hot tea."

"Dear Louisa, you're so good to me," Priscilla sniffled.

After the kitten had its little funeral, Ethan summoned the maid to his study.

"Come in, Louisa, and close the door." She did as he asked. A shadow of uneasiness crossed her florid, round face, as she approached his desk.

"Mrs. Pembroke is settled in her room?"

"Yes, sir. She fretted a bit over the accident but I fixed her some valerian root tea and put her to bed. She's resting now."

Ethan rolled his pen between his fingertips. "Did you see what happened in the cellar before you came for me?"

"Well, not exactly. There was some kind of tussle, some kind of accident—"

"You were down there with Mrs. Pembroke, weren't you?"

"I was, sir."

Ethan leaned forward with his elbows on the desk. "What *kind* of accident?"

The maid folded and refolded her hands. "I'm really not certain, Mr. Pembroke. But Miss Priscilla was only trying to help, I'm positive of that."

"Help—help what? Those cats have been getting along just fine in the cellar all these weeks. Why would the mother suddenly turn on her own kittens and kill one of them?"

Louisa looked miserable and on the verge of tears. "I don't know, sir. But Miss Priscilla didn't do anything wrong."

He considered the maid with a long, assessing gaze, hoping to pry more information out of her by sheer intimidation. But she remained silent.

Louisa bore unswerving loyalty to her mistress. She had come with Priscilla from the Driscoll home when Ethan married her, and he doubted that any kind of incentive, either money or the threat of unemployment, would make her betray that loyalty. Besides, if he tried such tactics and old man Driscoll got wind of it, Ethan would probably bring more trouble down on himself than the situation was worth. His father-in-law expected ruthlessness from Ethan in his business dealings. In fact, he almost demanded it. But that method did not apply to his home life. Ethan never forgot that Priscilla's father expected him to make her happy, no matter what the cost or difficulty.

And sometimes it was damned difficult.

He glanced around his well-appointed study, just one of the many fine rooms in his well-appointed house on Madison Avenue. Armistead Driscoll had played an important role in putting Ethan here.

"Miss Priscilla did nothing wrong," he repeated.

"No, sir. Not one thing."

He leaned back in his chair and, with a brisk wave of dismissal, released the maid from the spot on the carpet to which he'd fixed her. "Very well, Louisa. You may go."

She bobbed a quick curtsy and scurried out, closing the door behind her.

Strange, the maid's assurances of his wife's innocence told him more than he'd wanted to know.

Chapter Six

Zach poked at the fire he'd built just after sunup, and then stirred the bacon he was frying in the skillet. "There's no point in traveling on today. We need to take a day to get this mess straightened out. We'll just move closer to that stream down there so we don't have to haul water." He pointed at a meandering creek at the bottom of a distant slope. "Anyway, I figured you could use the time to, well"—he gestured broadly with a fork—"you know, take care of personal stuff."

Relief was obvious in Sarah's face. The fragrant smell of perking coffee had lured her from the wagon where she'd spent what Zach figured was a sleepless night with the baby. She looked as whipped as a horse run to exhaustion. Although she'd tidied her long braid, faint purple shadows underscored her eyes, and her clothes were as wrinkled as a turkey's neck.

Zach thought he knew why. By the time evening fell the night before, the wagon bed had dried out enough for Sarah and Danny to sleep on it, but the blankets were still damp. He'd made do by bedding down against the wall, and he suspected that he'd been the better off of the three.

Sarah nodded and took the cup of coffee that he offered to her. Looking around, she said, "At least the weather is better." And it was. The sky was clear blue, and the air, washed clean of dust and heat, smelled fresh.

Isabel, tied once again to a wagon wheel, let out a loud bleat when she saw Sarah. She eyed the goat and sighed, then set the cup down on the ground and prepared to rise, her movements stiff.

"Where are you going? This bacon is just about ready."

"Danny has to eat before I do. I've got to milk Isabel so I can feed him."

"Sit down. I've already milked the goat." He pointed to a bucket next to the wagon, covered with a clean white cloth.

She looked at him as if he'd told her he was from the moon. He shifted on the overturned keg where he sat. "What's the matter?"

"You milked Isabel?"

Stabbing with the fork, he gave the bacon another shove in the pan. "Well, yeah. I didn't think you'd mind."

"No, it's just that I didn't expect it. I got the impression that you hate Isabel."

"I don't hate her. That would be dumb." The truth was, he didn't like the animal at all and figured she'd be better off in a stew. But he'd look like an ass if he admitted it. "I didn't think you'd mind the help." Was she going to argue with him about that now?

"Thank you," Sarah said. Her expression softened and she smiled. It was a sweet smile that transformed her tired face. In the morning light, she looked so beautiful that Zach could only stare.

A halo of sunlight topped her dark hair, creating a black-cherry corona on the crown of her head. Fine strands around her face fluttered in the light breeze, rising and falling like flowers bobbing in a field. Her green eyes were framed with thick lashes and capped with delicate, expressive brows. Zach didn't want to notice these features but, hell, a man would have to be blind or dead not to. Hers was a simple beauty, one of rose-pink lips and softly flushed cheeks. It wasn't the showy sort that hit a man between the eyes like a poleaxe at first glance. Sarah's type of prettiness sneaked up and revealed itself at a moment like this—when the light was just so, when she looked up at him with a shy gaze and a suggestion of dimples.

And briefly it crossed his mind that some man, the father of her baby, had taken her to his bed, made her believe that he loved her—Zach was certain now that nothing short of love could have drawn her there—and then he'd abandoned her. She wouldn't speak of it, and he knew she was right, that it was none of his business. So why he was certain of the betrayal he couldn't explain to himself. But he *was* certain. And knowing that she'd been so taken advantage of made a hot spark of anger flicker through Zach before he crushed it.

Later, after she fed the baby, goo-gooed over him for a while, and got him back to sleep, she began stitching up the bigger tears in the wagon canvas. They had thought it would be easier for her to work on it if they took it off, but when Zach tried to untie it, the rotting fabric began to disintegrate in his hands. So it had to remain in place, stretched over the arches. He stacked a couple of crates for Sarah to sit on while she stitched, and he sat next to her on an upended barrel.

Despite the fact that yesterday's weather had improved the wagon's ventilation, heat was already beginning to build inside the small enclosure. Working this close to her, he could smell her soap and her hair. He could see fine blue veins in the creamy column of her throat and wondered what it would feel like to press his mouth to that place. Would her pulse beat beneath his lips, keeping time with the rhythm of her heart? Would her neck be as smooth as it looked? As she worked with her arms raised, the swell of her breasts came into full view, pressing against her camisole, which was visible through her thin white blouse. He felt like a dumb schoolkid when his body reacted to the sight. Jesus, what was wrong with him? He'd seen lots of women wearing far less, or nothing at all, and here he was, the crotch of his jeans getting tight over a female who was fully dressed.

He renewed his efforts to concentrate on the goal—to fix the damned canvas. The last thing he needed were sweaty dreams of Sarah Kincade complicating his life. "I'd like five minutes with that old guy who sold me this wagon. I'd get part of my money back," he groused while he struggled to pull together the edges of the old canvas for her to mend. It was tricky—if he pulled too hard, the material tore in a new place.

Already tired and irritable from another sleepless night, Sarah tried to ignore the ache in her arms from holding them at an awkward angle while she stitched. With an impatient sigh, she let them drop to her lap and glared at him. "Zach, I have a favor to ask of you."

"A favor—" He looked perplexed then his face took on a knowing expression. "Now, Sarah, if it's about leaving you in some town, I already told you I won't—"

"No, I know you won't, and I know why." She fixed him with a hard stare. Why had fate made this heartless man so handsome that her insides flip-flopped whenever she looked at him? "I know you told me that it isn't personal, that I got myself into this fix, and that your whole future depends on getting me and Danny back to Helena."

"Well, yeah . . ." He wouldn't look at her, but busied himself with the fabric. "Then, what?"

"Please stop talking about money!"

"What?"

"You've already explained that this is just a job to you, that Danny and I are just a means to an end, commodities to be sold so that you can get what you want for your own life. I know *all* of it. I don't need to be reminded of it several times a day. We're real flesh-and-blood people, but you seem to know only about money."

"There's nothing wrong with having a goal," he said quietly.

"No, there isn't, as long as you don't reach it on the broken backs of others."

His face flushed, but Sarah wasn't sure if it was from anger or the heat. She hoped it was the latter, since she didn't know what kind of temper he had.

"*I've* been through hell to get to this point. All that kept me going was the chance that someday I'd have a spread to call my own. I had it and lost it, and now I'm going to get it back. That didn't happen through good deeds. Good deeds don't get you anywhere. And when this is over, I'll never answer to anyone ever again."

She pulled a length of black thread from the spool in her pocket, bit it off with her teeth, and threaded her needle. "If you chase after goals with that kind of single-mindedness and blind yourself to everything around you, you'll *always* answer to someone else." She glanced at Danny where he slept in his basket. "Try to have some compassion."

He followed the path of her gaze and looked at her son for a long, thoughtful moment, as if a memory crossed his heart. "Compassion is for churches and charities. Just stitch the damned canvas, Sarah," he barked impatiently, "and I'll try to remember not to talk about money."

Sarah lapsed into insulted silence, wondering why she'd bothered to say anything to him. Zach Garrett was a baffling, infuriating, and unpredictable man. She pushed the needle through the crumbling canvas.

Three days and fifty miles later, Zach settled the Dutch oven in the campfire coals to bake his sourdough biscuits for their supper. The wagon had held together better than he'd hoped, and the cover had been patched fairly well. Some holes were beyond repair, but they'd created a canopy large enough to cover their supplies and give Sarah a little shelter at night.

They rode along without many words passing between them. But no matter what he did, he was very aware of her—the scent of her, a seductive blend of soap, sun-dried cotton, and another, indefinable essence that was her own— the curve of her cheek, the small slenderness of her hands. Sometimes he had trouble keeping his eyes on the road ahead of them.

At the same time, though, he felt both angry and, damn it all, guilty again. Sarah had all but accused him of being heartless. He really didn't want to be but—well, so what if he was? What did she know about a hard life, or what drove him? From the little she'd told him, it sounded like she'd grown up in a loving family. If she was in this predicament now, it was no one's fault but her own.

Warring with his conviction, though, was a nagging doubt that grew with each turn of the wagon wheels. What if Sarah was right about his hell-bent pursuit? Had money become so important to him that he'd shut his eyes and heart to everything else? The very question rattled him because until she'd mentioned it, he never once doubted that he was following his true destiny.

Right now she was on the other side of the wagon, washing herself, and giving Danny a bath too. She'd warmed water in a kettle over the fire and filled a galvanized washtub she'd taken from the wagon. Clear skies and a gentling of the heat made it a fine day to bathe a baby in the sun, she'd said. Zach could hear her murmuring to him in that voice mothers use to talk to infants, high and sweet, rising and falling on the wind. This was accompanied by the sound of splashing and the baby's happy gurgling. It was such a homey, domestic sound that Zach could almost imagine hearing it at his own place.

He closed his eyes for a moment, surprised to discover how easy it was to picture himself as part of the warm scene, riding in from a day on the range to find his wife and child on the porch, waiting for him. A nearby oak cast long shadows across the house. Its leaves rustled in the breeze and dappled the setting with light and twilight. Evening smells of supper and cool grass and clean wash flapping on the line came to his mind almost as if they were real. He hadn't experienced much of that in his own life, but he'd seen it as an outsider looking in, and he'd longed for it with a yearning so sharp it had hurt. Back then he'd wondered if one day they would be his. A home, a wife, children. Strange, though—he'd never really imagined it for himself. He'd always managed on his own and pictured himself alone, from his earliest days as a dirty, hungry kid running through the narrow, winding maze that was Mulberry Bend in New York. Although he was supposed to have been part of a family in Illinois, he'd been alone there too, and through the years that followed when he came west.

Now, as a man, the true meaning of *home* rushed over him like a river that had overflowed its banks.

Until this moment, he'd pictured himself sitting on the front porch of his ranch house, surveying his hard-won kingdom and watching the sunset in complete contentment and with a proud sense of accomplishment. Today a quiet voice in his head nudged him: without someone to share the accomplishments, would they be enough?

He shook off the question the way he would pull away from an unwelcome touch. Well, damn it, they would just have to be enough. He had plenty of other worries at this point—actually getting his land back, buying stock, building the house so there'd *be* a porch to sit on. He had a lot of work ahead of him and probably wouldn't be able to afford to hire help. Maybe someday, when there was more time, when his life was settled, he'd sort it all out.

More splashing and baby giggles came from the other side of the wagon, and he looked up from the fire. He felt as if he were fifteen again, living in that barn in Illinois, while the rest of the family sat around a big kitchen table at night, eating, talking, laughing. He'd known he wasn't welcome at that table, but sometimes, he'd sneak up to the house for a glimpse—

He rose from his crouch and quietly rounded the back end of the wagon. It was a beautiful afternoon, crystal-blue and clear, with the sun in the western sky already tracking in a southerly direction on its way to winter. Yeah, it probably was a nice day to give a baby a bath outside.

But when Zach stuck his head around the tailgate, although he heard Danny's giggles he didn't notice him. What he saw instead brought a flush of heat to Zach's entire body. He saw Sarah, naked and standing in the washtub, pouring water over her soapy, wet skin with a white enamel pitcher. Her back was to him and the low afternoon sun limned her in gold, her narrow back, the curve of her waist to her hip, her sweetly rounded buttocks. She'd twisted her dark hair into a knot on top of her head, but some long tendrils had escaped and hung between her shoulders like uncoiled springs. Her plain white underwear was draped over a nearby sagebrush next to her dress. She looked like a nymph in a painting, with an endless blue sky and the rolling green prairie of Montana serving as the backdrop.

Zach took two steps backward then pivoted and walked back to the campfire, sucking in a deep breath as he went. His heart felt as if it were trying to pound its way out of his chest and fire pumped through his veins right down to his groin where an uncomfortable erection made him try to remember just how long it had been since he last lay with a woman.

Grabbing the branch he'd used for a poker, irritably he stirred up the coals. He felt like a Peeping Tom, spying on her as he had. Damn it, he'd thought she was finished with her own bath and was washing the baby, the way the kid was laughing. But even stronger was the image imprinted on his memory. The sight of Sarah, sleek and glistening from her improvised bath on the plains, overtook every other thought in his mind.

He didn't want to think about her as anything more than a job. He couldn't. If she became more real to him, he'd get so confounded he wouldn't be able to complete this assignment Pembroke had given him. Pembroke wouldn't get the boy, Zach wouldn't get his note back, and all of his plans would go up in smoke.

He didn't want to daydream about Sarah, or see her face on his nonexistent porch, or have her visiting his sleep with the lure of silky skin, full breasts, and a long, slender neck. But it was already happening.

The smell of burning bread reached his nose. "Son of a bitch!" he cursed vehemently. Now the damned biscuits were ruined. Without thinking, he grabbed the Dutch oven's handle with his bare hand.

Sarah heard a sharp yelp of pain as she was buttoning her bodice. Her head snapped up. "Zach?"

She heard no specific answer, just some low-voiced cursing.

Leaving her shoes, she picked up Danny in his basket and hurried barefoot around to the camp side of the wagon. There she found Zach on his knees in the grass next to the campfire, his shoulders bowed, cradling his right hand, and rocking slightly. The Dutch oven lay on its side in the fire, and what must have been their dinner biscuits had tumbled out into the flames to become blackened lumps.

She put the baby down and rushed to Zach. "What happened?"

After a couple of heavy breaths, he ground out, "I burned my hand. I reached for that goddamned thing"—he indicated the kettle—"without a glove."

"Oh, no! Let me see it."

He pulled away. "No! Just leave it alone."

She bent over him. "Zach, for heaven's sake, it needs to be tended! Let me look."

Another heavy sigh. Without raising his head, he slowly extended his injured hand, then snatched it back. "Don't touch it! Just look."

Sarah hid a smile—it sounded just like something one of her students would say about a skinned knee or elbow that occurred during recess. The child usually relented when she offered to rinse the injury with cool water and wrap it with gauze. By the time she was finished, and threw in a piece of taffy as a reward for bravery, the tears had stopped.

"All right, I swear I won't touch. Now please let me see." How bad could it be? Having endured the rigors of childbirth, Sarah felt certain that many men had no concept of true pain.

But when Zach opened his fingers just enough for her to look at his hand, she stared.

"Oh, God." This was nothing like a playground accident. A gruesome horizontal line crossed his palm from edge to edge, red and angry-looking. Even as she examined it, huge blisters bubbled up from the burn. "Oh, dear God," she whispered and sank to her knees next to him.

"It's bad, huh?" Zach swallowed hard. Sweat inched its way down his temples and the color had drained from his face.

"Yes—well, no, maybe not . . ." Sarah didn't want to sound as frightened as she felt. But the burn looked horrible, worse than any she'd ever seen, and extremely painful.

"It feels like I grabbed the wrong end of a branding iron."

That just about summed things up, and she wasn't sure what to do for it. This went beyond her limited knowledge of the new technique called "first aid," a kind of emergency treatment of injuries. They didn't have beeswax or turpentine with them, or any of the other typical remedies used to treat a burn.

"What can I put on this?" she asked, talking more to herself. She mentally reviewed the meager contents of her valise, jumping from item to item. Talcum powder, diaper pins, nightgown, toothbrush, apron, *McGuffey's Reader*— they all flashed past her mind's eye, irrelevant and useless. Then suddenly, an idea occurred to her.

"Petroleum jelly—I've got carbolated petroleum jelly."

" 'Carbolated'? That's something good?"

Without replying, she jumped up and ran to the back of the wagon. She plowed through her belongings, flinging items around with no regard for where they landed. Glancing at a clean handkerchief she'd tossed aside, she retrieved it and jammed it into her skirt pocket. Finally, she closed her hand around a glass jar and withdrew the petroleum jelly and read the label—good for bruises, cuts, chapped skin, *burns*—

Hurrying back to Zach, she found him sitting cross-legged on the ground, leaning against a boulder. She sat down next to him and reached for his wounded hand where it lay, palm up on his denim-clad knee.

"I promise I'll be careful," she said, "but this is probably going to hurt."

He shrugged and nodded, obviously resigned. "Just have at it." He tipped his head back against the rock and closed his eyes.

Sarah worked quickly, her lower lip clamped firmly between her teeth, and perspiration trickled over her scalp. She tried to be gentle but she also wanted to make sure she spread ointment over the entire burn. It was a well-favored hand, she thought, or at least it had been until a few minutes ago. Long-fingered and strong, it bore a line of calluses along the top of the palm. She could tell it had done its share of work. The hot kettle handle would leave a mark long after the wound healed, but Sarah didn't believe a scar would detract from its handsomeness.

Glancing up now and then, she saw rivulets of sweat trickling down Zach's face too, and his color was no better than it had been earlier. His jaw muscles flexed in his temples and just beneath his ears, causing Sarah to clench her own teeth. "Are you all right, Zach?" she asked, alarmed by his pallor.

He nodded slightly, keeping his eyes closed. His dark lashes were uncommonly long, she noted foolishly.

"This really should be washed with soap and water, but hopefully the carbolic will be enough to keep it from festering. It's an antiseptic." At last she tied her clean handkerchief around his hand, leaving his fingers and thumb exposed. She didn't have a piece of taffy to give him which, of course, would have been silly anyway. She couldn't give candy to a grown man for being a good patient. Instead, ever so lightly, she squeezed his fingertips with her own. Perhaps it was too intimate, but it seemed like the only comfort she could offer.

He opened his eyes and looked down at the bandage,

starkly white against his tanned skin. Shaking his head, he said, "I've had a lot of things happen to me—I've been shot at, I broke a couple of bones, I've been whip—I mean, I've been in fights . . . But I've never done something this dumb." His gaze connected with hers, and suddenly he seemed too close. "Thanks, Sarah."

She felt herself blush. "We might need to fashion a sling for you so you don't bump it."

With his good hand, he pushed himself to his feet and swayed unsteadily before gaining his equilibrium. "Nope, no sling. I won't be able to work wearing a getup like that."

Sarah didn't see how he'd be able to use that hand at all, but she didn't voice the thought.

Zach had no appetite for the stew that Sarah had concocted after she patched him up. It tasted fine but his hand throbbed like a bitch in heat, and he ate just a couple of bites before he gave up.

How could he have been so damned careless? he asked himself again. It had been such a stupid thing to do, grabbing that hot handle. Of course, it probably wouldn't have happened if he hadn't been so distracted by the sight of Sarah standing naked in that washtub, pouring water over herself. Even now, the memory of it temporarily made him forget the pain in his hand and stirred up a hunger deep within him that had nothing to do with food.

He almost smiled. Women complained that men usually had the same single thought on their minds at any given time—maybe they were right. He glanced at her, fine-boned and delicate, eating her stew with as much dignity as if she were sitting at a dining room table instead of balancing her plate on her lap out here in this rough place. He wouldn't have guessed that so much beauty existed under her brisk, prim, schoolmarm exterior.

There was only one thing he could think of that might take the edge off both the hunger and the pain. He set the plate aside and walked over to his gear stowed beneath the wagon seat.

"You're not eating?" she asked, watching him. She seemed genuinely concerned.

He shook his head and, reaching into his saddle bag, pulled out a bottle of whiskey. "Maybe later." Lowering himself a bit awkwardly, he reclaimed his spot against the rock. He stretched out his legs and crossed his ankles, trying to get comfortable. His feet were just inches from the hem of her skirt. Then he pulled the cork out of the bottle with his teeth and poured a measure into his coffee cup.

"Is your hand paining you much?" she asked, eyeing the bottle. Next to her in his basket, Danny kicked and gurgled in happy contentment.

"Yes, ma'am" he confirmed with brittle enthusiasm. "Up to my elbow." Resting the injured limb on his knee, he took a drink and let the kindly fire burn its way down his throat.

Sarah sipped her coffee. "Maybe we should stay here another day. I'm not sure you'll be able to drive the team."

"I'll drive the team, don't you worry about that. We already lost one day, and we've been making lousy time, only eight or nine miles a day. I don't want to lose—" Their eyes met briefly, long enough for Zach to remember his promise to avoid the subject of money. He took another drink. This one slid down a little more easily. "Besides," he added, holding up his hand to examine the bandage, "you did a good job of wrapping this. You must have done some nursing in your time."

She put down her own tin plate and brushed nonexistent crumbs from her dark green skirt. "No, but a teacher has to handle the little emergencies that come up during a school day. Children get hurt, accidents happen. And my mother has some nursing talent. Sometimes she helps out in Stockett when Dr. Griswold is busy. She's delivered a few babies, set a couple of broken arms, that kind of thing."

"And your father?"

"Daddy owns the dry-goods store. He's the postmaster too, so he knows just about everyone in the county. They all come to get their mail from him and share news."

Once she warmed to the subject, Sarah went on to tell Zach about growing up in the small town, the sense of community she'd always known, and how close her family had been. Animated with the first real joy he'd seen in her, she talked about Sunday dinners, Fourth of July picnics, church bazaars, Christmas mornings. Zach had assumed, and reasonably so, that her background was vastly different from his own. But, hell, they were about as different as two lives could be.

"Sounds nice. Someday I'd like that kind of life ... slow-moving and steady, to wake up under the same roof every day. Maybe get me a wife and have some kids." He shifted his back against the rock and gazed at Sarah from heavy-lidded eyes, feeling a little fuzzy from the whiskey. "If I had a wife, I'd want a real lady, a Sunday-go-to-meetin' type with fancy manners and lace collars. A woman who could give my kids the home life and upbringing that I never had." A woman just like Sarah, he thought. He looked at Danny kicking and waving his fists in his basket, and nodded in his direction. "Didn't you think about taking him back to Stockett instead of running away to Lame Horse?"

Her smile of reminiscence had faded and now a look of outright horror crossed her face. "Dear God, no! I mean, yes, I thought about it, but I knew I couldn't. How could I go home? They were so proud of me and had such high hopes. My mother bragged to everyone she met about the noble work her daughter was doing in Helena. How could I break their hearts and let them see how wrong they were—how low I—" She broke off with a choked sound. Tipping her head, she gazed blankly at the ground, then in a quiet voice uttered, "How could I?"

Her question hung between them, open-ended and lacerating, asking for more than one answer.

Zach, exhausted by hard work and the pain in his hand, his defenses lowered by the whiskey, felt his heart clench. Also born within him was an overwhelming desire to take her into his arms and protect her.

Shifting his boot, he tapped her foot with his own. "Sarah."

She wouldn't look up.

He tapped again. "Come on, Sarah, don't be so hard on yourself."

"I'm not sure which is worse," she said in the same low voice, "having no one to turn to, or having family you *can't* turn to."

Zach pondered her statement. "I don't know either," he said in complete honesty. "But I think having no one is worse. At least you know you have folks in Stockett who care about you. When I went to the Gerlichs in Illinois, they were supposed to become my family. That's what I'd been told, anyway. All the way out on the train, I kept wondering, will they like me? It didn't take me long to figure out that liking me had nothing to do with it. I was like a draft horse or a yoke of oxen to old man Gerlich. He had three fat, homely daughters and no sons to help on the farm, so that's where I came in. But I wasn't his son and I was never treated like one." He tipped another splash of whiskey into his coffee cup.

"But wasn't it better than living at the reformatory?"

Zach sighed. "No. In New York, I didn't have any expectations or hopes. I got in trouble a lot, although that was my fault—I pulled my share of pranks. But I never felt like an outsider there. Herman Gerlich made sure I never forgot that I didn't belong. I lived in the barn, I wasn't allowed to eat at the table with the rest of the family . . . he said he didn't want his wife and daughters exposed to riffraff like me. He taught me some German though. *Sie sind ein fauler wertloser Hund!* 'You're a lazy, worthless dog.' " He shook his head and laughed, but the sound had no humor in it. "*Die Kuh ist intelligenter als Sie.* 'The cow is smarter than you are.' And those were the compliments. He didn't know that I'd found an old box of books in the barn, and that I could probably read better than he could. But even so, he knocked me around now and then, just to make sure I understood that I was his property, I guess."

Sarah felt her eyes widen. "Didn't the people who placed you ever come back to see how you were being treated?"

"Naw. There were too many of us sent out—thousands. And I think the kids placed with town families did a little better." He rested his injured hand in the crook of his left arm. "I don't know, maybe I'm wrong. Maybe I was just unlucky. Anyway, I was supposed to stay until I was eighteen. I ran away three years early. I learned one important thing from the time I spent with old man Gerlich. I learned that I wanted my own land and I was going to get it, no matter what. No one would ever beat me again, or call me stupid, and nothing would keep me from getting what I wanted."

"Where did you go?"

"I just started working my way west. Sometimes I was no better off than I'd been in New York, sleeping in doorways and stealing to eat. But in the West there are more possibilities. A lot of people have come out here, broke and down on their luck, and they all get the chance to start over. I had the chance to start over every morning. I took any kind of work I could get, and like I said, I've done all kinds."

He told her about grave-digging, ditch-digging, and well-digging. He talked about being a faro dealer, a cowhand, and a gandy dancer. That last was easy for her to imagine—she pictured him swinging a sledgehammer on a railroad crew, driving spikes. He'd survived by his wits and sometimes by the seat of his pants.

"About five years ago, I found the sweetest piece of land this side of heaven on the eastern face of the Rockies. Good water, knee-high grass, a nice hill to build a house on. But someone owned it already, a man named Ethan Pembroke. He was willing to sell it, and I had enough money for the land but I needed a loan for stock and some lumber to build a ranch house. Nothing fancy, just a little cabin to get me started. So I mortgaged the property. I put most of the money into the cattle. That was in 1886." He looked up at her with a suddenly weary expression that spoke volumes. "Then winter came."

"Ohh." It was all Sarah could say. It was all she needed to say to convey her comprehension. The winter of 1886–87. The Big Die-Up it was called now. A merciless arctic fist had held the territory in an icy grip for months. Entire herds froze to death. Large ranchers were hurt, but many small spreads lost everything.

"All those cattle that I'd bet my whole future on—dead as doornails. When the spring thaw finally came, I had nothing left but bloated carcasses scattered around that little piece of heaven and choking the stream." He drew a deep breath and cleared his throat, but she heard his voice crack with unmistakable emotion. "Of all the things I'd been through—being an orphan, living on the streets, being shipped off to the Gerlichs—that winter was the worst yet."

Dear God, Sarah didn't want to feel sorry for Zach. He was the man who was taking her back to Helena to break her heart. But she did feel sorry for him—how could she not? She gazed at him sitting across from her, pain making dark smudges form beneath his eyes while he gingerly supported his hand.

"I lost it all, but I still owe the money for it." He roused himself and glanced at her again. "Sorry—I know I promised I wouldn't talk about that anymore."

She shook her head to indicate it didn't matter right now. "So you owe the money to Ethan Pembroke."

"Yup. And he won't let me put one foot back on the property until the note is paid in full."

Damn Ethan, she though viciously. He was a snake, an evil viper of Old Testament proportions. How well he'd chosen the individual to deliver Sarah and her child into his hands—a man whose land was as important to him as Danny was to her.

As if knowing he was in her thoughts, the baby began to fuss. She plucked him from his basket and rocked him slowly with his downy head tucked against her jaw. When she looked at Zach, she saw that he'd dropped off into an uneasy doze, with his head resting on his shoulder at an awkward angle. In that instant, she wished she could do the same for him—rock him in her arms. No one had loved him in his entire life, or taught him to value the tenderness of the human heart.

But she wasn't the one who could fix that. And in case she'd forgotten, his earlier statement had reminded her of who she was now.

I'd want a real lady, a Sunday-go-to-meetin' type with fancy manners and lace collars.

Not a woman who'd been seduced by a married man

and had a child out of wedlock. She was about as far from being a lady as possible.

The sun dropped lower in the sky, pulling dusk over them like a star-flung blanket. Sarah finished her chores, tucked Danny in, and made sure that Isabel was securely tethered to a wheel.

Just before she climbed into bed, she glanced out at Zach, still asleep where she'd left him. Well, blast it, she couldn't just leave him like that. It would get cold before morning.

Wearing only her nightgown and shawl, she took a blanket from the wagon and climbed out to cover him. Tentatively, she brushed the backs of her fingers against his temple, then scampered back to the wagon, wondering if she'd taken total leave of her senses.

Zach Garrett sighed.

Chapter Seven

The tantalizing smell of coffee and bacon brought Zach slowly awake the following morning. The butter-yellow brightness of sunlight knifed into his eyes when he cracked them open. He lay on his stomach, he realized dimly, one side of his face resting against dew-damp grass, the crushed blades prickling his cheek. His blanket was wadded up around his waist, a lump of wool pressing into his belly. He blinked, yawned, and then winced when he tried to move. Everything ached. His head, his hand, his back, his neck. Oh, God, even his hair hurt.

His shoulder joints creaking like rusty hinges, he rolled over and managed to lift his head. There was Sarah milking Isabel. The woman looked fresh and rested and generally a hell of a lot better than he felt. He let his head relax against the ground.

He hadn't had much to drink, but that whiskey had sure loosened his tongue. God, he groaned inwardly, had he really told her the story of Herman Gerlich and that sorry stuff about the ranch? Well, no, he hadn't told her all of it, but more than he'd intended. She hadn't thought much of him before, so last night probably hadn't won him any points.

He rolled his head to the side and gazed at her again. Of course, his view was a little canted with his head turned that way, but there was no question in his mind that she was a fine-looking woman. More than that, though, he sensed a tender spirit dwelling within her. He'd felt it last night when she covered him with the blanket and touched his face. That realization just turned up the fire under the conflict raging in his heart and mind. Until he met Sarah, he'd never worried about doing the right thing. He'd just done what needed doing.

With considerable effort, Zach sat up. The mostly full whiskey bottle still stood next to the rock, its cork in place.

"Good morning." Her voice was soft.

Busily straining the goat's milk, she looked almost too pretty to be real, the folds of her skirt drifting gracefully each time she moved. This morning, she wore her hair tied back with a scrap of ribbon, its shiny length falling in a single cascade down her back. It reminded him of a pampered thoroughbred's tail, sleek and inviting a man's touch.

He glanced at the sun and rubbed his face. Damn it. Nothing like sleeping the day away. "You should have woken me up sooner."

She adjusted the cheesecloth over the funnel. "You were tired and needed the rest. How's your hand this morning?"

"Better," he lied.

She considered him with raised brows and a look that allowed him the exaggeration. "Really—well, that's good news. That bacon will be ready in a few minutes."

Zach pulled himself to his feet and went to the stream to wash up. Once he was upright he felt a little better . . . until he forgot his injured hand and bumped it against his leg. Searing pain flashed up his arm with an intensity that made him dizzy. The sky tilted at a sickening angle and he sat down hard on the gravel edge of the creek, grinding out profanities that would make a miner proud.

"Zach?" Sarah's voice sounded far away. He glanced up and saw her running toward him through the tall grass and late-blooming wildflowers, her skirts swishing against the serrated blades.

He didn't want her to find him knocked on his ass like some sissy. He plowed his good hand through his hair and struggled to his feet just as she reached him.

"Are you all right?" she asked, gripping his arm. Her quiet beauty, enhanced by the morning light, seemed to vanquish all his defenses and excuses.

"Yeah, I just . . ." He just wished he could rest his head on her shoulder for a minute, but he couldn't. He couldn't tell her that he was worn out and lonely and tired of struggling. "I'll be fine in a minute."

"Are you sure? You look a little peaked." Her hand remained on his arm, warm and gentle and strong.

Oh, hell, what was the use? He knew he wouldn't be able to do much in the shape he was in. Just the thought of wrapping lines around his hand to drive the wagon, even with gloves on, made his scalp prickle.

He gazed at the mules hobbled under the branches of a big oak, and then down at her. "Have you ever driven a team?"

"When you want them to go left, you say *haw!* If you want them to go right, say *gee!*" Zach sat next to Sarah on the wagon seat, his arm in the sling she'd convinced him to wear, and his thigh pressed against hers. She wore his leather gloves. They were huge on her and their shape conformed to his hands, but she needed some protection against the rough lines, and she had no gloves of her own.

"But what if I want them to go straight?"

"Well, say something like, 'Git up there,' and slap the lines on their backs. Go ahead, now, say it."

"Get up, there," she said and flicked the reins. Nothing happened. She looked at the stationary mules' rumps and then at Zach. "Why aren't they moving?"

He laughed long and hard. "Hell, girl, you've got to say it like you mean it. They probably think you're talking to yourself. Try it again, and slap those lines."

"Get up, there!" One mule shook his head and that was the only movement she saw.

Zach chuckled again, and looked out the other side of the wagon. "Maybe you should say *git* instead of *get*. They're mules, not scholars."

Oh, he was getting a big laugh out of this, wasn't he? she thought acidly. Sarah, accustomed to being the teacher rather than the student, felt her face grow hot with embarrassment.

"Git up, there!" she barked in her best schoolyard voice, and whacked the reins. The mules took off and the wagon lurched forward, catching them both by surprise. Zach uttered an oath and grabbed the edge of the seat with his good hand. Sarah leaned forward, planting her feet, and the whole business moved forward several hundred feet.

"Now, stop them."

Instinctively, she yelled, "Whoa," and pulled on the lines. The wagon came to a stop, and Sarah beamed triumphantly.

"Pretty good, pretty good," Zach affirmed, nodding. Then he made her walk the team around for a while, turning them right and then left.

This dress rehearsal gave Sarah no comfort. The whole vista of mules' rumps and the far horizon took on a completely different and more intimidating appearance with the reins in her own hands. Zach was beginning to look different to her as well, and that was even more disconcerting. Although his appearance today, unshaven and tired, was the roughest she'd seen on him, he was acquiring the comfortable familiarity of a normal man and losing the devilish proportions she'd first ascribed to him.

"All right, then," he said finally, "let's get going." Just as he spoke, Danny began crying in his bed behind them.

Zach looked back at the baby and then at Sarah. "What does he want?"

"Since his colic went away a couple of days ago"—she grinned like Lewis Carroll's Cheshire cat—"my guess is that his diaper needs changing."

That had been the agreement they'd reached. She would drive the team, and Zach would take care of Danny while she was doing it. It seemed a fair trade, especially since neither of them knew anything about each other's jobs.

Zach glanced behind him again, this time rather uneasily. "Diaper, huh?"

"Have you ever changed a baby's diaper?"

He made a wry face and sniped, "No, the opportunity never came up at the whorehouse or while I was laying track."

She set the brake as he'd shown her, and wrapped the lines around the handle. "There's nothing to it. You'll do fine." Gathering her skirts, she climbed over the seat, went to Danny's bed, and picked him up. As she suspected, he was wet.

Zach remained where he was. "Well, come back here, Zach. You can't do it from the seat of the wagon."

He stayed put. "Look, Sarah, I don't know anything about kids."

She put one hand on her hip. "So I should drive the team, do the cooking and washing—In other words, you want me to take care of *everything* while you sit back and watch me work."

"No, I didn't mean that. I just never learned how to take care of a baby."

She scowled at him. "Believe it or not, women aren't born knowing it either. And I certainly didn't learn how to drive a mule team in normal school! But I'm learning. You can learn too, can't you?"

He sighed. "Yeah, I guess." He followed her and sat back on his heels while she began the lesson.

She peeked inside the back of the baby's diaper, then laid him on a quilt where he kicked and cried. "He's just wet, so it's not too bad this time. I keep his diapers in here." She pulled a clean one from a small cracker crate and folded it into a triangle. "Take the wet one off him—it's pinned right there in front, see?"

Taking his hand from the sling, he struggled awkwardly with the safety pin, his face screwed up with the effort. "Now what?"

Sarah took the wet diaper and put it in a bucket to wash that night. Then she led Zach through the steps of putting the clean diaper on the baby, who thrashed his chubby legs and giggled. "All right, take it off and put it back on."

He shrugged. "What for? I saw how you did it."

She sat back on her heels too. "Have you ever taken a gun apart and put it back together?"

"Sure."

"Why?"

"So I'd know how to . . . oh, I get your point."

She smiled again. "You're a good student, Zach, even if you need convincing."

Now he was smiling too, and some of the exhaustion left his eyes. With a little fumbling he managed to unpin the diaper, get it off Danny, and then plant the baby's bottom in the center of it again. But before he had the chance to pull the corners together, the baby showered him with a geyser of urine.

Zach jumped back but not in time. "Jesus!" Danny gave him a wide, toothless grin, as if pleased with his accomplishment.

"Oh, no!" Now it was Sarah's turn to laugh. "Danny,

that wasn't very nice." Then to Zach, "Now you've been baptized!"

"This has happened to you?" he asked, obviously dumb-founded, plucking his wet shirt away from his body.

She laughed again, thoroughly enjoying the picture of tall, broad-shouldered Zach, the man who'd pushed her to her knees on the hotel stairs, literally brought to his own knees by a baby. "Yes, several times. You've got to be faster, but you'll learn."

She heard some grumbling, and then he said, "I'll take care of this. You get us going toward Helena."

She gave him a pointed look. "I'll wait until you come up front again. I found out you can stick yourself or the baby if you try to change a diaper while the wagon is moving."

By the time they stopped late that afternoon, Sarah was more tired than she'd ever been in her life. Slowly she sat down on an overturned keg beside the wagon, holding Danny in arms that shook with fatigue. A low groan escaped her when her backside made contact with the keg. God, she sounded like an old woman. Her shoulders and back ached from driving the team. Even her neck was stiff. She felt dirty and wished desperately for a real bath, in a real tub, and knew that nothing even close was available to her.

Zach was off taking care of the team. It was slow going for him now that he was reduced to doing the work with just one hand. He'd done a reasonable job of tending Danny, but in her heart she nursed a secret resentment that a day of closeness with her baby had been snatched away from her because of Zach's accident.

Above all, the irony of the situation was not lost on her: now she was forced to drive *herself* to the last place on earth she wanted to go. It seemed a little like making a condemned prisoner tie the hangman's noose for his own execution.

Sarah sighed and leaned her head against the wagon wheel, perilously close to tears. She certainly had the right to cry, considering her impending fate, but did everything she could to resist the urge. Her eyes burned and she squeezed them shut until the wave of emotion passed. If she fell apart now—well, she just couldn't. She had to stay strong to face the days ahead.

She looked out at the wide-open landscape, green and gold with a perfect blue sky hung above it, and for a moment wished with all her heart that she could just stop here and stay. Build a house, plant crops, raise her child in peace. Far away from her own troubles and those of the world, both grievous and trifling. Of course, it was out of the question, especially for a woman alone. And it was a silly daydream—she'd never thought of being a rancher's wife, out in the country and away from town. Lame Horse had seemed like the very end of the earth to her. She'd always loved the bustle of town life, especially in Helena where things were growing so fast.

Her memory carried her back, unwillingly, to promises whispered in soft, moonlit darkness by Ethan Pembroke, the man who would betray her. *I'll build you a grand house, Sarah, better than any you've imagined. We'll have a good life ... all of Montana will be at your feet.* The promises had been calculated lies, although she hadn't known it then. He hadn't needed to make those promises to lure her in—she had already fallen in love with him. Nor had she yearned for wealth or status. Still, the image he'd painted had intrigued her.

Now as she sat here relishing the late-afternoon hush, the idea of living in the country didn't seem so preposterous after all. Sarah had realized months ago that as long as a person had her dignity, it didn't matter if she lived in a boardinghouse.

She'd also learned that if she lost her dignity, living in a palace couldn't help.

When Zach came back to the wagon, he found Sarah asleep on a keg with the baby in her arms. She sat with her head tipped back slightly and resting against a wagon wheel. He couldn't help but stop and watch her. With the sun hitting her at this angle, her dark lashes and brows appeared to be dusted with gold. Her cheeks and lips were tinted the same color as the pink undersides of clouds at sunset. That rush of feeling, both physical and emotional, flooded Zach just to look at her.

With every passing day, she continued to amaze him. She was smart, she had grit, and she had courage. She'd driven that mule team today as though she had a lot more experience than just a few minutes' practice. No wonder she was worn out.

Zach, on the other hand, wasn't too sure how well he'd taken care of the boy. He hadn't been so nervous since the time he drove that nitroglycerine. One false move could mean disaster. As the day progressed, he'd gotten a little better at the diaper-changing. Well, at least he hadn't gotten peed on again. But one of the diapers had been so foul, he'd been tempted to put a bandana over his nose and mouth. All that had stopped him was his pride—he didn't want to look like he couldn't handle a woman's job. Sarah had just laughed again.

And feeding the baby—it had meant milking that mean-tempered Isabel, and he'd been puked on enough times to make him think Danny was sick with some horrible disease.

Sarah had assured him that all babies did that, and that the rocking wagon made it worse.

Smelling as bad as the goat, Zach had cursed his injured hand again. He'd taken off his stinking shirt as soon as they'd made camp and washed it in a bucket of water. He didn't bother to put on another—if he fed Danny again tonight and got puked on, it would be easier to wash himself off.

But he had to admit that he was fascinated, too, by this miniature human. A calf could stand on shaky legs soon after being born, but this little cuss was helpless and completely dependent on them for his survival. Zach had marveled at his tiny hands and feet with their little nails, and the huge blue eyes that watched him with equal interest.

Seeing Zach now, Danny smiled at him and began squirming on Sarah's lap. Although she had a pretty good grip on him, even in her sleep, Zach worried that she might drop him.

Carefully, as carefully as he'd loaded that nitro, he took the baby from her arms. "Come on, son, let's give your mama a little rest," he whispered. "We'll go get her something nice to look at when she wakes up. She's had a hell of a day."

Something was desperately wrong. Sarah moved in a dream world—she knew a malevolence lurked in the cold unknown surrounding her. It wasn't a fog or a mist or even darkness, and though she couldn't see through it, she knew that danger surrounded her. She bore Danny in her arms, trying to protect him and save them both, but the horrible Thing circled her. First it was behind her and then it was ahead of her—no matter which way she turned, it was there. And its sole purpose was to take her child.

Her heart thundered in her chest as she sought an escape

from this fearful place but could find none. Never had she felt so alone, so hopeless. Was there anyone here besides her and Danny and that which would destroy them? Up ahead she saw a brightness in the gloom . . . was it a friend, someone who would hear her call for help? The light grew brighter and she tried to run toward it, but her feet moved no faster than if she were wading through knee-deep molasses. Then suddenly her arms were empty and she was alone, the brightness gone. Sarah was alone in the nightmare world—

"Danny!" Her eyes flew open and she found herself where she'd fallen asleep by the wagon. But her baby was gone. Her dream had come true. Ethan was the malevolence and he'd taken him. *"Danny!"* Her scream bounced off the rock face of a nearby butte and swirled through the trees.

Zach came running across the field, carrying a bundle in his good arm. "Sarah!"

Sarah jumped to her feet, nearly hysterical and slightly disoriented. "Zach, oh, dear God, Zach! Danny's father came and took him!"

"No, it's all right—"

"We've got to find him!"

"No, no, honey, look!" He held up the baby, his badly pinned diaper sagging off one hip, his index finger in his mouth. He gave her a big, gummy grin.

She gaped at him, her sense of the nightmare receding. "Oh, my God!" She plucked the boy from Zach's strong arm. Clutching him to her, she sobbed once against his soft little neck. "I was having a terrible dream—Ethan was chasing us and I couldn't get away from him. And—and then I woke up and the baby was gone—"

"We were right over there." He pointed at a field of clover and Indian paintbrush.

She glanced at the meadow, then pressed anxious kisses to the baby's cheeks and soft hair.

Zach looked sheepish and gave her a self-conscious pat on the shoulder. "Aw, hell, I'm sorry, Sarah. I just took him so you could rest. I didn't mean to scare you."

She turned her gaze upon him, unable to keep the anguish out of her voice. "Zach, what am I going to do? How can I let him go?" She made a desperate appeal not for clemency, but for advice. She truly wanted to know how she could live without her flesh and blood, the child who had lain under her heart for nine months. This man had seen a lot more of life than she had. Maybe he had an answer.

But he only looked away, just as the men had in Lame Horse. Finally, he reached inside his sling and brought out a posy of pink wildflowers. "Um, we—Danny brought you these. I—he thought maybe they were prettier than the mules' behinds you looked at all day."

A bubble of laughter and tears swelled in her chest, looking for an escape. At last, the laughter won. She glanced down at Danny and jogged him in her arms. "You thought of that on your own, did you?"

The baby ignored the question and instead gripped a loose lock of her hair in his small fist as if it were the most intriguing toy he'd ever seen.

Hesitantly, she reached out to take the little bouquet from Zach and their fingers brushed. Only just now did she realize that he wore no shirt. "I'm surprised you found these so late in the season."

"Oh, I'm good at finding flowers." He stepped over to the water bucket hanging on the side of the wagon and sank the dipper for a drink. A trickle ran down his chin and neck, and Sarah let her gaze follow its path down his broad chest. It paused briefly on his flat belly and then continued on to the waistband of his jeans, where it disappeared. "When I was still living on the streets in the Mulberry Bend—"

Sarah interrupted. "You've mentioned that town before. Where is it? In Illinois?"

He chuckled, but there was no humor in the sound. "No, not in Illinois. And it isn't a town. It's a bend in a street, Mulberry Street. I guess it's the worst slum in New York. Life there is—" He looked at her and shook his head. "It's almost impossible to describe to someone who hasn't seen it."

He talked about rat-infested tenements—buildings that had been cut up into rooms, each no bigger than a line shack, where as many as four or five families, a total of fifteen or twenty people, lived and died. Some of the rooms were on inside walls and had no windows, and so no source of natural light or fresh air. Between the buildings ran a network of dark, narrow alleys that barely saw sunlight, even at noon on a summer day. Clotheslines strung between the buildings on every floor flapped with laundry seven days a week, the clean, ragged wash hanging on them a contrast to the utter filth and stench generated by boiling cabbage, dirt, garbage, and sewage.

Zach painted a graphic picture for Sarah of dying children, dead animals in the streets, a babble of accents and languages—Hebrew, Italian, Czech, German, English—and the misery of consumption, measles, poverty, murder, and starvation.

She could only gape at him. He was right, she'd never seen anything like that in her life, anywhere. She sank back down to the keg and put Danny on a blanket next to her, as engrossed by Zach's story as she was horrified. He sat across from her on the edge of the blanket and tickled the baby under the chin with a grass stalk gone to seed.

"The kids ran like abandoned animals. Some had families and some, like me, didn't. We didn't go to school so most of us couldn't read or write, and we all got by the best we could." He turned his eyes up to her. " One time, though, five or six of us pulled together. A bunch of us were pitching pennies in a hallway, and a man came out to chase us off, telling us that his wife was dead in their room and we should have some respect for the dead. He was heartbroken—you could just see it in his face, you know? He was crying and raging and so wild with grief he looked like he wanted to kill himself too. We couldn't help but feel bad for him. So we went out and started hunting for flowers. Even though it was summer, that was no easy job in the slums. Finally, we found some in a storefront window and begged for them. Not for ourselves, we told the owner. They were for the lady who'd died. I don't even remember what kind they were now.

"We carried them back to the tenement and knocked on the door. The man yanked it open, ready to kill us, until he saw the flowers. He let us file in and we put them in her hands. She looked old to us at the time, but I'd bet that she probably wasn't any more than twenty or twenty-five. Later that day the city hearse came and took her to potter's field on Hart Island in Long Island Sound. She was probably put in a common trench with a bunch of others in the Poor Burying Ground." He sighed. "But maybe they let her keep the flowers."

Already emotionally fragile, Sarah looked down at the pink wildflowers in her lap and her eyes filled with tears for all of them. For the dead woman, for herself, and for Zach. God above, no wonder he wanted his own land. He described a childhood that must have been conceived in hell. That he'd survived at all was a marvel. She would expect such a harsh beginning to show in his appearance.

But oddly, it didn't. He was strong and well built, with a handsome face and even, white teeth. The only hint of his early years sometimes showed in his eyes, in that peculiar, expressionless look they sometimes took on. She'd seen it the first day she met him.

Giving him a wobbly smile, she gathered her small bouquet and said simply, "Thank you."

That evening, after the diapers and dishes were washed, Sarah called Zach to her side so that she could change the bandage on his hand. He sat on the grass in front of her, and with her on the squat little keg, they were almost at eye level.

She'd hung a lantern on the side of wagon to work by. "Let me see how it's doing. Does it still hurt as much as before?" Cradling his hand in her lap, she untied the now dirty handkerchief and carefully unwrapped it.

"No," he said, and the lie nearly became truth. The touch of her soft, cool hands on his was tender and soothing, enough to make a man forget a lot of pain, both old and new.

"Then let's try to wash it." Leaning over, she filled an enamel washbowl with cool water and produced a cake of good white soap. Then she spread a towel across her skirt, wet and lathered her own hands, and took his very gently between them.

Zach bit back a profanity and even managed to avoid sucking in a breath between his clenched teeth, but he didn't fool her.

"I'm sorry, I know it's sore," she said. "I'm trying to be careful."

"It's fine," he ground out.

She did her best to avoid the actual wound and washed the rest of his hand, front and back. The slick, soapy touch of her fingers intertwined with his was the best thing he'd felt in a long time, better than a saloon girl's unimaginative ministrations in an upstairs room, even better than the eventual release brought on by those ministrations, and for Zach that was saying a lot. Despite the fire in the palm of his hand, for a fleeting moment he let his mind stray to the possibility of what that sweet, gentle touch would feel like on other parts of his body. It was an unworthy thought, he knew—what Pembroke was doing to Sarah was bad enough. But he was a heartless bastard who'd probably sell his own mother's soul to the devil if the price was right.

All Zach wanted was to feel close, not to just any woman, but to Sarah. He'd never forget what he'd seen and done in his life, but he sensed that she could take away the hurt that still surfaced when nights were too long and the memories too vivid. Circumstances being what they were, though, he knew he stood as good a chance with her as a rain cloud had in the desert during a drought.

She rinsed his hand by cupping water in her own hands and letting it run over his skin. After she patted it dry with the towel, she reapplied the carbolated petroleum jelly, the most painful part of the whole ordeal.

"Almost finished," she said, her head bent close to his as she worked. The yellow flame of the lamp cast a golden light on the rounded curves of her smooth face and long creamy throat. Her hair smelled like rainwater and flowers, and his mouth was close enough to kiss her ear. The picture of her standing naked in that basin, the very reason he'd burned his hand, pushed itself forward again. But if it had brought him this kind of delicious torture, it was almost worth it.

Jesus, just stop it, he told himself. He was being seduced by a woman's tenderness and the soft, mild night, one of summer's last. Overhead the stars were brilliant gems, twinkling and occasionally flashing across the dark blue sky as if shot from heaven's bow. The grass around them was as fragrant as new-cut hay, and his senses and emotions were bombarded—pain, pleasure, guilt, desire.

Finally, after what seemed like an eternity, she tied a clean handkerchief around his wound. "All right," she said, and looked up with a half-smile. His lips were an inch from hers, soft and full and there, and before the hand of reason pulled him back, he took them.

Sarah stiffened in surprise, torn by indignation and the most enticing sensation she'd ever known. All of her senses awoke—it was as if she could taste the scent of Zach and smell the tenderness of his touch as his mouth moved over hers. She could hear her pulse in her head and see the glow of the fire behind her closed lids. The kiss was brief, light, and then he pulled away.

"I'm sorry," he said immediately, and tipped his head down. "I didn't mean to—I'm sorry."

She didn't know how to respond. Propriety demanded that she erupt in a feminine fit of outraged modesty, but that wasn't how she felt. What she did feel was vague anger that after everything he'd put her through, and despite her kindness to him, he thought he had the right to take such a liberty.

And worst of all, she had liked it.

He'd already apologized, though, and his words rang with sincerity. Sarah's conflicting emotions frightened her.

Gathering her equipment together, in a cold, stiff tone she warned, "Don't do that again, Zach."

Then she climbed into the wagon and undressed for bed. Lying on her back, she stared up at the drying diapers hanging overhead. How could she have enjoyed the feeling of his mouth on hers when he was the very reason she was out here in the middle of nowhere? But she *had* enjoyed it, and she couldn't lie to herself. She'd enjoyed touching him. There had been his big hand, laid open and vulnerable in her lap while she tended his wound. She'd inhaled the scent of him, sage and male and even a faint whiff of Danny's talcum.

After her experience with Ethan, she had sworn that no man would get close to her again. At least not for a long, long time. She clutched the blanket in her fists—oh, God, she was actually developing an attraction for him. Just the memory of that kiss made her heart thump in her chest, and though she wanted to believe otherwise, she knew it wasn't from fear. It was because a voice in her head made her realize that she hoped Zach might kiss her again. From that her thoughts strayed to how he looked without his shirt, tall, straight, and broad across the shoulders and chest. Oh, how could she? Hadn't she learned anything from her experience with Ethan?

No, she resolved. It wouldn't happen again. It couldn't. There would be no more kisses, no more wanton thoughts, no more—*anything*. She rolled over and took her sleeping child into the shelter of her arm. Then she stared at the side of dark wagon, confused, annoyed, and lonely.

Chapter Eight

The miles continued to roll past, with Sarah managing the reins and Zach managing Danny. The countryside was beautiful, marked with hills that gave way to great expanses of grassland and shallow, pebble-lined rivers sparkling like fire under the afternoon sun. A steady, gentle wind, clean and fragrant, threatened the fragile, carefully mended canvas but it kept them cool too.

Secretly, she was rather proud of her improving skill with the lines. She maneuvered the mule team over areas that, for the most part, had no roads. They crossed streams and climbed low, grass-grown hills, and as the days went on, she turned to Zach for help less and less often. He merely pointed her in the right direction, always toward Helena, and demanded that she put more miles behind them.

Unfortunately, his skill at tending the baby kept pace with hers and the team, and a gnawing, white-hot jealousy, as fierce as a mother cat's, took hold in Sarah's heart. So fervent was her resentment, it blocked out any other thoughts and feelings she'd previously held about Zach.

How dare he? she asked herself every time she glanced over to see him patting Danny on the back, every time he made those ridiculous baby-talk noises, whenever he hoisted the child to his shoulder. Her emotions were in a greater turmoil than ever.

He didn't do things the way she would have, she grumped to herself. That diaper wasn't pinned exactly right, the front of the baby's dress was wet with drool—God, had Zach actually *kissed* the top of Danny's head? Nothing he did pleased her, and she had trouble hiding it.

What made things even worse was the fact that with each passing day, Danny looked less like her and more like his father. She swore she saw Ethan's face in her son's, especially when he was cranky. It seemed that fate had conspired against her in every way possible to take Danny from her.

One evening after they'd stopped to make camp, Sarah was coming back from a nearby river with a bucket of water. As she neared the wagon, she heard snatches of a peculiar one-sided conversation and a voice she didn't recognize. Zach and Danny were nowhere to be seen, but she didn't panic quite as easily now as she had that first time.

She put down the bucket and stole closer with her hands pressed against her skirt, trying to hear who was speaking in that high, improbable tone.

"Then the littlest of the three pigs asked, 'Who's been sleeping in my bed?' 'Not me,' Red Riding Hood said. 'I just came to see my grandma.'

What on earth? Sarah wondered. She crept around to peek inside the back end of the wagon. Inside she saw Zach with her best apron on his head like an Indian war bonnet, the ties secured under his chin. Danny lay in his basket and watched while the grown man gesticulated wildly.

" 'Well, *I've* been sleeping in your bed, little pig. And you, Red, I've been waiting all day for you! Where's my basket of goodies?' Grandma was mad as a wet hornet, no two ways about it, because she craved the hot cross buns that Little Red had brought with her. The pigs were pretty upset too. *Then* Papa Bear came home. 'Fee fi fo fum, what are all these strangers doing in my parlor?' "

Sarah stared in disbelief. Zach was a sight with the white apron flowing down his back like a veil, and she never would have suspected his hidden talent for mimicry. The tone of his voice alternated between his own, a cranky crone's, and the booming rumble of Papa Bear's.

She glanced at her son again and saw that he was utterly enchanted by the mixed-up story. She didn't know whether to laugh or cry. Zach was funny and engaging, despite the confused plots, but he'd taken one more step toward robbing her of the pleasure of mothering her own child. She hadn't had a chance to tell Danny any stories, or sing to him, or to experience all those other delights that mothers enjoyed. She'd been too worried, too busy, too distracted. And at the rate things were going, she wasn't going to get that chance either.

"Zach, I could use your help out here," she snapped.

He jumped, obviously unaware that she'd been watching him, and a red flush crept up his face when he turned to find her standing there. He quickly scraped the apron off his head and tossed it over a crate.

"Um, well, partner, looks like we've been found out," he said to Danny as he lifted him out of his basket. He carried him to the edge of the tailgate and put him in Sarah's arms. "Maybe we'll get a chance to finish the story later." He leaped down and prodded Danny's stomach. The baby waved his slobbery fists enthusiastically.

"I just thought he'd like a little—"

Stifling her resentment, Sarah turned to walk away while he was still talking. She knew it was rude, and plainly, so did Zach.

"Sarah—"

She waited, hating herself for her insecurity.

He caught up with her and gripped her arm, forcing her to look at him. "What the hell is eating at you?"

"I don't know what you mean." Her nose was up and she couldn't meet his intense hazel eyes for fear of what she'd see there.

"I think you do. You've been as pursed up as a mouthful of alum, and as cross as—"

"As cross as Grandma?" she supplied huffily, feeling awkward now too.

He narrowed his gaze and crossed his arms over his chest. "Yeah, I know I didn't tell the story right, teacher. If it hadn't been for that box of books I found in old man Gerlich's barn, I probably wouldn't know how to read much at all. But there weren't any fairy tales mixed in with the Dickens and Thackeray and Cooper. Sorry." The sarcasm was unmistakable and, regardless of the secret heartache she nursed, she knew it was deserved. Her hand fluttered over Danny's dress, smoothing, smoothing, looking for something to do.

"I'm not mad about the story."

"But you're mad. So it must be about the other night. I already apologized for that too, and I'm not going to do it again."

The kiss. Of course, that's what he was talking about. The memory of it had crept into her heart and mind a dozen times or more since it happened. It had felt . . . it had felt like her very first kiss, sweet, desperate, tentative. She didn't know why he'd done it—maybe because he thought she was a loose woman. And she hated herself for remembering it with any pleasure.

She let her gaze slide up the buttons on his shirt to his eyes. They had that odd, fathomless look that she so disliked. Reflecting only her own vulnerability back at her, it was worse than anger. Hastily, she shifted her focus back to the baby's head.

"No," she uttered miserably. "I'm not mad about that anymore. Not that one, at least."

"That *one*?" She heard a gusty sigh. "Well, goddamn it, Sarah, I'm not going to play a guessing game over this. If you've got a gripe, speak up. Otherwise, do me a favor and quit acting like a horse with a burr up your—under your saddle." His tone was as brittle and unfeeling as it was the day she'd met him.

Sarah was horrified to feel hot tears flood her eyes, especially when she worked so hard to keep her emotions under control. The words tumbled out. "You're trying to take my child!" She pressed her cheek to Danny's soft hair.

Another sigh, this one laced with impatience and bordering upon dangerous. "Haven't we been over this? You know all the reasons." He pointed in the general direction of his gear stowed in the back of the wagon. "I've still got that contract in there with your signature on it. You made the deal with the Pembrokes, not me, and that's what it all comes down to."

That was the last thing she needed to be reminded of, and she hated his choice of words. Deal. It made it sound as if she'd agreed to make a trade for a cow or case of preserves. "I'm not talking about my *deal*!" she lashed out. "I'm talking about you—spending all that time with my baby. Feeding him, changing him, telling him stories, *kissing* him!"

He pulled back as though she'd whacked his hands with a ruler. "Well, yeah—so, wasn't that what I was supposed to do? In other words, I'm taking care of him too well?" he demanded, angry and plainly baffled, his arms hanging at his sides. The low sun revealed a variety of colors that made up his dark hair—mahogany, chestnut, auburn—and picked up matching bristles in the shadow of his day-old beard.

"Yes! No—but he's my child and that's my job. Instead I have to drive the team, and at a pace that leaves not even a spare minute. You're so anxious to get to Helena and trade us for your precious land, you've got us traveling from sunup to nearly sundown. If there was a way the mules could see at night, I'll bet we'd never stop. You fixed it so I can't even have my last few days with Danny. You and—and that hand of yours." It sounded like such a feeble, petty complaint, even to her own ears. How could she find fault with Zach for his accident and then for taking good care of Danny? But it was how she truly felt.

"So it's my fault that I burned my hand? Jesus, what do you want me to say, Sarah, that I'm sorry I'm so clumsy?"

"It doesn't matter how it happened! It just did and now—" Her voice broke on the last word.

Zach's escalating anger fizzled away. Dumbfounded, he stared at Sarah, at the wind that tore strands of her hair from its ribbon binding, the dusting of freckles on her nose from days in the sun, her large green eyes swimming with tears. He might have seen a lot in his life but he hadn't expected to deal with a mother's jealousy on top of every other trial this trip had thrown at him. And yet, there it was, as plain as day. He supposed he could see her point. Sort of. In all his years, no one had ever cared enough about him to argue over who'd get to take care of him, so he had no real point of reference.

He let his shoulders relax and he rubbed the back of his neck with his good hand, feeling damned squirmy. "Well, hell, I was only doing what you told me to do." He held out a finger to Danny, who reached for it, but then with a look at his mother, Zach dropped his hand.

It was hard for him to admit, even to himself, that he got a kick out of looking after the boy. He liked the way the baby smelled—when he was clean, anyway—the soft feel of his skin, and the way his tiny fingers curled around Zach's own. He liked the way the boy's mother smelled too, and he hungered for her gentle touch again, like the night she'd brushed his face with her fingertips.

For a fleeting moment, he envisioned that ranch house porch again with these two waiting there for him at the end of a long day. He saw her at the stove, and Danny playing on the floor. He pictured Sarah next to him in his big bed, snuggling beneath warm quilts on icy-clear winter nights, and naked and beautiful in a shaft of summer moonlight, the breeze from an open window playing over her body. He clenched his jaw.

"Do you want me to drive the wagon tomorrow?" he asked, looking at her. His hand, although better, still ached with the layers-deep injury it had sustained. But if she was going to be this upset—

There was a pause and then she shook her head with obvious regret. "No. I know you aren't ready and if you got blood poisoning out here, it would probably kill you. I don't want to be responsible for that."

Zach watched her turn and walk away, feeling that he'd committed the worst offense of his life.

All right, Garrett, how bad do you want it? he asked himself as he stared at the stars overhead. How much did he want to hold a handful of soil from his own land and shake his fist at the sky in triumph? There had never been any doubt. He'd always wanted it very badly, and he still did.

But now, something new had become part of the picture. No matter how he tried, he couldn't get Sarah Kincade out of his head, and it scared him in a way that little before ever had.

He sat with his back against a wagon wheel, trying to doctor his own hand with the petroleum jelly and clean handkerchief she'd given him. He wasn't having much luck. The firelight was barely adequate, although he'd daubed the ointment on well enough. Getting the handkerchief on just right was another matter. Whenever he got the two ends ready to tie, they seemed to slip loose and the whole business fell off. Since Sarah was disinclined to offer help, he'd be damned if he'd ask for it. Unceremoniously, she'd dumped the items in his lap while he'd sat rechecking the numbers in his bankbook, glaring at him and downright shooting flaming arrows at the little double-entry ledger on his knee.

She was up there now, in the wagon. Not much shelter was left after they'd put the canvas back together, but she'd hung a couple of blankets to give herself some privacy. He could hear her brushing her hair and humming to Danny. It was an unmistakable sound—the whisper of boar bristles through long strands—and purely feminine, one he'd heard plenty of times at Lady Rose's.

He could imagine how she must look, with her arms raised gracefully to her head as she held the brush in one hand and her hair with the other. Her skin would be the smooth color of an apricot in the glow of the lamp, her shape womanly and gently curved. As beautiful as she'd been at her bath that afternoon he'd stumbled upon her. In his mind, she wore a low-cut chemise he'd once seen undulating in the breeze on her makeshift clothesline, laying bare to the night her long, slender neck and arms, and inviting him to press soft kisses to the column of her throat. To let him take her into his embrace, once and for all, to conquer her mouth with his own, and then strip away all the barriers between them and join his body to hers.

Zach felt a familiar arousal, hard and hot and insistent. He cursed himself for his train of thought and made the powerful effort to redirect his attention to his hand. Gripping one end of the hankie between his teeth, he tried to hold it while he attempted another knot. Damn it all, when had he become so clumsy? he wondered. He'd tied all kinds of knots to secure loads, haul sledges, and lasso animals, and now he couldn't even manage this simple task.

But he knew why. The reason was that the woman in the wagon behind him had *him* tied up in knots. That was the unvarnished truth of it, no matter how he tried to get away from it or put a different face on it. She was always in his thoughts, and regardless of how he justified his actions, he knew he was doing a lousy thing to her. He glanced down at his bankbook, still resting on his knee. All this time he'd had them pressing on across the prairie at top speed, worried about the poor time they were making, because he was so set on getting back to Helena and claiming his reward. He was still set on it. But . . .

A woman brushing her hair, the taste of a good sourdough biscuit or a drink of whiskey, the sound of crickets in the night—they were all simple things he had long ago begun to ignore because he hadn't had time for them. In letting them go, he'd lost something of himself as well, including his conscience. And now he was forcing Sarah to miss out on the simple act of mothering her baby.

The wheels that had set this trip in motion started rolling long before Zach came onto the scene. Eventually, it would advance to its predestined conclusion, with Sarah giving up Danny and Zach moving out to his ranch. Eventually. But maybe not right away.

With an impatient tug, he jerked at the knot in the handkerchief and tied the bandage in place. Then, tucking his bankbook inside his shirt, he stood and went to the rear end of the wagon, keeping his back turned to the opening in case he stumbled upon another intimate scene.

"Sarah, can I talk to you?"

The brush fell still and the humming stopped. "I guess." He heard the rustle of what he supposed were her skirts and she emerged from her little cubbyhole. "What is it?"

Venturing a glance, he saw that she was still dressed so

he turned to face her. But that didn't make this easier. In fact, it almost made things more difficult, as he looked up at her pretty face and smooth, loose hair in the firelight. He backed up and jammed his good hand into his pocket, then withdrew it. "Well, I've been thinking about what you said earlier."

She sighed tiredly. "I said a lot of things, but since none of them were about dollars and cents, I don't imagine they carried much weight."

He decided to rise above the comment. "I realized that you're right—since I burned my hand, you haven't been able to spend much time with your boy." He took a deep breath. "Look, I can't change what's happened, or what is to be. But here's what I can do. We can stop here for a while, if you want, or somewhere else along the way."

A puzzled expression crossed her features in the low light. "I don't understand."

"It's true, I've pushed us along to make good progress, and we've done some hard traveling. What I'm saying is that if you want to have some time with Danny before you have to give him—before we get back to Helena, we'll make camp for a while. It'll give my hand a chance to heal too, so that you won't have to drive anymore. And anyway, you can probably tell him better stories than I can. We've got enough provisions to last us for the extra few days, and the Pembrokes will still be there if we get back a little late."

She leaned toward him slightly. "Oh, Zach—really?"

"Sure, Sarah."

He saw so much gratitude in her eyes he wasn't sure if he was a hero or the lowest snake on earth.

Maybe he was a little of both.

"Ethan, I'm sorry . . . I just can't." Priscilla Pembroke lay in her bed, a slash of moonlight falling across her torso.

She looked like a nighttime still life done in grays and charcoals. Ethan, wearing a rich silk robe, sat on the chair next to the mattress and peered at her in the dark, since she would allow no lamp to be lighted. Disgruntled and tight-jawed, he drew on a slim cigar and watched the orange-red coal as it waxed and waned.

"Surely you're feeling better by now. You were in bed for days after the incident with the cat." He made no attempt to keep the impatience out of his voice.

She sat up, dragging the crisp linen sheet with her to cover her bare breasts. He had managed to get the night-gown off her unresponsive form, but that was where proceedings had come to a halt. "Yes, I'm better. I just had a bit of a headache tonight, that's all."

Headache—that's what Louisa had told him, too, when he'd encountered her just leaving this room a few moments earlier. She'd put Miss Priscilla to bed, she'd said, because she had a touch of a megrim.

Priscilla continued with an edge of distaste in her voice. "And—and I always feel a little timid when you, well, your touch is a bit rough—"

"Have you ever wondered why we don't have children of our own?"

"I suppose that providence has not chosen to favor us." Her words had a dreamy, wistful sound that only further irritated him.

"Christ, Priscilla!" He barely overcame the urge to throw the cigar to the floor and grind it out on the polished oak. "Providence has nothing to do with it. You can't lie there in your bed like a dying swan in a melodrama at the Ming Opera House. Where do you suppose the baby will come from when you turn me away?"

Ethan had no burning passion for his wife, but she *was* his wife, by God, and as such that gave him certain rights.

Even his father-in-law couldn't argue with that. Wooing virgin queens like Priscilla, or worse, Sarah Kincade, was tiresome to the extreme, and it was much easier to get what he wanted from the girls at Chicago Joe's or Belle Crafton's, his favorite sporting houses. Actually, he'd liked Lady Rose's the best, but he'd been barred from there after a tussle with an uncooperative whore.

Sometimes, though, it was just a damned nuisance to dress and go out, and why should he have to when his legal spouse was right here under his own roof?

The moon highlighted her hair with gray-white glints and caught the corner of her jaw as she turned her face away. "But we have a child coming now, if that roughneck Garrett ever gets back here with Sarah Kincade and the baby. Our baby."

"It's not *our* baby, yours and mine." He took cruel pleasure in the pointed reminder.

"Yes he is. It doesn't matter how he came to us. He will bear the name of Armistead Ethan Pembroke, and he will be our child."

For all that she was a practical woman in many ways, Priscilla had a stubborn, narrow blindness to certain realities that had only annoyed him in the past. He'd accepted it as part of her personality. Now, though, his suspicions made him question that blindness, nagging him to find answers that he might not want to deal with.

"Our child more than Caroline or Eleanor were?"

Her dark silhouette wilted visibly. "No, of course not, God rest their blameless souls. How I loved those poor little girls. I had such grand plans for them. They would have gone to the best schools and female academies. There would have been Paris and London. I miss them every day."

"What do you think was wrong with them? They seemed

healthy enough when we brought them home."

"Oh, Ethan," she pined, her voice full of bitter distress, "I've asked myself that a hundred times. A thousand. What was wrong? They had the best of care and attention. Little Caroline, baby Eleanor, both of them simply wasted away, unable to draw nourishment from their food. That constant flux—Dr. Nash was at a loss to treat it. None of the specialists he consulted could understand it either. They all said it was some abnormality of the bowels, or some mysterious contagion, but they couldn't do anything about it. I felt so helpless."

Although he'd absented himself from his wife and the daily goings-on of the foul-smelling sickrooms, Ethan remembered those days—Priscilla pale and anxious, wringing her hands, lingering over the cradles of first Caroline and then later Eleanor, barely sleeping or eating. After Dr. Nash had admitted defeat, at her insistence Ethan brought in a cadre of expensive medical consultants from Denver and San Francisco. They, too, had all shaken their heads in bafflement, and privately, she had dismissed them as incompetent fools. But they'd been very sympathetic and just as concerned for Priscilla as they were for the children, and she seemed to take great comfort from their attention. In fact, as each child worsened, she had needed as much care as the patients. And when the end came, she'd had to be sedated both times and required round-the-clock attention. Nash had expressed the private concern to Ethan that she might pine away to the grave.

On the face of it, Priscilla appeared to be an ideal mother, concerned to the point of collapse. Yet Ethan couldn't shake the sense that something was wrong. And if his darkest suspicions were correct, perhaps no child, adopted or of her own blood, would be safe with her.

The moon continued its trek across the night sky, and a

widening slash of light poured through the window, cutting across her bed. She drew up her knees and swept her unbound hair behind her shoulders. The gesture reignited Ethan's flagging interest. She could be a striking woman, he remembered. Sometimes never more so than when she was vulnerable. It was a fine line to walk—if he was too rough, she might withdraw completely. But occasionally, when he played his cards right—The idea of conquering her cool unwillingness further aroused him.

He rose from the chair and dropped the cigar into the pitcher that stood on her washstand. It extinguished in the water with a brief, sharp hiss. Then he returned to the side of her bed and unbelted his silk robe, letting the garment fall open. He stood in the moonlight to reveal his heavy erection to her.

"You know, Priscilla, you have certain marital obligations besides acting as my hostess."

She clutched the sheet to herself and eyed his body. He sensed her fear. His pulse pounded in his groin. "But Ethan, I—"

Savagely, he ripped the sheet from her hands, leaving her naked in her chaste bed. Her gasp of surprise filled the room.

"No more coyness tonight," he ordered from between clenched teeth. "Do you hear me, *wife*?" He lashed out a hand and grabbed her slim ankle, pulling her to the edge of the tall bed so that her thighs flanked his. She struggled to draw her knees up and close them, but he kept a firm grip on one leg.

"Then bring me my child."

"I *am* bringing you your child. Garrett is bringing him."

"He's taking too long, Ethan. He should have come by stagecoach or the train instead of by wagon. He should have been here by now." She relaxed her knees. "You could send a rider to fetch him . . ."

Reaching down, Ethan forced his hand between her legs and pushed two fingers into her tightly guarded femininity, eliciting a gasping shriek from her that probably reached the servants' rooms. He lifted a brow when he discovered her to be slick and moist. "Headache, was it?"

"Will you send a rider to bring the baby back on the stage?" she uttered between gritted teeth.

His pulse pounded in his brain. "Yes. Tomorrow."

She turned her face away and let her legs fall open. "Then do as you will," she murmured.

That was good enough for Ethan.

The next morning, Ethan shoved a sack of gold coins across the top of his polished teak desk to the rough-looking hulk of a man standing on the other side. "One hundred dollars, Bettinger, to find the baby. When you bring him back, you'll get another hundred. Get back within the week, I'll double it and throw in a nice piece of ranch land I hold the title to. Right at the base of the Rockies."

Everything in life was a matter of negotiation and bargaining, it seemed. Priscilla promised she would grant Ethan access to her bed every night between now and the time the baby arrived if he sent someone to look for him. She was a remarkably dull lover, but Ethan snapped at the bait like a trout. Why, he wasn't even sure.

"Yessir, Mr. Pembroke. You say Garrett and the woman are between here and Lame Horse?"

"They should be close to Helena by now—that's what I need you to learn. If you can't find them, report back here immediately. If you do find them, I don't care how you get the baby, or what you have to do. The *only* one whose safety I'm concerned with is my son's. Not one hair on his head is to be harmed. Do we understand each other?"

Bear Bettinger grinned at him, revealing teeth so rotten they were black. "I b'lieve we do, Mr. Pembroke. I b'lieve we do. I'll leave today."

"Good." He should have hired Bettinger in the first place, Ethan thought sourly, as he watched the hefty brute leave his study. He might be a bit slow in the head, but as far as Ethan could tell, he had even less conscience than Zach Garrett.

A valuable asset, to his way of thinking.

Chapter Nine

Sarah woke up, the sun bright against the thin blanket that she'd hung for privacy. Pinholes of light created a speckled effect over her, and she sat up with a start. It must be very late. Zach would make some smart remark and then nag her to hurry the team all day long.

But then she remembered—they were still camping. They'd been here for three days, and they weren't going anywhere today either. She could spend more time with her baby. Danny hadn't even woken her with a wet-diaper complaint or a call for a bottle. He was just now stirring next to her, probably as tired as she'd been. She flopped back against her bed of blankets and stretched. This was one of the few days since she'd run away from Bozeman that she had nothing to do. Well, she still had her cooking and washing chores, but there would be no driving again today. What heaven!

"Oh, how's my little lamb?" she crooned, taking the baby into her arms. He was wet but she hugged him to her anyway. "Oh, look! My little lamb has little piggies!" Cradling him, she took each of his toes in a gentle grip and recited the nursery rhyme about the piggies, talking about going to market and having roast beef. "And this little piggy went *wee, wee, wee,* all the way home!"

Danny giggled and Sarah did too.

But, much as she longed to lie there lazing the day away, they all had to eat and cooking was her job. She pulled on her clothes, changed Danny's diaper, and emerged from her little shelter with her apron. Although the sun was bright, there was a decided nip in the air that hinted at a crisp autumn and a cold winter yet to come.

That chill didn't seem to bother Zach though. He stood on the other side of their little camp, his shirt off, peering into a piece of mirror he'd propped on the shelf of a rock. His razor glinted in the morning light, flashing like a cavalry saber. Now and then, she saw him gaze off into the nearby hills, as if looking for something.

"Good morning," she called as she tied on her apron. It was the same one Zach had worn on his head, and despite how upset she'd been at the time, she had to smile at the memory. "I'll have breakfast ready soon."

Turning toward her, he gave her a little salute in acknowledgment, and she felt that odd quickening again, a slight breathlessness, just as she had the night he'd tried to kiss her. As she'd demanded, he'd never tried *that* again, thank heaven. The sight of his lean torso framed with muscles that embraced his ribs brought a delicious, frightening flutter of sensation to the pit of her stomach. She wanted to chalk it up to timidity at seeing a half-naked man.

But she couldn't, and she knew it.

Well, so what if he was attractive, she asked herself as she poured water from the bucket into the coffeepot. Some people were homely, others not—his looks didn't have to mean anything to her.

But they did, and she knew it.

Regardless of what lay in store for her in Helena, she and Zach would go their separate ways. He would have his ranch and she would have . . . emptiness. At least she would no longer have to worry about her confused, ambivalent feelings for Zachary Garrett. He would be out of her life. That would be good.

But it might not be, and she knew it.

The aroma of coffee had just begun to perfume the air

when Zach came to the fire, shaved and shirted. Plucking a tin cup from their small store of dishes, he poured himself a steaming cup. He glanced over his shoulder again.

"What are you looking for?" she asked. Using the wagon tailgate for a worktable, in an earthen bowl she whisked together flour, some sourdough, water, and salt to make splatterdabs, a rough version of pancakes her mother used to make. They took more time than bacon, but today she had all the time in the world.

He hunkered down, sipped at the hot coffee, and shrugged. His inky hair was wet from a morning dousing and the ends curled intriguingly against the back of his neck. "I don't know—I just have a funny feeling, like we're being watched from up there."

She followed the path of his gaze and looked into the beige hills but she found nothing unusual. "Have you seen someone?"

"No, not a soul. Like I said, it's just a feeling. But I think we ought to move on."

She stopped the fork in mid-whisk. "Move on! Zach, you said we could stop for a few days."

"We can still stop. I'd just like to do it somewhere else, on flatter ground out in the open."

"But you admitted that you haven't seen anything. And it's so pretty here. This little valley, all green and gold, with the creek running through it. There's Queen Anne's lace and sage and clover—"

He grunted, apparently unimpressed. "That stuff grows everywhere. Besides, none of it is worth risking our necks for." He shrugged, as if trying to push an unwelcome hand from his shoulder. "I just don't like it here."

She almost laughed. "If *I* told you I felt like someone was watching us and that it was my woman's intuition at work, you'd wave it off without a second thought."

He turned a sharp look on her. Then he grinned over the rim of his cup. "Yeah, I guess I might."

She pointed her fork at him. "Might! You know you would."

He glanced up at the hills again. "Okay, we'll stay. But I'm going to keep my eyes open, and I want you to do the same."

That afternoon, Sarah sat in camp, the baby in his basket next to her feet making fussy noises. Zach perched on a keg nearby and cleaned his shotgun. Her hands were busy with mending while she tried to soothe Danny at the same time.

Although part of him chafed at the delay he'd granted her, Zach had to admit that this was the most relaxing time he'd spent in years. And despite his misgivings, she was right—this was a pretty spot to make camp. A flat, slow-moving stream gurgled next to them, the grass-lined edges busy with grouse and the occasional prairie dog. At night, the stars overhead looked so close he swore he could put out a hand to grab one, and crickets and frogs serenaded them. It was all so different from Mulberry Bend, and even different from the Gerlich farm. It was *peaceful* here. The realization was downright surprising to him. Life for Zach had never been about peacefulness, or even peace of mind. It had been about survival. He glanced at Sarah's smooth, dark head as she took careful stitches, and knew that she and Danny had something to do with that sense of well-being.

Leaning over, Sarah adjusted the child's blanket, tucking him in more warmly against the light, cool breeze. "Hush, now, Danny. You've been fed and changed." The baby screwed up his face into an unsatisfied scowl and whined.

Zach dropped the rag he'd been oiling the barrel with

and stared at the baby's irritable expression, thunderstruck. "Jesus Christ!"

Sarah's head snapped up. "I'm sorry—you know he's really a good baby most of the time."

"It's not that . . ." His reply trailed off. Sometimes, when the light had been just right, or when a certain expression crossed the baby's face, Zach thought he'd seen a resemblance to Ethan Pembroke. He'd also thought it was a crazy idea, that he'd imagined it. But no, it was there in the kid's frown. It was there now, obvious and unmistakable.

His gaze shifted back and forth between Danny and Sarah, wishing he might find the answer to the question without asking it. But before his brain could rein in his tongue, he blurted, "Ethan Pembroke is that kid's father!"

It sounded like an accusation fired from a gun.

And Sarah sat frozen, like a doe caught in a hunter's rifle sight, her mouth slightly open. "W-what—?"

"I can see it in his face—it's right there in the way he frowns."

She looked down at the baby and back at Zach. Her own face crumpled—obviously she couldn't deny his words.

Now Zach understood everything. At least he thought he did. "So it's not about the money Pembroke gave you," he said quietly, looking at her ashen face. "He wants the baby—his baby."

She snatched Danny out his basket and clutched him to her, much the same way she had the day he first saw her in Lame Horse. "He's *my* baby."

His mouth turned down at the corner and he chuckled. "No offense, Sarah, but you weren't able to make him by yourself."

She gaped at him. He could see the heartache in her eyes, and worse, the shame, and he wished he could take back the cynical comment. He hadn't meant to make her feel bad, but of course, he had. Christ, it seemed like he was always apologizing to her, and for things that *she'd* done. "Oh, hell, I didn't mean—"

Her face was a rigid mask of anger. The baby howled in her arms, and her movements were tight and stiff. "Yes, Ethan Pembroke is Danny's father, and I curse him for it. But you don't know *anything*! You can't know. He wouldn't have dared tell you the truth. And I'm not going to because it's none of your business." Her eyes narrowed to furious slits. "You think I'm a whore, now, don't you?" she demanded. "That was why you kissed me that night."

Zach felt as if he'd pulled the lid off a box of hornets and stuck his head into it—suddenly, he was put in the position of defending himself. "No, I don't think you're a whore!" All right, he might have thought that before he'd met her, but he couldn't now that he'd gotten to know her.

"Oh, really? How else can it look?" Grief and remorse poured out in a torrent of merciless self-description. It was worse this time than the last, when she'd talked about her parents, so proud of their daughter. "A schoolteacher willingly lets a rich man seduce her, a rich, *married* man, and she bears his child out of wedlock! You tell me how it looks, Zach." Her breath came in hard, rasping gulps.

She protested that it was none of his business, but he had the feeling that she really wanted to tell him, tell someone, about what had happened. He put down the shotgun and rested his elbows on his knees, letting his hands dangle between them. "Well, why did you do it?" he murmured.

Her mouth fell open and then snapped shut again. "I told you, you wouldn't believe me." Danny's screeching tapered off to occasional snuffles.

"Try me."

Her voice dropped. "No. I can't. You're working for Ethan. I can't trust you."

That last remark hit like a punch in the stomach. It bothered him that she didn't trust him, but then, why would she? He *was* working for Pembroke, although he'd sincerely begun to wish otherwise. He leaned over to pick up the rag where it had fallen between his feet and idly turned it in his hands. Then hesitantly, he reached across the narrow space separating him from Sarah and touched her arm. "Listen, I've done some things in my life that I'm not so proud of. I admit that. But it wouldn't do me any good to keep kicking myself about them. It won't do you any good either."

She considered him with those green eyes, although she didn't pull away from his touch. "Maybe we all have our crosses to bear, Zach. But some are heavier than others."

He could think of no response.

Danny had fallen asleep in her arms, and she put him back in his basket. "I've got washing to do."

He loaded the shotgun and stood up, anxious to get away from the tense scene that he'd created. "I'll see if I can find some game for supper tonight."

She nodded and climbed into the wagon to gather the laundry. Watching her, he knew she was right. Some crosses were heavier.

With Zach off looking for fresh game to roast for their supper, Sarah sat beside her wash bucket, rinsing the last diaper of the day. Her skirt was soaked from the hem to her knees, and her chapped hands stung from constantly being in hot, soapy water. Still, as hard as it was to live out in the open with no decent shelter and no conveniences, she was grateful for these days that Zach had given her to spend with Danny.

Letting the diaper fall back into the bucket, she rose from her seat and looked over the side of wagon at the baby, who slept under the canvas canopy in his basket. Her heart swelled with love. Could there be a sight sweeter than a sleeping child? There was no guile on his face, no worry, and now, no resemblance to his father—only the tender innocence of babyhood.

She sat down again and plucked the diaper out of the water and began wringing it. So. Zach had seen Ethan in Danny's frown, something she'd hoped wouldn't happen. It galled her that the baby bore any resemblance to Ethan— an innocent child shouldn't be marked with the looks of a man who had such a black heart. God, she'd rather that her child take after Zach Garrett.

Her head came up when she realized the direction of her thoughts. What on earth had prompted such an idea?

Zach had. He rose in her mind's eye, tall, straight, and lean, more handsome than any man had a right to be. After her experience with Ethan, she swore she'd never put her faith in another man again. And yet, Zach, someone she had no reason to trust, or even like, had been honest with her from the first day she met him. He'd never pretended to be anything or anybody other than what he claimed—a mercenary with a personal mission. But there was more to him than that, she'd discovered. His beginnings had given him compassion, and while she'd resented him taking her place with Danny, she knew he'd developed an affection for the boy.

She would have hated to admit it until now, but Zach Garrett was a good man. And she hadn't been completely truthful with him when she'd said she didn't trust him. She did, up to a point. And she enjoyed being with him, re- gardless of the reason and their ultimate destination. He told her fascinating, harrowing stories about his childhood and youth. Some of them were even funny, and she realized that it was a miracle he'd survived with his humor and spirit mostly intact. Many people, she suspected, would have grown up to be cruel and permanently scarred, with no regard for human feelings or life.

His image still filled her mind's eye when she heard Zach's footsteps approaching on the hard-packed earth. Assuming it was him that she sensed on the other side of the fire, she didn't look up right away.

"How do, ma'am."

Sarah clapped her eyes on a stranger, a ragtag giant with a barrel chest and a round head. He swept her figure with tiny, dark eyes that were sunk deep into his fleshy face like two shirt buttons in a bowl of bread dough. His shaggy, short-cropped hair stood up like the dirty roots of an unearthed onion. He wore a gun belt strapped beneath the overhang of his belly, and the butt of the revolver gleamed dully in the afternoon sun. Everything about him bespoke danger. He nodded at the cold coffeepot sitting outside the fire pit. "I could sure do with a cup of coffee."

Startled, she froze, her throat suddenly as dry as parchment, the diaper in her hands halted in mid-twist. "There isn't any," she managed evenly. Although she kept her voice steady, a dozen thoughts bounced through her mind, and her gaze skittered around the campsite, searching for Zach's shotgun—no, of course, he'd taken it with him—for Danny, for Zach himself. She hadn't seen another human being since they left Lame Horse, and she sensed that this one did not mean well.

The drifter gave her a lolling smile that revealed teeth so rotten his mouth looked like a black hole. "Now, I know that ain't true. Last couple days, I've smelled it morning and evening since the wind's been right. I've been watchin' this camp from that high land yonder." He pointed to a tall, craggy hill some distance away. "I said to myself, Bear, you go on down there and see that woman. She looks like a mighty fine woman, and pretty too, with that dark hair. She wouldn't begrudge a man a cup of coffee. An' mebbe a little something to eat." His tiny, close-set button eyes traveled over her again from her hair to her feet and back. "I worked up a powerful appetite studyin' you."

So Zach had been right when he'd said he felt as if they were being watched. Dear God, where was he now? The plains beyond seemed as huge and desolate as the biblical valley of the shadow of death. She was in trouble and she knew it. Calm, stay calm, she told herself, even though her heart pounded so hard she could feel it in her throat.

"If you noticed the coffee you must have also noticed my husband," she replied carefully, sounding much steadier than she felt. She barely realized the title she'd given Zach. "I'll call him so you can talk about this with him."

He shrugged and waved off the suggestion. "Hell, he ain't your husband, not 'less you married him in Lame Horse. Anyway, he won't be back anytime soon. Maybe not at all."

Lame Horse. Convulsively, she squeezed the diaper. "What do you mean? Who are you?"

"Oh, I tracked him down while he was huntin' game. Got himself a nice rabbit for your supper, he did. I snuck up on him in that wash down there and gave him a right smart wallop on the head. I got a little Injun blood on my ma's side—I can creep up on a man without makin' a sound." He seemed to be waiting for her to applaud his talent and his deed. Sarah could only stare at him in horror, but he laughed amiably, as though he were reporting good news that she'd been waiting for. "He wasn't movin' when I left him, and I don't think he was breathin'. But leastways he won't be botherin' us any. I walloped a few other skulls in my day, 'cause they laughed at me on account of I'm slow in the head. Some of 'em got up again, and some didn't. So," he said, rubbing his hands together, "it's just you an' me."

"Who are you?" she repeated.

"Why, I'm Bear Bettinger," he replied, as if surprised that she didn't already know. But the name suited him—he was a ragged bear of a man, and looked as dangerous as a grizzly. "Mr. Pembroke paid me to track you down. I guess he didn't think that Garrett was gettin' you and the boy to Helena soon enough. But he'll give me an extra reeward if I bring the baby home within the week. And I intend to do just that."

Think—*think!* she commanded herself. Desperately she lied, "We aren't the ones you're looking for. I never heard of this man Pembroke you mentioned. Zach is my husband and we're making our way west to—to Idaho. We're going to ranch there." Sarah swallowed and swallowed, but if anything, her throat was more papery than ever. Dear God, was there no end to what Ethan would do? *"Zach!"* she shouted. "Zach, there's someone here to see you!"

Bear shook his head and laughed again. "I'm tellin' you, lady, that man ain't comin' back. Anyways, I know Zach Garrett—me and him worked at the same copper mine for a spell. You're the one he was lookin' for and the one I found."

A horrible feeling of a recurring nightmare swept over her. "And how will we be getting to Helena, Mr. Bettinger?" She asked the question, not because she really cared, but to stall him while she groped for a plan, any plan.

"Not *we*, ma'am. Just me and the boy. You'll only slow me down. I've got a horse waiting up in the hills and I'm gonna ride like hell for the train line south of here. At a gallop it shouldn't take me more'n a few hours. I'll be back in town before you can say lickety-split."

Sarah tried to swallow the painful knot forming in her

throat. Surely it was her heart . . . "How did you plan to feed my son?" she asked. "Babies eat every two or three hours."

He waved off the information. "No need. He'll do fine for a few hours till we make the train."

Her stomach fell to her feet. She had to do whatever it took to protect Danny. Remembering from her teaching experience that height commanded respect, she rose from her seat, picked up the coffeepot, hoping for the perfect chance to "wallop" *him* on the head. She kept the pot close to the folds of her skirt to hide her trembling.

"I want you to leave," she said with far more bravado than she felt. It was a futile order, but she had to try. "Right now."

"Oh, no, ma'am! You and me, we're gonna have a fine time here first." His peculiar affability frightened her more than downright hostility would have. "Mr. Pembroke said he didn't care what I do to you or Garrett, just so's I bring back that boy. So I want to have a good, long look at you before I go. Up close. You peel off them duds."

Outrage made her snap out the first thing that came to mind. "I will do no such thing!" Lunging forward, she swung the coffeepot toward his head with all the force she could muster, but he deflected her arm with no effort. Then he wrenched her weapon from her hand and lobbed it into the brush.

The black-toothed smile faded and he drew his gun. "Don't do that again." He stepped over to the wagon and looked in. He picked up Danny with one meaty paw, like a grizzly plucking a salmon out of a river. The baby waved sleepy fists and made protesting noises at having been awakened so rudely. "Now, you'll do as you're told, ma'am, or I'll put a bullet in your head and take this young'un of yours. You won't never see him again, ever, 'cept maybe in the Promised Land. I'm gonna have my way with you, and it's either gonna be easy on you or hard. Don't make no difference to me. It might to you though."

Sarah's heart stopped in her chest as if gripped by an icy fist. Oh, God, what an idiot she was! Zach had wanted to move their camp to an open place but she'd said no, that this was a pretty spot to rest for a few days. Why hadn't she listened to him? And where was he? Lying in a ditch someplace with a critical injury? Or—or worse? She couldn't bear to think about him being dead, not now, not on top of this crisis. If she did, she wouldn't be able to keep her own wits about her, and she needed them now like never before.

Groping at a passing thought, she offered, "But what about that meal you wanted? Nothing is ready, but it wouldn't take long at all to get some beans and bacon going."

Bear actually seemed to consider her offer for a moment, but then he shook his head. "Nope. I got my druthers, and I want my fun first. So get to it. Oh, and untie your hair. I want to see it loose."

She looked around wildly, searching for another weapon, an escape route, anything to rescue her child and stave off this horrible inevitability that she faced. Strangely, the sound of everything was muted in her ears except the sound of Danny's fussing and her thundering pulse as it rushed blood through her head. No birds twittered, the nearby stream moved silently over its rocky bed, and even the wind that fluttered through the grass made no whispering noises.

"Come on, lady. I ain't got all the time in the world. And neither do you." Bear waved the revolver at her with one hand and jogged the baby on his other hamlike arm as if he were an indulgent, jovial uncle. She wanted to scream at him to put her baby back in his basket, but thought better of it.

With hands that shook, she reached up and pulled the scrap of ribbon holding her hair back.

His button eyes seemed to gleam. "Shake it out now."

Furious, she shook her head and viciously raked her fingers through the long, dark strands.

"That's right pretty," he commented, and then to Danny, "Your mama has nice hair, don't she, boy? And I bet she's got smooth skin too. Let's see what's under them clothes." He lowered his lardy butt to the keg that Zach had last occupied, keeping the gun trained on her. When she made no move to comply, he ordered, "Go on, ma'am. I'd hate to have to shoot you in front of your kid, here." He was grinning again, sending another shiver through Sarah.

Her fingers were cold and numb, and she fumbled ineffectively with the buttons on her bodice. To her horror, she found Bear enjoying what he seemed to believe was a coy display. "That's real nice," he murmured, a faint sheen of sweat on his pumpkin-round face. "I saw a dancin' gal in a Fort Worth saloon one time—she took off her clothes the same way. Slow like. Say, we ain't got any music, but you could shimmy some like she did. And smile too."

Sweet Jesus, this was too much! Sarah thought. Fury and fear warred within her. "I don't dance."

He cocked the revolver and lifted it a bit higher. "That's all right. I ain't picky. Now *shimmy,* goddamn it!"

With no options coming to her frantic mind, Sarah dragged her way through a disrobing that gave her one more reason to hate Ethan Pembroke with every ounce of energy she possessed. While she swayed more like a scarecrow in the wind and less like a siren, she divided her attention between the filthy oaf before her, Danny, still on the man's arm, and the perimeter of the camp, hoping for deliverance.

When she was down to her mended drawers and thin camisole, and trembling with rage and humiliation, Bear put Danny back into the wagon. "Now, then"—he grinned again, displaying his rotting teeth—"we're gonna have us a good time." He stepped closer to her and she saw his stinking open mouth coming toward hers. At the same time, his beefy hand gripped the strap of her camisole and pulled it down to her elbow to expose her breast.

"Keep your hands off me, you dirty pig!" Automatically, her hand lashed out and she slapped the man's coarse, bristled face with all the strength she could put into her arm.

Neither her comment nor her action met with Bear's approval.

After recovering from his obvious surprise, he grabbed her upper arm and squeezed so hard she feared he would break it. Then he shook her as if she had no more substance than a rag. "We was gettin' along just fine! Now, bitch, I'm gonna show you what happens when I get mad."

He flung her to the ground. She landed hard on her side, the wind knocked out of her. Small rocks and dirt gouged her bare arm and tore into her underwear, and her loose hair blinded her. She tried to scramble beneath the wagon, but Bear hauled her back by her wrist, further scraping her skin. Then he retrieved Danny from his basket, putting the baby on the ground next to her. Sarah snaked out an arm to grab him but, before she could, Bear stepped on her hand with his full weight. She couldn't suppress the loud moan of pain that escaped her throat.

"Keep still, damn it!" He transferred his boot squarely to her stomach, and fumbled with his belt buckle.

From Sarah's viewpoint, all she could see between the locks of her hair was a big foot pinning her down, a huge

belly, and what he brought out from beneath it. Every
gnawing fear she'd originally had about Zach was coming
true now with the arrival of this despicable fiend, increased
a hundred times over. She could do nothing to protect
Danny, or keep Bear Bettinger from taking him. Escape
was impossible at the moment, and even if it became possible, it might not do her or her child any good.

All she could hope for was insensibility, and the uncertain desire to live through what was sure to be the worst
event of her life thus far.

Chapter Ten

Zach rolled onto his back and opened bleary eyes to wispy clouds overhead. The moon rode across the afternoon sky as a duo, two pale, slim crescents, side by side. After a moment, the moon became one again, and he realized that his head ached as if he'd been kicked by one of the mules.

God, what the hell had happened? He hadn't simply fallen, he felt pretty sure about that. He'd been out here, hunting game so they could have fresh meat for supper. His memory sharpened. Yeah, that was right, he'd gotten a rabbit and was busy dressing it out. Then . . . and then he'd seen a man's shadow fall across his own, and before he could react he'd been whacked on the head. Why, he had no idea. Who had done it was as big a mystery.

With a leaden arm he reached up to touch the crown of his head and winced. Dark blood stained his fingertips, but he counted himself lucky to be alive and conscious again, considering how hard he'd been hit. Then he touched a tender place on his cheekbone, where he must have scraped the hard, dry earth when he'd landed.

With some effort and an audible groan, he sat up and looked around. The world tilted sickeningly a couple of times before it settled into place. He was still in the dry creek bed. His shotgun lay next to him where he'd dropped it, and a few feet away was the big jackrabbit. Slowly, he rummaged through his pockets, expecting to find himself stripped of every possession and dime on him. Nothing was missing. His bankbook, his money, everything was still there. If he hadn't been robbed, what had been the point of the attack? What kind of cowardly son of a bitch stole up behind a man and nearly cracked open his skull for no good reason?

Suddenly and unbidden, Sarah flashed through his mind. Sarah alone with Danny back at camp, where Zach had felt the eyes of an unseen danger in the hills, watching them.

He had to get back. The wagon was about a mile east of here, and he had no horse to carry him. He'd have to run for it. Mortal fear filling his chest to compete with his galloping heart, he lurched to his feet and spots burst before his eyes like the champagne bubbles at Lady Rose's. He staggered around for a moment as he worked to get his bearings. Finally, his vision cleared and he risked leaning over to pick up his shotgun. Then he checked his rounds and reloaded. He could see the camp from here, although in his condition it seemed as far away as that crescent moon overhead. But Sarah and the baby could be in one hell of a fix, and she didn't even have a gun. Of course, as far as he knew, she couldn't fire one anyway. If Danny was threatened, though, Zach was certain she'd put herself between him and any danger. Maybe get herself killed. God, he had to get back to them. He took a couple of tentative steps, then set off loping across the plain back toward camp, every step thundering up his spine to his skull.

Why hadn't he followed his own instincts? he cursed himself as he trotted over the yellow grass and silver-gray sage. He should have insisted on moving to a safer place instead of listening to Sarah's praise of the natural beauty of the trees, the babbling creek and wildlife, and all that other schoolteacher bunk. He supposed he'd wanted to please her, a stump-dumb thing to do.

Women . . . they could throw a man off and get him to do something that was in no one's best interests. He dragged a forearm across his sweating brow, his lungs burning with the exertion, his head pounding like a hammer on an anvil. There wouldn't be any more indulging her, he determined. They were going to do things his way, god-damn it. He was the man—he was in charge, and if she didn't like it, that was just too bad.

If only she was all right . . .

But when he neared the camp, his anger congealed into worry. There was the wagon, but the abbreviated canvas blocked his view of whatever might be happening on the other side of it. Quietly, he slipped up alongside, using the cover as a screen, taking careful steps and listening as he went.

"See this here? This is Big Charlie. Big Charlie's made women faint when they seen him. You'll like him fine. Or I'll shoot this young'un of yours."

Zach knew that man's voice from somewhere. And Big Charlie—he'd heard that before too, and there was no question in his mind as to what it meant.

Swiftly, he crouched to look beneath the wagon bed be-tween the wheels to determine which direction the man faced and how many other enemies he might have to deal with. He saw just two big, booted feet, one of which pinned Sarah to the ground. She was stripped to her underwear, and the shoulder of her camisole had been torn off to reveal a smooth, round breast.

Rage, hot and volcanic, bubbled up within Zach so that he could think of nothing but revenge. He gripped the shot-gun until he felt joints pop in his hand, and the pain in his head was forgotten as he struggled against the fury. He had to keep his wits or he wouldn't be able to help Sarah. If he did something dumb and reckless like charge in with the shotgun blazing, he'd probably get himself killed, leav-ing Sarah alone. Defenseless.

He had to act fast though—Big Charlie's owner wasn't

going to wait. Sliding around the wagon so that the man's back would be to him, Zach got a glimpse of the bastard. Like a fool, the man's pants drooped halfway down his legs, and his big, hairy ass hung out for all the world to see. But he held a revolver on Sarah, and there was nothing ridiculous about that. It was personal now. Still, he wouldn't shoot a man in the back. Zach wanted the son of a bitch to see who shot him, face to face. He drew a deep, steadying breath.

"Hey!" Zach barked, his shotgun leveled on his enemy's head.

Startled, the other man turned, his near nakedness making him look even more ridiculous.

"Zach!" Sarah cried, her voice high with terror.

Zach had no time for her at this moment. All of his attention was focused on his enemy and whatever he needed to do to defend those he'd come to think of as his responsibilities. "Bear Bettinger," he said, hiding the shock of recognition. He glanced down at the man's privates, nearly buried beneath the belly that obscured them. Now he remembered hearing Bettinger use the reference before. Until now, he'd never had any desire or opportunity to see if the name was accurate. Zach smiled. *"This* is Big Charlie?"

Bettinger sputtered, lifting his pistol to aim at Zach's head as he struggled to drag up his pants at the same time. Zach's fury controlled to a low hum in his head, he shot the man's gun hand, which exploded with a spray of red.

Sarah screamed and Bettinger yelped, his pants falling to his knees again. The gun went flying into the brush, and Sarah grabbed Danny and rolled beneath the wagon.

The wounded man gaped at his hand and then at Zach. "Garrett, you son of a bitch, look at my hand!" Blood ran from the shattered limb. "Look what you did to my hand!"

Somewhere, Zach heard Danny crying but he ignored it. He pumped another shell into the chamber. "Back away now, or I'll start blowing off parts of you, one at a time." He grinned again, feeling a macabre humor. "I'd go for Big Charlie first, but I just can't see him."

The other man yanked up his pants again and got them fastened this time, leaving bloody smears all over the denim.

"What are you doing here, Bettinger?" Zach took a step forward. "Raping women and bushwhacking—aren't they a little low, even for you?" He remembered that what the man liked more than anything was a drink of whiskey, a plump, loud saloon girl, and a chaw. Zach wouldn't have considered him harmless—he'd seen Bear start deadly fights over good-natured insults. And he was disgusting—he smelled like a dead cow, and those rotten teeth, God! But stalking and attacking chosen prey were beyond his limited abilities. Or so Zach had thought.

"Damn it, Mr. Pembroke sent me to finish the job that you started, and I aim to do just that!"

Zach focused sharply on the ugly man's face and advanced on him, his shotgun held close to his shoulder. "He sent you here to crack my skull and rape Miss Kincade?"

Bettinger had to back up. "He sent me for the kid. He said you're takin' too long, and that he don't care what I do to either one of you just so's I bring the brat. He give me a hunnert dollars and promised me another hunnert and a ree-ward if I get back by the end of the week. And I want it, goddamn it! That piece of land would be mighty nice."

The cold in the pit of Zach's stomach turned icy. "What piece of land?"

"Like it's any of your business," Bear grunted, trying to wrap his ruined hand in a dirty bandanna. "It's over near the Rockies. I got me a hankerin' to live there, maybe even start a little ranch. And I will too!"

His land. Pembroke had offered Bettinger Zach's ranch, just as he'd offered it to Zach himself, like a whore angling for the best price. Zach glared at him, so enraged it took all his willpower to keep from blowing the man's head off and mashing his boot into the remaining stump of his neck. But despite what Bear had done to Sarah and him, Zach realized that his true anger, and the blame for what had happened today, lay squarely on that double-crossing bastard, Ethan Pembroke.

"That's *my* ranch, you sorry son of a bitch, and you'll never live there. Unless you walk away right now, you'll never live anywhere again. I'll shoot you so full of holes, you won't even make good crow bait. Then I'll ship you back to Pembroke's front door."

"You ain't part of this anymore, Garrett! And I ain't walking away."

"If you don't, I'll blow a hole in your leg and you'll crawl." Zach knew it would be lower than a snake's boot heel to take advantage of a slow-witted, unarmed man with a wound, but Bettinger was pushing him to the limit. And anyway, he'd left Zach for dead out there in that wash.

After a tense moment of locked gazes, Zach saw angry frustration in Bear's tiny eyes. Then suddenly, without warning, the big man dropped to his knees and made a swipe at Danny where Sarah hid with him under the wagon. Unbelievably, he had the boy's leg in his massive, uninjured paw and was pulling him out. Sarah screamed and pulled just as hard, kicking at her child's kidnapper with her bare feet.

It all happened so quickly, Zach reacted automatically and without thought. He had one clear shot at Bear Bettinger's head and he took it. Fire exploded from the shotgun's barrel and the man toppled over sideways, like a fir tree felled in the woods, dragging Danny with him. The hole in his temple oozed blood and brains, and the baby's leg remained clutched in his death grip.

As Zach ran to Sarah, she scrambled out and pried open the big fingers to release Danny. Her face was pale and fixed, her hands smeared with Bear's blood, her breath coming in wheezing gasps. He kicked the dead man's hand away from her and dragged them both from the grisly scene. Danny wailed at the top of his lungs. Still gasping and clutching her child to her, Sarah twisted her head to stare at Bettinger's body.

He took her by her shoulders, unnerved by her wild, staring expression and her rigid stance. She felt as stiff as a store window mannequin. "Sarah! Are you all right?" She didn't respond. *"Sarah!"* He shook her lightly. "Did he hurt you?"

Finally she dragged wide eyes up to his. "Oh, Zach," she uttered, her face a mask of terror. Her breath came faster as reaction set in. "Dear God, Zach!" She began to shake as if she stood in a Montana blizzard.

"Are you hurt?" Now that he was closer, he could see a bruise on her face and various scrapes on her pale arms. Her thin underclothes were ripped and grass-stained. The child in her embrace hid her bare breast. Damn it, Zach thought again, he should have listened to his instincts and moved them when he'd wanted to, before Bear Bettinger could come down from the hills to carry out Ethan Pembroke's dirty little orders.

Orders that weren't much different from the ones he'd hired Zach to complete.

"Is Danny hurt?" He looked at the baby's leg, and although the tender skin was a bit red from Bear's rough grasp, it seemed fine.

Sarah gave him a frantic once-over as well. "N-no, I don't think so. Zach, he told me you were dead. He told me he killed you and—and he was going to—if you hadn't gotten here, he—" She pushed lamely at her disheveled hair with a trembling hand.

He put an arm around her and drew her against himself. "I know. It's okay, he can't hurt you now. He can't hurt anyone."

Sarah sagged against Zach's tall, straight form, allowing herself a moment of exhausted weakness. She took a small measure of comfort from his unyielding strength, and despite her confusion and panic, she noticed the smell of him, clean and male, and took comfort from that too.

Would her life ever be sane again? she wondered. These things that were happening to her—nothing had prepared her for them. To be standing here in the middle of a wilderness, in torn underwear that barely satisfied modesty, a dead body mere feet away, and the man who at once served as her captor and her savior holding her in his arms . . . these were events that nightmares were made of, not daily living.

Most of her life she'd been strong and decisive, but lately she'd found herself powerless, at the mercy of men who all wanted something from her. She could be strong for Danny. For herself, though, she felt she had nothing left.

"Let's get the hell away from here," Zach said grimly next to her ear.

She nodded and hoisted the baby higher on her hip.

"Will you have more roast beef, Father?" Priscilla signaled her serving maid to present the platter of rare meat to Armistead Driscoll. She was cool and lovely at her place at the table, dressed impeccably in pearlescent rose taffeta, with not one hair out of place. Yes, if nothing else, she was a very satisfactory hostess, Ethan reflected again.

The old man waved off the girl and leaned back in his chair. "No, no, I've had plenty, my dear. It was a wonderful meal, as always." White-haired and white-bearded, he reminded Ethan of a bald eagle when he turned an inquisitive eye on him. "What I'd really like is to talk business with you, Ethan."

Ethan swallowed the starchy lump of potato in his mouth and chased it down with a big gulp of wine. He sensed this wouldn't be a typical or enjoyable conversation.

Priscilla pushed her own chair away from the table. Her skirts rustled pleasantly. "Well, I'll say good night, then, and leave you gentlemen to your discourse. Amy, you'll serve the coffee and brandy in the study, please?" Ethan watched her go, wondering if she'd let him into her bedroom again tonight. She was not an exciting lover, or even an interesting one. But there was something about the idea of accessing that sanctuary and breaching her cool, smooth, marblelike façade that made the blood pound in his body.

The serving girl bobbed a quick curtsy and backed away into a corner of the dining room, making herself as properly inconspicuous as possible as Ethan and Armistead made their way past her and down the hall.

"Ethan, have you had any luck finding the Kincade woman?"

He'd known the subject was bound to come up when Priscilla had told him her father would be joining them for dinner. From the glint in the old man's eye, he sensed that Armistead viewed Sarah's escape and continued flight with the boy as evidence of a bungled failure on Ethan's part. He waited while the serving girl, who had appeared as quietly as a cat, brought a tray of coffee and brandy. She left, pulling the doors closed behind her.

Ethan poured the brandy himself and handed a short-stemmed glass to his father-in-law. "I've got two men on Sarah Kincade's trail. One of them is accompanying her. I've sent the other as a backup. I expect to have her in Helena by the end of the week."

Armistead settled himself into one of a pair of deep leather wing chairs by the fireplace. "By God, she'd better be here. My brother didn't want to sign that court order, you know. With elections coming up, he was afraid word might get out that he'd struck a blow against motherhood and all that nonsense, and jeopardize his cozy seat on the judge's bench. It took a lot of reassuring to convince him that I'll see that his reelection is in the bag." Armistead inhaled the aromatic fumes of his brandy. "Priscilla needs and deserves to be a mother, Ethan, despite those earlier tragedies. Maybe even because of them." He shook his head. "Such warmhearted, motherly devotion. She wore herself out over both of those children, learning everything she could about their conditions. I swear she knew more than those idiot doctors. Sat by their beds every waking moment—the best nurse I've ever seen. She even had to be put to bed herself that one time."

The seed of doubt that had begun growing in Ethan's mind sprang forward now. "Yes, I remember. Oddly, while she was away from Eleanor, the doctors said the child seemed to get better. Then when Priscilla insisted on getting up to be with her, she grew worse again."

"Bah, doctors!" Armistead carped. "What do they know? You just get my girl a baby, Ethan—" Here the old man bent a riveting, knowing eye upon him. "That is, since you haven't been able to give her one yourself."

Ethan clenched his jaw, and his face grew as hot as the coals in the fireplace. What would the old man say if he told him his "girl" was a cold, unresponsive prude who made him bargain his way into her bed and seemed to be deliberately obtuse about how children actually arrived?

But he couldn't say that. He couldn't say anything to his father-in-law.

Ethan's project, the wonderful hotel he planned, was to be his alone, an accomplishment that would allow him to stand on his own two feet and out of Armistead's shadow. But he needed to remain in the man's good graces to see it through to completion.

The three of them—Ethan, Priscilla, and her father—were locked in a dance that involved too much money, too much power and influence, for Ethan to jeopardize.

Armistead held out his glass for Ethan to refill. "Maybe you'd better ride out and see what's happened to that woman and baby. Too much is at stake to trust the riffraff you've hired. Priscilla is looking quite wan these days. I'm worried that she's pining away for want of a child."

Ethan gave the old man another drink and bolted down the contents of his own brandy glass, swallowing any sharp retorts with it. "I'll get her a child, Armistead. Don't worry about that. I'll do whatever it takes."

Chapter Eleven

Zach lashed the mules with regularity and the aged wagon moved across the plain at a pace faster than he'd ever set before. That made for a bumpier ride, and Isabel complained from the back. But his face remained set and grim, emphasized by the scrape on his cheek edged with dried blood. If his injured hand still pained him, he gave no indication of it. Sarah hugged Danny to her and glanced at Zach from time to time. For the most part, though, she gazed unseeing at the landscape ahead, dull-eyed and dull-minded, trying to block out the image of Bear Bettinger. She'd never been in such danger till today, had never seen a gun fired in self-defense, or a man killed. And she felt forever changed by the experiences.

While she'd put on clean clothes in the back of the wagon, Zach had buried Bettinger in a shallow grave where he'd fallen. "Better than the lousy bastard deserves," he'd grumbled when he climbed up to the seat.

They'd ridden for several miles and darkness was falling when he brought the team to a halt in a wide-open, grassy field. "We'll stop here," he said, scanning the horizon. "We'll have a good view of anyone coming."

Sarah was weary to the point of exhaustion and wished for nothing more than the luxury of a bath in a real tub to scour Bettinger's touch from her skin. Then, if she could, she would lie in bed—a real bed—for three whole days, and when she rose, she'd bathe again and put on better clothes than her torn, travel-beaten garments that were turning into rags. But there was no bathtub and no bed, and she had to go on with what she had. She wasn't hungry but she knew they ought to eat so she climbed into the back of the wagon, put Danny in his basket, and tied on her apron.

After the fire was started, she sat peeling potatoes and watching Zach as he milked Isabel. Lord, but he was handsome, she thought with resignation. Much bigger than Ethan—taller and broader through the shoulders and chest. Not only was he a handsome man, he was a good man too. And she didn't want to care about him, but her feelings for him were growing. The memory of him rescuing her with that shotgun still dazzled her, despite the horror of her situation. A true knight in shining armor could not have seemed more noble to her, or more chivalrous. She gazed at his lean, straight features and hazel eyes. Even the gash on his cheekbone seemed to enhance his good looks.

He straightened uncomfortably, then touched the back of his skull and winced.

"How's your head?" she asked, a long ribbon of potato peel trailing from her knife.

He dropped his hand. "Harder than I thought. Lucky for me, I guess."

He was so quiet and introspective, she wondered if he'd ever killed a man before, and if the weight of Bear's death sat heavily on his conscience. She couldn't bring herself to ask though. It seemed too personal.

She looked out into the gathering darkness beyond their campfire. Frogs sang their twilight song and crickets accompanied them. Somewhere in hills too distant to be useful to bushwhackers, a coyote called to the night, lonesome and solitary. It was quiet here, peaceful. But one question that had nagged at her since this afternoon came to elbow her again.

"Zach, when Bear Bettinger doesn't show up in Helena, do you think Ethan will hire another man to come out here?" One glance at his expression told her he'd already considered the possibility.

"He might—we aren't that far from Helena now. Just three or four days by wagon." He gave her a long, thoughtful look. "You probably know him better than I do."

She turned her eyes back to the potato in her hand. It wasn't a sarcastic comment, it was a probing one. He didn't come right out and ask, but she knew he still wanted to hear the story of how Ethan had come to be the father of her child. She sighed.

"Do you think I'm like Bear Bettinger?"

Her head came up at the question. "What do you mean?"

Zach finished with Isabel and began straining her milk into Danny's bottle.

"I mean, Pembroke made just about the same offer to me that he did to Bear. My land in exchange for Danny." He shrugged and made a careless gesture with his free hand. "Well, I guess he offered Bear more money, but basically, it was the same. And we both came after you with the same goal. That could have been me today who tracked you and Bear, if Pembroke had hired him first."

Sarah considered him, and the possibility of what he'd proposed. What if Bear *had* gotten to her first? She'd probably be dead by now, or wish that she was. She shuddered. "I'm glad you were the one who came for us. If he'd hired Bear first, you probably wouldn't have found much left of me. Oh, back in Lame Horse, I was very worried about what might happen to Danny and me once you got us away from town. As far as I knew then, you *could* have been like Bettinger. But you're not. Not at all."

He connected his gaze with hers, as if looking into the mirror of his soul. "Do you think I'm like Pembroke?" He spoke quietly, as if he were afraid of how she would respond.

The question alarmed her. "Good Lord, no! You're nothing like him. I've never known anyone like Ethan and I hope I never do again! What would make you ask such things?"

"I asked them of myself first, maybe a dozen times over. Some nights by the fire run long, and I have a lot of time to think." Fitting the tubing and attached nipple over the neck of the bottle, he gave her a wry half-smile. "I didn't like the answers I came up with. I wanted to see if I'd get different ones from you."

"And did you?"

"Yeah, but I'm not sure you're right. Maybe I'm not so different from Pembroke."

"I sincerely doubt that Ethan has ever lost a minute of sleep over the things he's done to people. And I'm positive he's never wondered if he was doing right or wrong. That alone makes you a better man."

How odd that Zach Garrett, the one who had dragged her and Danny to the wilderness, had now put her in the position of defending him. But he was nothing like Ethan, and he deserved to know it. Carefully, she put the potato in the pot of water that contained the others she'd peeled, then put them on the fire to boil. Sitting down again, she laced her fingers together in her lap. "I guess I ought to tell you how I know Ethan."

He let a moment pass, then said, "You didn't want to before. Why now?" Standing, he lifted Danny out of the wagon and, to Sarah's amazement, sat on the keg and proceeded to feed him. He'd never done *that* before, at least not when she wasn't busy driving. The baby stared up at him with big eyes while he suckled greedily at the bottle, clearly contented. In Zach's strong arm, Danny had never looked so protected, so sweet and precious.

She tightened her clasped hands, and instead of jealousy,

her heart swelled with unwanted affection for Zach as he cradled her child. "It wasn't any of your business before. But after what you did for us today . . . risking your own life and saving us from that horrible man, maybe you've earned the right to hear the story. Then you can decide for yourself how much you are like Ethan Pembroke."

"All right," he agreed.

Taking a deep breath and reaching back into her secret heart, Sarah commenced. "I met him about two years ago at an ice-cream social at church."

"Pembroke?" Zach hooted in disbelief. "At church?"

She nodded. "He told me he was from the East and had just come out to Helena."

Zach frowned. "He's not from the East. He's from Butte."

She inclined her head, acknowledging Ethan's first lie.

She went on with her story, telling him about her spinster teacher's life, how Ethan wooed and seduced her, all the while hinting at marriage but withholding his proposal.

When she told Zach about Ethan's request to invest her savings, he stared at her with wide eyes and raised brows. She flinched. A man who checked and rechecked the figures in his bankbook would likely think that she had done a very foolish thing by giving Ethan access to her money. "I didn't have a vast sum in that account, at least not by Ethan's standards, but it had taken me a long time to accumulate it." Then as if to justify her decision, she hurried to explain. "I expected to marry him, and I planned to trust him with my *life*. So I believed I could trust him with my savings. And he seemed so sincere—about everything. But after that, he began to change and I started to think that maybe Ethan and I weren't a match made in heaven after all."

Night had fallen around the campfire and Sarah hugged

herself against the chill. Zach sat across from her with the baby asleep on his lap as he waited for her to continue. "But by the time I realized that, well, Danny was on the way. It didn't matter whether Ethan was right for me or not." She told Zach about the note she sent to Ethan.

The memory combined with the chilly evening sent shivers coursing through her, until she shook almost as violently as she had earlier in the day. She rubbed her temples and kept her gaze trained on her lap, unwilling to look at Zach.

"When Ethan came to see me, he brought his wife with him. He was already married and I didn't know it."

"What?" Zach demanded with a start, unable to maintain his silence any longer. Danny murmured in his sleep, and Zach glanced down to soothe the child with a tender touch. He'd listened with growing fury to Sarah's story, one that seemed to get worse with every passing minute. She nodded and shivered again. He stood to put Danny in the wagon and grabbed her shawl while he was at it, draping it over her thin shoulders.

"I was mortified, so aghast I couldn't get my breath. Ethan had lied to me and betrayed me, and I'd believed him. And he was married. I couldn't understand why any woman would agree to her husband's philandering, but what was even harder to understand was why he had brought her along to meet her husband's pregnant mistress." She said "mistress" in the same tone of voice with which she might have said "leper." "But Priscilla Pembroke wasn't upset. In fact, she was happy about it."

Sarah soon learned why. Priscilla revealed the purpose of their scheme. Childless but desperate for a baby, she and Ethan had *chosen* Sarah to bear one for them. She'd even made a point of staying out of Helena so that her identity wouldn't slip out and scare off Sarah.

Zach stared at her, a muscle in his jaw working as he listened. "Chose you? Without telling you?"

Sarah nodded. Leaning forward, she put her head in her hands. "Of course, they knew the scandal would destroy my reputation and my teaching career, which was my only means of support. So they made me an offer. They'd pay my expenses to leave Helena to have the baby. I refused. I'd leave, all right and move somewhere else, because I couldn't stay in town. But when I went to the bank, I learned that Ethan had emptied my bank account. I was flat broke, trapped in Helena by the Pembrokes. What kind of life could I give a child under those horrible circumstances?"

"So you agreed to sign their contract," Zach supplied quietly.

"Yes, I signed it. Then I went away to Bozeman and got a room in a boardinghouse with every intention of making good on my word. I posed as a widow, hoping with all my heart that I'd made the best choice for my child. But when Danny was born, I held him in my arms and I knew I couldn't give him up. Three days after I had him, I grabbed a few belongings and ran away. I found the job in Lame Horse, and that's where you found *us*. And no matter what happens in the future, good or bad, I know I'll never be the same." She paused a moment and turned tortured, haunted eyes upon him. "So tell me, Zach, do you think you're like Ethan Pembroke?"

Silence fell between them, the desolate sound of her voice replaced by the soft popping of the fire and crickets calling beyond the circle of its light.

Zach couldn't answer. Now he understood why Sarah had said that he wouldn't believe the story—it was incredible. He did believe her though. And the vague guilty sensation that he'd been carrying all this time settled firmly in his gut and grew into remorse, leaving him with a sick, empty feeling. He could tell himself that he was a different man than Bear, a better man than Pembroke, but in the end, his pay would have been the same. The result would be the same.

Sarah Kincade would lose her baby, and he was the reason.

He could no longer excuse what he'd done by telling himself that he was only trying to get his land back. He couldn't push the subject to the back of his mind just because he didn't want to think about it. He had to think about it now, and he knew that regardless of whatever contract Sarah had signed, this whole thing was wrong. Ethan Pembroke thought he could buy and sell people as if they were real estate or heads of cattle.

Zach couldn't change Pembroke, but maybe, just maybe, he could manage to get his land and save Danny too.

He stood and dropped to his knees in the dirt in front of her. "Sarah," he said, looking into her face, forcing himself to accept whatever anger or accusation he saw there. "I didn't want to care about your problems—I didn't want to care about anything. I wake up sometimes and for a minute I think I'm still sleeping in an alley, or that I'm back in the Gerlichs' barn. All this time, I've done what I thought I had to in order to get what I wanted—a place of my own. I didn't deliberately cheat anyone but . . . most of the time I looked the other way when I saw others being cheated or robbed or taken advantage of. After all, there are crooks and thieves everywhere a man turns, and I told myself I was minding my own business. I tried to look the other way with you. But I can't do it any longer." He pushed a strand of hair from her face. "I did a bad thing to you, tracking you down in Lame Horse so that Ethan Pembroke could take your son away from you. I've brought even more trouble down on your head than you already had. Jesus, Sarah, I'm sorry, for everything. For making you fall on the steps, for dragging you out of Lame Horse like a criminal, for all of it. I can't excuse what I did, and you were right all along—not everything is about money. I—I just—" Mortified to hear his own voice break, he cleared his throat, hard, and took her work-roughened hands in his own. Leaning forward, he pressed his forehead against them on her lap. "I just wanted a home."

"Home," she repeated, parrotlike. She sat unmoving for a moment, then she pulled one hand from his grasp and he waited for her to shove him away or punch him or serve up some other kind of punishment. Instead, she stroked his hair, her fingers tentative and as gentle as a night breeze in the strands, and he realized this was the worst punishment of all. His heart twisted in his chest and his eyes burned as he knelt before her like a penitent.

"You're not like Ethan. I hope you understand that." She laid her hand flat to his head. "You're a good man." Her pronouncement fell upon his soul like a benediction, an absolution that he didn't deserve. He would have to earn it. And he knew how he must do it.

He straightened again and tucked the ends of her shawl around her. She was beautiful in the firelight, weary and wise, yet she retained a sweetness that many would have lost long ago. And, despite everything that had happened to her, she still found room in her heart for forgiveness and compassion. She gave them both to him.

"Sarah," he intoned, savoring the feel of her name in his mouth. He lifted both of her hands to his lips to kiss them. "I've never known anyone like you. Never. I can't change what has already happened, but I can do something about the future. Tell me where you want to go. I'll see you and Danny safely to any place you say."

Sarah gaped at Zach with wide eyes. "Do you mean we aren't going to Helena?" It was too much to ask, too much to hope for—

He shook his head. "How can I take you back there and surrender you to the Pembrokes after what they did to you? No, I won't take you to Helena."

"But what about that note Ethan is holding on your land? He might be so angry he'll never give it back to you."

He sighed and sat back on his heels in front of her. "Look at what he's done already—he gave it away to Bear Bettinger, when I still had every intention to make good on our agreement. There's no doing business with Ethan Pembroke. He's one of those vultures I was talking about, always ready to stick a knife in a man's back, always ready to double-cross someone, steal from someone." He took a deep breath and his expression darkened. "I'm going to have to fight him on his own level. But you don't need to be part of that. After I see you on your way, I'll come back and dance with the devil."

"Oh, Zach," she whispered. It outraged her to think that Ethan would take that ranch from Zach, when she knew he probably didn't give a tinker's damn about it. "Don't you have enough in that bank account to just pay him what you borrowed from him?"

"Yeah, if he hadn't charged me a lot of interest too. It's been piling up for two years. I probably owe him more than the land is worth. But this isn't over between him and me. On top of everything else, he sent Bettinger out here to kill us both—or at least he didn't care if Bear killed us. So I've got more than one score to settle with him, and I'll do it, after you're safely away."

Sarah stopped to consider the wonderful gift that Zach was giving her. He was giving her back her son, her freedom—

Overwhelmed with gratitude, impulsively she flung herself at him and threw her arms around him. "I don't know how to thank you," she said, kissing him on both cheeks like a European diplomat. "You can't imagine how my heart was breaking—I don't think I ever would have recovered from it."

His arms closed around her and it felt like the most natural thing in the world to be in Zach Garrett's embrace. He pulled back slightly to look at her, and suddenly, the air between them became charged with more than a mother's gratitude or a lonely man's need for redemption. There sprang up between them a heat that had been building since they'd first laid eyes upon each other and had made itself felt in sidelong glances, a lingering of fingers on fingers, a single stolen kiss, the nurturing of trust.

This last came as a surprise to Sarah. She hadn't expected to believe any man again for years to come, perhaps not ever.

But she trusted Zach.

By virtue of his beginnings, he had the right to be as callous and unfeeling as Ethan, the potential to be as underhanded and dishonest.

He was none of those.

And now, with the low-rumbling passion came wonderment. Sarah, emboldened by the banked fire she saw in his eyes and the kindness she knew dwelled in his heart, dropped her gaze to his lips and shyly touched her own to them.

Zach drew in a swift, sharp breath and held it, and Sarah pulled back, horrified by her forward behavior. What would he think, especially after the story she'd just told him? Of course, he had to be disgusted by her. What else could she seem to be but a woman of easy virtue?

"Zach, I beg your pardon," she uttered, ashamed, her

eyes fixed on her lap. "I shouldn't have . . . I know you
must think I'm just a loose—"

Swiftly, he took her face between his hands and forced
her to look at him. "No, Sarah! No. You've got to stop
telling me what I think of you. You're the finest, most
decent woman I've ever known. You've risked everything
to save your child—that's more than I can say about a lot
of people I grew up around." He hugged her to him again,
almost fiercely, cradling the back of her head with his hand.
"And even though I'm sorry about the way we met, I'm
glad that we did." He eased her back and gazed into her
eyes. "So glad."

Slowly and with exquisite care, he rubbed his temple
against hers. The sensation astounded her, sending chills
down her arms and back. Growing more bold, he pressed
soft, feather-light kisses to her cheeks and brow, her jaw
and ear. At last, his lips claimed hers, gently at first, then
as the kiss deepened, more hungrily. Tightening his arms
around her, he reached up to plunge his fingers into her
hair. The tangy scent of him, of fresh air, wood smoke, and
some other undefinable essence that was his alone, filled
her head, both comforting and exciting.

"Sarah," he muttered, between nibbles on her lips. "I've
dreamed of kissing you again ever since that first time.
Dreamed of it every day and every night."

Should she be embarrassed or shocked by his confession? she wondered idly, as he moved his lips to a sensitive
spot on her neck. She was neither. Rather, she was bash-
fully pleased. "I've wished for it too," she admitted, her
breath coming faster. She felt that she could tell him anything now. He'd heard the worst about her, and thought
none the less of her. If anything, his opinion of her seemed
to have improved.

His fingertips grazed her cheek, then held her chin and

jaw as he investigated her mouth with his tongue, slick and warm and intimate. Sarah's pulse took off at a gallop, thundering through her like the pounding hooves of a wild horse. Ethan had never thrilled her so easily—he had been rougher, more impatient.

From her chin his hand slid down her neck and inside her shawl to stroke her shoulder with a touch that was both tender and demanding. He followed the trail of his hand with a line of soft, moist kisses on her throat. When the backs of his fingers grazed the side of her breast, she sucked in a deep breath. Through the tissue-thin fabric of her bodice his caress was like fire, and with unerring skill he sought her nipple and teased it until it rose to meet his fingers. She couldn't stop the small, anguished moan that escaped her throat.

"I'm going to make love to you," he whispered, his breath ragged against her ear. "Is that all right?"

Ethan had merely seduced her when he'd taken her virginity. He'd been very smooth about it, plying her with flowers and wine, but he'd never sought her permission or asked what she wanted. Overcome with the tenderness, the passion, of Zach's request, she couldn't speak. She lifted his hand and placed a kiss in his palm to indicate her assent.

Still on his knees, Zach parted her legs so that her thighs bracketed his and he pressed his hips to her as he embraced her again. Despite the layers of fabric between them, she felt his arousal, hard and hot and demanding. Waves of heat poured off him, from inside his shirt, from his head, carrying his delicious scent to her nose.

Keeping his eyes on hers, he reached for the buttons on her bodice and unfastened each one with such slow deliberateness, she was tempted to bat his hands away and do it herself. Then she realized that his measured movements were having the precise effect he wanted—her arousal grew with every button he opened.

At last, when he'd made his way through the fastenings on her dress and her camisole, he reached in to cradle her breast in his hand, and Sarah leaned into it as if he'd willed her to do it.

His lips sought hers again, greedily, and this time she raked her nails over the length of his back, pressing just hard enough so that he'd feel it through his shirt.

Zach felt it, all right, clear down to his fly buttons, where his body throbbed for the want of this woman. Sarah was both an innocent and a temptress, and although she'd had prior experience and had even borne a child, there remained about her an untouched core of sweetness that he wanted not to take from her, but only to taste. "Wait right here," he said, dragging his mouth from hers.

Rising to his feet, he climbed up to the wagon and gathered every blanket he could find. While he was there, he did a quick check of the sleeping child and bundled him more securely in his basket.

When he jumped down, he saw Sarah limned by firelight, her hair freed from its braid and hanging around her shoulders like dark, rippling satin. She seemed to blossom into a beautiful, night-blooming flower as he watched.

Barely able to take his eyes from her, he quickly made a bed for them next to the fire. She followed his actions with great interest.

"Is Danny asleep?" she asked.

"Sure, he's fine—warm and in dreamland." He pulled back the top blanket and held his hand out to her. "Come here, Sarah. This is our time—we've had a hell of a day." She smiled as she took his hand and sat beside him on the blanket-bed.

"Yes, we have. I think it was the worst of my life." She

touched cool fingertips to the edge of the scrape on his face. "It was the worst and yet . . ." She looked into his eyes and he thought he saw a glimpse of her heart and the affection she carried in it. Affection for him. He didn't want to hope it might be more than that, or to acknowledge that he felt more than that for her.

He glanced at the battered canopy on the wagon. "You don't know how many nights I sat out here and thought about you. Up there."

"I thought about you too," she admitted. "I didn't want to, but I couldn't help it." Her confession pleased Zach enormously.

He held his arms open to her and, with a little cry, she fell into them, and he took her mouth again with a passion that would no longer be denied. Laying her back against the blankets, he parted her clothes to reveal her breasts to the stars. The warm, lush woman who lay in his arms outshone the diamond-hard, faraway radiance in the night sky.

"Sarah, sweet Sarah—you're so beautiful," he murmured, at once awed and ignited by the sight of her gentle curves and dusky nipples. He dropped his head and nuzzled the soft flesh, planting kisses beneath each breast. Her breathing deepened, and when he closed his lips over a ripe nipple, she arched beneath him. God, he'd been months without a female, and his slow-burning desire for Sarah made it seem even longer. It took all of his willpower to keep from pulling off her clothes and raining kisses on her body, then taking her as a stallion took a mare. It wasn't a bad idea, but he knew that women needed more than that from a man, and Sarah *deserved* more.

So he reined in his hunger and stroked the length of her, arms, legs, and torso, unbuttoning and untying as he went. At last, she lay before him, naked and goosefleshed and golden in the firelight. With great regret, he flipped the blanket over her to protect her from the night chill. In response, she opened his shirt and timidly began caressing his shoulders and ribs, working her way down, with slow, torturous sweeps.

Zach caught her hand between his own and the bare skin of his belly, feeling as if he would burst. He skimmed out of his shirt but the cool air didn't bother him. All he felt was her hand on him, leaving fiery trails wherever she touched him. He rolled her to her side and pressed her smooth body to his.

"Shall I stop?" she asked against his neck.

"Yes . . . no. God, no," he groaned deep in his throat, and pushed her hand lower between them.

Sarah was confronted by the obvious heat of Zach's arousal, pulsing just behind his fly buttons. Working those buttons wasn't easy with him outlining her ear with his tongue. Shivers coursed through her in waves as he dragged his fingertips up her spine, over her shoulder to the indentation above her jaw . . . then down, slowly, around the outer curve of her breast until he brushed the spot just inside her hipbone that made her jump out of her skin whenever it was touched.

With trembling fingers, she released him from the confines of his jeans. He kicked off his boots and pants, and at last they lay beneath a jewel-flung sky, their limbs entwined under the blanket. The hot, hard length of him prodded her hip, and again she was struck by his sheer maleness. Ethan had been nothing like Zach, nothing.

Everything about Zach was utterly masculine, stripping away any shyness that lingered in her. Where he was hard and muscled, she was soft and curved. Where she was smooth, he was rough.

Dipping his head again, he suckled at her breast and Sarah wound her fingers in his long, dark hair. Her senses were swamped with fire and wonder and love. The realization came as no surprise to her, but as right and natural as the stars overhead. She loved Zach Garrett.

Flushed with rapidly growing desire, she once more regretted that she'd had to wean Danny so early. She wished not only for a mother's right to feed her child, but for the intense intimacy of sharing her milk with Zach as well. It was a wanton, immodest thought, she knew, but it was true. If she couldn't have that, though, she would have the feel of him under her touch, his hard-muscled arms and shoulders, the broad expanse of his chest, his long-boned legs, his full erection. She dug her fingers into the strong muscles in her back and felt them flex. Zach responded by grazing the insides of her thighs with a feather-light touch.

But when his seeking fingertips moved higher to probe her tender flesh, she jumped, bumping his hand away. It felt as if a jolt of electricity had sizzled through her. Ethan had never touched her like that, and Zach seemed to realize it immediately.

"It's all right," he whispered to her, returning to the slick, sensitive bud.

Fervent hunger overtook all reason. The tiny place he caressed created a tightness low in her belly, as tight as a clock's mainspring. Every slow, deliberate stroke wound the spring another turn, and Sarah lifted her hips to reach for more of this delicious torture he inflicted upon her, not knowing where it was going, or how much more she could take.

Zach whispered to her, tender endearments and the promise of something wonderful waiting for her. She couldn't imagine what he referred to except perhaps some reward in the afterlife, because surely her pounding heart would burst in her chest and kill her. Then the strokes increased in speed, like the beats of a hummingbird's wings.

"Zach—dear God, Zach," she cried. He murmured to her again, but she didn't know what he said. Her entire being concentrated on the tightness between her legs and in her belly. When she was certain that she would die, he pulled her up to the top of some ethereal peak where she hovered between life and death, and then he flung her into an abyss of pleasure so profound, she sobbed his name. Swift contractions racked her again and again.

Zach felt the quivering flutters beneath his hand and they increased his own need to the breaking point. He could wait no longer. He parted her thighs with his knee and with a long, smooth thrust sheathed himself in her hot moistness. Sarah gasped and wrapped her legs around his waist, pulling him in deeper.

He looked down at her face in the firelight and saw tears running from the corners of her eyes to her ears. For the first time in his life, his body wasn't the only part of him involved with having a woman. His heart competed with the fierce need coursing through him.

He forced himself to lie still within her. "Sarah, I don't know what's ahead for either of us," he whispered. "But tonight—I want you to know that you mean more to me than anyone ever has." She smiled up at him and touched his cheek, and he saw tender regard again in her eyes.

"Oh, Zach, I *love* you." He stared into her pretty face and swallowed hard. It was the first time in his life he'd ever heard anyone say that to him, and his response caught in his throat. So he did the only thing he could think of. He lowered his head and kissed her, then withdrew slightly to push home again. She moaned and tightened her grip on his waist.

That was all Zach could take. He hiked himself up to the full length of his arms. His thrusts came faster and harder, and beneath him, he watched Sarah as another climax overtook her. She clamped her fingers onto his back and called his name, while her muscles inside clenched him again and again. He pushed harder and harder, seeking his own release. When it finally came he swore that his heart and soul burst out to touch hers, riding on the waves of spasms that made him strain against her.

He dropped his head to her shoulder and she relaxed beneath him, running a soothing hand down the length of his back. This was where he wanted to be, with Sarah Kincade. It was a startling realization, but a comforting one as well.

The stars traveled across the sky, looking down from the cold firmament on the man and woman who lay by their campfire on the Montana prairie. In the grand scheme of the universe, they were no more than two grains of sand.

But in their own hearts at that moment, they were the only two people in the world.

Chapter Twelve

Pearl-gray light stole over the landscape as Sarah woke and found her head pillowed against Zach's shoulder. They lay under the wagon canopy, she and Danny snuggled against Zach's strong, warm body. His shotgun rested along his other side, in case, he'd said, someone else came along with evil intent.

Right now, though, even yesterday's hellish events faded when she thought about last night. Remembering what she'd shared with Zach, she felt herself blush like a girl. They'd made love twice. The second time he'd lingered over her, attending her with a slow hand and bringing her to a fever pitch of passion that had left her trembling and sobbing. After idling in each other's arms until the moon hung low in the sky, they'd moved their bed up here to be with the baby.

Sarah propped herself up on her elbow to look at Zach. He lay on his back, his breathing slow and even as he slept, his broad chest rising and falling. She studied his handsome face in the low dawn light, and she saw none of the worry and years of struggle that sometimes showed there. Sleep smoothed his features and let him rest with the boneless ease of a baby.

Her gaze traced the line of his sinewed arms, up to his shoulders, over his strong chest, dusted with dark hair, and down the ridged muscles of his flat belly. The wool blanket cut a horizontal line low on his waist. From there, she saw only the outline of his long legs and at their apex, a frank suggestion of his maleness. Wicked temptation—unusual to her, the proper schoolmarm—prodded her to take a quick peek under the blanket. After all, it had been pretty dark last night and she hadn't really seen him. She glanced around as if someone might catch her. Then quickly she lifted the cover to find that he was as finely made below as above. His was not the body of a man who spent his time behind a desk, deciding people's lives and fates, like Ethan did. Lowering the blanket, she smiled a private smile and looked at his features again. Even when he was awake and wore a guarded expression, Zach's face held no guile, no duplicity.

Pondering the thick fringe of his dark lashes, she marveled at the improbable turn of events that had brought her to this moment—sharing her heart and her bed with the man she'd had every reason to regard as her enemy. Just a few short weeks ago, she had been worried and uncertain, hiding with Danny in Lame Horse with a fear that had made her heart pound until she felt sick. To top that off, this man—this *fiend*—had appeared on her doorstep to steal her child.

But Zach wasn't a fiend, after all. He had turned out to be her champion, as chivalrous as a knight of King Arthur's Round Table. He'd renewed her faith in people, proving that not everyone was like the grasping, deceitful Pembrokes, or the stone-hearted nurse in Bozeman, or judgmental Clarice Flanders, her landlady in Lame Horse. As long as Zachary Garrett was in the world, there must be other good people too.

While she watched him, Zach stirred and rubbed his nose without waking. The funny little gesture sent a rush of tenderness flowing through Sarah, so strong that she felt it in every part of her being.

She had to decide what she was going to do. He'd offered to take her wherever she wanted to go so that the Pembrokes would never find her and Danny. Even more than the gift of tenderness and passion that he'd given her last night, he'd offered her the moon and the stars by saying he'd see her safe with her child.

Out here on the plains, it was easy to pretend that they were a family, the three of them. How could she tell Zach that she wanted more—that she wanted him to stay with them? Especially when she knew what *he* really wanted— his own place, the one he'd worked so hard for? If he gave up his chance to get it from Ethan, he would have to start all over again, and even though she suspected he truly cared about Danny, he wouldn't want the two of them dragging at his coattails. Of that she was certain—after she'd blabbed her feelings about him he'd said nothing. She wished that she'd kept her mouth shut. And besides, he wanted and deserved a better woman, one who was, as he'd said, a real lady, one who could bear his children and set them upon a straight path. She didn't qualify for that job. She would have once, but she had allowed Ethan to lead her down a primrose path that had no destination but shame. She would only pull Zach down. She had to leave Montana, for her child's safety and her own peace of mind. It would be best for Zach too.

Taking Danny on her arm, she lay down again and cradled his softness to her. She was grateful to Zach for his help. He could have taken the easier path to his goal by sacrificing her to the Pembrokes. Instead, he was choosing the hard way. And though she might love Zach with all her heart, he owed her nothing else. He was about to give her the unspeakable joy and satisfaction of raising her child to adulthood.

She would have to be content with that.

When Zach opened his eyes, the sun was up and he was alone in the wagon. He heard the clank of metal against metal and sat up to investigate. Sarah, combed and dressed, busily scraped the cast-iron pot that held the remnants of their uneaten, overcooked potatoes. He rested his elbows on the edge of the wagon side to watch as she worked in the early morning light. Her back was turned and he smiled at the insistent sway of her hips, keeping time with the big cooking spoon she used as her weapon to attack the burned-on food.

The goat, tethered to the back wheel, saw him and sounded a baleful *eh-eh-eh*, but he smiled at her as well, feeling too good to scowl. He gazed out across the open country, at the cottonwoods that rose like specters from mist that lingered along a streambed, and the hawk swooping down to snag his breakfast. Putting his arms behind his head, he lay down again on his bed of blankets, awash with the unfamiliar sense that for this moment, anyway, all was right with the world.

God, what a woman, that Sarah Kincade, he marveled. She was smart, practical, and brave, but tenderhearted with a kindness that he believed could heal almost any wound of the body or spirit.

He felt renewed this morning, as if he might finally be able to pry loose the memories that had gripped his soul with sharp claws all this time. His early years of starvation and fear and desperation . . . the hope kindled and damned when he went to live with the Gerlichs . . . his struggle to put down roots and find his place in this world. He'd never be rid of them—they were part of him and made him the man he was, for better or worse. But today, for the first time, he thought he might be able push them into a back corner of his heart and shut the door on them.

This morning, more strongly than ever, came the feeling that he had the chance to start over, that life was full of possibilities.

And he realized why. Sarah had said she loved him. Loved *him,* Zachary Garrett, an orphan with a last name he'd given himself at the age of seven because someone had told him that he couldn't go around without one. A nobody who'd slept in doorways, then had graduated to sleeping in a barn while he watched his adopted family sitting around their cheerful kitchen table, knowing he hadn't been welcome.

But none of it mattered because Sarah loved him.

His elation dimmed. He'd hungered for someone's love his entire life, even while he'd told himself he needed no one and had built a shell around his heart. Now he had what he'd yearned for, and damn him, he hadn't a clue what to do with it because he'd never learned.

Oh, he knew he was grateful. Sarah's love was a precious gift. Mostly, though, it scared him. That was why he hadn't answered her last night. He didn't know if he ever could.

"Zach, I've been thinking about where Danny and I should go." With the baby in her arms, Sarah tried to feed him and herself at the same time, taking a forkful of fried potatoes and bacon now and then. They hadn't eaten supper last night and she was starving.

Everything was different between them. She felt shy around Zach now, almost bashful. She had to stop herself from ducking her head when he turned his gaze on her. But he seemed a little awkward too, which she found surprising. Zach was a man who'd seen and done everything, good and bad. Now he acted as if he'd been called in from roping cattle to sit in a lady's brocaded parlor and balance a teacup and cake plate on his knees. He'd already inhaled his breakfast and now he sat on his keg, fidgeting like he didn't know what to do with his hands or where to look.

Oh . . . of course. She realized he was worried that she'd have expectations of him now, that she must think last night implied some kind of commitment, more than he intended to give. She might wish for more, but she didn't expect it, and certainly wouldn't ask for it. Sadness weighed on her heart and she sighed.

"So, where do you want to go?" he asked, pulling at a loose thread on his shirt.

Sarah had agonized over her choice, but she knew she didn't have much time to think about it. She had to get away soon. "I need to leave Montana. It's—it's a difficult decision for me, and I don't know what I'll tell my family. But I have to put a healthy distance between us and the Pembrokes."

His head came up sharply. "Leave Montana?"

She nodded. "For Oregon. I've read some good things about it."

He wore a peculiar expression, almost stricken. "Well— but where in Oregon?"

"Maybe Portland." She shrugged. "Or I could settle somewhere along the way."

He jumped up and paced around the camp, seeming almost angry. "No, no, I don't think this is a good idea. I don't like the sound of it."

Baffled, she hoisted the baby to her shoulder to burp him. "Why not?"

He stopped and turned toward her, then jammed his hands into his back pockets and started walking again. "Because, well, because it's too goddamned far. Do you know how far away that is?"

"No," she admitted, but she knew she'd be leaving part of her heart here, and it would seem like half a world away.

"It's hundreds of miles."

She shook her head. "You don't have to take us all the

way over there. If you could just get us to the train I'm sure we'll be fine." She felt that lie in her soul. She was sure of no such thing, and she didn't want to be separated from Zach, but what else could she say? Plainly, he didn't want to go the entire distance and she couldn't blame him. It would be asking too much—he had his own life to get on with.

He continued to pace in long, irritated strides. He still wore the same shirt that Isabel had destroyed—well, after all, he had only one other. Between them, she supposed they looked like ragpickers, dressed as they were. Maybe he didn't wear expensive clothes, but she'd never seen a man more handsome. It was there in the way he carried himself, tall and lean and straight-backed, as if he would always meet the world and life head-on. She began to wish that he looked more like Bear so it would be easier to turn her back and forget him when the time came.

"Why don't you go to another small town in the territory?" he asked.

"Zach, you didn't have much trouble finding me in Lame Horse." Was her plan such an inconvenience to him? She wished she had the courage to ask, but judging by his dark expression, she already knew the answer. To hear him say the words would complete her heartbreak. "Do you really think that Ethan will give up searching for Danny and me? He'll send someone else when Bear Bettinger doesn't come back, and someone after that until he either catches us or I'm worn to a frazzle and old before my time from worrying." She rubbed her forehead with her fingertips. "As it is, I know I'm going to have nightmares about him for months. I have to get away from here. Far away."

He stopped pacing and stood in front of her, his face now clouded by a frown that made her wince. It reminded her so much of how he'd looked when he'd grabbed her skirt on the stairs that first day, the day he'd held her contract up to her face and said that she had to pay the piper.

"I don't want you to go to Oregon."

Panic swamped her. Dear God, he couldn't take back his offer to help her. Not now, not when he knew how much she needed it. "But why?"

"Because if you do, I—you'll be too far away."

"That's the point! I have to be far away—from Montana and from the Pembrokes." And from him, so she wouldn't run the risk of seeing him and remembering how she had come to care about him. Or how he'd made her heart and body sing.

"Yeah, but—If you go, you—I—Damn it, Sarah, you'll be too far away from *me*!"

Comprehension dawned on her—he wouldn't be able to protect her across three states. Some of her sadness lifted. "Oh. Well, if I'm careful, with any luck Ethan won't figure out where I've gone. We should be safe, Zach."

He dropped to one knee and gripped her arms in his big hands, squeezing almost painfully, his very manner begging for understanding. "I'm not talking about just being safe. I mean—" His face was a mask of frustration, reminding her of a student she'd once had with a stuttering problem. He'd known what he wanted to say but hadn't been able to get it out. He looked at her hem and took a deep breath, then lifted his head again. The pain in his hazel eyes went straight to her heart, even though she didn't know its source, and she held the breath that he'd exhaled, waiting.

"Oh, hell, Sarah, I don't know what I mean," he mumbled. Leaning forward, he took both Sarah and Danny into his arms, and her throat grew tight with emotion. She buried her face against his neck.

They stayed that way, the three of them, until Danny complained with a loud squawk. Zach released them. "I just

want you and Danny to be safe and happy. I guess if going
to Oregon is what you really want, then that's what's best."

She gazed at Zach with wide eyes, letting a glimmer of
hope bloom within her like the first wildflower after a long,
dark winter. "Do you mean you want to come with us?"
Maybe if they went somewhere else, a place where no one
knew her, he could forget her past and that she was no
longer a lady.

He sat back and looked at her, obviously puzzled. "Hell,
no. I mean to get my ranch back from Pembroke, and I aim
to live here." His dark expression lifted. "You can stay here
too."

"In Montana?"

Pulling up a grass stalk, he began ripping it into long
strips. "Yes, in Montana."

"But I can't. I told you why I can't."

"And I can't leave. Look, I've always expected to have
a spread here. That parcel near the Rockies . . . it was like
my idea of the Promised Land, you know? I thought about
it day and night, I *dreamed* about it."

"But there are ranches in Oregon," Sarah offered, "and
thousands of acres of country. I've seen advertisements in
the newspaper about it. You could come with us, start
over—"

He looked at her as if she didn't understand English.
Tossing aside the blade of grass, he rose to his feet and
said, "And let Pembroke win? Sarah, I can't just walk away
and start over *again*. That parcel kept me going when nothing else could have. For the first time in my life, I own
something. It's mine and I want it back."

Now it was Sarah's turn to feel frustrated. Possessions,
money, winning—was that all men cared about? "If it's that
important to you, how do Danny and I fit into this? Why
do you care where we live?"

His throat worked, but no real words came out. Then he said, "Because . . . well, just because." And no real answer.

She swallowed hard, struggling with that awful feeling that came when hope fizzled away. "Zach," she said, gazing into his suddenly unfathomable eyes. It broke her heart to speak the words, but she had to. "I have to leave, but if you're just as determined to stay, then—" Her throat was as dry as chalk.

He nodded. "My offer is still good, Sarah. I'll see you and the baby safely on your way."

"There's something else." She put Danny in his basket next to her feet. Leaning forward, she rested her elbows on her knees and looked directly into Zach's face. She had to say this, no matter how awkward she felt, and even if it meant he would change his mind about escorting her. She had to tell him so that she could begin rebuilding her self-respect and heal the wound that Ethan had left on her soul. Even if he were to pledge his love right now, she wouldn't change her mind. She wanted actions, not words. "Last night . . . it was wonderful." Her cheeks grew warm when she saw a smoldering light in his eyes. "But I will not be any man's mistress ever again. *Ever*. And last night won't happen again."

"No." He sighed, sounding regretful. "It won't. You don't have to worry about that."

They sat in camp the rest of the day making plans. Sarah didn't like it, but Zach told her he had to go to Helena to move his money from the First National to another bank.

"Pembroke has a lot of influence at First National, and if he's bearing a grudge against me, or thinks I'm dead, I don't want him to tie up my cash. He could do it too. I don't trust that bastard, especially after what he did to you."

Going into town was a risky thing to do, and though he

wouldn't admit to the danger, she saw a shadow of doubt in his eyes.

"Don't worry," he said. "We'll stop on the outskirts of town—I know just the place. You'll be safe and no one will see you. Then I'll slip into Helena and go to the bank. I won't be gone more than a couple of hours at the most."

After that, he'd drive her to a place where she could catch the train and head west.

"What if Ethan sees you, or someone who knows him? He might have a man follow you."

Zach placed a hand on his chest and drew himself up, his expression one of mock indignity that almost made her laugh. "*Me*? Follow *me*? Sarah, you cut me to the bone. Have you forgotten that I regularly dodged the police on the streets of New York? One time they chased me for three blocks and through four alleys. I was running with a whole leg of lamb I'd pilfered from the Greek butcher shop—that thing was almost as big as me. At first, old man Karamanos chased me up the street in his blood-spattered apron, waving his meat cleaver and swearing at me in Greek." He grinned. "Well, I couldn't understand all of it, but I knew enough to pick out the bad words. Then he flagged down the coppers and they took over. I got away, though, and I didn't drop the lamb even once." He looked proud of himself and now they both laughed.

It was easy to picture him, a dirty-faced street urchin dragging the lamb along. "What did you do with it?"

He shrugged. "Of course, I had no way to cook it. So I took it to Frankie Callaghan's mother. She had four kids besides Frankie, and a husband who spent most of his time and money in the saloons, so she was only too happy to get it. She blessed me and said, 'God love ye, Zachary, and may all His saints watch over ye.' She didn't figure that God would hold with my stealing, but she was certain a hungry child who shared his food with other hungry children would be forgiven. I got a good dinner, and so did she and her kids. So, see"—he grinned again—"I shouldn't have any trouble getting into my own bank account."

Zach was more optimistic than Sarah. She decided not to mention the fact that he *was* eventually caught for stealing and sent to reform school.

The idea of him going to Helena worried her, but it was a risk that he swore he had to take.

That night, Zach and Sarah lay in the wagon bed fully dressed, with Danny between them. Although she and the baby slept, the air under the canopy was electric with tension and suppressed longing.

He'd wanted to kiss her good night but knew that he didn't dare, fearing that his desire would get away from him and he'd do something that she would see as a breach of the promise he'd made.

Zach had never felt so torn, so divided. Damn it, he didn't want her to go to Oregon. But he couldn't give up on that land of his. He just couldn't.

It sure played hell on him, her lying so close and yet out of reach. He could hear her every breath, every swallow, every whispering shift of fabric against skin. If he wasn't concerned about Pembroke sending more henchmen, he'd be sleeping by the fire and away from the temptation of her warm, gently curved body. But after Bear's attack, Zach knew they might be in more danger than he'd first guessed, and he had to stay close to Sarah and Danny.

He rolled over to his back and gazed at the blue-black night sky, trying to distract the stubbornly insistent lust that throbbed away in his groin. It didn't work.

Zach was no stranger to women's bodies but Sarah's could be compared to none that he'd ever known. In his mind's eye, he followed the silken, sweetly rounded planes of her flesh with his hand, working his way up from her small feet. Her legs and thighs, slender and well turned, flared to womanly hips that were trim but not sharp-boned. At the apex of her thighs was a warm haven that invited a man to plant his seed there and offered a safe, comfortable cocoon for that seed to grow into a child. Continuing up past her tiny waist and sleek flanks were her breasts, smooth and weighty in his palm, crowned with tight, rose-pink nipples that begged him to suckle—

Groaning, Zach turned over to face the side of the wagon, the ache low in his belly, heavy and demanding. God, why was he torturing himself like this? It would take only the slightest encouragement from Sarah to make him rip open his fly buttons, unleash himself, and find his way beneath her skirts to the slick cleft he'd visited just the night before. But she slept beside him, trusting him, and there was that promise he'd made. After tomorrow, maybe the day after, she'd be gone, and though he'd miss her, that would put an end to the most agonizing celibacy he'd ever known.

He still had to get through tonight though.

Twisting his thoughts away from Sarah, he concentrated on an imaginary meeting with Ethan Pembroke. It would be ugly, he knew that, especially when he showed up in Pembroke's office without Sarah and Danny. But Zach had never backed down from a worthwhile fight.

For the past two years, he'd taken every action, made every decision, with the single-minded intention of securing his place under the vast expanse of Montana sky. He'd viewed those acres with nearly the same regard as he would a lover, a pure, wild lover that would accept him as he was, despite his wretched beginnings and more recent question-

able deeds. He would be baptized and made new in miles
of good grass and water.

And his goal to acquire a place of his own had now
expanded into a yearning for a family of his own. He
glanced over his shoulder at the baby sleeping against his
side. This child could be his son, he realized. It didn't matter that the boy resembled another man, or that he wasn't
related by blood. He could teach Danny to ride and rope
and to face his responsibilities like a man. To be fair-
minded, honest, and upright in his dealings with people,
and especially with women.

Beside him, Sarah made a tiny whimpering noise in her
sleep. Gently, Zach reached over and stroked her hair with
his finger, his heart so full of tenderness he marveled at the
sensation. He'd never known the feeling until he'd met her
and Danny. Maybe it was love, this joy, this despair when
he thought of her leaving him.

But she was bound to go, and he must let her.

If he could only tell her how he felt.

"Miss Priscilla isn't feeling so well tonight, Mr. Pembroke." Louisa had answered Ethan's knock after a pro-
tracted moment, her apron in her hand. Stepping into the
hall, she closed her mistress's door behind her to guard the
portal like a stout-breasted Wagnerian sentinel. Her unspo-
ken but obvious purpose was to keep Ethan out of Priscilla's bedroom. Her flushed face was a noticeable contrast
with her white cap, which was askew.

Ethan crossed his arms over his chest. "Really, Louisa?
And what would it be this time? Some female complaint?"

She tied on her apron, centering it over her plump waist.
"No, sir. It's one of them headaches again. The ones the
doctors can't figure out."

"The ones that no one can figure out," he snapped. After

sending Bettinger to comply with Priscilla's request, Ethan had come to his wife's bedroom every night. Bettinger was now overdue, and she still had no baby. Ethan intended to make her keep her side of the deal they'd reached, damn it, whether or not Bettinger was late. But tonight, she'd installed her guard dog at her door.

The maid's face fell into mildly reproachful lines, highlighted by the harsh glare of gaslight. "Mr. Pembroke, you know that Dr. Nash said if she doesn't get better he'll have to send her to a sanatorium in Denver to see what's wrong inside her head."

Of course, what else could the good doctor offer to an unsatisfied, wealthy patient? Ethan grumbled to himself. Dr. Nash had found nothing "wrong inside her head" during his examination of Priscilla, which turned out to be simply a medical fishing expedition. How could the man see into her head, anyway? But in fact, Ethan was beginning to think that a sanatorium might be the perfect place for her if his suspicions were true. He couldn't bring his son into this house and leave him in her care.

For the time being, though, they had made a bargain. He was glad that his robe was securely belted—underneath he wore nothing but a throbbing erection that grew harder with each passing minute he was denied entrance to Priscilla's sanctum.

"Louisa, step aside. I have the right to enter my wife's bedroom."

"No, sir, Miss Priscilla told me she couldn't be disturbed tonight. I massaged her head and she's resting now. She said that she's the luckiest wife in the world because she has such a kind, understanding husband. Why, just the other day I overheard her telling her father the very same thing."

Ethan clenched his teeth until his jaw popped. Machiavelli had had nothing on this woman. But Ethan had amassed a small fortune thanks to ruthless solutions. He employed one now with nary a twinge of conscience. "Louisa, remember that day in the cellar a while back?" he asked in a confidential tone. "The day that Priscilla killed the kitten?"

The maid blanched under the gaslight flickering in the wall sconce. "She did not! She tried to help that poor little thing! He'd stopped breathing and—and—"

"The way that Eleanor and Caroline stopped breathing?"

Louisa stared at him. "Mr. Pembroke! What are you saying?"

"I'm saying that if you don't step aside, I might ask the county prosecutor to look into what I feel are the suspicious deaths of my two daughters. And I'll tell him to start by investigating my wife's maid."

Her jaw dropped. "I didn't harm a hair on either of those two children! I was never even alone with them. Miss Priscilla wouldn't allow anyone to get near . . ."

Ethan locked eyes with Louisa in a battle of wills, but he knew he'd bested her. Loyal she might be, to the point of an almost loverlike devotion to Priscilla. But he doubted that she was willing to sacrifice her life for her mistress. And Louisa, regardless of her innocence, surely had no doubt that with his connections, he could engineer her trip to the state penitentiary. No one, not Priscilla, not even Armistead, could save her.

Her round face crumpled and she wept noisily into her apron as she fled from Priscilla's door and ran down the hall.

Ethan didn't bother to knock. This was his home, goddamn it. Bought and paid for by him. Gripping the brass doorknob, he flung open the door and found Priscilla lying back on her pillows, lighted by the glow of a single candle on her bedside table. She wore a gauzy dressing gown and a look of astonishment upon seeing him.

"Ethan, didn't Louisa tell you that I'm not well?"

He closed the door behind him. "She did. And I've sent her off to do something more useful than act as your sentry. We certainly don't need her for what I have in mind."

She sat up and squared her shoulders. Her hair tumbled over them in a pale cascade. "I have a headache, Ethan."

He approached the bed, opening his robe as he did so to display himself to her. "Damn it, no you don't. You and I have an agreement, Priscilla."

She kept her eyes on his face, refusing to look any lower. "I agreed to submit to you if you brought me my child. I don't have him." Her growing dissatisfaction was giving her a bit of newly acquired grit—a quality that only made his desire burn hotter.

He reached down and yanked back the bedclothes, making the candle gutter. He discovered that her flimsy peignoir was open and that she wore nothing beneath it.

"You are not welcome here tonight!" she snapped and tried to cover herself, but the blankets were now on the floor.

"It looks to me as if you were expecting my visit."

"I don't know what you're talking about."

"Really? You're certainly dressed for the occasion. And will I find that you're ready for it too?" He passed a swift hand between her legs and she recoiled, but not before he discovered slickness and swollen arousal. He smiled, ready to burst at the thought that she had been pleasuring herself. "Why, Priscilla, I never would have guessed. Don't let me interrupt." He sat on the edge of the bed.

She glared at him, color filling her wan cheeks. "How dare you make such a disgusting accusation? I have never—"

Then more weakly, "I despise you and your filthy mind." She clamped her knees together.

He had to admit that he rarely bothered trying to satisfy her. There never seemed to be any point. Still, it might be interesting . . . "Open your legs," he commanded.

She lay rigid and unmoving, her soft, creamy body displayed before him.

"Priscilla, do as I say."

"Where is my child, Ethan? Where is he?"

He was ready to promise anything at this point, he was so inflamed. "He'll be here. If I have to go out and find him myself, you'll have your baby."

"Swear it."

"I swear."

She turned her face to the wall and relaxed her knees. He lay down beside her, pushing his erection against her thigh while he stroked her engorged flesh. She wept softly when he touched her, but he was unable to hold back, and with no more control than a youth, he released himself against her leg in hot, spurting jets.

Priscilla continued to weep. Thoroughly annoyed, Ethan put his robe back on and left his wife's room.

He went to his own bedroom and slammed the door, flinging off the robe and throwing it to the floor. Almost immediately, he heard Louisa return to Priscilla.

Through the adjoining door, which she kept locked, Priscilla uttered a soft, indistinct welcome to her maid. It was more than he ever got from his bitch of a wife.

Ethan poured himself a large brandy and flopped in a brocade chair. He fell asleep before the gentle blur of female voices in the next room faded away.

Chapter Thirteen

Zach and Sarah traveled in the disintegrating wagon for three more days, through green forests of lodgepole pine, spruce and fir, and arid stretches of sagebrush. Although Zach did his best to avoid ruts and rabbit holes, every time the wheels crashed over one or the other, their axles made threatening noises, sounding as if they would snap off. The entire conveyance shuddered and groaned in its joints, and Sarah expected the canopy to come crashing down and all four sides of the wagon box to fall away. In the back, Isabel complained as well, adding to the general racket.

When Sarah saw the faint outline of Helena's buildings that marked the town's perimeter, she swallowed hard. She felt as if she were approaching the jaws of hell, and that while she waited for Zach to return from his trip to the bank, she and Danny would be taunting the very devil to come and drag them in.

At the top of a rise, Zach brought the wagon to a halt under the shelter of a large oak. Setting the brake, he wrapped the lines around the handle and leaned his elbows on his knees while he considered the town, spread out below under the afternoon sun.

"It looks different from up here, doesn't it?" he asked absently.

Yes, it did, Sarah thought, holding Danny in her arms. There was Last Chance Gulch, a street that ran diagonally through town, the Bristol and International Hotels, sitting side by side, Gans and Klein men's clothiers on Broadway and Main. It was all so familiar—it had been her home.

But now she didn't belong there. Her own naïveté and Ethan Pembroke had seen to that.

"God, Zach, I wish you wouldn't go. Something could happen while you're down there. Someone might see you. I have such a bad feeling about this. Can't you move your account later, after you take us to the train?" She tugged on his arm. "Please, Zach, let's just keep going."

He pulled off his gloves and took her hand. "Now listen, honey. I know you're worried about this but I won't be gone long. I can't take the chance of losing that money. Anyway, I don't think I have enough cash on me to buy your train ticket. I have to go." He pointed in the general direction of First National Bank. "You can see the roof of the bank from up here. You won't be able to see me but you can watch for me. I'll leave the shotgun here too."

The possible danger his offer implied made her shudder. "I don't know anything about firing a gun."

He pulled the weapon from its boot beside him and quickly showed her how to operate it.

"I'll probably forget everything you've taught me in two minutes flat," she warned him in a shaky voice.

"If you need it, you'll figure it out fast enough."

True. If she'd had his shotgun the day that Bear Bettinger had come calling, she would have somehow managed to use it. Remembering how close they'd all come to disaster made her blood run cold.

He went through another quick lesson about loading it. "You don't need as accurate an aim as with a pistol or a rifle. Just point the thing and pull the trigger."

Her fear must have shown on her face. He shook his head. "You're *not* going to need it. I'll be back before . . ." He groped around for an end to the sentence. "Before you can name all the state capitals, teacher. How many are there, anyway?"

She smiled. "Forty right now. Montana should achieve statehood before the year is out. Then we'll have forty-one."

"Count on you to know that right off." He laughed, and she melted inside at the sight of his smile. "Okay, then, you recite them to Danny. That will make the time fly while I'm gone."

"I doubt that," she said, giving him a wobbly smile.

His expression turned more serious, but the light in his eyes, the hope, burned on. "When I get back, we'll bypass the town and catch the train at one of the stops farther west, maybe Red Mountain. You'll leave all the trouble and bad memories behind, and start a new life." He glanced down at his boots on the footboard, then back up at her. She saw his heart in his hazel eyes. "Sarah . . . I want to tell you . . . it doesn't seem right to . . . aw, hell." He tapped his fist lightly on her knee. "You just keep your eyes open and watch for me. I'll be back as soon as I can."

He jumped down from the seat and started to walk away. Sarah's heart clenched in her chest and she put her hand to her throat, trying to ease the ache there. Maybe he'd felt her longing and fear, because he stopped. Turning around, he leaped up to her side again in two running strides to kiss her with all the passion he had shown her during their one night together. He grabbed the back of her neck and pulled her mouth to his, hard and desperate, as if he could never get enough.

As if he would never have this chance again.

The idea brought another cold chill to her and she clung to him, with Danny squeezed between them. But she had to put on a brave front for both of them. She didn't want Zach to know how scared she was.

Zach drew back and searched her face as if he knew though. "It's going to be all right. I swear." Looking at

Danny in her arms, he kissed the baby's head and stroked his velvety cheek.

He leaped down again and lingered a moment, staring up at them both.

She wanted to tell him again that she loved him. But the time for that had passed and they were moving inexorably toward a parting of the ways.

"Please, please be careful," she added.

He nodded and his throat worked, as if a robin's egg were stuck there preventing some reply. Finally, he waved and called, "Look for me."

She kept her eyes on him, on his dark head and wide shoulders and long legs, as he descended the hill toward town. She watched until he was just a speck that finally disappeared among the buildings in Helena.

Then she began watching for his return.

Zach stood in the understated confines of the First National Bank, looking at clerk Jacob Mullins on the other side of the latticework teller's cage. Mullins compared Zach's withdrawal ticket against the balance in his account book.

"Mr. Garrett, are you sure you want to close this account? This is the first withdrawal you've made since you opened it." He was a small, fussy-looking man, who smelled faintly of the hair oil with which he plastered down his mouse-brown mop. Most of the ornate Spencerian entries in Zach's bankbook had been made by Mullins.

"That's what I want, Mr. Mullins."

Now the teller regarded him with a disappointed *tsk-tsk* and an expression of grave concern. It was almost closing time and the bank was busy with other customers. He glanced around and dropped his voice to a discreet level. "But to carry this much money in cash—you've got nearly a thousand dollars here. If you're planning a large transaction, perhaps a cashier's check would be safer."

"I don't need a check, I just need the cash. This is my grubstake." Zach decided to keep it to himself that he was moving the money to a competing establishment.

The little man sighed with obvious regret. "First National Bank will be sorry to lose you as a customer, but—very well. I'll have to get approval from Mr. Carpenter, the bank manager. If you'll just wait here a moment—"

As Mullins left the cage, Zach leaned against the counter. The walk into town had taken him more than an hour. He'd stayed to side streets and had kept a sharp eye the whole time, watching for anyone who might recognize him. Though he'd passed people on foot, on horseback, and on streetcars, he didn't think he'd seen a familiar face.

Still on his guard, he glanced around the bank. There were a couple of other men dressed as he was—jeans, boots, and trail dust—but the rest of the customers were prosperous-looking merchants and businessmen in dark suits and boiled shirts. Not the type he typically had dealings with.

One, though, caught Zach's attention when he felt the man's eyes on him. With an air of pomposity and snowy hair and beard, he puffed on a fine, slim cigar as he lounged in a guest chair at the bank manager's desk. Mullins hovered deferentially, waiting for Mr. Carpenter's blessing on Zach's request. Although Zach couldn't hear what was being said, conversation between the old man and a sour-looking Carpenter, who also glanced up at Zach, seemed very intense.

To the best of Zach's knowledge, he had never seen the old goat before, not even at Lady Rose's sporting house. But the man studied him with suspicion, as if Zach were still the light-fingered guttersnipe he'd once been and had no business being in this place. Zach returned his even, direct stare before turning away, but he knew a paralyzing pang of inadequacy, just the same. The feeling changed into resentment as he waited for Mullins.

It was just fine and dandy for a man to wear an expensive suit, smoke a good cigar, and look down his nose at the rest of the world, or at least Zach's corner of it. What did that stuffed shirt know about desperation and deprivation, about sleeping in a doorway or in a barn? Not much, Zach figured, judging by his well-fed paunch and his cozy conversation with the bank manager.

Despite the obstacles he'd overcome, Zach wondered if he'd ever rid himself of the grubby, insecure orphan kid who yet hid inside him. Not without Sarah, he didn't think. The boy in his heart still talked tough, calling names and making obscene gestures at the world, all the things that Zach, as an adult, couldn't do. But mostly, like the adult, the youngster was scared and lonely. The only thing that had ever made him feel secure was cash. To be alone *and* broke in the world was, in Zach's opinion, the worst thing that could happen to a person.

As if in response to his dilemma, Sarah materialized in his mind's eye and took the insecure boy into her arms. The sensation was so vivid that his throat tightened. He swore he could feel her embrace, as warm and real as if she stood right beside him, the sun-made, black-cherry corona on the crown of her head like a halo. Sarah . . . maybe if he had her gentle spirit watching over him, the frightened child would finally quiet within him.

After what seemed like an eternity, the teller returned with a leather wallet from which he withdrew a stack of paper bills and a few gold coins. "All right, sir, here we are." Quietly, Jacob Mullins counted out the sum of nine hundred sixty-seven dollars and twelve cents. Mullins returned the money to the wallet and pushed it under the bars to Zach's side of the counter.

Zach tucked it inside his shirt, his confidence restored. "It's been a pleasure, Mr. Mullins."

"Good luck to you in your new enterprise, Mr. Garrett," the teller called.

When Zach turned to leave, he saw the white-haired man talking into the bank manager's newfangled thingamabob, a telephone. To him, the old man, holding the earpiece to his head and speaking into a little tube, looked as ridiculous as a peacock carrying a parasol. He'd probably never gotten his hands dirty in his life, not in the literal sense, anyway, and no doubt suffered from gout, biliousness, and all the other complaints common to idle, wealthy men.

Zach smiled to himself as he strode past the two men and out of the bank. He yearned for the peace of the countryside. Progress and people were bearing down upon Helena, bringing the demand for streetcars and gadgets. Let them have it all, he thought, the champagne, the telephones, the stomachaches.

When Sarah and Danny were on their way to Oregon, he'd come back to Helena and confront Ethan Pembroke to get his ranch back. Just how he would accomplish that, he wasn't sure yet. But when he did, he'd have a future brighter than gold. And there was no room in his heart or head for anything else. Except, perhaps, for a dark-haired woman and her child who kept nudging their way into his thoughts.

Emerging into the sunlight, he took a deep breath and looked down the street. Then he set off for Montana National Bank.

Sarah had taken to striding in circuits around the wagon as she waited for Zach. She didn't suppose he'd been gone an

awfully long time, but it seemed like hours and hours. Now
and then she stopped to absently pat Isabel on the head, or
to check on Danny, who slept on unconcerned, but time
dragged.

She glanced up and noticed the low, southerly angle of
the sun. The change of seasons was fast upon them. The
weather was already beginning to turn. The days had grown
noticeably shorter and the nights were getting colder. Soon
the fields would turn gray and dormant as the earth rolled
over on its belly to rest against autumn and sleep through
winter. The trees would lose their leaves and stretch dry,
bony fingers toward a sky pale with snow clouds. She
would have to find a place to winter soon, and please God,
let it be somewhere far from here.

Growing weary with her pacing, she tightened her shawl
around her shoulders and settled on a boulder that over-
looked Helena and the road that would bring Zach back to
her. Thinking of fall, with its sharp fragrance of dry leaves
and first frosts, carried her back to her hometown. This was
the time of year when her mother would be putting up her
vegetables and preserves. The kitchen would be redolent
with the aroma of tomatoes, pickles, and fruit, simmering
on the stove. In between, she'd make up a batch or two of
her sovereign cough and sore throat remedy, which consisted of garlic bulbs soaked in a quart of good-quality
whiskey. Better to be ready than reaching when sickness
came, her mother would say.

She'd bring the heavy quilts out of storage, and have
Sarah's father carry the rug down from the attic to roll out
in the parlor to help ward off the cold nights to come. At
Christmas they'd bring in a spicy-smelling Ponderosa pine
to decorate. Except for two years, when the snow had been
impassibly deep, Sarah had always gone home for Christmas. They'd sung carols and sipped hot cider while she

played the old upright piano. Outside the snowdrifts sparkled like stardust under the winter moon, and made the words *silent night* exquisitely descriptive. She had wonderful memories of her family in all seasons and a wealth of traditions that she wanted to carry forward in her own life.

But this Christmas, she wouldn't go home. She sighed and rubbed her forehead with her fingertips. Although she loved Zach and wished she could stay with him, she recognized the possibility that this Christmas she might have no home at all if something happened to him and he couldn't come back for her. She didn't have enough money to buy a train ticket, and God knew there was no place in Helena where she could hide.

No, she couldn't think about that. Zach could do this. He could do anything. To distract herself, she returned her thoughts to her family, but in its own way, that was just as distressing.

What she would tell them, her parents and brother—about everything—she didn't know, exactly. They must be worried by now, having had no word from her for months. At the first opportunity, she would have to write to them and at least let them know she was alive and well. Beyond that, what? That she had a child? No, she couldn't tell them about Danny. It didn't matter how dear he was to her. The circumstance of his birth was still a shame that she couldn't burden them with.

Sarah stood up and began pacing again. She couldn't think about it now. That she'd deceived and worried those who loved her still weighed heavily on her heart. Eventually, it would all get sorted out. Perhaps the exact truth, which would only hurt them, might be blurred to spare their feelings and her own.

Once again, she peered down at the road below, looking for Zach. Finally, when her head had begun to ache from her squinting, she saw a tiny, solitary figure approach the base of the incline. She kept staring until it began to take on a familiar appearance—the dark hair, the confident, long-legged stride, the lean, masculine grace of movement. The late afternoon sun cut across his form, giving him a long shadow and outlining him in gold. God, how she loved him, almost as much as she feared Ethan Pembroke. At last he lifted a hand in greeting and, weak with relief, Sarah waved back with all her might. Not that long ago, she had dreaded the sight of him. Now she wondered if she'd ever be able to fill the void he would leave in her heart when they parted.

Zach climbed the steady rise to the top of the hill where she waited and held his arms open wide. "All right, Sarah girl, we're all set."

Laughing and near tears at the same time, she fell into his embrace and flung her arms around him. He twirled her in a circle, making her feet fly and her skirts swish. She giggled with a girl's delight. He smelled wonderful, she thought foolishly, and comfortingly familiar—like road dust and clean sweat and faintly, of soap. "No one saw you or tried to stop you?"

He set her on her feet and once again gave her the mock-offended look that made her laugh. "Me?" He touched his hand to his chest. "*Me?* Did I ever tell you about the time I ran for six blocks and through seven alleys with two legs of lamb?"

Though she tried to keep a stern look, it was hopeless. "I thought it was three blocks, four alleys, and *one* leg of lamb."

He shook his head and waved off her protests. "The details aren't important. I got away then, and I got away today. The new account book is right here, along with money for your train fare and some extras." He patted his shirt pocket.

"So, Danny and I—we're really free to go?"

He looked down at her with an expression of dawning realization in his eyes. "Yeah, I guess you are. You're free." Lowering his mouth to hers, he hovered above it for an instant. "You've got the rest of your lives to look forward to. Together."

Together, but not with him. Sarah meant to pull away. To have him kiss her and know that they would soon part . . . But her eyes drifted closed. "Free."

Then he kissed her with such soft tenderness, Sarah's legs turned to water. "I really do care about you, Sarah," he whispered over her lips.

And she wilted against him. "Oh, God, Zach . . ."

Holding her chin and the point of her jaw just below her ear, he deepened the kiss, teasing her mouth open with his tongue. His other hand traveled from the small of her back, over her hip and up her ribs to graze her breast. She knew she should pull away and stop him. She had to stand by the vow she'd made to be her own woman and no man's mistress. She had to make Zach keep his own promise.

But his touch was like fire and the feel of his mouth on hers, slick and warm, was so difficult to deny. He pressed her to his body and even through all the layers of their clothes, she felt the evidence of his arousal. She was drawn to him by ancient rhythms as old as the pull of the tides and the moon's phases, as basic as the need for food and drink. When he darted his tongue into her ear, her knees nearly buckled at the sensation, and a moan escaped her. His hands and mouth dared her to forget the rule she'd placed upon herself and him.

Maybe it didn't matter, after all, she thought dreamily, letting her hands wander over his back and brazenly tug at his shirttail. She would never see him again, and she could cherish the memory of their joining during all the lonely nights to come.

But with an anguished sound in his throat, he reached around and gripped her hands in his own, stopping her questing fingers from caressing the bare skin along his flanks.

"No." He released her and they backed away from each other, wary, wanting, breath coming fast. Every nerve under Sarah's skin called to Zach, defying both of them and their self-imposed restrictions. The very air around them seemed to pulse with its own heartbeat, keeping time with hers.

When he spoke, his voice was rough with frustration and unsatisfied desire. "I said I wouldn't ask to make love with you again. And I meant it."

She nodded and took a deep breath, putting her hands to her hot cheeks.

He raked a hand through his hair and fixed her with a look that could have set fire to the brush. "But, by God, woman, you're hard to resist." He grinned suddenly. "You're a hot-blooded little swatch of calico."

Desperate embarrassment coursed through Sarah, making her feel small and common and lewd. Looking at his smile though, she realized he was complimenting her, not criticizing her virtue, and her face grew even warmer. Instead of shame, she felt love for this man who would put aside his own pleasure to keep his word to her when her own resolve had wavered.

From the wagon, Danny started whimpering, and Zach stepped over to pluck him out. He held him in one strong arm and gently bounced him, and the baby immediately quieted. "What do you say, son? Do you think you can convince your mama to stay in Montana?" Zach leaned his ear down to Danny's mouth as if listening very carefully, and he grinned. "He says he might try."

The two dark heads looked so natural together, Sarah interlaced her fingers and pressed them to her mouth, her heart filled to bursting. Why couldn't they have met under different circumstances, in another time and place?

Clearing the emotion in her throat, she said, "I'd better get supper started. If you'll hand me my apron—"

Zach shook his head. "No, we should probably leave right now. We'll eat farther along the trail."

"But Danny has to eat. Don't we have a little time for—"

There came a sound then that made her pause, one that she almost felt before she heard it. The distant rumble of hooves and the rattle of harness, rising and falling on the wind, grew distinctly audible. Zach turned his head, obviously hearing it too.

He handed the baby to Sarah and retrieved his shotgun.

"What is it?" she asked, her pulse beginning to race. Clear and vivid memories of Bear Bettinger sprang to her mind. Not again, dear God, she pleaded, not again—

Zach shook his head to indicate he didn't know, and approached the edge of the rise to look over. Sarah followed at his elbow and peeked around his shoulder. What she saw made her wish that Bettinger had returned.

"Oh, God," she gasped, suddenly winded. "Oh, my God."

Riding up the hill were two policemen, flanking a four-seated surrey. Ethan Pembroke drove the horses himself, and Priscilla sat beside him. In the rear seats were two other men Sarah didn't recognize.

Zach recognized one of them though—the white-haired man he'd seen at the bank. Zach had led these vultures right to Sarah and Danny. He'd thought he made a clean getaway, he'd thought he was so damned smart with his tales of leg of lamb and outrunning the police. Gripping the shotgun, he uttered a low profanity and pulled Sarah behind him.

The whole cavalcade drew up to the campsite and halted. The horses stamped and shook their manes, and Ethan jumped down from the surrey.

"Well, Garrett, I'd given you up for dead."

"After you sent Bear Bettinger to see to it."

Pembroke shrugged. "I'm a businessman. I hired you to do a job for me, to find my son. When I thought you failed, I hired another man. You've cost me some money, but luckily, my wife's father saw you at the bank today. You must have recognized him—everyone knows Armistead Driscoll."

Zach spared a glance at the father. "Sorry, Driscoll, your name doesn't mean anything to me." He couldn't resist the dig. He'd learned the hard way that men like Pembroke and Driscoll expected to be treated like kings. It pricked their egos when their celebrity and power went unnoticed. "Our deal is off, Pembroke. I'm taking Miss Kincade and her son away from here."

"Ethan—" Priscilla began and leaned forward as if preparing to step down.

Over his shoulder, Pembroke signaled her to silence. Then he fixed Zach with a glacial stare. "Oh, yes, indeed our deal is off. You can bid farewell to that ranch land. And I'm willing to let Miss Kincade go anywhere she likes, but the boy is coming with us." From his inside coat pocket he withdrew some papers which he flipped open with the snap of his wrist. Zach recognized a duplicate set of the documents he carried himself—the contract Sarah had signed and the court order issued to enforce it. Holding them up for Zach's inspection, Pembroke added, "These are still binding and I've brought both Judge Driscoll and the police to make sure this business is concluded right now."

One of the "police" looked very familiar to Zach, although for the moment, he couldn't remember why. He heard a faint strangled sound from Sarah but he couldn't break eye contact with Pembroke to comfort her.

He remembered the name Driscoll now, though, and not because of the father-in-law. Judge Wallace Driscoll had signed the court order. Jesus, Pembroke had the whole damned family involved, from his wife to the judge. What a cozy arrangement.

White-hot anger sluiced through him and he struck Ethan's arm to push the papers away from his face. "Goddamn you, Pembroke, Sarah is the boy's mother. And from what I understand, you trapped her like a rabbit in a snare to get a baby for your wife." He let his gaze stray to the pale, thin woman sitting in the surrey. Priscilla wore a righteous look, though, as if Danny were her own child who'd been kidnapped.

Ethan's expression was stony. "Everything that Sarah did was of her own free will. *Everything*. That includes rolling in the sheets with a man she wasn't married to."

By God, Zach would kill this bastard with his bare hands. He launched himself at Ethan and grabbed his expensive lapels, lifting him off his feet. Priscilla screamed in the surrey, and in an instant, before Zach was able to get in even one good punch, the two policemen were off their horses and chaos erupted. One grabbed Zach by his hair to pull him off Pembroke, while the other, as big as a seed bull, yanked the shotgun out of his hand and delivered a hard uppercut to his jaw. Zach landed on his back at Sarah's feet. The other copper kicked him in the ribs and flipped him over on his face, twisting his arm painfully behind him. One false move and it would break. The big copper planted his boot on Zach's neck, and shoved the barrel of his own gun against Zach's temple. Rocks and pinecones tore through his shirt and dug into his flesh, but he felt no pain. Only rage. Worse yet, he was unable to do anything.

Christ, these couldn't be real policemen, he thought. They behaved more like hired thugs in costumes. Zach wouldn't be surprised if that were true. He twisted his face out of the dirt, trying to see Sarah.

She screamed too, and dropped to his side, still clutching Danny to her. In turn, the baby began crying, and Isabel bleated.

Armistead Driscoll climbed down from the surrey to add his piece. "You try that again, Garrett, and I'll order your arrest for assault and battery."

Priscilla descended from the surrey and approached, her plum moiré skirts rustling and her hands extended. "Let me have my baby, Sarah. I've waited far too long for him. I should have had him months ago."

Surging to her feet, Sarah glared at Priscilla. A mix of wild emotions and a ferocious maternal instinct raced through every fiber of her being, making her blood boil in her veins. She pressed Danny's head to her shoulder. "He is *not* yours. I must have been out of my mind to let you trick me into signing that damned agreement, you barren, wicked monster!"

Priscilla gasped and stared at her with her jaw open, plainly insulted. "How dare you!"

"On the contrary," Sarah lashed out, "how dare you?"

Ethan interjected. "You're in no position to call names, Sarah. Now give me the boy."

When Sarah had first learned of Ethan's deception and Priscilla's existence, she had been too hurt, too overcome with breathless disbelief, to speak up for herself. Now, looking at Ethan Pembroke made her stomach roil, and she wondered how on earth she had ever believed the promises and lies he'd told her, how she had ever allowed him to touch her, to—God, it made her ill just to think of it.

With a mother's protective anger humming through her like electricity through a wire, Sarah vented that fury. "So badly did you want a child that you stole from me, pauperized me, and threatened me with social ruin to get your own way! Fool that I was, I believed my reputation was important. Well, I was wrong, and so are you if you think I'll let you take my child! You'll have to kill me first!"

Priscilla turned to her father. "Daddy—Uncle Wallace— *do* something!"

Armistead Driscoll, his face the color of a rooster's comb, thumped the point of his walking stick on the ground. "Enough! Miss Kincade," he said, glaring at Sarah, "release the child to the Pembrokes' custody as you agreed to in the contract, or I'll see to it that he's taken from you right now and made a ward of court, pending adoption proceedings. Ethan, for God's sake, get the boy and let's finish this business. I have a meeting this evening and I have to get back to town."

"I'm handling this, Armistead!" Ethan barked. His father-in-law strode back to the surrey and settled heavily next to his brother, the judge, who looked distinctly uncomfortable.

Zach struggled to rise, but the policeman holding him down with his foot jammed the point of the shotgun barrel under his chin. The other tightened the grip on his arm. "You try to get up, Garrett, and I'll blow a hole through your jaw with your own gun and log it in the books as a suicide."

From the surrey, Armistead, plainly vexed, brushed at

his sleeve. "Priscilla, get back up here. This is no place for you. You should have stayed home."

Shaken, Priscilla did as she was asked.

Sarah backed up, fearing for Zach but terrified for Danny. "Stay away from me!" she snarled at Ethan. "I won't give up my son."

Ethan advanced on Sarah and Danny, and she turned and tried to climb to the seat of the wagon. Before she could get one foot on a wheel spoke, he pulled her back. Danny shrieked and hid his face against her neck.

Sarah looked around wildly, terror eating her alive. Desperately she hoped for someone, anyone, to intervene, for God's vengeance to storm down out of the sky like a bolt of lightning and burn up her persecutors. This was even worse than the day Bear Bettinger had appeared in their camp. At least there had been just one of him, but now she was so outnumbered, how could she possibly escape? She glanced at Zach, struggling against his captors, his face red with anger and pain while he watched Ethan.

Ethan closed his hands around Danny's warm little body and tried to pull him from her arms. She tightened her grip and kicked at this dreadful monster who would steal her child, connecting with his shins and feet.

"You goddamned bitch!" Ethan barked, and then slapped her so hard tears sprang to her eyes and bright spots of light swam before them.

She heard murmurs of protest from a man—who, she didn't know—and Zach growled in wordless protest on the ground. But he couldn't help her. Taking advantage of her disorientation, Ethan snatched Danny from her and ran to the surrey. Handing the baby to Priscilla, he vaulted to his seat, took up the reins and snapped them on the horses' backs. They took off at a lurch, and the fringe on the vehicle's cover shook mightily. Danny continued to scream, tearing out Sarah's heart.

Sarah howled with the unholy sound of a trapped animal and ran after the surrey. "Danny!" she sobbed, "Oh, dear God, don't take my baby!" The police sped past her on their horses, churning up clouds of choking dust as they galloped to catch up with the Pembrokes.

She stumbled on a tussock and fell, scraping the palms of her hands and tearing her skirt. Picking herself up, she began chasing them again, but the entourage grew smaller and smaller as they pulled ahead. "Give me back my baby!" she called frantically, tears blurring her vision.

Finally, they were just pinpoints on the road below and then they were gone.

"He can't drink cow's milk," she sobbed, breathless and heartbroken. Unable to run anymore, her feet dragged over the sage and bunch grass. "He needs goat's milk."

Falling again, she didn't bother to get up. She stayed on her knees and wailed.

Chapter Fourteen

As the night wore on, Zach feared for Sarah's sanity.

She sat on the ground by the fire clutching one of Danny's gowns. Though the crackling campfire gave off considerable heat, she trembled inside her shawl as if she couldn't get warm. She alternated between dull-eyed grieving—staring vacantly as if in a trance—and sobbing inconsolably. The sound of it tore at Zach's heart. She refused to speak, and she wouldn't let him comfort her. When he'd put his hand on her arm, she'd shaken it off and given him a look that would have frozen hell's lake of fire.

He knew he deserved it.

The side of her face was bruised where that bastard, Pembroke, had slapped her. Her hands were scuffed up from her falls, and he suspected that she'd skinned a knee too, judging by the rip in her skirt. But she seemed aware of none of her injuries, and he could understand that.

She'd run a good half mile by the time Zach caught up with her. He'd found her on her knees, gasping and wailing like a banshee. The bloodcurdling sound of it had made every hair on his body stand on end.

He'd led her back to camp and cleaned up the scrapes on her hands and face with soap and cool water. She'd allowed him to do that much. But now she would have nothing to do with him.

Anger at Ethan Pembroke, like a hot, slow-burning coal, sat in the pit of Zach's stomach. He'd known this kind of consuming hatred only once before in his life. That had been when Herman Gerlich beat him. He'd been just a kid then and he'd run away. Now the anger took a different, more malignant form. It was probably a good thing those uniformed thugs had taken his shotgun with them—if he had it, he might be tempted go down into Helena tonight and shoot Pembroke.

Short of killing him, which would only put a noose around Zach's own neck, he wanted to see the bastard ruined.

He sat in the shadows of the wagon, listening to the sounds of the night and Isabel's ruminant, champing jaws as she munched on the grass around her. The fragrant smell of chewed grass blended with the cool air, and any other time, Zach would have enjoyed the peace. Not now, though. All he could do was keep vigil over Sarah, since there was damned little else he could do for the moment.

He'd never felt so helpless in his life, or as bad. He actually welcomed the pain in his sprained arm, and the fiery sting of the scrapes and gouges on his face and torso he acquired in his struggle trying to defend Sarah and Danny. He was certain they were hired imposters and not real police—he now remembered one of them briefly working as a bouncer at Lady Rose's place. Pembroke or old man Driscoll probably used them when they wanted to intimidate someone who wouldn't know the difference between genuine coppers and a pair of thugs. With a judge in the family, who was there to complain to, anyway?

Gingerly, he tried to flex his arm, and a hot ache shot up to his shoulder. The pain of his injuries was part of his punishment, he figured. The retribution he had coming to him for trying to profit from Sarah's misfortune.

That was really why he and Sarah were here in this place right now, nursing wounds of the flesh and the heart.

All of this was his fault, he thought, twiddling a dry stick he'd found next to his leg. Somewhere along the trail that had brought them to this point, his conscience, which he'd suppressed for so long, had stirred to life and he'd recognized what a crappy thing he was doing, separating Sarah from Danny.

At first he'd told himself that she'd made her own trouble and then compounded it by failing to hold up her end of the bargain she'd made with the Pembrokes. After all, a deal was a deal. Seeing them together, mother and child, day after day, had made him realize that he, not she, was in the wrong.

He'd almost made it up to her though. Out here, he'd come to care not only for the mother, but for the child as well, and had grand, magnanimous plans to let them go free.

But he'd been worried about losing his money in the bank. Cash meant security. It turned out that not everything was about money, he realized with dumb surprise. Hadn't Sarah told him that? Hadn't she practically begged him not to go to Helena? He snapped the stick in his hand.

Not everything was about money.

He wished with all his heart and soul that he'd remembered the lesson before he'd gone into town. If he had it to do over, he'd have left the cash in that bank account. Between what he had in his pockets and whatever he'd make from selling the mules, he'd have had enough to buy a train ticket for Sarah.

But, that wasn't how it had happened. Today, full of bluster and bravado, he'd marched into town, into the bank, almost into the very lap of Sarah's enemies, and led them back here. Of course, he hadn't recognized Priscilla Pembroke's father at the time. Zach realized now that when he saw old man Driscoll using the bank manager's telephone, he must have been talking to Ethan Pembroke. They'd set their wheels in motion to steal Danny.

On foot, Zach had been easy to follow, slow-moving

prey, unable to outpace a horse or that lightning-quick contraption, the telephone.

He cursed himself for that idiocy too, going to town on foot. He wasn't some ten-year-old kid anymore, who resembled all the other dirty-faced ten-year-olds around him, able to blend into a crowd. He'd walked right into the First National and stood there while the teller had trumpeted his name for all to hear.

He looked at Sarah, slumped by the fire. Hell, he couldn't just sit here and watch. His heart ached too, and if they couldn't comfort each other in this crisis, there wasn't much point in being together. In fact, he carried the very real fear that Sarah would no longer love him, considering everything he'd done to her. Still holding the broken stick, he rose from his keg and went to her side. Settling cross-legged next to her, he put an arm around her.

This time she didn't shake off his touch, but she pulled away from it, and he let his arm drop. Her eyes were puffy from crying and in the gold-red of the firelight, it seemed as if she'd aged twenty years since this afternoon. Still beautiful, but tragedy heaped upon tragedy gave her a bloodless, embittered look that ate at his soul. His throat closed.

She buried her face in Danny's dress and inhaled. "It smells like him," she said, her voice ragged and thin. "Like talc and that wonderful baby smell he has."

He reached for the dress, but she snatched it away from his hand.

Tears burned his lids. "You know I feel like he's my son too."

She considered him with narrowed eyes. "Well, he isn't," she snapped, her chin quivering. "He's not Ethan's and he's not yours. He's just mine. He came from me, and I bore him alone."

The well-aimed reminder was as sharp and cold as an ice pick.

"I know this is my fault," he began, feeling the need to purge the demons of guilt that plagued him. "If I'd listened to you . . . if I'd never gone into town—if I hadn't been so damned worried about that bank account—" He pulled his bankbook from his pocket and looked at it as if it were a vile enemy. "God, Sarah, you were right about that—I've been a fool, worrying about money, worrying about all the wrong things."

She held up a shaking hand to silence him, her eyes brimming over. "I made mistakes too. But right now I don't want to talk about whose fault this was. I already know."

He snapped the stick into smaller pieces in his lap, then let them fall to the ground. "Mine, you mean."

She huffed at him like an angry house cat, as if trying to hold back and then no longer could. "Yes, if you insist on hearing it! Money has been your top priority all along, and I've paid the price for your greed more than once. I cared about you, though, and I could overlook . . . forgive. But this—*this*!" She shook her head and gestured wildly with Danny's dress. "I can't overlook it and I can't forgive it."

Stung by the force and truth of her accusation, Zach jumped to the offensive. "You don't think you were lured by Pembroke's fancy champagne dinners you told me about? Those promises he made to you of a big house and a life of leisure? None of that comes for free, you know. Some things *are* about money and—"

She cut him off, her eyes narrowed to slits. "Don't you dare tell me again that I got myself into this, and that you came along after the fact. I was minding my own business in Lame Horse, or at least I was trying to, when you barged into town and dragged us out here."

Angry and hurting, Zach snapped out a profane curse, picked up a pebble near his knee, and threw it into the darkness with all the force he could put into it. They were bent on punishing each other, it seemed, maybe because there was nothing else they could do. They couldn't fight a well-oiled, powerful machine like the Pembrokes and the Driscolls. The Sarah Kincades and Zach Garretts of the world were just ants under their heels to be stepped on.

All they could do was mourn the loss of a child with dark, downy hair and a toothless grin that could make anyone's day better. Zach wasn't sure which was harder to bear—losing a child in death or having him stolen away.

"What do you want to do tomorrow?" he asked, rubbing his temples, determined not to let the conversation degenerate into an argument. "Do you still want to set out for Oregon?"

She stared at the flames, silent for a long time. Then looked up at him. "No, now I don't have any reason to. I want to go home."

His heart felt as if it had stopped. It gave him a funny, breathless feeling, as if someone had punched him in the chest. Maybe she'd changed her mind about staying with him. "Meaning?"

"I gave you my heart, but the Pembrokes took it with them when they stole Danny. I just—" She breathed a shaky sigh, then looked at him with accusing, haggard eyes. "I don't want to spend one more day with you. Not one."

He flinched, pushing back the torrent of pain and emotion her words stirred up. God, but it hurt. Waiting to get control of what he was certain would be a rough voice, he said finally, "I promised I'd see you to wherever you wanted to go. I'm standing by that promise."

She pressed the baby's dress to her cheek again. "I want

to go home to my family in Stockett." It was about a hundred miles north of Helena.

He nodded. "I'll take you."

"No! Just get me to a stage stop. That will be good enough."

He swallowed hard. "I'll do that and make sure you get on safely."

Her mouth was tightly pursed. At last she muttered, "Thank you, Zach."

Still clutching the offensive account book, he pulled her into his arms and she let him. Stiff in his embrace, she wept silently, her shoulders shaking, as if she sought comfort from a stranger. He pressed his cheek to her bowed head and rocked her, holding her close.

When he thought of what he'd nearly had, a woman's love, his stomach knotted. Yeah, he'd almost had it, and then at the last moment, he'd thrown it all away by worrying about the goddamned money. His life had crumbled around him and now he sat in the ruins. He lifted a hand to dash the back of his hand over his own wet eyes.

It was the hand that held the bankbook.

An idea, as startling as an electric shock, zigzagged through his mind. "Hey . . . *hey!*" He pushed her back to look at her. "You said you had an account too, the one that Pembroke emptied."

She gazed at him, dumbfounded and uncomprehending. "Yes. So what?"

"Which bank?"

"First National. Why?"

"Do you still have the book?"

She shrugged and gazed at the fire. "Oh, God, I don't remember. I don't want to talk about—"

He closed his hands around her upper arms and forced her to meet his eyes. "Sarah, listen to me. This is important.

You've got that beat-up old valise. Do you think the book is in there?"

She scowled at him. "There's no money in that account, Zach! It's empty! Money, money, mon—"

"Goddamn it, I'm not talking about money!"

"What are you talking about, then?"

"Do you have the book?"

She locked her gaze with his. "Well, maybe," she fretted, "but what can it matter?"

"We might be able to get Danny back, and that bankbook is one of the weapons I'll need."

She stared at him, suspicion in her eyes and utter desperation in her voice. "How?"

"I have an idea. I can't promise anything anymore, Sarah. But, by God, I'll sure as hell do my best. Someone has to rescue Danny and topple those sons of bitches off their high-and-mighty pedestal." He shook his head, amazed at the position he was putting himself in. "I guess it's going to be me."

Animated by a glimmer of hope, regardless of how faint, Sarah tore through her valise, pulling things out and throwing them everywhere. She found underwear, her hairbrush, her precious *McGuffey's Readers,* Danny's extra clothes—which made her break down again.

But no bankbook.

She couldn't remember packing it, and after all, why would she? The thing was as worthless as Confederate bonds.

Just when she was ready to give up, her frantic, questing fingers hit upon the little ledger wedged in the bottom corner of the bag. When she gave it to Zach, he leafed through the pages and smiled.

"Jacob Mullins made these entries. I'd recognize that curlicued handwriting anywhere."

Zach said he had a plan. Tomorrow morning, they would travel into Helena. He would get her a hotel room where she could rest and wait for him. While he did what, she didn't know, and he wouldn't tell her. Not yet.

It was a long and sleepless night for Sarah. She never dozed even once, and though she couldn't have sworn to it, she didn't think Zach did either. He turned restlessly and sighed a lot. They lay in the wagon, as close to the opposite sides as they could get, as stiff as store window dummies.

Anger did not describe how she felt about Zach, but blame—oh, blame was perfect. Her lacerated mother's heart had no room for clemency or compassion. If Danny had died from an illness or an accident, she might have been able to understand Zach's pain. But Danny hadn't died. One moment she'd been holding him, the next he'd been taken from her, and all because of Zach's actions. Even though he'd offered valid reasons for going into town, he should have known better. He should have known the risk was too great.

She'd known it.

She watched the stars cross the sky, reliving the scene from that afternoon again and again, and each time she'd remember some horrifying new detail. The venomous look in Ethan's eyes—why hadn't she seen it from the beginning? Priscilla, odd and spoiled and demanding—this woman would be taking care of her child. And worst of all, oh, dear God, the worst, Danny's terrified expression when Ethan had pulled him from her arms.

She wrestled with one other thought that was equally difficult to consider. Zach's remark about her being seduced by Ethan's lavish, expensive dinners and the promise of a fancy house hit closer to the truth than she would like to admit, even to herself.

But there it was.

She *had* been dazzled by the side of life Ethan had shown her, one generally unavailable to a schoolteacher, and in fact, to most other people. She'd been impressed by his knowledge of fine wines and food, his impeccable dress, and his sophisticated ways. But decency of character wasn't born of knowing which wine to order or a talent for financial dealings.

A real man, an upright man, could just as easily dig ditches for a living, and barely know the difference between a teapot and an inkpot. His true measure lay in his heart and in his soul. To do what he'd done to her, Ethan Pembroke must possess neither or they were both as black as tar.

Everyone needed *some* money to live. After all, one of the reasons she'd gone to Lame Horse was to earn a living for herself and Danny. She'd often heard people say that it was the root of all evil, but money, by itself, wasn't a bad thing. Rather, the correct Bible verse said it best.

The love *of money is the root of all evil.*

And that, Sarah believed, was where the difference lay.

Under a slate-gray sky that threatened rain, Zach and Sarah drove the sorry wagon and tired mules into Helena early the next morning.

The wind had kicked up and a sharp breeze blew through Sarah's thin shawl, chilling her to the bone. As if knowing her grief, the sun refused to shine, refused to warm her.

She had been away for just about a year. The town looked the same and yet, after the slower pace of Bozeman and Lame Horse, after the utter peace of the plains, the bustle of civilization was jarring to her. Some of the newer buildings, three and four stories high, seemed as tall as Chicago's famous skyscrapers that she'd read about. As people hurried over the sidewalks, and carriages, wagons, and horses vied for space on the street, she was struck by a hubbub and urgency of purpose that she realized she hadn't missed.

People stared at them as they traveled down Main Street in their groaning conveyance, the rotting wagon canvas flapping in the wind. God, they must look like hard-luck sodbusters, newly arrived to the big city from some remote mountain cabin, bringing their goat with them. Although she'd changed clothes, what she wore this morning was nearly as threadbare as the torn dress she'd taken off. She'd barely bothered to tidy her loose braid and she hadn't been able to take a full bath since leaving Lame Horse. If anyone recognized her now, they would certainly wonder what misfortune had befallen their upstanding Miss Kincade, dedicated teacher, church organist, and bake-sale planner.

In her other life, she would have perished from embarrassment to be seen in this state. She'd worried about what others thought of her conduct and how she looked to them. Now, it didn't matter because the woman she'd been was gone forever. Nothing mattered, except the possibility that she might get her child back. And if Zach couldn't accomplish that, trivial things like clothes and appearance would never seem important again.

Her innocence and idealism had been stripped from her peeled away in layers, with each treacherous betrayal, each disappointment, leaving a woman who looked at the world with a view unfettered by girlish dreams. Only hope remained, a feeble, flickering light in what was the darkest moment of her life.

She and Zach had spoken very little since last night. She

was exhausted and had retreated into herself. Anyway, she didn't know what to say or how she felt about him. Even though she'd told him differently, she hadn't stopped caring about him, exactly—but anger, grief, and blame crowded out every other emotion.

Glancing at him now with numb detachment, she saw his set face as he sat forward with his elbows on his knees and the lines in his gloved hands. He looked as bad as she felt, tired and haggard, with dark circles underscoring his eyes, and the shadow of a two-day beard dark on his jaws. But inner strength radiated from him. It was there in his clean, even profile, and the symmetry of his broad shoulders and straight back. Zach was capable, a survivor, as immutable as the Rockies. She should find comfort in that, if only she could feel something.

He pulled the wagon up to the front of the International Hotel, one of the town's more famous and elegant establishments. It had been destroyed by fires and rebuilt so many times, it was sometimes referred to as the Phoenix of Helena.

Zach set the brake and jumped down, then came around to help Sarah to the ground.

"Come on, I'll get you settled." He held out his hand.

She looked at the imposing four-story structure. "I can't afford to stay here!"

He gave her a long, steady look. "No? And what can you afford?"

Sarah couldn't answer. Of course, she had no money at all. He would have to pay for any hotel room she rented.

As if reading her mind, he said, "Consider it a down payment on the debt I owe you."

Exactly which debt that was, she wasn't sure but she wasn't about to discuss it here on the street, under the gaze of curious onlookers. With great hesitation she put her hand in his and let him take her elbow to help her down.

After he grabbed her valise from the back, he escorted her into the hotel lobby. The desk clerk considered them with brows that nearly scraped his receding hairline. At first Sarah worried that he'd recognized her, but then she realized they must look far worse than she thought. Expecting the clerk to ask them to leave, she was relieved when the man recovered his dignity and hid his surprise.

"A room for me and my wife," Zach said.

She turned and gave him a sharp look and was about to object when he pinched her elbow hard enough to silence her.

"Very good, sir. That will be two dollars." The clerk spun the register around on its turntable for Zach to sign, and plucked a key from a rack behind him. Zach scratched his name in the book—he had nice handwriting, Sarah noticed inanely—and threw fourteen dollars on the counter.

"For a week," Zach said.

The clerk turned the register around and read Zach's name. "Room 307, Mr. Garrett. A very nice room it is too. Shall I have a boy bring up your, um, bag?" He indicated the scarred valise that looked as if it had been kicked all the way into town.

"Nope, thanks." Zach grabbed it and took Sarah's elbow, steering her toward the stairs.

When they were out of earshot, she fixed him with accusing eyes and demanded in a hissing whisper, "What are you doing, saying I'm your wife? If you think that paying for the room means you get to sleep in it as well—"

"I'm not going to stay here at all."

"You're not?"

"No. Would you rather that I'd told the clerk your real name?"

She dropped her gaze. "Well, no, I guess not . . ."

"I'll need to be able to talk to you and I don't want to have to worry about someone thinking that a strange man is visiting Miss Sarah Kincade's hotel room."

She couldn't think of an argument for that. Being registered as Mrs. Garrett gave her anonymity, a respite that would postpone the awkward questions sure to come when someone eventually recognized her.

They reached the third floor, quiet and carpeted and lit with flickering gaslight. Zach led her to a door with the brass numerals 307, put the key in the lock, and opened the door. Inside was a clean, spacious room with flowered wallpaper, nice furniture, a real bed, and lace curtains.

Dear God, this was what she had yearned for during those weeks on the trail. Of course, she'd always pictured Danny with her.

Zach ushered her in and put the valise on the floor.

"What are you going to do now?" she asked.

"First of all, I'm going to sell the team and the wagon and buy a horse. Then I'll get a room next door at the Bristol Hotel. After I get cleaned up, I'm going to pay a visit to a bank teller." He reached into his shirt and withdrew several coins. Extracting a twenty-dollar gold piece, he picked up her hand and pressed it into her palm.

She held it out to him. "I can't take this."

He sighed and closed her fingers around the coin. "Sarah, you have to eat. You need something else to wear. None of that will be free."

He was right once more, and she wondered if her brain would ever clear enough to let her think on her own. Through the fog of her despair, one thought did occur to her though. "What about Isabel?"

Zach wasn't sure whether to laugh or utter a profanity. That damned goat. "I'll try to sell her with the mules."

"Oh." Sarah looked so crestfallen, so defeated, he felt like an ogre all over again.

"What else can we do with a goat? You can't keep her in a hotel room."

She dropped her gaze to the carpet. "No, no, I understand. I—I just got used to her, I guess."

Zach understood too. One by one, everything that was dear to Sarah was being taken away from her. Now she stood bereft and dispossessed in this room, with all of her worldly goods in a valise.

Reaching behind him, he closed the door. He put his hands on her shoulders and kissed her cheek. Its chill worried him. "Stick around here so I can find you and let you know what I learn. Sarah, I'm going to do everything I can to get Danny back."

She stared into his eyes. "Why won't you tell me how you're going to do it?"

"Because I'm not sure yet myself."

Chapter Fifteen

Ethan Pembroke slumped drunkenly in the chair at his desk, staring at a crystal decanter of brandy in front of him. Actually, it was a half decanter. Had he really finished off that much? He must have—it had been full when he sat down an hour ago.

Pouring another healthy measure into his glass, he took a large swallow without bothering to savor the fumes, and considered the last twenty-four hours. He'd accomplished the difficult mission that Priscilla and Armistead had pressured him to complete. Armistead Ethan Pembroke, his son, was safely ensconced in the house. But even with the doors to his study closed, and a floor between himself and his wife's bedroom, he could hear the baby yowling. The child had cried almost nonstop since they brought him home.

Ethan had wanted to get a closer look at his son. Everyone who saw him, even those who didn't know the details of the boy's parentage, had remarked on the uncanny resemblance he bore to Ethan. But Priscilla and her maid had whisked him away upstairs yesterday as soon as they'd gotten home. They'd moved the cradle into Priscilla's room and now she was in there fussing over him, with Louisa acting as her lady in waiting.

He'd seen his wife just once since then, which, he admitted in his inebriate state, was fine with him. She'd already looked worn and frazzled. Well, it was probably hard to sleep with that baby crying hour after hour.

What Ethan knew about children would fit on the tip of a gnat's eyelash, but he supposed it was possible that the child, young though he was, missed Sarah. During the mad dash away from Garrett's camp yesterday, he'd glanced over his shoulder and seen her running after the surrey, screaming and wailing.

Ethan took another drink and sank lower into his chair.

More than once he'd wished he'd never laid eyes on Sarah Kincade. His conscience wasn't troubled in the least by what he'd done to her, the promises he'd made, and the lies he'd told her. A conscience was only an obstacle to success. But the whole business had turned into a much bigger bother than he'd ever anticipated.

First he'd had to maneuver Sarah into a vulnerable position, a process that had taken months. Oh, he hadn't minded bedding her. At least she'd been more responsive than Priscilla. And the money he'd emptied from her bank account had more than covered her expenses that he'd agreed to pay when she went to Bozeman. But the rest of his carefully laid plan had backfired when she decided to run.

He'd spent a considerable amount, advancing money to that cowpoke, Garrett, to find Sarah and the baby, paying Bettinger to find the three of them, and then hiring the two beefy thugs yesterday who'd ridden alongside the surrey. He smiled when he thought of them—they'd been a bargain compared to the other expenses. Their very presence had been effective, inarguable. No one wanted to tangle with what they believed were policemen. Coupled with the judge, they'd given the whole entourage an official look. But it had been a lot of trouble, just the same.

All because Priscilla insisted on being a mother, a role which Ethan seriously doubted she was suited for. And those doubts had only continued to grow over the past several months.

Upstairs the crying continued, and he drained his glass. Dusk brought a gloom to the study and he sat in the gathering darkness, muzzy and tired, his chin resting on his chest. Things around here had better be quieted down by tomorrow night. He and Priscilla were hosting an important dinner party, and Helena's most influential people were invited to listen to his proposal to build a hotel and natatorium at the site of a natural hot springs. The project would require investors and he needed to make an impressive showing. It wouldn't do to have the house in an uproar with the sound of a screaming baby overriding conversation in the dining room.

A sudden tapping on the door brought him around. "Ethan?"

God, he groaned to himself, Priscilla again. Would the woman give him no peace?

"Come in, Priscilla," he commanded impatiently.

She opened one of the double doors, and a wedge of gaslight fell across the polished hardwood floor.

Approaching his desk, she eyed the decanter but made no comment about it. Instead, she twisted her handkerchief in her hands. Even in the dim light, he could see that her usually tidy hair straggled a bit, and her blue silk dress was stained with infant excretions that he could smell from where he sat. "Ethan, there's something wrong with the baby."

A vague unease crept over him. He'd been down this road before with her. "*What's* wrong?"

"He just won't keep his milk down and he has the most terrible flux. Who knows what kind of hardships he endured out in the wilderness, what kind of disease he might have been exposed to? Can you use your telephone to call Dr. Nash?"

It was starting already? he wondered. Just like with the other two children? Then he caught himself. No, it was possible that Priscilla was right. Perhaps the baby had contracted some illness on the trail.

He pushed himself upright in his chair and reached for the telephone on the desk. "All right. I'll call. But this house had better be in order by tomorrow night, Priscilla. You know how important that dinner party is to us."

She gazed at him with eyes that said so much more than her response. "Yes, Ethan. I know."

Zach eyed the sun sliding down the western sky. As it dropped the wind grew colder and he was glad for the sheepskin coat he'd bought that afternoon.

Lingering in blue shadows at the mouth of an alley next to the First National Bank, he watched as the employees left for the day. He imagined some heading off to warm supper tables and others to solitary rooms. He studied each face, looking for bespectacled Jacob Mullins. He could have gone inside before closing, but he waited here, hoping to talk to the man away from the eagle eye of the bank manager, who would probably grill Mullins about the conversation and report Zach's presence to the Pembrokes or the Driscolls.

This stop at the bank was one of many that had made up Zach's day. After he'd checked into the Bristol Hotel and cleaned up a little, he'd sold the team and wagon to a livery on the edge of town and bought a sturdy, five-year-old gelding. The livery owner had even agreed to take Isabel, saying a body never knew when a nanny goat might come in handy. Zach had almost felt bad when he'd walked away from her. He'd hated that animal from the first day he'd laid eyes on her, but over the weeks, they'd reached a truce. She'd even let him hand-feed her now and then.

Oh, hell, he thought, cursing his soppy sentimentality. He shrugged inside the big coat. She was just a damned goat. Sarah's feelings were probably rubbing off on him.

After that bit of business, he'd gone to Gans and Klein to get himself some clothes. Nothing fancy, but his old shirts and jeans were just about falling off. Then he'd stopped at a gunsmith's to buy a Colt revolver, which he now wore strapped to his hip. The next few days could be dangerous, and he wasn't about to remain unarmed.

In his pocket, he gripped Sarah's bankbook, which showed only deposits and no withdrawals. The last entry noted a balance of almost three hundred dollars. It wasn't a vast fortune, but from experience, he knew how difficult it would be for her to accumulate that sum, especially on a teacher's pay. Ethan Pembroke had stolen it from her and kept it, the no-good bastard.

The bank doors opened again, and at last Jacob Mullins emerged. The bowler hat he wore made Zach look twice, but no, that was him. He looked even smaller out in the open, away from his teller's cage, and Zach wondered if he stood on a box behind that counter. He stepped out of the shadows.

"Mr. Mullins."

The little clerk jumped, a startled expression fluttering across his bony face. "Mr. Garrett—I didn't expect to see you again. I thought you were leaving Helena."

"Something came up. If you have a few minutes, I need to talk to you." Zach looked around and spotted a saloon across the street. "Do you have time for a beer?"

Mullins adjusted his lapels primly. "My, no, I don't drink."

Of course he didn't, Zach thought sourly. "Coffee, then. We can get something at a café."

Mullins fussed, "No, I'm sorry, I can't. If I don't get to my boardinghouse in time, I'll miss supper. The food goes pretty fast and—"

Frustration made Zach bark, "Hell, I'll buy your damned supper! In a restaurant!" Mullins jumped. Zach held up his hands, immediately backing down and lowering his voice. "I'm sorry. Look, if it weren't important, I wouldn't bother you. But it *is* important, Mr. Mullins, and so is your part in this. Please . . . the future of a woman and her child hangs in the balance, and I think you can help them."

"Me! Well, I—" The clerk glanced around at the evening traffic, as if seeking permission from someone, anyone.

Detecting his advantage, Zach sweetened the offer. "How does steak and fried potatoes sound? And maybe apple pie for dessert?"

Jacob Mullins practically licked his lips. "It sounds very good, Mr. Garrett. Very good, indeed."

Seated at a back table in a busy chophouse, Zach watched as the bank teller carefully cut a steak into precisely equal pieces, and then savored each bite as if it were manna from heaven. Zach was sure it beat the hell out of any boarding-house fare. He also doubted that the man's bank job paid more than two or three dollars a week, tops, so he'd probably never eaten like this in his narrow little life.

Zach jabbed his fork into a pork chop, but the strong smell of Mullins's hair oil robbed him of his already flimsy appetite. Mostly he waited with barely concealed impatience for the teller to finish. He figured he'd nail him with his questions between dinner and dessert.

At last, after Mullins had mopped clean every square inch of his plate with a piece of bread, he sat back in his chair. Wiping his mouth with the white linen napkin, he wore a look of utter satisfaction.

The waiter appeared to take the dishes. "Gentlemen, we

have three kinds of pie tonight for dessert, apple, cherry, and peach."

Mullins sat up. "Wonderful! I'll have—"

But Zach interrupted. "In a few minutes. Just coffee for now, thanks."

After the waiter cleared the table, Zach reached into his pocket and produced Sarah's passbook. "Down to business, Mr. Mullins." He unbuttoned his coat in the warm room, purposely letting Mullins see the Colt. "What we're about to discuss needs to remain between us, is that understood? That means you can't tell Carpenter, the bank manager, or anyone else who might ask."

Mullins's gaze dropped to the revolver and his eyes widened behind his wire-framed spectacles. Though he whispered, Zach could hear his sudden agitation. "Mr. Garrett, are you going to ask me to do something *illegal*?"

Zach almost laughed at the man's horrified expression. "No. But I think a crime has been committed by someone else, and you can help me figure that out." He opened the book to its first page, which listed Sarah's name and her first deposit. "Does this look familiar to you?"

After great hesitation, Mullins took the book from him and studied it. "Hmm. Well, I see I opened the account . . . oh, yes, I remember now. Miss Kincade. A very nice lady, and a diligent saver. She added a little to her savings each month. A schoolteacher, I believe. I think she taught Sunday school too." He glanced up at Zach. "How did you get this book?"

"She gave it to me."

Mullins shrugged. "Of course, it has no value now, anyway. The account was closed well over a year ago."

"But not by her. The balance shows nothing but deposits."

Zach thought he heard a note of regret in the teller's answer. "No, not by her."

"Tell me about it."

"Oh, I— Really, this is personal business between Miss Kincade and First National Bank. It wouldn't be right for me to—"

Zach leaned forward. "Please. Something about the *whole thing* isn't right. You know it and so do I, and I'm trying to help her."

Mullins glanced around the busy restaurant, as if now understanding the need for confidentiality. Putting his elbows on the table, he also leaned closer and began haltingly. Finally, the words came more easily and he went on to describe the day that Sarah came into the bank with Ethan Pembroke to add him as a cosigner to the account.

"He said that he would take very small sums from the account to invest for her. They seemed quite ... close, I suppose one might say. I had the impression that perhaps marriage was in their future, and she gave every indication that she trusted him implicitly. Although he was newly arrived in Helena, he was a well-established First National customer, with long-standing accounts with the bank. In fact, he was and still is one our larger depositors.

"As time went by, Miss Kincade continued to make her own small deposits and Mr. Pembroke left the account untouched. Then one day several months later, he came in alone and closed it."

Mullins removed his spectacles and polished them on his napkin. "I have to admit that I was concerned, but Miss Kincade had made him a signer on the account, and he had the right to withdraw every penny."

"Without this?" Zach asked, tapping the passbook in front of the teller.

The man blanched. "Well, no, not strictly speaking.

When I told Mr. Pembroke he must present it, he became quite annoyed and reminded me that he had a great deal of money on deposit at First National. Even Mr. Carpenter objected to the transaction, but after a long, private discussion between him and Mr. Pembroke, he approved it, and I had to liquidate the account."

A day or two later, Sarah had come into the bank, plainly distraught about something, and became even more so when she learned that her account had been closed.

"Pembroke robbed her, you know," Zach said quietly. "He left her penniless and in a very bad spot." He waited a beat and then added, "Her and her child."

Jacob Mullins stared at him, apparently grasping his meaning. He swallowed hard and handed back the passbook. "I couldn't prevent it. I had to follow orders."

Zach knew that but he didn't reply. There was nothing to say. He merely pocketed the book, a slim but valuable piece of evidence in the whole sorry mess.

"What happened to her—Miss Kincade? Is she all right now?"

Zach put his napkin on the table. "No, she isn't. Not at all. She's a broken woman."

The waiter reappeared at that moment. "Have you gentlemen decided what kind of pie you'd like?"

Mullins sat back in his chair, looking stunned and waxy. "I don't believe I'll have dessert, after all."

Late that night Zach lay naked in his bed at the Bristol Hotel and listened to the occasional horseman riding by in the street, or the jingling of harness and creaking wheels that signaled a wagon rolling past. Sometimes he heard faint murmuring and footsteps in the hall outside his door, as guests staying on the same floor entered or left their rooms.

He was dead tired after everything that had happened and all the people he'd talked to. But sleep eluded him. He lay on his back, staring at the shadows thrown across the wall next to him, created by the streetlight and the crossbars of a telephone pole.

Considering the places he'd slept in his life—in doorways, in barns, and bunkhouses full of snoring, farting men, he should have enjoyed wallowing in the good bed linens, feeling their cool crispness against his clean, bare skin. Tonight, though, he had just one thought on his mind.

Sarah.

He'd had years of practice being a scared survivor of the streets and life in general, long enough to learn how to shut out his emotions. She had restored his humanity and his heart, only to leave both yearning for her. What the hell was he supposed to do with his thawed feelings without her?

It didn't take much to imagine her lying next to him on the sheet, her skin as smooth and pale as churned cream, and her black-cherry hair draped around her like a cloak of satin. He could picture her, full breasts that fit his hands so perfectly, the coral nipples, the rounded belly, feminine and womanly.

He'd had just one tantalizing night with her, a night of desperate need and a melding of souls so profound it sucked the breath from his lungs just to remember it. His body remembered as well, responding with an aching hardness that only made him want her more.

But she wasn't here. She was in another bed, in another hotel room. Not that far away. But considering the gulf that had opened between them yesterday, she might as well be on the other side of the world.

In the darkness, his hand drifted downward beneath the sheet, answering an urgent physical demand to put a quick end to the torturous desire pulsing through him like liquid flames. Maybe after he eased the throbbing heat, her face and form would recede to a quiet corner of his heart, and sleep would come to him.

No, it wouldn't. He knew it wouldn't.

Uttering a profanity, he pulled his hand away. His touch on himself wasn't like hers. She was there, etched on his soul like a tattooist's ink beneath the skin, and nothing he did, either right now or in the future, would change that. With a groan of frustration he flopped over on his belly and viciously punched both ends of his pillow, savoring his raging discomfort almost as much as he wished it away.

The following morning, Sarah stood at the washstand in her hotel room and looked at her reflection in the mirror above the sink. The bruise on her cheek was fading, thank God, although it still felt tender to the touch. But she believed it had diminished enough to let her go out without drawing attention.

She needed to buy a few necessities. The piece of soap she'd carried out to the prairie had melted down to the size of a button. Her clothes and underwear were worn to ribbons, and the fall she'd taken yesterday had finished off the skirt she'd mended many times over. So, although she'd resisted Zach's offer of twenty dollars, she was glad she'd agreed to take it.

Pinning up her lusterless hair, she stared at her ashen face and sighed. At least she felt a little stronger than she had last night. All she had wanted to do then was crawl into bed and lie in the arms of her new companion: heartache.

Danny was gone and she had no idea where Zach was. If he was working toward rescuing her child, she knew nothing about it. She missed them both desperately, and would give anything to hear the baby's gurgle or Zach's knock at her door.

But that heartache—oh, it stuck beside her, as faithful and constant as the sunrise, and almost as tangible.

Last night, she'd ordered some soup and tea brought up to her room for dinner. As she'd sat at the round, marble-topped table by the window, sipping her meal, in a fit of macabre humor she'd considered inviting heartache to sit down and join her.

The memory of it frightened her because she knew it hadn't been rational. Understandable, perhaps, but not rational, and she had to hang on to her reason. Sometimes it seemed it would be very easy to release her grip and slip away into a quiet, peaceful place.

During the long night, though, she'd begun to realize that anger was a better friend than fear. Anger gave a person strength. Fear only paralyzed. And rage was waking up within her—a burning, white-hot rage against Ethan Pembroke and his whey-faced wife.

So she stood here at the mirror, resolutely pushing her few hairpins into place, determined to leave this room, and maybe even heartache, if only for a while. She had to keep some spark of strength and hope alive within her, she had to carry on. Going out to shop was a good first step. She glanced at the bed, and the pile of Danny's clothes, neatly folded, waiting for his return.

Heartache was patient. She knew it would be here when she came back.

"Why, my stars! Sarah Kincade, is that you?"

Sarah froze before an artful display of Ivory Soap at Sands Brothers Dry Goods, two large cakes gripped in her outstretched hand. She thought she recognized the female voice behind her, but she didn't want to confirm her suspicions. Pretending not to hear and without looking back, she took the soap to the counter, where she'd collected a reasonable order of clothes and toiletries.

"Please," she whispered urgently to the shop girl, "have all this delivered to me at the International Hotel." She wrote her name and room number on a slip of paper and pushed it across the countertop.

"Yes, ma'am," the clerk replied, and began wrapping her purchases in brown paper.

Sarah hurried toward the door, her worn heels thundering over the plank flooring.

"*Sarah!* Wait!"

Oh, damn it, Sarah thought hopelessly, realizing that escape was impossible. She stopped and turned, and saw Matilda Gumble, one of her church's biggest gossips, advancing on her. Fortunately, none of the other patrons nearby seemed to notice Matilda bugling her name like an elk.

"I thought that was you!" Matilda exclaimed. She bustled closer, carrying a wicker shopping basket on her arm. Fashionably dressed in burgundy-gold changeable taffeta, she looked as if she were going to an afternoon tea. Her usually high-colored face heated up to blazing red with excitement.

"Matilda . . . how nice to see you," Sarah lied. She could almost feel the woman's eyes on her as they raked her up and down, touching every detail of her shabby appearance.

"My dear, *where* have you been all these months? We had to find another organist, and neither of our bake sales went well without you. You contributed so much in your own little way. I heard you were going off on a grand tour or a holiday, but, well—" Her raised brows and critical gaze adequately expressed her disbelief. "You simply vanished and no one heard from you."

Matilda had terrified Sarah in the past, always looking for a breath of scandal among Helena's citizens, just as she was doing right now. The slightest hint of disgrace set the woman on the trail like a bloodhound. For years, Sarah had lived in fear of saying or doing the wrong thing, of jeopardizing her reputation. Pleasing others, and their opinion of her, had once been so very important. It was also one reason why she'd kept her affair with Ethan a secret. While she was glad she had, after everything she'd been through she finally realized what a petty tyrant Matilda was.

"There was an emergency in my family." It wasn't a lie.

Matilda put a hand to her mouth in exaggerated distress. "Oh, no, I'm so sorry to hear it. Then that would account for your poor color and the worry lines on your face." The comment was typical of one of the woman's well-aimed barbs. A true Job's comforter, that was Matilda Gumble. "I hope everything is all right."

Sarah only gave her a faint smile. "You're looking tidy and prosperous, Matilda. I really must be going, though—"

The woman beamed, ignoring Sarah's attempt to leave. "How kind of you to say so. We're doing very well, indeed." She leaned a bit closer and confided smugly, "My husband, Wendell, and I have been invited to a big dinner party tonight at the Pembrokes'. He and his lovely wife are wonderful hosts and such upstanding citizens. The cream of society. Anyway, Wendell's lumber company has been doing a lot of business with Mr. Pembroke and his father-in-law, Mr. Driscoll, so of course we're included. It's going to be quite a lavish event, from what I hear. All of Helena's best will be there." She nodded briskly, making the ostrich feathers on her hat bob as if they were still attached to their original owner. She rattled on about the Pembrokes' fabulous brick mansion on Madison Avenue, with its stained-glass windows, then interjected, "And I learned this morning that they've just adopted a baby. Oh, I hope we'll get a look at the little darling."

Sarah gaped at her, her throat tight and dry. Of course, before dinner was served, they would bring out Danny to show off to everyone as their own. The guests would cluck and coo and congratulate Ethan and Priscilla on their good fortune and the baby's beauty.

Her child! The child they kidnapped from her.

"Dear, please don't look so stricken," Matilda said, wearing that smug smile again. "Now that you're back, you might eventually get an invitation to one of the Pembrokes' dinners, considering all of your charitable works. Wealthy people are always involved in one charity or another." She shifted the basket on her arm, and continued. "Thank goodness you're back. I'm so relieved that we'll have a capable person to take over the bake sales again, and heaven knows, for all that she tries, Gerty Norton can't play the organ to save—"

"Excuse me." Unable to stand there and listen to Matilda one minute more, Sarah spun on her heel and walked away. She had to reach the door, to get outside, to get back to her hotel room. If she didn't, she'd either kick Matilda in the shins or begin crying hysterically, or both.

"Well, land's sake, Sarah!" Matilda huffed.

Sarah yanked open the door so hard, the overhead bell was knocked off its bracket and tumbled to the floor.

But she kept walking, and she didn't look back.

"Zach! By God, I never expected to see you again. And don't you look fine! Just fine."

Zach stood in the doorway of Lady Rose Malloy's office and smiled at the flame-haired, milk-skinned madam who had once been his employer. Rising from her desk, she came forward to greet him with a swish of silk skirts, and put her soft, white hand in his. He bent and gave it a gallant peck, inhaling the familiar scent of her French perfume.

Lady Rose was one of a kind—ambitious, tough, compassionate when it suited her, a practical businesswoman. And despite her line of work, which was vilified by local churchgoers and social reformers, but frequented by town fathers, in his opinion she was a hundred times more ethical than the Pembrokes or Driscolls. If anyone could help him, he thought he might be able to count on her.

When he straightened, she gave him a look of frank appreciation. "Lordy, you're still a handsome devil with those dimples and big hazel eyes. Why, there were times when I was tempted to invite you upstairs myself." She tweaked one of her red curls. "I still might."

Zach actually felt himself blush, but Rose only laughed and reached up to pinch his cheek.

"How have you been, Lady Rose?"

"Can't complain at all—business is always good. But you come on in and sit down, and tell me about yourself. I couldn't believe it when Pompey told me you were here."

Pompey, a giant black man, was Lady Rose's personal bodyguard and butler. He stood in the background, silent, but as unobtrusive as a grizzly. Zach remembered hearing a rumor in the house that when he was a slave, Pompey's owner in Louisiana, in a fit of jealousy, had ordered him castrated when that man took a liking to Pompey's wife. Whether it was true was anyone's guess. No one had been inclined to ask him.

Lady Rose signaled the man to leave and he exited, closing the door behind him.

Zach let her lead him into the plush office, with its dark paneling, thick carpet, and expensive furniture. She sat on a green and gold striped settee and patted the cushion next to her.

"Looking for a job?" She reached for the decanter on a table next to her and poured drinks into two heavy crystal glasses.

He sat down next to her and took the whiskey. "No, something else."

"What? A woman? Jesus, Zach, you're an old friend. You don't need to come in here to ask me for that. It's on the house. Just tell whichever girl—"

"I need information, Lady Rose."

She leaned back against the cushions and gave him a long, steady look. "What kind of information? If it's about one of my customers, this might be the end of our little meeting. You know very well that they count on my discretion."

Zach sat forward, his elbows on his knees, and rolled the whiskey glass between his palms. "Yeah, I know that. I'm counting on it too."

She lifted her russet brows, obviously intrigued. "All right. Ask your question. I'm not promising anything, but if I can answer it, I will."

"It's kind of complicated. I have to give you some background first, but this has to stay between you and me."

She nodded, probably long accustomed to the role of confessor.

He took a deep breath and a big swallow of the whiskey. Without asking, she poured him another drink, and he began. He started at the beginning, telling her about the job he'd accepted from Pembroke, and about tracking Sarah and Danny to Lame Horse. He told her how the Pembrokes had set up Sarah and stolen from her, taking her money and her child. He revealed everything, except his feelings for Sarah and the night they'd made love.

"It's not right, Lady Rose." He took another drink and muttered, "Hell, I'm ashamed of my own part in this, and I told Sarah I'd do whatever I could to get Danny back."

She drummed her fingers on the arm of the settee for a moment. Finally, she said, "It isn't only that you're ashamed. I think you're in love with Sarah. And the boy too."

His face grew hot again. "Well, it's not that. I just feel responsible for—"

"You love her." Her pronouncement was final.

Yes, he did, and the realization struck him like a thunderbolt. Loved her—he couldn't get her out of his mind. He couldn't forget the night they'd shared under the stars, the way her curves fit his hands, the sweetness of her smile, the lulling sound of her voice. That he'd lost her was eating him up inside.

He shrugged and nodded, keeping his eyes on the flowered carpet. He wasn't comfortable discussing something so personal, even if it was with a woman who'd seen just about everything in life, good and bad. He'd had enough trouble just admitting his feelings to himself. "But it didn't work out between us. She's going back to her hometown, and I'm leaving Helena too, I hope."

Lady Rose sighed. "The world is a hard place for a woman alone. A woman alone with a child is in an even worse spot."

He lifted his gaze to her powdered face. "So, what do you think? Can you help me?"

Lady Rose took a sip from her own glass. "Maybe. Pompey threw Ethan Pembroke out of here a couple of months ago after he tried to beat the living hell out of one of my girls. He's barred from my house—you know I won't put up with that. I hear he goes to Chicago Joe's these days, so I guess he's her problem now. At any rate, I don't feel any loyalty to him or his secrets."

Zach straightened. "Secrets?"

She poured another dollop of whiskey into both their glasses. "I know a couple, but there's one that I think you can use. I might even be doing someone else a favor by telling you about it."

Chapter Sixteen

What you want me to do isn't ethical. I have to draw the line somewhere, Pembroke, and I'm drawing it here." Willis Carpenter's brows met at the bridge of his nose, and his face turned a fascinating shade of vermilion as he glared at Ethan across the desk in his private office at First National. Although he was dressed like a banker, in all, Ethan thought the man's expression lacked the cool detachment that bankers strived for.

Ethan, unimpressed by the threat, merely laced his fingers together. "First National Bank stands to make a lot of money when the Springwater Hotel project goes through. You know I've been in negotiations with Great Northern Railroad to bring in a line to service Helena. That isn't finalized, but they're so interested in the idea that they've committed to featuring the place in their travel pamphlets. I have to line up investors to get this thing up and going, and I want to know who I should even bother to approach. For God's sake, think of the money *you* could make, Carpenter. I'm not asking you to embezzle funds. I just want a list of your largest depositors and their balances."

"I tell you it's dishonest. It's a breach of the trust our customers have placed in this bank. What good is money if you have to sell your soul to earn it? I won't do it!"

Ethan gave him an even look. "It wouldn't be the worst thing you've ever done. At least not by your standards. Remember? There was the night at Lady Rose's Sporting House that your wife doesn't know about. I imagine you'd like to keep it that way." He shook his head. *"Tsk-tsk."*

Carpenter clenched his jaw, making the muscles jump

in his temples. Another man might have reached across the desk and grabbed Ethan by his lapels. But not Carpenter. "How long do you think you can dangle that threat over my head?"

Ethan laughed. "I suppose as long as I need to. I seem to recall that you begged me not to tell another soul what I saw you doing there. You were pretty drunk, but I don't suppose you could forget the two women, shall we say, entertaining you? It was quite a sight, with one of them perched naked over your face and the other—"

Carpenter thumped the desk with his fist, making his pen jump on the blotter, nearly strangling on his own anger. "You son of a—You bast—I never would have been in that place to begin with if you hadn't insisted on meeting there! A business deal, you said. You set me up. I'm a happily married man with a wonderful wife and three children."

"Yes, I remember them." That had worked to Ethan's advantage, as had Carpenter's profound sense of morality. It had gone exactly as he'd hoped. The man couldn't hold his liquor worth a damn—he'd gone down like a leaky boat, landing on a bed of silk sheets and perfumed females.

The poor devil must be writhing inside over the favors Ethan had demanded to buy his silence. But Ethan's plan had worked. He truly believed that Carpenter would rather die first than have his wife learn his guilty secret.

Ethan knew Jessica Carpenter. She'd been a guest at the Pembrokes' dinner table several times, before and since the night at Lady Rose's. Jessica adored her husband with a syrupy devotion that Ethan both envied and loathed. After the escapade at the sporting house, Ethan had prepared a carefully and graphically worded letter to her, describing Carpenter's night in detail. He'd showed the horrified banker a copy, then he locked the original in a wall safe at home where it still reposed. Only he knew the combination.

Ethan knew how to gain and keep the upper hand. That bit of blackmail had been a convenient tool to help him get a number of concessions from Carpenter.

"Wouldn't it be a shame if your wife learned of your indiscretion?"

Carpenter paled and then turned scarlet again, his fury palpable but contained. A vein throbbed in his forehead, and finally he said, "All right. You'll have your damned list. But one of these days I might surprise you, Pembroke. I might tell Jessica about that indiscretion myself."

Ethan considered him a moment, then stood and chuckled. "No, not you. Not in a thousand years. I'll see you and your lovely wife tonight at dinner."

With Carpenter's list tucked safely in the breast pocket of his coat, Ethan rode home on his new chestnut gelding. It was a fine animal, full-blooded and from good stock, and had cost him almost five hundred dollars. He wanted to see what he'd gotten for his money, how the horse would do on flat, open land away from town. But there was no time for that now. His grand dinner party was only a few hours away.

It had been good to get out of the house and leave behind the chaos that had descended upon his well-ordered life now that a baby was under the roof again.

Charles Nash had come out last evening, bringing with him his doctor's bag and the night cold into the entry hall. Upon careful examination of the baby and questioning Priscilla, he'd said something about the child being intolerant of cow's milk, that they must give him goat's milk or find a wet nurse. Ethan had gone out himself and found a livery owner with a nanny goat.

But now, as Ethan rounded the corner to his street, he

saw Nash in front of his house again, climbing into his buggy. The doctor's mare stood patiently at the Pembroke's ornate hitching post, waiting while Nash adjusted himself on the seat.

After the diagnosis last night, Ethan had supposed that would be the end of it. Today the doctor was back.

Ethan nudged the horse forward to the front of his house. "Dr. Nash! A moment of your time, please."

Under a cold, fine drizzle that had begun earlier, Ethan dismounted and stepped down into the muddy street. Keeping a tight hold on the horse's reins, he hurried to speak with the physician.

Nash turned and waited. "Mr. Pembroke, I was hoping I'd get a chance to talk with you."

"Come into my study. We can warm up with a brandy and get out of this rain. Is everything all right? Is the baby getting better?"

The doctor glanced up at the imposing brick-and-stained-glass mansion. "Can you come with me to my office? I think it would be better if we talked there."

"Is it about the boy?"

"Partly, but it has more to do with your wife."

That vague, uneasy sensation washed over Ethan again. "She's ill?"

Nash adjusted his bag on the seat next to him. "Not exactly, and certainly with nothing acute. I'd really rather not discuss it here."

Ethan had a feeling that Nash was going to tell him something he didn't want to hear, and he almost declined. But the look he saw in the doctor's eyes made him change his mind.

"All right, I'll follow you over."

Nash's office was located in his modest home several blocks away. When they arrived and walked in through the clinic entrance, Bessie Crandall, the doctor's sturdy nurse, was at her desk with a stack of files. Several patients sat on benches along the walls waiting to be seen, and their rain-wet clothing steamed up the windows. Some with early colds and cases of influenza sniffled and hacked into handkerchiefs. They all looked up expectantly at Nash's entrance, their eyes following him through the parlor.

The whole aura of sickness made Ethan want to turn around and walk out again. He despised sickness.

Bessie gave Nash a questioning look.

"Give us a minute, please, Nurse Crandall," Nash murmured and led the way to his private office at the end of the hallway. Along the way, Ethan glimpsed a couple of examination rooms, all tidy and medicinal. But the office was another story.

The room contained a desk and shelves, mostly hidden by assorted medical journals, loose papers, and books. A chaos of overflowing patient records littered the floor, and jars of suspicious-looking liquids and preserved specimens—of what, Ethan couldn't tell—filled a glass cabinet.

"You'll have to excuse the mess, Mr. Pembroke," Nash said, removing his damp hat and coat to hang them on a clothes tree in the corner. Then he moved a crate of some kind of tonic from the guest chair that faced his desk. "Bessie's been after me like a cavalry sergeant for quite a while to get this straightened up, but my practice keeps me hopping. I've always felt that it's more important to tend a child sick with the croup or a woman in her confinement than to clean house. Please, sit." He gestured Ethan into the now empty chair.

Looking for a place to put the crate of tonic and not finding one, Nash set it on a stack of yellowing newspapers.

It was a good thing that Charles Nash was one of the most highly regarded physicians in western Montana, noted for both his expertise and his compassion. Otherwise, after seeing this horror of an office, Ethan would have dismissed him immediately. But he believed that Nash knew his business, and that he'd brought him here for a serious reason.

The gray-haired doctor closed the door and flopped his long, bony frame into his desk chair. "I'm sorry to drag you over here, but as I said, I think it will be easier for us to talk here, away from your house."

"Did Priscilla call you back?"

Nash leaned back in his chair. "No, I dropped by to check on the baby. He's not improving as I'd like, although I have hope for him. Your wife told me how he came to you." Though he made no further comment about that, the doctor paused and gave Ethan a look that made him distinctly uncomfortable. He also wondered how much of their personal information Priscilla had revealed. "Last night, she expressed concern that the child might have been exposed to a contagion or suffered from neglect. In fact, he looks like he was thriving until now. And that brings me to my point, Mr. Pembroke."

Ethan tightened his jaw. "Which is?"

"As I said, I have hope that the baby will recover—" He leaned forward. "But not if your wife continues to care for him."

Ethan sat up as straight as a flagpole, as if tied to one of those newfangled electric chairs used for executions. "Exactly what are you implying, Dr. Nash?"

"When your first child died, of course, I was saddened and baffled, but there are a lot of things in medicine that we still don't understand. People die and we might not know the reason. And infants are especially susceptible. When the second child died, I wondered how an identical tragedy could visit the same household twice in such a short period of time." He had tended both children when Ethan and Priscilla still lived on Helena's outskirts, after they'd moved from Butte. Now he stared at Ethan with a piercing gaze. "A third time, though, is too much. Based on my past examinations, I believe that Mrs. Pembroke is suffering from an emotional condition. One I've never seen before in all my years of practice, but one that causes her to inflict harm on her children, for what reason I can only speculate." Nash pushed aside a human skull that sat at his elbow, as casual an ornament as a glass paperweight. "She seems to enjoy the attention she receives as the fretful, suffering mother."

Nash only put into words the very same worry that had nagged at the back of Ethan's mind. But hearing it so baldly stated triggered a defensive reaction. "That is a very presumptuous statement to make, Doctor. I've never seen a more dedicated mother than Priscilla."

He nodded and held his hands wide, affirming Ethan's statement. "Oh, yes, indeed. On the surface, I would be inclined to agree with you. She appears to be a loving mother, and I think that she believes herself to be one too, worrying herself into a state of collapse over her children. But I have attended three youngsters in Mrs. Pembroke's care, all from different backgrounds. Two of them died of exactly the same mysterious symptoms that this little boy is exhibiting now. It isn't easy for me to tell you that I fear this child will suffer the same ultimate fate as the two girls who went before him."

"But last night you said that it was simply a problem of the wrong milk."

Nash rubbed his chin. "Yes, I did, because Mrs. Pembroke told me she was feeding the boy cow's milk. But if she followed my instructions and got goat's milk for him, he should have made considerable improvement by now. He hasn't improved at all. And infants can fade very quickly, sometimes in a matter of days. Either he is still getting cow's milk, or she is dosing him with something that she won't admit to. Believe me, I have asked her in every single case if she was giving the children anything I didn't order. She denied it. But druggists' shelves are full of purgatives and other elixirs that can kill a baby." He shrugged. "Or mimic an illness."

Ethan swallowed, but his throat was so dry he longed for that brandy bottle sitting in his study. "What would you suggest?"

"At least several months' rest in a sanatorium. I've thought of this before, especially in light of the headaches she seems to suffer with. A sanatorium might do Mrs. Pembroke a world of good. It will certainly save that baby's life. I can recommend one or two that are very good."

God, a sanatorium, Ethan thought. The notion had flittered across his mind once and Louisa had mentioned it, but Nash was serious this time. What in the hell would her father say? Ethan didn't even want to think about that. Nash's recommendation was out of the question. "Dr. Nash, that really isn't an option. Armistead—our social position—well, it's just not possible."

Nash put both elbows on the desk and leaned so far forward, Ethan backed up. All traces of friendly, compassionate doctor disappeared from his lined face. "Understand this, Mr. Pembroke. I don't give a damn about Armistead Driscoll's opinion or your social position. Either Mrs. Pembroke receives treatment—and I mean immediately, make no mistake—or I'll report her case to the authorities. My suspicions are strong enough to get their attention, and I have the documented case histories to back up my concerns. I cannot stand by and watch a third child die. And I won't."

* * *

Sarah's hotel room was beautifully luxurious compared to the severe conditions she'd endured on the trail. Instead of wagon planks, she had a comfortable, clean feather bed to sleep in. She'd bathed in the well-appointed bath just down the hall, and she wasn't cold, hungry, or sore.

But she paced over the braided rugs and hardwood floor, her stomach tied in as many knots as a tatted doily. On the bed sat her still-wrapped parcel the dry-goods store had delivered to her, but she hadn't bothered to open it.

All she could think of was Danny and Zach, and her infuriating encounter with Matilda Gumble. Tangled thoughts darted through her mind, speculative and worrisome. And anger, deep and hot and strong, continued to grow within her. Rage at the Pembrokes, fury at smug Matilda, simmering impatience with Zach.

Where was he? Why hadn't he come back to tell her what he was doing as he said he would? For all she knew, he could have left town.

She stopped dead in her tracks, her hands laced together into one tight fist.

What if he never came back? What if—oh, God—Zach could very well have gone to Ethan, telling him he'd held up his end of their agreement. The Pembrokes had Danny, and he wanted his ranch back. He could have gotten on a horse and ridden out of Helena, and she'd sit here in this room, never knowing he was gone.

It was an unworthy thought, Sarah knew, but at this point, and given the circumstances, no one was above her suspicion. Experience had made her wary.

She went to the window and looked at the street below, muddy and slick in the rain. Zach—thinking about him made her heart ache as much as thinking of her child. Would he abandon her here after his promise to help her? Could he do that? Maybe. He'd never lied to her, as far as she knew. But she'd misjudged almost everyone else she'd encountered in the past two years; perhaps he'd fooled her too.

He had nothing to lose.

Yet even as she coldly imagined Zach shaking hands with Ethan and pocketing the deed to his land, her heart protested. Why would he even bother with such an elaborate charade? He could have taken her to the stage stop, sent her off to her family in Stockett, and that would have been the end of it. If he was going to force Ethan to make good on his offer, he hadn't needed to drag her to Helena with him.

She leaned her forehead against the cool glass. She'd seen the caring in his eyes, she knew she had. Caring that she realized had never been in Ethan's eyes when he'd looked at her. She'd felt the sweetness of his touch, which could, by turns, soothe and comfort, or drive her to a blade-sharp edge of desire and push her over into its fiery, breathless expanse.

A beer wagon rumbled by in the wet street below the window, but she paid it no attention. Her mind was focused on Zach and the time they'd spent together. He'd brought her wildflowers, he'd milked Isabel when she knew he disliked the goat intensely. When danger had threatened, he'd been there to defend her. And he'd cared for Danny, if not with as much skill as she did, at least with enough affection to make up for the lack.

In her grief and anger, she'd said some hard things to Zach. She'd as much as told him that she didn't love him after all, and that she didn't want to be with him. She was beginning to realize that she hadn't meant it. She loved him to distraction. Despite his decided aura of danger, surely the result of a childhood that could have sprung from the pages of Dickens, there was a corner of tenderness in his hard heart that he'd given to her and to Danny. She missed both him and her child in equal measure.

But where was he now? Every time she heard footsteps in the hallway, or the murmur of voices outside her door, she tensed, hoping it was Zach.

Hoping. Sarah straightened. Hope was a fine thing, but it often wasn't enough to get a job done. She wasn't going to just sit here like a fool, waiting for news that might never come.

She was sick to death of allowing life and events to happen to her, doing as she'd been told, as had been expected of her. She would go out there herself and look for Zach. With a population of almost fourteen thousand, Helena wasn't a small town anymore, but she couldn't wait here any longer.

With renewed energy and determination, she went to the bed and tore open the brown paper package from Sands Brothers Dry Goods that contained, among other things, new underwear, two new dresses, and a pair of shoes.

After washing quickly at the sink in her room, she dressed and pinned up her hair. She'd chosen the new dresses with an eye toward function more than style. But now that she looked at herself in the cheval glass in the corner of the room she was pleased to see that she had managed to satisfy both. The outfit she'd put on was made of blue figured sateen and trimmed with lace, as was the matching apron that draped gracefully over the skirt, front and back. The hem was edged with a deep row of knife pleats. It was a far cry from the much-mended, cut-down dresses she'd been wearing for the last several months. The new clothes made her want to lift her chin and straighten her shoulders, to take on the world.

Throwing her old shawl over her shoulders, she left the room and headed down the hall.

In the lobby, Sarah felt the curious gaze of many eyes—
a woman alone in a hotel was a novelty and a cause for
speculation. She also caught the attention of the desk clerk,
who, she knew, hadn't seen her "husband" since the day
he came in and paid for their room, a week in advance.
She didn't have time to care about what any of them
thought.

Out on the sidewalk, Sarah pulled her shawl over her
head and looked both to the right and left, trying to decide
where she ought to begin. Her gaze lit upon the façade of
the Bristol Hotel—that's where she'd go. She'd start there
and leave a message for Zach. In this weather, it might be
all she could do for now.

A heavy rain fell from the low, dark sky and bounced
off passing wagons and carriages. The sidewalk was slick
and muddy, but she moved with a determined stride. She
didn't look into the faces of those she passed, but merely
stepped around them as she went. After she brushed by a
nicely dressed man to reach the front door of the Bristol,
she heard her name.

"Sarah!"

She whirled to look at the man she'd just passed. "Zach!
Oh, God, Zach!" He looked so different in a black wool
frock coat, matching trousers, a burgundy vest, black boots,
and a black hat, she hadn't even recognized him. His appearance reminded her of a wealthy cattleman. He was certainly the handsomest man she'd ever seen. There on the
street, without thinking, she flung herself into his embrace.
His arms closed tight around her, and he tipped his head
down to hers. "Where have you been?" she asked, her voice
shaking. "I've been worried sick about you! And why are
you dressed like that?"

He released her and smiled down at her. "Come on, let's
get out of this rain and go back to your room. I was just

coming to talk to you. I have lots of news." He took her elbow and turned her around. They made their way back through the lobby of the International Hotel, and the desk clerk noted their entrance with a smile and a nod.

"I think he suspected that I was abandoned," she whispered.

His grip on her elbow was firm and comforting. "I'm sorry I didn't get back to you sooner. I've been talking to people all over town."

"And shopping, apparently," she added tartly, as they climbed the stairs.

"Yeah, well, there's a good reason for that."

At Room 306, he took her key and opened the door. She stepped inside and flung off her wet shawl to hang over the towel bar at the sink. But Zach lingered in the doorway, as if waiting for her to invite him in. Looking at him standing there, breathtaking in his new clothes, she felt a surprising flush of shyness and an unexpected rush of desire.

Heavens, she'd seen him with no clothes at all, but this costume gave him the appearance of a fascinating stranger, dangerous and desperately attractive. The coat accentuated his lean height and broad shoulders, and it looked as if it had been custom-tailored for him.

"Zach, please—come in and sit down." She indicated a small rose-colored settee by the marble-topped table near the window. She tried to sound calm when she felt anything but. She needed to tell him how she felt, to apologize for what she'd said, but his next comment distracted her.

Stepping inside, he tossed his hat on the bed and closed the door, and suddenly the room seemed very small. "You look good, Sarah. I'm glad you got something new to wear too. You're going to need it."

She settled next to him, inhaling the scent of shaving

soap and slightly damp wool. "Why?" She gestured at his suit. "What is this all about?"

"Like I said, I've been talking to people around town, about the Pembrokes. I don't like most of what I've heard—Ethan's made quite a few enemies. But that'll work to our advantage. They're having a party tonight. All of Helena's high rollers will be there, although I don't think they know why."

"Yes, I heard." She told him about her infuriating encounter with Matilda Gumble. "Do you know the reason all those people have been invited?"

"As far as I can tell, Pembroke is hoping to interest investors for some scheme he has to build a fancy hotel and heated swimming hole at the hot springs out on the west edge of town. He's going to unveil the plans tonight at dinner."

Sarah wasn't following Zach's line of thinking. "What does that have to do with us being dressed up?"

He grinned. "Hell, honey, we're going to the party too."

She stared at him. "W-what? Why? We'll never get past the front door."

"I think we will. The Pembrokes won't be answering it themselves. If we look prosperous, we might be able to blend in and fool the servants."

"Ethan will have us thrown out of the house like—like vagrants tossed out of a hotel lobby."

He ran a hand through his dark hair. "Yeah, well, I have some experience with that. Oh, we might not be there very long. But long enough, I hope, to get Danny and leave."

Sarah was still not clear about his plan. "We'll storm in and demand him?"

He shook his head. "I've learned a lot more the son of a bitch than I ever wanted to know, and more than he'd like me to know. That's our ace in the hole. He won't want his dinner guests to hear about his misdeeds. Plus, I've still got that contract and court order that Judge Driscoll signed. He's up for reelection and I don't think he'll be too anxious for people to learn about his part in this. On top of that, I have your bankbook with a supposedly untouched balance." He told her what he'd learned from Jacob Mullins and Lady Rose.

"Zach, do you really think we can do this? Walk right into the Pembroke house and get Danny, just like that?"

He took her hand in his own, strong, warm, and vital. "I don't know. But we've got to try, Sarah. Let me do this last thing for you before we go our separate ways. I owe it to you."

. . . go our separate ways . . .

Yes, of course. She'd told him she didn't want him, and by the sound of it, he'd already made other plans to move on without her. After all, he'd been on his way someplace when she met him. Now he would go back to his old life, and he looked pretty pleased with his decision.

Tears gathered behind her lashes and she turned her head, trying to force them back. She wanted to tell him she hadn't meant it, that she took back everything she'd said. But how would she do that without seeming like a fickle, inconstant woman who couldn't make up her mind?

Even if she had the courage to speak, she suspected that he'd already made other plans—plans that no longer included her. Her heart was too fragile to take the chance that he would reject her. She'd had her fill of rejection and humiliation.

Obviously misunderstanding her distress, he said, "I admit it isn't much to go on, but I think it'll work. You're going to have to be brave, but I know you can do it. You've got the heart of a wildcat." He put a finger under her chin to turn her face back to his. "Are you worried about facing Pembroke again?"

Gathering her resolve to be strong, she dashed a hand across her eyes and shook her head. She didn't have much hope for this plan Zach had concocted, but he was right. They had to try. And she had nothing better to offer as an alternative. "No. I look forward to it. I never had the chance to tell him what I think of him and his lies."

He nodded, satisfied. "Good girl. All right, then. We've got a couple of hours yet. Let's get supper down in the dining room."

Sarah thought she might never be hungry again, but she agreed.

Chapter Seventeen

Zach tried not to stare at Sarah as she dipped a spoon into her soup, but he couldn't help it. She was beautiful, and God Almighty, he adored her. It was bitter knowledge, knowing that just as he realized he loved her, she no longer felt the same about him.

Chatting diners and the busy clink of silver on china was the only sound around them. They both sat in edgy silence at their table, barely eating their food. It wasn't as if he didn't have enough to worry about with the coming night—even though he sounded confident about his plan, it was a flimsy one.

This dining room was a hell of a lot different from anything he was used to. White linen and candles on the tables, porcelain serving dishes, more knives and forks than he knew what to do with. But Sarah . . . she looked liked a rose at a garden party.

She'd never been more desirable.

Yes, she had, his memory nudged. The day he'd stumbled upon her, bathing on the prairie, pouring crystal sheets of water over her naked curves. That day, she'd had no fancy trappings around her. Just miles of grass and blue sky and the wind. The mere thought of it made the fly of his new wool trousers tight.

"Zach, what are you planning to do?" Sarah's interruption of the silence startled him.

"Do? We're going to the Pembroke party—"

"No, I mean after all of this. After I go back to Stockett."

"Well, you know I'm going to try to get my property back from Pembroke."

"What if you can't? What will you do then?"

He'd been torturing himself with the same question ever since she'd made her announcement about going home. To hear her ask it made it all the more painful. Sometimes he wished his conscience and his heart had remained in their state of numbness, because this was hell.

Incredible though it was, his long-cherished dream of having his own land had lost some of its luster without Sarah and Danny in it. No matter how he tried to focus on it, to shine it up again, it just wasn't the same. It was as if he'd found that his golden dream was really just brass. Even if he could make Pembroke knuckle under, what was he going to do? Sit out there on that porch he'd imagined all by himself? Regardless of which direction his life took, it would seem hollow, without Sarah and Danny.

"I'm not thinking about—" He glowered at her. "I don't know anymore, *damn it*!"

Sarah jumped at the vehemence of his response. She stared at him with wide eyes, then glanced around as if to see if anyone else had overheard him. But her question started another slow-burning fire in him. He tried to spear a chunk of potato, but it slid across his plate, and he dropped his fork with a clatter and gave up.

Sarah had the right to be mad at him, no two ways about it. They wouldn't even be sitting here right now if he'd done things differently. But Zach hadn't gotten this far in a hard life by lying down and accepting what fate doled out to him.

He wasn't going to let her just walk away from him after everything that had passed between them. "Are you finished with that soup?"

She looked at him across the top of the candle flame, achingly beautiful, her hair dark and sleek in its chignon, with wispy tendrils curling at her temples. She'd only been dabbling at her dinner and he'd lost what little appetite he had. "I guess so."

"Good. Because we need to talk. And we need to do it before we go to the Pembrokes'." With short, impatient motions, he pulled a couple of bills from his pocket and threw them on the table. "Before we rescue Danny. This is about *us*."

"Us—"

He stood and walked around the table to pull out her chair. Taking her elbow, he escorted her to the ornate, acid-etched doors, where an anxious-looking headwaiter asked, "Was your meal satisfactory, sir?"

Zach blew past him, propelling Sarah along with him.

"Please let go of my arm," she whispered furiously. "What is the matter with you?"

But he didn't let go, and didn't respond as they climbed the stairs and strode down the hall to Room 306. He unlocked the door, followed her in, and slammed it behind them.

Once inside, Sarah backed away from him, truly fearful. He was a big man with a dangerous side she knew was there, even if she'd rarely seen it.

"Zach, what's gotten into you?"

He paced the floor, much the way she had earlier. But his stride was like that of a long-legged, caged animal, tense and threatening. His was a formidable presence.

"You know," he said, his hands jammed into his trouser pockets, "when we were out on the trail, I asked you to stay here with me."

She retreated behind the settee and gripped the top edge of its carved mahogany back. "I know, but I told you why I can't. Ethan—"

"He's not part of the problem anymore."

She gaped at him. "He's nearly all of the problem!"

He stopped and glared at her. "What does he have to do with how we feel about each other?"

"But that's just it. I don't know how you feel about me. All I know is that Ethan has your precious ranch that you won't let go of! I asked *you* to come with *us,* but you said no. Then you let your pride and swaggering get in the way of your common sense. Danny is with the Pembrokes now because of it! You might have been right—maybe you're more like Ethan than I thought!" The words were spoken in anger and fear.

He stepped back, looking as if she'd slapped him. "That's a rotten thing to say!"

The carving on the settee frame dug into her clenched fingers and she scowled at him. Frayed nerves and fatigue turned up the fire under her anger. "You and your boasting—you could steal a leg of lamb and outrun the police." Her anger edged toward bitterness. "But you couldn't save my baby."

"I know what I did! I know they took Danny because of me. It damned near killed me when they drove off with the boy." He paced the length of the room and then returned to stand in front of the settee. After a moment, he gestured at her impatiently. "Damn it, Sarah, come out from behind there. I'm not going to hurt you."

She sidled out carefully, keeping her eyes fixed on his. Even in the face of this fiery tension, the hope she'd been nursing along in her heart stirred as if awakening from a coma. Maybe he did care about her—maybe he even loved her? He took her upper arms in strong hands that gripped tightly but didn't hurt. He still looked angry though.

"Jesus, Sarah, don't you know how bad I feel about everything that happened, and the pain I've caused you and Danny? Why else would I have brought you here and hatched this plan to save him?" He spread his arms wide and looked down the front of his vest. "Why else would I have bought this damned suit?"

Silence hung between them for an endless moment. Only the sound of their breathing filled her ears. Their gazes were still locked, the tension between them as heavy as the air before a storm.

Without warning, his arms went around her and his mouth came down on hers, hot, hard, insistent. A single, brief thought of resisting him fled her mind as if he'd stolen it and any willpower she possessed. He pulled back then, his breath coming faster. "I want to make it all up to you. Let me do this."

"Oh, Zach." She chanced a look into his hazel eyes that revealed the heart of a good, decent man, and the energy fizzled out of her anger. Even if they had to part, for whatever reason, she would be glad that she'd known this man.

Finally, he said, "Come on. We've got business to take care of."

He released her and held out his hand. She withdrew a handkerchief from her pocket and dried her eyes, laughing a little. "And just so you'll know, you look wonderful in that 'damned suit.' Like a cattle baron."

He smiled, self-conscious and boyish, and her heart swelled. "Good, I'll need the disguise. Ready to walk into the lion's den?" he asked.

She took a deep breath and straightened, feeling as if she were, indeed, going into battle. He hadn't said the words she longed to hear, but he was a brave warrior by her side. With his courage and strength, she could face Ethan and rescue Danny. "Yes."

"All right, then. Let's go get your son."

Zach and Sarah drove to the Pembrokes' in a buggy he'd rented from the livery. Located on a corner lot of Madison

Avenue, theirs was the brightest house on the block, even behind the veil of misty twilight. Nearly every one of its stained-glass windows was full of color and light in the evening.

"God, look at the size of that place," Zach marveled.

Sarah had to admit that it was impressive—three floors with as much ornamentation as she'd ever seen on a house. It was more than a house. It was a mansion. "And probably every brick bought with money made from cheating and stealing," she observed bitterly.

The curb in front was already crowded with carriages and Zach had to find a place to park the buggy farther down the street. He jumped down and then came around to hand Sarah out.

Her hands were as icy as the pit of her stomach, her fears as dark as the coming night. Every step brought her closer to a confrontation that might prove horrific, and worse, unsuccessful. Would they be able to do this? she wondered. Would they even get one foot past the entry hall? Only her fierce desire to save her child and Zach's rock-steady arm under her hand kept her from running back to the buggy.

Luck was on their side when they reached the front walk. Two other couples approached the house just ahead of them, all more lavishly dressed than she and Zach. Another couple followed them, making it a bit easier to blend in with the group. She climbed the staircase, her feet like lead, her heart fluttering in her chest like the wings of a hummingbird. Zach, though, nodded to one or two of the men, acting as if he were an invited guest.

"Good evening . . . good evening." The solicitous tones of a butler reached her before she saw him. As she and Zach neared the doorway, he squeezed her hand on his arm.

"Good evening?" This time the greeting sounded more

like a question. The haughty, withered butler looked them over with a quizzical gaze, as if trying to identify them. But Zach only handed him his hat and breezed through as if he owned this house and a dozen more just like it. He pulled Sarah with him before the old man had a chance to protest.

The marble entry hall was bright with gaslight from a sparkling chandelier, and fresh flowers in crystal vases flanked the door on matching Corinthian stands.

Zach led her deeper into the group of guests who were drifting toward a side parlor, where more fresh flowers graced side tables and a warm coal fire burned brightly in the fireplace. The scent of the flowers mingled with various colognes and pomades.

Two uniformed maids moved through the guests. One passed around a tray that held glasses of champagne and sherry, and the other offered dainty little sandwiches without crusts, cut in fancy shapes. In a discreet alcove, two men in evening clothes played a violin and a grand piano. It was a warm, elegant scene, but Sarah found it as bitter as bile.

This was the home of the man who'd used her and tricked her, the home of the pair who'd stolen her baby.

As Zach edged her toward the wall next to a window, Sarah glanced up at him. He appeared to be searching the crowd. Apparently finding the one he sought, he nodded slightly.

"Who's that?" she whispered, following his gaze.

He leaned down. "Willis Carpenter, the bank manager."

Sarah eyed the man again. He looked as pale as a fish belly. Next to him stood a woman with her hand on his arm, obviously his wife. She was just as chalky, as if she had recently suffered a great loss or an extended illness.

Looking up, Sarah saw Matilda Gumble coming toward

her with a glass of sherry. Oh, God no, Sarah groaned inwardly. That dreadful gossip was the last person she wanted to see.

"Why, Sarah, you slyboots, you didn't tell me you'd be here tonight!" Matilda eyed Zach with an appreciative leer that was downright vulgar. "And who is your companion?"

"We have business with the Pembrokes," she replied shortly, not bothering to introduce Zach. It was rude, Sarah knew, but this wasn't a social event for her, and she didn't give a damn what the woman thought.

The slight was not lost on Matilda, who now turned her slashing gaze upon Sarah. "What a sweet dress, dear. It's not appropriate for the evening but, then, a schoolteacher can't be expected to own something really fashionable. She'd never have the chance to wear it."

She glided away with a satisfied smirk, and Sarah clenched her back teeth to keep from snapping out an equally petty remark at the woman's retreating back.

"A friend of yours?" Zach asked, a hint of humor in his eyes.

Sarah huffed out an annoyed, noncommittal humph.

Most of the guests were prosperous-looking and fashionably dressed. Some she recognized. Charles Nash, a local physician. Famous Montana cattleman Granville Stuart. And of course she knew Cornelius Hedges, the man responsible for establishing Montana's school system and Helena's library. Other important people mingled in the luxurious parlor, such as Anton Holter, whose varied business interests and personal contributions were responsible for many improvements to the territory. Those like Matilda Gumble and her husband she knew to be rather shallow.

The women wore beautiful clothes, and sparkling jewels hung from their ears and graced necks that were either crepey with age or youthfully smooth.

And standing at the center of them all, like a benevolent queen, was Priscilla Pembroke.

Seeing her, Sarah stiffened like a pointer and her nervousness fell away. She was filled with a hatred so profound she wanted to charge through the group and claw out the woman's eyes.

The conniving kidnapper, she fumed inwardly. The selfish, whining—*bitch*! Just thinking the word was hard for Sarah. She usually didn't consider people in such terms. But there was no other way to describe Priscilla. Never in her life had she been confronted with such treachery as that she'd experienced at the hands of the Pembrokes.

Apparently sensing Sarah's rage, Zach squeezed her hand again, hard, as if to say, *not yet ... not yet*. She glanced at him quickly. He remained poker-faced, revealing nothing of his thoughts, and pushed into her hand a glass of champagne which he'd snagged from a passing tray. She drew a deep breath and struggled to follow his example, to maintain her mask of composure while Priscilla, dressed in sky-blue silk and pearls, greeted her guests. It seemed to Sarah that she, too, appeared strained and uneasy.

"Where the hell is Pembroke?" Zach whispered tensely.

Ethan was nowhere to be seen, nor were the Driscoll brothers, Armistead and Wallace.

The babble of conversation rose in the room, and finally the three men entered, nodding to the other guests. When Ethan made his way to Priscilla's side, he whispered some comment to her and then lifted his voice to be heard.

"Priscilla and I are so pleased that all of you could join us this evening. We'll be going in to dinner in a moment, and afterward, I have an exciting business proposition to discuss with the gentlemen. But first, I have an announcement to make." He glanced around the room, and Sarah drew back, her shoulder brushing a wine-colored brocade drapery panel.

"Just this week, we became the proud parents of an adopted child, a son. Lucinda—" He turned in the direction of a side door that apparently led to the hall, and a maid entered carrying a blanket-wrapped bundle. Sarah uttered a small cry, lost under the murmured comments of the guests, and lurched forward a step, spilling the contents of her glass. Zach pulled her back.

"Ladies and gentlemen, I present Armistead Ethan Pembroke." He took Danny from the maid and held him up for all to see. The group broke into polite, enthusiastic applause and offered congratulations and compliments.

"Ethan, what a striking resemblance he bears to you."

"He looks like a strapping young man."

"Oh, the dear little thing!"

But even from here, Sarah could see that Danny looked sickly and listless. Oh, God, what had they done to her baby? She'd been away from him for only two days—it felt like two lifetimes—and he was already ill. Never in her life had she known the urge to hurt another human being, but she swore if she had a gun in her hands right now—

"Zach—"

Zach glanced once more at Willis Carpenter, and with a voice that rose above all others, he thundered, "Why don't you tell your friends how you came by that boy, Pembroke? They'd probably be very interested to know the lies you told to his mother, how you cheated her, and then tore the baby from her arms only days ago."

The challenge was unmistakable. Zach was calling out Ethan Pembroke, and in front of his own dinner guests. The man dared not back down. The charge was too conspicuously damaging to dismiss. Sarah's heart swelled with admiration for Zach.

Silence blanketed the room. Necks craned and eyes turned to look at Zach. He took Sarah's icy hand and squeezed it. She clung to his warm, firm grip, allowing him to pull her forward.

Seeing them, Priscilla let out a squeak of distress, and Ethan shot both Zach and Sarah a murderous look. "What the hell are you doing here, Garrett? And you've brought that slut with you to my house?"

A ripple of gasps and murmurs rolled through the group like the wind sighing over an acre of grass. Some recognized her as the former schoolteacher, and she heard her name spoken here and there in the room.

But Ethan's insult glanced off Sarah. His words could not hurt her anymore. And she was far beyond worrying about public opinion. Her sole interest lay in getting Danny back. If the Pembrokes' reputation was ruined in the bargain, that would be a bonus.

Sneaking a glance at Zach's set face, she realized that he looked even more threatening than Ethan did. Ethan was accustomed to paying others to do his dirty work, manipulating people like pieces on a chessboard, while keeping his own hands clean. Zach was different. Literally growing up in the streets of New York, he'd experienced all kinds of situations, faced every conceivable type of person, and dealt with them all. His approach was far more personal and direct.

Now his hazel eyes glittered with a feral danger that Sarah thought only a fool would fail to recognize.

Hearing Sarah called a slut fanned the hot ember of fury that had been burning in Zach's insides. "I've brought *Miss Kincade* here to get her child." Reaching into his coat pocket, he retrieved the creased, dog-eared contract and court order that Pembroke had given him on a summer day that now seemed like years ago. He held them up like royal proclamations for all to see. "You tricked her into signing this contract to surrender her baby to you. Tricked her by stealing her life savings from her. When she changed her mind, Judge Wallace Driscoll signed this court order to bring her back to Helena." He turned to the judge. "Aren't you running for reelection in November, *Your Honor*?"

More buzzing, louder now. While some of the ladies appeared shocked by the scandalous disruption, the whole scene was too delicious to miss.

Ethan's face turned crimson with rage. "Louisa take the child back upstairs!"

"No!" Sarah cried. "Don't you take my baby!" But the maid scurried out with Danny, and only Zach's hand on the back of Sarah's skirt stopped her from running after them.

"Garrett, this isn't the time or place to discuss any of this," Ethan responded tightly. "And your false accusations made in front of all these witnesses will get you nothing more than a lawsuit. Slander, defamation of character—"

Zach stepped closer, until just a small table next to the sofa separated them. "That's only one way you're wrong, Pembroke," he uttered with a smile. "This is the *perfect* time and place." He heard a few muttered objections among the guests but their obvious curiosity kept the rest of them downright spellbound.

His eyes flicking around the group, Ethan said, "Perhaps the best way to get you and this woman out of my house is to call the police."

Zach pocketed the contract and court order for safe-keeping. "Sure, you call them. Will they be the same two whorehouse bouncers in fake uniforms I met the other day when you kidnapped Miss Kincade's son? Maybe your guests and prospective business partners would like to hear about how you convinced her to make you a cosigner on her savings account, and then emptied that account without her knowledge." Again reaching into his breast pocket, he withdrew Sarah's bankbook and flipped it open to the last entry, the one that showed a balance of almost three hundred dollars. "Does this look familiar to you?" Zach chuckled humorlessly when he saw a flash of apprehension cross with the anger in Ethan's eyes. It took all of Zach's willpower to keep from smashing his fist into Pembroke's malevolent face, the no-good son of a bitch. "Probably not, since you withdrew all of her savings without it. That's not legal, now, is it?" Zach turned his head and looked straight at Willis Carpenter. But the banker appeared so pasty and weak-kneed, Zach thought he might faint before he spoke up, damn him for a coward.

"Gentlemen." Ethan, now purple, addressed the other men in the room. "Will you help me escort these two intruders to the sidewalk?"

Several men stepped forward then and grabbed Zach and Sarah, and began pushing them toward the door. He struggled against them, trying to reach her. How many times would they be roughed up and pushed around by Pembroke and his toadies?

The butler, still in the entry hall, opened the door with an expression so snooty, Zach wanted to smash his face too. He'd been on the receiving end of plenty of those snooty looks in his life.

"You're nothing more than a good-for-nothing drifter, Garrett, and a bald-faced liar on top of it!" Ethan shouted after them from the safety of the hall.

"He's telling the truth! Let him go."

Zach recognized Carpenter's voice, and there was general confusion at the door. Viciously, Zach shook off the hands that gripped him and smacked away those that held Sarah. Taking her hand, he pulled her back to the parlor.

"Carpenter," Ethan warned. Moaning, Priscilla sank to the sofa behind her with a whisper of silk.

The nervous banker moved to the center of the room, and with a quick, apologetic glance at his wife, he said, "Mr. Garrett is telling the truth. I authorized that transaction for Pembroke, and several others, even though I knew they were wrong." He touched shaking fingertips to his temple. "He threatened to tell—" He turned to Ethan and straightened his shoulders. "You cannot blackmail me any longer, Pembroke. I told you I'd turn the tables on you, and I have." Jessica Carpenter, pale as milk, stepped forward to stand next to her husband, and he seemed to draw a bit of strength from her gesture. To the rest of the group he said, "I—I have tendered my resignation from First National Bank, effective immediately."

Now the low buzzing in the room erupted into chaos, with everyone speaking at once, asking questions and demanding answers.

"Do you mean to say that you've cheated people, Carpenter?"

"What about Pembroke? What has he been up to?"

"Whose baby is that?"

"He looks like Ethan, but Sarah Kincade says she's the mother. Good heavens, do you suppose—"

Sarah spun to face the woman who'd posed the question with genteel horror. "Yes, Mrs. Stewart, the baby is my child and Ethan is his—sire." She couldn't bring herself to refer to Ethan as a father.

Priscilla shot up from the sofa and fled the room, sobbing.

"Sarah, don't!" Zach said. "These people will eat you alive."

She turned grateful eyes on Zach. He was like a rock, strong, steady, and she drew courage from him. "No. They've known me longer than they've known Ethan Pembroke. They need to learn what kind of man he is. I believe they'll recognize the truth when they hear it."

Sarah held her anger before her like a shield and marched up to Ethan. She would speak her piece, and in front of these witnesses, regardless of how they viewed her. She was long past caring. Looking at Ethan, she realized what a superficial, wicked-hearted man he truly was—nothing but vanity and an expensive suit of clothes.

"I made a mistake," she said, speaking to him, but also to the whole room. "I was a spinster schoolteacher who foolishly believed a handsome man's lies when he told me that he was a bachelor, that he loved me and wanted to marry me. I also foolishly trusted him when he told me he could make some smart investments for me using my savings. When he asked me to add his name to my account, I agreed. Then when I learned that—that—" She swallowed hard, and raked him with a disgusted, unforgiving gaze. "When I realized there would be a child and told you about it, you brought your wife to meet me." She poked Ethan in the chest with a stiff index finger and he actually flinched. "Your wife! You two had *selected* me to bear your child, without my knowledge, without my permission. Then you emptied my bank account so that I would have no choice but to do what you wanted—give up my baby to you to raise as your own. Say it isn't true, and I'll call you the filthy liar that you are, Ethan!"

He sputtered, and for the first time since she'd met him, he couldn't come up with a smooth, practiced answer. "I— well—you make it sound worse—And anyway, you signed that contract—"

Her words grew in power and conviction. "Yes, I signed,

under duress, after you pauperized me and threatened to expose my 'shame' to the whole town, as if you'd had nothing to do with it." She drew herself up to her full height. "Ethan Pembroke, I have come to get my son."

Again, the room erupted in a babble of questions, angry now, and more than a few considered Ethan with suspicious eyes. Oddly, it gave her strength. Perhaps she and Willis Carpenter were not the only ones present who had been bamboozled.

Ethan Pembroke felt as if the floor had suddenly turned to quicksand beneath his feet.

"Armistead, what is this all about?" Cornelius Hedges demanded, putting his champagne glass on the mantel. "Has your son-in-law been seducing decent women and swindling people? And you, Wallace," he added, turning to the judge, "you signed a court order to drag Miss Kincade back here like a criminal? Why not just build stocks in front of the courthouse and have her pilloried?"

Wallace, Ethan thought sourly. He'd always been an unwilling, weak link in Ethan's entire plan. In answer to Hedges's question, he simply turned and left the room with a great show of injured dignity.

"I certainly intend to get to the bottom of this, Hedges," Armistead harrumphed. "And I'll start by returning the child to Miss Kincade, his rightful mother. Ethan, have Priscilla bring the baby in here."

Ethan stuttered, "Y-you can't be serious!"

The old man fixed him with a hard, unblinking stare, reminding Ethan once again of a bald eagle. "By God, I *am* serious."

Ethan's jaw remained tight. "Make Priscilla happy, you said, no matter what the cost. I did what you wanted!"

"I didn't expect you to sacrifice the Driscolls' good name in the process. I will not permit you to ruin us with the outrageous schemes you've concocted." His father-in-law's public disavowal and abandonment left him nearly speechless. God, the old bastard was even more ruthless than Ethan had ever guessed. He'd thrown Ethan to the wolves to save his own hide. And after everything he'd done for the Driscolls, including Priscilla, the ice princess.

As he gulped down another glass of sherry, the only spirits at hand, Ethan noticed Charles Nash standing next to the piano. Christ, another uninvited guest. The doctor made straight for him, fixing him with a knowing look that completed this disastrous scene. "Armistead is right, Ethan. The baby belongs with his natural mother." He added, "And, of course, Mrs. Pembroke must be sent to a sanatorium, as we discussed."

"Sanatorium!" Armistead barked. The word echoed through the room. "You'd better explain yourself, Nash."

The doctor and Armistead moved to a corner to engage in a terse, low-voiced conversation while everyone in the room stared at them and then Ethan. Society matrons craned their necks for a better view, as eager as vultures discovering a new, delectable feast. And he was the feast.

Furious and flabbergasted, Ethan watched as his entire world crumbled around him, the little empire that he'd so carefully constructed brought down by an insignificant drifter and a dark-haired schoolteacher whom he'd seriously underestimated. The well-appointed house, the façade of respectability, the satisfactory wife—they all meant nothing now. He was ruined in Helena. He saw it in the eyes of most of the guests as they began calling for their wraps: he'd suddenly become a social leper. A few others hung around, drinking his champagne and eagerly waiting for the next lurid development.

Sarah Kincade stared at him too. "Well, Ethan?"

Defeated, he signaled impatiently to one of the maids to

bring Priscilla and the baby back to the parlor.

His wife came, but not quietly. Wild-eyed and downright frightening, she stood by the fireplace and held the baby in her arms while he wailed. Louisa followed, hovering and wringing her hands. Priscilla had always been a bit odd, Ethan knew, but now she was a complete stranger to him.

"You can't take him! He's mine now, do you hear? Mine!"

Sarah approached her, and the baby's shrieking increased when she held out her arms and he seemed to recognize his real mother. "Priscilla, he's not yours. I carried him under my heart all those months. I bore him, alone in Bozeman, while you and Ethan schemed and plotted."

Ethan watched as Priscilla's slender grasp on reason appeared to slip away from her like a bar of wet soap. "You harlot! You slept with my husband!"

Sarah gaped at her, plainly incredulous. "And you urged him to do so!"

Zach Garrett stepped between them and gently pulled the baby from Priscilla's grasp. "Mrs. Pembroke . . . you have to let him go now. You know that. Miss Kincade is right—he isn't yours and he never was. She is his mother and she loves him. No contract or court order can change that." Zach handed the baby to Sarah. "Here, son. Here's your mama." Immediately the child began to quiet. Then Zach turned on Ethan. "I want my ranch. I'll pay you what I owe you but not a damned penny more—no interest, no penalty."

Ethan nodded wearily—what difference would it make? Giving up that insignificant patch of grass paled in comparison to the business about the baby and the social ruin that had befallen them tonight.

The three of them, the drifter, the teacher, and the baby, drew together, triumphant and exalted. They embraced and kissed, becoming a family right before Ethan's eyes. He resented their joy and the private whispers they exchanged, just as he'd resented Jessica Carpenter's unswerving devotion to her husband. It was the kind of happiness that no amount of money in the world could buy, and no maneuvering or sharp dealing could acquire.

Seeing the three as well, Priscilla covered her blotchy, red face with her hands and sobbed.

Louisa tended her, stroking her hair in a way that captured Ethan's attention like a blow. "There, now, sweetheart, it will be all right. We still have each other, don't we?" she murmured with intimate affection. "You know I'll never leave you."

"Yes," Priscilla sniffled dreamily, dropping her hands, "you've always loved me, Louisa, even when no one else did." The maid led his wife away, still petting and comforting her.

It all made sense to Ethan now, their fierce, inseparable loyalty, and the feeling he'd always had that there were three people in his marriage. Why had it taken him so long to realize the nature of his wife's relationship with her maid?

Ethan Pembroke dropped to the sofa recently vacated by Priscilla, stunned and nearly destroyed. He watched as Garrett, Sarah, and their son—Ethan knew that he himself would never be the boy's father—left the room without even a glance in his direction.

Before he had a chance to draw a breath, his father-in-law and Dr. Nash approached him. One look at their grim faces, and he knew his destruction was now complete.

Chapter Eighteen

Zach, Sarah, and Danny returned to her room at the International Hotel. She felt drained but so exalted, so relieved, by the turn of events, she couldn't help but dance around the room with the baby.

Her child, the flesh of her flesh, was safe in her arms again. And although he looked sickly, she would restore his health with the right food and all the love he could handle. Heaping kisses upon the small, sweet face, she gazed upon her son with so much love she thought her heart would burst.

Watching from the settee where he sat with his ankle crossed over his knee, Zach laughed gently. "It's good to see you smiling again, Sarah."

She turned to look at him. He was a true knight in a frock coat and boots, and she loved him for it. "I have you to thank for that, Zach, rescuing Danny that way. You were *wonderful*! Ethan practically disintegrated right before my very eyes. And that Priscilla—when I think of what might have happened to Danny if he'd stayed with her . . ." Sarah shuddered and paused in front of Zach.

"You did a pretty good job of speaking your mind too. I was proud of you."

Sarah ducked her head, pleased.

"So—you have Danny again, and I got that promissory note back from Pembroke. Now you can live wherever you want." He rose from the settee.

Sarah tucked Danny's blanket around his silky head and lifted her eyes to Zach's handsome face. "We've been through a lot, you and I," he continued, and reached briefly

for her fingers where they held the baby. His touch was
warm, vibrant. "I guess you're not mad at me anymore,
huh?"

He still had the same effect on her as he'd always had.
Her femininity yearned to respond to his maleness. "No,
not anymore. I *was,* though. Plenty mad." They tiptoed
around each other with awkward questions and responses.
"I suppose you'll be going off to your land. Now that you
finally achieved your goal, I mean."

"And you'll be going to Stockett?" His expression was
earnest and open, touching her heart.

"Yes, I will. There's no reason to do anything different."

"But you don't have to. You could stay with me. What
I mean is . . . I mean I don't want you to leave. I care about
you and Danny." He stretched out a tentative hand to stroke
the baby's cheek with the back of his finger. "After our
trial by fire, I sort of feel like, well, you belong with me
now. And especially after our night together, the night we
made love. And *not* just because of what we did."

Sarah swallowed, a riot of feelings coursing through her.
"W-why else, then?"

"Because of what you said to me that night."

A gulf of silence opened between them. What had she
said? Then the memory came flooding back. "You mean,
that I love you?" Her voice sounded like a child's to her
ears.

He nodded. "Nobody ever told me that before. I've
never heard it."

"Oh, Zach," she mourned. Of course he'd never heard
it. There had been no one to love him. She turned and laid
Danny in his basket so that she could take Zach's hand.

Suddenly he sank to his knees in front of her and
clutched a fold of her skirt. His head was bent like that of
a damned soul's, waiting for a punishment he had no hope

of escaping. "Sarah, maybe I don't have the right to ask this—" He looked up at her, the hazel eyes now wet, and his pain went straight to her heart to become her pain too.

"Please don't leave. I need you and Danny in my life. You made me know what it is to feel again, to have a conscience again. For the first time in my life, I know what it means to—to love and be loved back. I love you."

Her throat grew so tight, it ached. "Zach . . . Zach, I wanted to tell you I was wrong, to take back what I'd said about leaving you. But I didn't know how. And I thought that since I'm not the highborn lady you want to raise your children, you wouldn't want me."

He stared up at her. "Not want you! You're exactly the kind of woman I meant. A real lady, with fine manners and a good sense of right and wrong. Sarah, Sarah, I never thought less of you because of what Ethan did."

She took his head in her hands, twining her fingers in his long, dark hair, and dropped to her knees as well, facing him. "Zach, I do love you, with my whole heart and soul."

"Then will you do me the great honor of becoming my wife?"

Wife! It was crazy. How could she marry a man she'd known only a few weeks? But she'd known Ethan for almost a year, had followed the accepted rules of courtship—most of them, anyway—and in the end he'd turned out to be more of a stranger to her than Zach was now.

"I've seen and done a lot in my life, Sarah. Some good and some not. But there is still a lot I don't know, and I need a good teacher to help me. What do you say?"

She loved him, she felt certain that he loved Danny. They'd make a good family. Her eyes blurred with tears, she smiled and replied, "I say yes."

A look of profound relief crossed his features, and he took her face between his hands and kissed her.

Tears streamed down her cheeks as he wrapped her in a desperate embrace. They clung together, there on the braided rug, two lost souls, stripped of their dignity, who'd found each other in a harsh, unforgiving world and had that dignity restored. Their lips met again, and an anguished sound rose in his throat. Then they rained urgent kisses on each other's face and ears, exchanging muffled vows in between.

"... never let you go ..."

"... I only want to be with you ..."

"... mine now and always, you and Danny ..."

Sarah reveled in his vows and was so grateful for the chance to reaffirm her own.

Straightening, he reached into his vest pocket. "I bought this yesterday. I've been carrying it around with me, hoping that everything would turn out all right." He withdrew a ring that he held out to her on his open palm.

"Ohh ..." Carefully, she picked it up. "It's beautiful." And it was. The center stone, a modestly sized emerald, was surrounded by five brilliant white diamonds. Not large and gaudy, but certainly not small.

"The emerald reminded me of your eyes. And I thought the size of it was right for your hand." He took the ring back from her and held it. "I took a big chance, I guess, when I bought it. I'm asking you again, Sarah, just to make sure. Will you marry me?"

She laughed and sobbed at the same time, so relieved that this wonderful, kind man had been stubborn enough to refuse to walk out of her life. "I will, Zach. I will."

"Then you won't go to Stockett?" he asked, his voice rough.

"Well, yes, I'd like to. I want my family to meet my child and my husband."

He slipped the ring on her left third finger. It fit snugly. "Is it too tight?"

"No, no, it fits fine." It was a little snug, but nothing could make her take the ring off again.

"In case you're wondering, your wedding band is in here." He patted his other vest pocket. "You'll get that when we see the justice of the peace. And until we're properly married, I promise that I won't do anything more than hold your hand, and maybe steal a kiss now and again. Is that all right with you?"

She nodded, unable to give voice to the jumble of feelings galloping through her.

He leaned forward and sealed his promise with a kiss that was at once fervent and gentle. His lips moved over hers, slick and sensual and conquering, plainly stating that their one encounter on that starlit night had been only a sample of all the joy they would share in the nights to come.

"I know a justice of the peace on the other side of town." Zach reached out a hesitant hand to lift her chin. "I know that's not the kind of fancy church wedding a woman wants."

"It doesn't matter," she replied. "What's in our hearts is more important than anything else. And God already knows that. He doesn't need a fancy wedding to bless us."

Leaning close again, he stroked her cheek and smiled at her, with a sweet, tender smile that touched her soul. "Maybe He doesn't hate me, after all."

"No, Zach, of course He doesn't."

He kissed her again. "We'll get an early start in the morning. After the ceremony, I want to put some distance between us and Helena. And by tomorrow night, come hell or high water, I want to sleep with Mrs. Sarah Garrett in a real bed."

Zach closed his arms around her, warm, reassuring, protective. Sarah relaxed in his embrace. Here they were, on their knees in a hotel room, with their child in a basket. They might have only a hotel roof over their heads right now, Danny might not have a cradle, and they didn't have a stick of furniture to call their own.

But in this man's arms, she was home.

"By the authority vested in me, I now pronounce you man and wife." Harlan P. Rodgers, JP, looked up from the book of civil ceremonies he held in his liver-spotted hands and peered expectantly at Zach over the tops of his spectacles.

Zach stood rooted to the spot, gripping Sarah's hand in his, and quaking in his boots and cattleman's suit with a case of nerves such as he'd never known in his life. Off to the side, stout-breasted Mrs. Rodgers jogged Danny on one arm while she swiped at her streaming eyes with her handkerchief.

They'd come to Rodgers's office in Helena, a man Zach figured to be the only honest official left in town, after Wallace Driscoll's fall from grace.

"All right, son," Rodgers prodded Zach, "you can give your bride a little peck." To his wife, he chided gently, "Mother, you always get yourself into such a state during these ceremonies." She nodded with happy misery and issued a muffled little whimper while she patted Danny's back.

In the stuffy confines of Rodgers's small office, Zach took Sarah into his arms and kissed her, wishing he didn't have to do it here. He'd never known a shy moment in all of his years. But what he felt for Sarah was so intense, so intimate, that even the simple act of kissing her in front of anyone else seemed vulgar. He inhaled the subtle fragrance of her skin, savoring the softness of her body beneath his touch, ripe despite the corset that restrained it and the dress that covered it. At last she was his, this steel-spined woman who had fought him, surrendered to him, and then fought him again, all for the sake of her son. He admired her for it, loved her for it—Zach knew what it was to have no one care about him. Danny was a lucky boy.

For his own part, Zach had so much to make up to her, so many ways he wanted to thank her, and all of them were private.

Eager to leave the kindly justice of the peace and his wife who wept like a paid mourner at a funeral, Zach released Sarah. She gazed up at him with long-lashed green eyes and a shy, tip-tilted smile that shot arrows straight to his heart and groin. God, they had to get out of here.

He made short work of paying Rodgers and accepted the couple's good wishes as he hustled Sarah and Danny into the buggy he'd rented to drive them to Dennison. Mrs. Rodgers offered them a little wedding breakfast, but Zach politely declined. They'd spend the night in Dennison and then catch the stage to Stockett, as Sarah wanted.

"Good luck, you two," Mr. Rodgers called.

Mrs. Rodgers alternately waved her hanky and dabbed at her eyes.

"Thank you for everything." Sarah smiled and waved, and held Danny up for a last look.

Under the clear autumn sky, Zach climbed into the seat beside them and flapped the reins on the horse's back. The buggy lurched forward, and as Rodgers's office dropped away behind them, Zach breathed a gusty sigh of relief.

"As painful as all that, was it?" Sarah asked, wearing a faintly amused expression. Danny giggled in his mother's arms as if following the conversation.

"No, but God—it wasn't—I thought—"

"I love you, Zach," she said simply.

He gazed at her. "I love you too, Sarah. That was what I wanted to tell you. But I couldn't say it in front of those strangers. I guess it sounds funny, but I felt like it was none of their business. It's personal business, between you and me. Do you know what I mean?"

She smiled again, a contented, secret smile, and tucked her hand in the crook of his arm. "I know."

Yes, he believed she did. Life was never trouble-free, but Zach felt certain that if he could wake up every day next to Sarah, he'd have a kind of wealth that none of the Pembrokes and Driscolls of the world would ever possess or understand.

More than ever, Zach realized the truth of the words Sarah had flung at him that day on the trail: not everything was about money.

Daylight was nearly gone when Zach lay on the bed in their hotel room in Dennison, just north of Helena. It rather reminded Sarah of the rooms they'd had in Lame Horse all those weeks ago, and certainly bore no resemblance to the stately International Hotel. But they were all together, she, Zach, and Danny. They were a family, and that was all that mattered. She sat in a rocking chair by the window, letting the baby finish a bottle of goat's milk that Zach had gotten for her from somewhere.

"He's eating all right?" Zach asked. He hoisted himself to his elbow and the bedsprings screeched alarmingly.

"Yes, thank God." Sarah rocked Danny until his eyes grew heavy and he fell asleep with the boneless innocence that only babies knew. "Dr. Nash said he thought that Priscilla was feeding Danny cow's milk, even after he'd told her not to. But he gave Danny a quick examination and said he should recover completely." She shuddered as she stroked his downy head, trying not to think of what would have happened to her child if he'd been left with the Pembrokes. "I can't imagine what on earth she was thinking of, especially when she could see how sick he got." She glanced up at Zach. "Where did you find goat's milk in this place?"

He got up from the bed and came to her side. "Look down there," he said, indicating something beyond the window.

Sarah sat up and leaned toward the glass. "Where? I don't see—" Then below, tied up in a little lean-to against a woodshed, she saw a goat. "Isabel! Oh, Zach, Isabel!" She spun in the chair to face him. "Where did you find her?"

"This morning, I went back to the same livery where I'd left her. The owner told me he'd sold her to the Pembrokes." He shrugged. "I paid him a little bonus to get her back and have her delivered up here."

She stood up and gently laid Danny in his basket. Then she went to her husband and flung her arms around him, tears burning her eyes. "Thank you, Zach." It seemed stupid to get weepy over a goat, but it wasn't just getting Isabel back that touched her. It was Zach's thoughtfulness.

"I have one more thing for you." He reached into his coat pocket and withdrew some folded, dog-eared papers. "Come on over here." He led her to the stove in the corner of the room where a low fire burned.

Sarah followed him and he put the papers in her hands. She stared at three copies of the contract she'd signed and the court order he'd been given. He opened the door on the stove. "I got all of Pembroke's copies last night and added them to my own." She looked up at him, her throat closed with emotion. "Go ahead, honey," he said, "throw them in."

She pushed the papers into the flames and watched as

they curled and caught fire, watched until they were nothing but white ash.

He shrugged. "Maybe this will give you some peace of mind. The Pembrokes belong to the past."

"Zach, I don't know how to thank—I can't tell you what—" She hugged him again. "I love you."

Looking into his eyes, she felt a subtle shift and saw a fire smoldering there that called to her. She must answer.

After rescuing Danny from the Pembrokes, they'd spent last night in Sarah's room. She and the baby had slept in the bed and Zach had made himself as comfortable as possible on the small settee because he'd respected the edict she'd established on the road to Helena.

Now they were married.

Now she could welcome him to her bed. The very notion made her heart thump in her chest.

Taking her face between his hands, he lowered his mouth to hers and kissed her. Oh, how he kissed her, with lips and tongue and heat. Passion, born of anticipation and needs too long denied, ignited between them.

Hands worked quickly to unbutton, unhook, untie, all the while competing with lips that reached hungrily for more kisses. At last, they faced each other, naked, and yet she reveled in the undisguised desire she saw in his face and body.

He was beautiful—the broad chest and shoulders, lean flanks that tapered to tight hips and buttocks, his long, powerful legs. Just to look at him made her yearn for his touch on her flesh.

Slowly, he reached out and pulled the pins from her hair, tossing them aside. They hit the bare wooden floor with a light ticking sound. Then he sank his fingers into the long strands to comb them out. "Sarah," he uttered roughly, "my pretty Sarah. Come to me now."

She stepped into his embrace. His fingertips left trails of fire as they grazed her skin, traveling over her neck and arm and breast. When he dipped his head to suckle her nipple, the sensation left her so breathless, she thought her knees would buckle.

In turn, she stroked the hard-muscled planes of him, over shoulder, chest, and belly. Finally, she closed her fingers around his erection, and a low, tortured groan escaped his throat. He pushed against her hand once, twice, and then withdrew, disentangling himself.

Going to the bed, he dragged the feather tick from the noisy springs and put it on the floor. When she gave him a puzzled look, he explained, "This is private, between you and me. I don't want everyone in the building to know what we're doing, and those springs make a hell of a racket." Then he took her wrist and pulled her down next to him.

She fitted herself against his side but he rolled her over to her back.

"Sarah, honey," he whispered, looming over her in the twilight, "you gave me back my heart." It was the dearest thing he could have said to her.

She touched his cheek. "And you gave me my dignity and my child."

When he parted her thighs and sheathed himself within her in a single powerful stroke, she gasped with pleasure and arched against him. He filled her, became one with her, and as he pushed her to the brink of rapture, he completed her.

The night passed in a glory of love and desire and wonder. Zach amazed Sarah. He conquered her body and heart, taking her, mastering her, in ways that left her trembling and sobbing, and not doubting for a moment who the man of this family was. But he also vanquished her with his vulnerability, offering himself to her with fierce tenderness and an appeal for her love and acceptance. Urgent whispers and vows flowed between them like the ebb and flow of their bodies.

For a man who'd grown up as he had, with a brittle shell that protected him from the rest of the world, Sarah knew very well the value of his gift to her. It was priceless.

When dawn was only an hour away, Zach woke to find Sarah's head pillowed on his shoulder. Her long, dark hair spilled over both of them and her leg was tucked between his. They lay wrapped in the bedding he'd dragged to the floor, a faded old quilt and two lumpy pillows. He was sore as hell from lying on the floor and exhausted and replete with a sense of well-being that he'd never known before.

He pulled the quilt closer around her and she stirred. Her eyes fluttered open and she smiled at him.

"Zach," she whispered happily, half drugged from sleep and, he supposed, her own weariness. "You're still here."

It seemed like an odd thing to say, until he realized that except for her family a hundred miles away, she'd had no one but herself to depend upon for a long time. When he thought of her, trapped by Ethan and his insane wife, pregnant and frightened, running first to Bozeman and then to Lame Horse . . . when he thought of his own part in her unhappiness . . . He shut out the images.

She had been deceived at every turn, but he'd see to it that it never happened again.

He tightened his arms around her. "Of course I'm still here. I'm not going anywhere without you." He planted a tender kiss on her forehead. "Oh, by the way, I thought you'd like to know—I got back your three hundred dollars."

She turned her head to look up at him again, more awake now. "How?"

"When I met with Willis Carpenter before the Pembrokes' party, I reminded him about the damage he'd brought down on people through his shenanigans with Ethan Pembroke. And I made sure he knew exactly what position he'd put you in by letting Ethan take your money. I guess he felt so bad about it, he sent it to me at the hotel this morning. It came from his own pocket. He put in a note along with the money, saying that he and his family are going to leave Helena. He said he can't change everything he's done, but he'll try to atone, and he started with you. I put the money in your valise, inside your *McGuffey's Reader.* I thought maybe you'd like to save it for Danny."

"Oh, Zach. You're such a good man," she said simply, running her fingertips along the rough stubble on his jaw. "I am so glad you found us in Lame Horse. For a long time, it seemed like I had no one in the world I could turn to."

Danny stirred and she reached into the basket next to them to pull him into the nest they'd made on the floor. He lay between them, kicking chubby legs and smiling that toothless smile that went straight to his parents' hearts.

"He looks better already," Zach said, and leaned down to kiss the baby's cheeks. "We'll make sure that you're fat and sassy, little buckaroo." Danny gurgled and reached out to grab Zach's nose, making him laugh.

Watching Zach and Danny together, Sarah's heart swelled with love and contentment. They were a family now, a real family. She thought of Ethan and Priscilla, prisoners of their own misery and greed in their beautiful, cold mansion on Madison Avenue, and could almost feel sorry for them. They'd never know this kind of happiness.

As if he'd read her thoughts, Zach looked up at her. "I swear, Sarah, that I'll do my best to make you happy every day. And Danny will be *my* son now, a fine strong son,

Montana born and bred. Ethan Pembroke will never again
be referred to as this boy's father." He lifted Danny carefully with one big hand behind his baby's head, the other
holding his back and bottom. He smiled at the boy, then
turned to Sarah again. "He'll be Daniel Kincade Garrett. Is
that all right with you?"

"Oh, God, yes," she uttered, her voice trembling with
emotion. Love and gratitude washed through her, wave after wave.

He gazed at her in the coming dawn that was bright with
the promise of a new day. "I'll always love you, Sarah
Garrett." He kissed her lips lightly and added with a teasing
tone, "That's something you can take to the bank."

She reached out to stroke his hair, then rested her palm
against his stubbled cheek. "No. I'll take it to my heart."